RACE WITHOUT RULES

By

N.A.T. GRANT

Llumina Press

This book is a work of fiction. Names, characters, places, and incidents are the product of the author's imagination or are used fictitiously. Any resemblance to actual events, locales, or persons, living or dead, is coincidental.

© Copyright 2003 N.A.T. Grant

All rights reserved. No part of this publication may be reproduced or transmitted in any form or by any means electronic or mechanical, including photocopy, recording, or any information storage and retrieval system, without permission in writing from both the copyright owner and the publisher.

Requests for permission to make copies of any part of this work should be mailed to Permissions Department, Llumina Press, PO BOX 772246, CORAL SPRINGS, FL 33077-2246

ISBN: 1-932560-52-1
Printed in the United States of America

Library of Congress Cataloging-in-Publication Data

Grant, Nat.
  Race without rules / by N.A.T. Grant.
    p. cm.
  ISBN 1-932560-52-1 (pbk. : alk. paper)
  I. Title.
PS3607.R364R33 2003
813'.6--dc22   2003021848

In memory of my father, CHARLES FREDERICK GRANT

Also, with thanks to LUISA BROUSSEAU

Prologue

Berlin, 1941

Karl Treiger, late from what he called a mission, stepped onto his street. Right in front of his parents' house, a trademark black automobile skewed itself at an awkward angle. He blinked in recognition. What a fool he'd been. Never once did he imagine anyone being caught, and this vehicle tolled the Gestapo death knell. His breath started coming in gulps so he clamped his teeth shut, praying this was all a stupid mistake.

With a fake shrug of his shoulders, he changed course for the street behind his home. In the fading light of dusk, he was barely able to see the entry to his secret tunnel. Karl wondered if he would still fit through the chimney grate at the end. Two years before, he'd found a cramped brick cubicle behind the fireplace wall and used it for 'private thought' until about six months ago, when the missions started.

School had become a boring drill about devotion to the German Reich with explicit instructions to report anyone, even family members, who might be disloyal. He'd also been taught that Jewish people were evil, unclean and carried diseases. Once he'd seen a group of Jewish women stripped naked and forced by the Gestapo to walk down the street. He had felt sorry for them, but some other children had pointed and laughed. In his cave, he began thinking of the other students and teachers as followers, especially any older boys who joined the Hitler Youth, *Hitlerjugend*. They swaggered in their uniforms, foolishly puffing out their chests like proud roosters and shouting with straight-arm salutes, '*Heil* Hitler!'

In particular, he disliked their pushy ringleader, Walther Bergermeyer. Karl had seen Hans talk to Walther a few times, but was pretty sure his brother wouldn't join the bullies. Brilliant at school, but dumb with people, Hans was mostly focused on one thing, Luisa Weiss's body. On summer nights, Hans and Luisa had gone at it in the backyard. While hiding, he'd seen her underpants off and glimpsed her curly crotch hair before Hans rolled on top. His brother was astonishingly clumsy, but it somehow worked; Luisa doted on him.

No one knew of his secret place, not even his parents, and in order to keep it that way, Karl had dug several metres of trench under the overhanging hedge leading up to the chimney and made a roof of old tiles and brambles.

But now, squinting to see, caved-in gaps made the cover look pathetic. Karl forced his lanky frame into the tunnel and, usually proud to tower above his eleven-year-old schoolmates, found size was his enemy. Awkwardly, he elbow crawled ahead until, within feet of the chimney, the back door banged open. Karl flattened himself. He couldn't have been at a worse point. Cold air filtered through a huge hole over his head. He shivered and peered out.

A broad-backed overcoat with epaulets stood like stone at the corner of the house. The official wearing it began a self-important strut as if this task was beneath him, but searched with a frightening thoroughness right down the yard. As Karl watched, the coated official turned his hawk-like stare onto the hedge. The eyes burned in his direction. Terrified, Karl's gaze dropped to the heavy hem of the black coat as the jackboots strode irreverently forward, thumping to a stop inches from his face. Branches strained and the tiles over his head seemed to shift. Deafened by a thunderous rush of blood in his ears, he saw a black leather glove grab down.

Unable to do anything else, he clenched his eyes shut.

After what seemed an eternity, the back door slammed. His eyes flew open. The yard was empty. The officer had only slashed his coat free from some brambles.

Karl inched forward to the grate where coarse stone gouged his shoulders as he forced first one, then the other, through the hole. With another push forward, a rogue cobweb clamped onto his face, fusing his lips. He spit uncontrollably—a stupid move. Silence was vital. He carefully tugged and dragged the rest of his torso through the opening until finally, through sheer determination, he crammed his legs against the far wall. There seemed little room left for air. A panicked faint grabbed at him until his brain admonished, 'smarten-up!' and a sharp stone dug into his hip reminding him this was real.

He knew he could find out what was happening to his parents here, because soon after finding the chimney space, he had become intrigued by barely audible talking on the other side of the brick wall. Using a penknife and a rusty file, he had scraped out a few bricks from the back of the fireplace, allowing a view into the salon. He had worked out another brick at the top of the firewall. Then, using pieces of mirror, he had devised a periscope system with a wide visual field. He then had a great view inside and often eavesdropped on his parents, Herman and Freda; even sneaking here at night after stomping jackboots in the street woke him. Their muffled dialogue deciphered into scary stories about abandoned children...Jews gone...interrogated...dead.

It dawned on him that, even though they were German, his parents were afraid, using words like political brainwashing and torture. His father clearly didn't believe that Jews were evil and spoke of the Third Reich as an insane 'reign of terror'—a reign that did not allow the least whiff of dissension. Simply questioning the actions of the Reich was treason.

One discussion ended with his father saying that, even though he hated the iron fist of indoctrination and coercion, he would hate himself more for doing nothing. Soon after, strange men had started meeting with his father at night. They discussed how to transport children out of Germany, often mentioning dates and times as they looked at a map. After one such meeting, his father had an anguished discussion with his mother. The next day, Karl was summoned to the salon and excitedly accepted their request, trying to act surprised. He had outgrown his cave and they were offering him a place back in the real world. His father emphasized that Hans was never to come with him. Proud to be singled out, Karl figured that Hans had been passed over because he seemed so focused on masturbating, French kissing, and fucking.

From then on, after his school day finished, Karl had regularly escorted one or two children to different sites. Someone always joined the children only after he walked away.

Now squished in his cave, he heard pounding, shouting, and crying from inside the salon. How stupidly innocent he had been. His right arm was pinned against the wall, but desperate to find out what was happening, he forced his hand to reach the brick that covered his observing mirrors. To his relief, the brick slid out easily. He craned his neck to look up at the image on the mirror above. He was not prepared for what he saw.

His father's face was barely recognizable— eyes blackened, blood dripping from his disjointed nose onto his jaw sagging. Karl's eyes burned with helpless tears, as he realized no sensible move on his part could help his father.

A sharp-faced interrogator in a stiff officer's hat swept into view. He had numerous Nazi emblems on his uniform, but more noticeably, a distinctive ring of polished gold with a death's head outlined in diamonds flashed in the mirror. He shouted so vehemently that spittle landed on his father's pummelled face; then suddenly calm, suggested in a reasonable tone that all the abuse and suffering could easily end, if Herman Treiger gave them the names they were asking for. Otherwise, until they found out, his men could entertain Mrs. Treiger. He said the words lightly, with a hint of humour. His father winced as the ringed hand grabbed his jaw and wrenched his head round to look at his wife. Karl arched his neck bringing his mother into view.

Nothing like the competent, loving woman who had always been there to comfort him, she stood quivering in her simple dress, pale and frightened, tears streaming down her face. Her soft brown hair, usually so tidy, straggled over her forehead and cheeks.

When the man holding his father's face nodded, the officer grabbed his mother's neckline and tore, stripping her in one stroke to the waist. With one last vicious tug, the front of her dress fell away. Karl could not take his eyes away. The tears falling from her terror-filled eyes burned mercilessly into his heart as a choking impotence engulfed him.

Karl couldn't believe what happened next. The man grabbed her between the legs. She pulled away so he stunned her with a cruel punch then dragged her in front of his father and cradled one of her breasts, sweetly whispering, *"Das ist shöne"*. With his other hand, he grasped her ample nipple and twisted the vulnerable flesh between his fingers. His mother convulsed. Her screeching cries echoed into his soul, violating any remnants of youth. Time stopped for Karl as the next image became indelibly printed in his mind. The officer pulled a baton from his belt and clubbed Freda Treiger so viciously that in place of her screams, there was dead silence.

The man with the ring spat out a command to halt. "She can't be any use to us if she is unconscious, or worse, dead," he snapped, and pushed her body over on its back to see if she was breathing. He turned to Herman Treiger and said in a conciliatory tone, "Look at what you are making us do to your poor wife. We really don't want to hurt anyone, but we have little time and if you don't tell me soon, neither you nor your family will be of any value. Think of the relief you will feel once you tell the truth. Your effort will assure me of your loyalty to the Reich and to our dear *Führer*."

His father moaned, but didn't say a word.

Karl now really understood what his father meant by 'reign of terror'. His eyes darted from the mirror. Hans! No, Hans would never knowingly unleash this indescribable agony on their own parents. He always got top marks. He couldn't be that stupid.

"Bring in the boy!" The command shattered Karl's thoughts.

The salon door opened. Hans, dressed in a Hitler Youth uniform, strode proudly forward, but stopped abruptly. Karl saw his brother gasp in disbelief at their mother, stripped and unconscious on the floor, at their battered father in the chair.

The ring-fingered officer also watched Hans react, and then, obviously knowing when to twist the blade, said, "Why did you not tell us of this—of the deceit and dissension of your parents? You are to blame for this."

Karl's father tried to speak, but a slap silenced him.

The ring-fingered man continued. "Yes, you are to blame. You did not do your job. You have made a very grave error, my young friend. The Reich wants to be proud of our German boys, and you are a great disappointment. Because you did not tell us, look at what we have had to do. You should be very ashamed."

Hans started to cry. "But I know of nothing, Herr...Commandant," he sobbed. "My parents are innocent."

The man stepped forward and struck Hans across the face making him stagger sideways. "Don't be a fool. Answer my questions. If you don't, it will only make things worse for you and your parents." The man's stern voice softened, grew friendly. "I understand you have a brother. He should be home from school. Where is he?"

Hans couldn't keep his eyes from shifting to his parents, which made him look all the guiltier. Karl knew what was in Hans's mind. Hans had thought his parents would be proud of him, proud of his uniform, proud that he was doing something. Now he was frightened and bewildered. Karl could see his brother lower his eyes before forcing out some words. "I . . . he—well, he's only a young boy and he goes off on his own a lot. He's a loner. I never know where he is." Hans's voice became stronger, as if to sound bold and strong. "I have better things to do than baby-sit my brother."

Karl knew Hans didn't grasp what was going on, but, instinctively, he had protected Karl. Pride flooded him.

The officer, however, looked at Hans in disgust. "Well, we have something very important for you to do now." He pulled out his pistol and thrust the grey handle in Hans's palm. "Shoot your parents for me. Put them out of their misery." He paused as if to let the full impact of his words sink into Hans's confused brain, and then continued. "This is what we do to enemies of the Reich. Prove to me you are not also an enemy."

Hans's fingers tightened around the gun as he stepped nervously backwards. He flung the gun against the wall and dodged for the door. The other officer caught him by the neck and slammed him face-first into the wall.

"You make me sick," said the ringed man as he walked over to pick up his gun. "Get him out of here!" He then moved in front of the fireplace. The only thing Karl could see clearly was the gun, but he could hear the man's harsh voice. "Unfortunately, it is too late for you and for me. I don't like mistakes and you have made me make one. I needed to know where those children are being kept and which route they will be taking before six o'clock. That," he said glancing at his watch, "is now impossible." He stepped sharply around the chair, levelled his gun with a straight arm, and fired into the back of Herman Treiger's head.

Blood splattered to the back of the fireplace landing on Karl's mirror. His head recoiled against the hard stone, but his eyes stayed riveted on the man and his gun.

"You are lucky. This is how we treat disloyal German citizens. Fast and easy." The ring flashed amidst the blood on the mirror as the officer pointed the gun to his mother's forehead and fired. "We are finished here," he said, and walked out the door.

Karl stared into the darkness. He felt he should cry, but no tears came; only numbness—a numbing vice of outrage that he vowed to keep for the rest of his life. Youth and innocence were now strangers. He shut his eyes for a time, hoping that he would die. His friend the cave would be his coffin, but the deadening numb enveloped his thoughts. It became clear what he must do and, without looking again into the salon, he extracted himself from his hide. He carefully dusted himself off, then walked deliberately over to the home of Walther Bergermeyer. He needed someone who was in a position of authority, and who better than a leader in the Hitler Youth.

Karl knocked on the door. When it was answered, he politely asked if he could disturb Walther from his supper. Walther marched to the door dabbing his mouth with a cloth napkin, eyeing Karl scornfully.

Karl looked Walther directly in the eye and said, "My parents are enemies of the Reich. I refuse to go home and will have no more to do with them."

Chapter 1

Westmount, Québec: Wednesday afternoon

"So, for you, the rape was only a secondary thing?"

Megan Brodie stared straight ahead and after a deep breath, exhaled, "You see, I didn't care what they did to me. I just wanted them to let Emily go, but she . . . died." The last word fell out like a dead weight, but hoping talk would get rid of the haunting memories, she forced herself to continue. "My daughter fell off that cliff trying to get away from them, but the court ruled her death accidental because she ran away on her own. The bikers, I found out, belonged to a drug cartel. They hired a sophisticated defence lawyer who argued the scum were trying to help Emily. Can you believe it? In the end, they charged me!"

"With manslaughter?" The psychologist's eyes remained focused on Megan.

"Yes. The charges were reduced from first-degree murder because of the rape. My lawyer said the prosecution had a strong case and tried to convince me to plea bargain. I couldn't believe the whole mess was happening. He wasn't very specific about the ruling, but there was some inference that my mixed blood had something to do with the outcome."

"You're not wholly Caucasian? It's difficult to tell."

"I have a long Scottish heritage, but my father was a Mohawk native."

The psychologist nodded for Megan to go on.

"At that point, I really didn't care anymore. The trial seemed such a mockery of what really happened and I ... I felt so alone. I didn't want to live after Emily's death."

"No one helped you?"

"Well, there was one detective who told me that his partner was going to testify against me and suggested that I reconsider the plea bargain. His name was Ménard, Danny Ménard. Oddly enough, he recently tried to contact me."

"Why is that?"

"I think he wants to go out with me ... but I really don't want anything to do with men now and—I don't want to talk about it. The trial!" she flared, "I want to talk about the trial."

She stopped abruptly, gritted her teeth and began again. "I was about to accept their deal so the charade would end, but the prosecution dropped the charges. I was out scot-free. Boom. Just like that. It was a government thing about immunity and Native treaties. To me, it sounded contrived, but I didn't care, didn't ask, and didn't really want to know. Perhaps Ménard had something to do with the outcome, but that's irrelevant. He doesn't really matter."

"What makes it difficult to focus on how you feel about Ménard, or other men?"

Megan looked away trying to hold back the surging swell brimming her eyes. "I never told anyone, but... I offered myself to them. To the bikers, that is." That did it.

Burning drops spilled down her cheeks as words tumbled out. "I was certain they were going to . . . to rape her. Don't you see? I had to do something—I was desperate. I figured if they focused on me, Emily would have a chance. 'Don't you want a real woman?' That's what I said. They were such . . . such pigs. She was young— only twelve and that was her last image of me. It's so disgusting. I'm so humiliated." The tears made any plea for composure a farce. She wished she had the nerve to get up and walk out, but instead, stared in a blur out the window.

The psychologist proffered, "In the past few sessions you've told me so much about Emily, but this is the first time you've ever talked about the rape itself."

Rape. The word resonated wildly in her head. "Yes, I was raped! The rape isn't the point. I couldn't save my daughter. I can't forgive myself. That's the point!"

"I know you're having great difficulty talking about this." The psychologist paused as if to let some of the tension between them ease.

Shaken, Megan looked into the psychologist's eyes and said, "Yes, very difficult. I don't know if I'm strong enough to deal with this. I want to be strong enough, but I'm afraid I'm not."

The psychologist waited.

Megan silently begged her to speak, but, in the end, grabbed for a tissue in defeat. "It was dusk and we were rushing home after our walk on the mountain. Then I heard the motorcycles. I expected them to just ride by, but they stopped. The air was thick with dust. I remember Emily coughing. One of them, the leader I guess, got off his bike and walked over to Emily, looking her up and down. She clung to my arm. I can still feel her." Megan trembled as a shiver ran through her. "I was so scared . . . but part of me felt ferocious, like a lioness protecting her cub. I felt a power rise up in me and whispered to Emily, 'When you get a chance, run as fast as you can.'

That's when I offered myself to him and . . . it worked. He grabbed my arm— his hand—like a vice, dragging me near their headlights. I can still smell the gas and oil. He shoved me to the ground and pinned me down. He stank of booze and sweat and . . . and piss. I wanted to throw up, but I swallowed it back. Deep inside I knew I had to be aware of every move. " The words spewed out and she didn't care whether the psychologist understood or not. She just wanted to get the horrible, bitter story over with— get the revulsion, fear, and pain out. "He laid a knife by my head. Said, 'you fight—I slice' then he . . . he ripped open my shirt. I heard them cheering—like it was a game; I lay stone still, trying not to feel him paw me. I couldn't see Emily so I prayed that she had run. That prayer killed her." She paused for a breath then continued. "He slapped my face— said 'I want to ride a movin' bitch!'—undid my jeans and forced himself... in me. I didn't want to feel anything, but it hurt . . . dreadfully."

With shallow, quick breaths, another choking surge followed. "I focused my mind on the knife, but couldn't help seeing the filth around me panting for their turn. The panic...panic searching for a—a chance. I waited...that horrible grunting went on and on...ugh...I heard him gasp, but couldn't move because of his weight. I ... I pretended to faint. Finally he knelt up with his hands raised for applause... so sick... I made my move."

Megan looked at the psychologist, hoping for a comment. None came. She forced herself to continue through the tears. "I grabbed the knife— energy just poured through me. My arm swept up—the knife slashed across his neck. Blood spattered all over, but he was still upright. At that moment, I couldn't have hated anyone more. His—his penis was right there—in front of my face. I brought the knife down." She shuddered, remembering all the blood.

"You mean you mutilated his penis?"

The question frightened her. She didn't want to think about the horror of that moment in real terms. She swallowed hard. "Well, in a manner of speaking."

The psychologist probed, "Are you trying to deny the reality of what happened?"

"Alright then I'll say it! I cut the damn thing off. So what! Everything I did was to save Emily, but she died all the same." A flood of endless sobs cut off her words.

The psychologist took a deep breath. "Enduring such a horrific experience with no one to protect you is harrowing. I think it is very difficult for you to reconcile your feelings of helplessness concerning your inability to save your daughter. In fact, no one should ever be put in such a position. On the other hand, while you recounted your actions after being raped, there was a trace of triumph in your voice perhaps to indicate that, in some way, you felt you did win. You did get revenge, but that triumph was short-lived because, tragically, your daughter died. Worse, you were charged for defending yourself. Then, after your whole ordeal, the court dropped the charges. Isn't that right?"

Megan, trying to fathom where the psychologist was going, tilted her head uncertainly.

"The court didn't try you, but are you not putting yourself on trial because you survived? You said to me a few moments ago that you are not strong enough. In fact, you are strong—perhaps stronger than most people. Faced with overwhelming odds, you survived. The harshness with which you judge yourself needs some exploration."

"Others judge harshly, too."

"And who might that be?"

The psychologist had caught her off guard. She sat staring at the other woman like an animal trapped in headlights. There was a part of her life she would never revisit and in here she intended to focus solely on the court case. Hidden anger pulsed through her pain. "Ménard's partner—I heard him saying after the verdict, 'Damn half-breed cuts off a man's dick, murders him, and gets off.' Half-breed! I've had to live with that kind of prejudice all my life."

The psychologist looked candidly at Megan. "You've had an unimaginable experience that has caused you great pain, both physically and emotionally. I can see how extremely difficult it is for you. However, I'm afraid our time is up for today, but if you are able, we can continue this next time."

Megan left the building feeling swept up in a black hole of pain. Shivering despite the warm air, she walked away still fighting tears. Dusk started to fall as she grimly walked uphill towards home. The time to experience emotional agony was with the psychologist and outside that office she had to get on with life. It was a brave front, but misery lurked close by.

Just past a ravine that cut deeply into the side of Westmount was her street, Roxton Crescent. It held only three houses, all immense and built right into the mountainside. One belonged to Fiona Kendall who, when Megan wandered onto Roxton a year ago, was the catalyst enabling her to move here. On that occasion, Fiona had described the architecture of each home on the curved street. Two were of a similar style, patterned after elegant Scottish manor houses, but the central one, belonging to Deirdre Ogilvy, was reminiscent of a sumptuous Val-de-Loire chateau of the French Renaissance. The third property belonged to a family named Treiger and was set apart from the other two by the mountain terrain. Fiona had mentioned that Deirdre Ogilvy, too kind for her own good, took in lodgers periodically and happened to have a vacancy because the prior tenant made a 'nocturnal exodus' in a stolen pick-up stuffed with booty.

Megan vividly remembered meeting Deirdre. She hadn't even rung the bell when the massive front door swung open revealing a rotund elderly woman enveloped in a floor-length fuchsia negligee draped with a black feather boa. That had been startling enough, but the incessant yapping of a miniature poodle half-concealed behind the gown made thought difficult.

"Welcome, dear," Deirdre had said with such sincerity that Megan wondered if she meant just the opposite.

The only thing she could think to say was, "I'm Megan Brodie."

"A Brodie—Scottish! I've been waiting for you," was added without explanation, where upon she turned to the yapper, "Shush, Monzie, don't frighten our visitor!" The admonishment, delivered with the force of a powder puff, caused the little poodle, obviously miffed, to plunk his curly white butt down and glue his sceptical eyes on Megan.

Deirdre looked down with a proud scrunch of her face. "I named him after a fierce Scottish warrior. And you live up to the name, don't you Monzie." Switching topics abruptly, she had announced, "You're just in time for tea. It doesn't seem proper to have tea alone, does it? I do love company."

Next thing Megan knew, she was sitting by one of the bay windows in the front drawing room pouring Deirdre tea from a sterling silver tea service. Deirdre ignored the inquiry about a room to let and reclined in an oversized armchair giving a randomly detailed summary of her life. The great Scottish warrior lay attentively at her feet, whimpering and panting for bits of shortbread. She interrupted her story to say, "Oh, Monzie, my sweet, you will get fat," but more than once dropped a morsel between his sharp little incisors.

Deirdre completed her story and her tea with, "Oh, how I do go on. You seem to have the patience of an angel and the listening ear of the loyal. I am certain you would love living here. You must see the basement rooms." A slight frown creased Deirdre's forehead as she slowly added, "I do hope you find them acceptable. I had some difficulties with the previous lodger. Such commotion! Still, I don't enjoy coping alone in this big house. Now, just walk down the hall and take the first door on the right, just before the kitchen."

Amazed that this elderly woman trusted a stranger to wander unattended through the house, Megan headed off. She had given a self-conscious glance into the oversized kitchen having seen a larger one only in Scotland and happened to glimpse a stunning conservatory on the far side. She looked away quickly and took the wide oak staircase to the lower level where a stunning complex of rooms opened off a huge central area. Apparently, Deirdre didn't know the meaning of the word 'basement'. Through the panoramic windows at one end, Mount Royal extended dramatically to the west and, across the ravine, spanned Westmount before it blended into downtown

Montreal. Viewed with her artist's eye, the mountain gave strength as well as an enduring quality to the city— inspirational and a perfect spot for an art studio. Her decision to stay took one second. And now, after the gruelling therapy session, she was glad to have a home.

Megan let herself in through her patio door entry and kicked off her moccasins. She had just enough time to change before going out with Fiona. A good laugh and a few numbing drinks was exactly what she needed. Even before turning on the light, she saw the answering machine blink in the dark. She strode over and pressed play. "Hi, Meggie. Fiona here. Can't meet you tonight, Hun. How about a coffee on Greene Avenue in the morning? About nine-ish? Usual place. Don't call back if you can make it!"

Disappointment shoved depression back onboard. Alone in the dark, she flopped into a chair and began to cry all over again. A small wet tongue started licking her ankles. She cried even harder as she scooped the little poodle from under the chair and hugged his warm little body. Out of the blue, Deirdre's voice drifted down the stairs. "Megan? Is that you? Come up for a sherry. I feel like a chat." Monzie promptly squirmed down and scooted up the stairs.

Oh, dear. Not quite what the doctor ordered, but Deirdre would be a good distraction. Her face was still hot by the time she made her way up to the drawing room, so she turned towards the handsome sideboard and said as casually as she could, "I'll get the sherry, shall I?" With her back to Deirdre, she took a few control-mustering breaths and walked over with the crystal decanter and a glass, setting them on the walnut table between the armchairs.

Deirdre clucked with delight, waving her fingers towards the crystal flask. "Help yourself, dear!" But when their eyes met, Deirdre settled uncertainly back in her chair.

After Megan filled her glass to the brim and downed the sherry in one gulp, Deirdre broke the hollow quiet with, "Oh my, you must not sit with an empty glass. Have a refill. Perhaps, dear, while you are at it, you could add some to mine."

Megan knew that Deirdre would ask no questions, but would be desperate to know what was wrong. Not tonight. She wouldn't get into her past, even though Deirdre was dear to her. Megan glanced about awkwardly, feeling the weight of the silence. Her eyes fell on an old, ebony framed picture of two men shaking hands. "Who's that?"

"What a good question. That is my first husband, Donder Black. And do you know whom is he with? None other than Nobel Prize winner Sir Frederick Banting. You must have heard of him?"

"Didn't he discover penicillin or something?"

"It was insulin, dear. Discovered by a Canadian. Now, how often do you hear that! Let me see. That picture must have been taken the summer before Banting was killed. Poor Donnie died after that—well, a few years after the war, but it was linked to his work with Banting. It was a very tragic death, and full of mystery at the time. I was too young when we married—eloped at seventeen. Of all my husbands, though, I loved him the most."

"Whoa, Deirdre. The sherry must be taking effect. You'll have to start at the beginning. Tell me more about him. Your husband, I mean."

"Well, Donnie was extremely intelligent, you see—a brilliant medical intern at McGill University. During the war, he worked day and night on a special research project. I barely saw him for weeks on end. Then, when he did come home, he only slept. We lived here, in fact."

"After you were married you lived here with your parents! Well, I suppose in wartime, it would make sense. This is a big house."

"My mother insisted on it as, you see, Donnie was not well off. And, to tell you the truth, it was all such a scandal— with me so young, the war, and, worst of all, Westmount gossip. My mother was very protective and determined. She got her way, but father never accepted Donder. To say Donder's relationship with Father was tense is an understatement. I sometimes think that's why Donnie stayed away and worked so hard."

"Why was he so special?"

"Donder was a very passionate man, the most passionate I ever met. The problem was, he could only be passionate about one thing at a time. In the beginning, I came first. Once he had me, he switched to his work."

"That must have hurt."

"Well, I was too young to realize it at the time and I was in love. Anyhow, Donnie was excited about his research and considered his input vital to the whole war effort."

"What were they were working on?"

Deirdre blinked once and looked furtively towards the door before leaning over with a hushed whisper, "germ warfare," and cast Megan a knowing nod.

"Really? I thought all of that only started with Saddam Hussein."

"No, it was going on much earlier than that and very hush-hush. In fact, Donder himself never breathed a word to me. I didn't even know where he worked in the university. At one point, I was so lonely I went to find him. It turned out he wasn't even in the Department of Medicine anymore, but had holed up in one of those obscure laboratories; I forget which—botany, genetics... zoology? Hmm, well one of those newer departments. They wouldn't even let me in to see him. I came home and sobbed my eyes out."

"How devastating. What did you do?"

"Well, I was miserable. I remember Mother being very worried about me. Then all of it worsened after Banting died. Donder became irritable and more reclusive. I thought his career had gone off course without Banting; that he had lost access to the higher levels without the great man. If that was true, he had been cut out of the research he loved, just as he was cutting me out of his life. I decided, rightly or wrongly, to have Father make inquiries."

"Why would it have been wrong?"

"Well, Donder was livid at my interference. He hated Father knowing anything about him. Anyway, my father had many connections, both political and otherwise, but he got almost nowhere with his questions. That just wouldn't do. Once Father was on the trail of something, he never gave up so, in a fit of anger, he extended his investigation to his links overseas because, you see, Banting was on his way to England when he was killed. In fact, I believe the person who found the information for Father was the son of a Brodie from Scotland. What an odd coincidence . . . what was that name? Goodness! I usually have a good memory for the past… Douglas, Dirk—D something . . . are you all right, dear? Your face has turned white."

Megan drained her glass, then swallowed hard. "I don't suppose Duncan Alexander Brodie rings a bell. He was a young major back then."

"You know, I think that's him. Is he a relative?" Deirdre hesitated, but there was hunger in her eyes.

Megan felt a hesitant frown crease her forehead. Deirdre wasn't to blame. After all, she had always avoided talking about her personal life, but, at this point, there was probably no harm in revealing a little something. "Duncan Brodie is my grandfather."

Deirdre seemed to perch on the edge of her chair; her mouth opened as if her tongue held a flood of questions. "I gather you don't know him well?"

Hoping Deirdre would get the hint, Megan tendered a few reticent particulars. "I know my grandfather all too well. He brought me up. Well, at least part of the time."

"I thought you were raised on the Kahnawake reserve here in Quebec."

Megan skirmished to plug the leaking story of her life. "Listen, Deirdre, it's a long story and not one I feel like getting into tonight. In fact, yours is far more fascinating." Blinking back tears, she quickly refilled her glass and took a long sip before asking, "What did your father find out?"

Deirdre reached over and patted Megan's hand before speaking. "Well, as I said, Banting, Donnie, and others were working on bacteriological warfare. It was all very new back then and very top secret. Barely anyone knew the Canadian government was involved, even after the war. I don't think it is common knowledge today. Nevertheless, your grandfather found out that Banting had been en route to a top-secret British lab in Porton Down to discuss a major breakthrough in his research, but he never made it—his plane crashed.

When Father found out about the top-secret work, he confronted Donnie. It was all very nasty. My father accused him of conspiracy because he had kept us all in the dark. It wasn't any of my father's business, but he did not see it that way. I thought Donder would walk out, but he didn't. He went to our room and doused his digestive tract with over-proof rum mixed with wine, a cheap concoction popular during the war. I thought the taste was quite disgusting, myself. Where was I? Oh yes, he got thoroughly intoxicated—soused to the gills. He muttered many things to me and begged my forgiveness, I guess, for neglecting me." Deirdre paused to take another sip of sherry. Her eyes strayed to another picture hanging on the wall.

"Well, what did he tell you?" Megan pressed.

"To be honest, I don't have any recollection. In fact, ridiculous as it sounds, for several years we continued with the same dreary relationship, but I remained devoted to Donder until he left for a conference in Europe. That was the last I ever saw of him. Apparently, in the end, he died horribly. After Donder's death I vowed never to love anyone as much again." Deirdre gave a little smile and squeezed Megan's hand again. "I hope I am not focusing too much on myself."

"Of course not. It's quite a story, but you mentioned something before, about a connection between your husband's death and Banting's?"

"After Donnie died, Father got drawn in again because they refused to release Donder's remains. Being denied information about his own son-in-law enraged Father—you must know that rage being Scottish. He got Duncan Brodie involved again. I think your grandfather was working with some sort of very secret agency in Scotland. I guess he was the James Bond type." Deirdre's expression grew inquisitive again.

"I don't really think of him in those terms, but his work did involve more than just information retrieval. Military intelligence, I think they call it over there." Megan searched for another question to redirect Deirdre. She poured a little more sherry in each glass and asked, "Did Donnie continue to work on the project after Banting died?"

"Well, I still didn't see much of him, but he did strike up quite a friendship with the Treigers across the street. Donder spent a lot of time with the older one Hans, a kind, quiet man as you may have noticed. Drink ruined his life though. The other one, Karl, was never home—though I believe he's the one with the money. He looked very young when he bought the place. I was extremely jealous, thinking that Donnie was attracted to Hans's wife. On the other hand, Hans and Donnie had the same interests— germs and genetics. That's it! Donder was in the genetics lab. Hans was younger than Donnie, very intelligent . . . a genius, I guess—until he turned out to be a drunk. It took a lot to impress my Donder and he was disappointed by the man's weakness." She sighed, "Of course, genetics was pioneer territory, back then."

"And still is," Megan reflected. "Just think of the cloning issue. We just have faster technology, which makes us feel more intelligent and in control; however, making the unknown into known fact is just as hard as it ever was."

Deirdre seemed to let the last comment settle in her mind for a moment. She took a little sip of sherry before continuing. "After Donnie's death, Hans and his wife showed up at the memorial service, but that was the last time I have ever been in their presence. They've kept to themselves, and to tell you the truth, I prefer it that way." Deirdre hesitated then seemed to have an after thought. "I have to admit, though, I have always had a crush on the younger brother, Karl. He is still so terribly attractive, and I do not think he has reached seventy yet."

The remark made Megan start an uncontrollable giggle. "Trying…to…rob the cra-aa-dle now! That'd be—what? Husband number se-ee-ven or eight?"

Deirdre looked curious as if trying to decipher the choked words before leaning back into the chair jiggling with laughter. Monzie leapt to his feet, barking crazily.

Chapter 2

After a restless sleep Megan got up, and still feeling down, decided a run on Mount Royal would perk her up. Even though it was just dawn, she tossed on her jogging attire and did a few warm-ups on the deck outside her door. A large staircase connected her deck to a larger one above. She glanced up to the conservatory windows where Deirdre would normally have her morning tea, but it was too early for that. She headed down the stairs onto the back lawn.

After moving in, Megan had made her own private access onto the mountain. This morning was balmy and she figured, with any luck, Indian summer might hang on for a day or two. She cut across the sloping backyard along side the mist-filled ravine where a cedar hedge, backed by a stone wall, kept the rear of the property from eroding into the ravine. With ample time before meeting with Fiona, she decided to head for the Mount Royal cross. The trail would be a challenge, but she wanted to drive out invading memories of the eminent and all-powerful Major Duncan Brodie; heart of stone and morals of iron. She hadn't contacted him since leaving Scotland, hadn't even let him know about Emily's death. He had a lot to answer for— her mother, her Uncle Dekanewidah, but in the end it was... No! Cut it off now. Emotional survival meant she had to erase the past. At least iron-faced Jeannie with the marshmallow heart had made life bearable.

Her foot dipped in a rut tripping her back to the present. Just ahead the upper part of the massive cross came into view; its metal girders cut through the overcast sky. She'd often admired the structure at night when, lined with lights, it shone elegantly over the city. In Aboriginal culture, before the arrival of the missionaries, young braves were tortured on them in tests of endurance and bravery making the cross a symbol of strength. For a closer look, she veered onto a side path and heard someone else ahead. She considered turning back, but speeded up, thinking to pass whoever was there. The runner in front stepped up as well.

She couldn't see who it was until she reached the clearing where the cross towered high above. On the other side of the enclosure, was her neighbour, Karl Treiger, all in black—shorts, T-shirt and runners. Deirdre's description of him the previous evening had been accurate; he had a great physique for an older man. Every muscle was contoured as if he had conditioned his body all his life and his feet fell in a graceful rhythm over the uneven terrain. His form captured her artistic approval. He obviously took meticulous care of his health. She couldn't think of many men, even younger ones, that were in such good shape. He didn't look back as he disappeared into the woods, but he must have known she was behind him. She decided to jog around the circular fence. She wanted to be alone and, obviously, so did he.

This morning the huge cross didn't look like the holy structure that shone across the night sky. The fence that surrounded the cross seemed forbidding. Wrought iron spikes rose two metres before curving over to form a menacing overhang, and the downward-pointing spikes prevented anyone from trying to scale the cross. The mass of black iron seemed to absorb the morning light and up high, the vast arms of the cross cast themselves out with a martyred heaviness. She stumbled slightly, as if the atmosphere weighed her down. A shiver ran down her spine as she left the area taking the same route Karl Treiger had used.

Cracking branches made her stop and crouch behind a tree, hoping to spy a raccoon waddling out from the brush. Once she had seen a deer. The undergrowth obscured her view so she carefully stood up and arched her body forward. A glimpse of black quickly vanished, along with the sound. She probably would have dismissed the incident if she hadn't just seen Karl Treiger. An eerie thought that he had been watching made her take a shortcut home.

Soon Megan found herself cutting up the far side of Fiona's property, along the high stone wall that lined the perimeter. The wrought iron side-gate was ajar. Megan had seen Fiona out gardening the day before; as usual, she must have forgotten to lock it. Megan slipped through the opening, and scooted up one of the garden walkways towards a rounded solarium at the end of the house. The only eyesore was at the back where Fiona's husband, Richard, had being doing renovations on their old coach house.

As she neared the back entry to the kitchen, Fiona's irate voice wafted through an open window. Another row with Richard, no doubt. Megan halted and put her head down, placing her hands on her thighs to give her hamstrings a stretch and catch her breath. She knew she shouldn't eavesdrop, but Fiona's voice was very clear.

"You spend more time on those renovations than you do on me, you inconsiderate bastard. Not only that, I went out to the carriage house and it's all locked up. I couldn't even find the key. Am I supposed to divine its under a plant pot? You are so secretive! Where do you spend the rest of your time? It can't all be at the office. You're a bloody dermatologist, for God's sake! Looking after moles and rashes can't take that much time. What about me? Am I no longer a priority?" She heaved a deep breath before resuming her rant. "Don't give me the silent treatment! Speak to me, you . . . you—I'm not, not just a piece of porcelain you married—a statue or..."

"No, you're certainly not even close, dear." Richard's dry, unemotional voice drifted from the terrace window. Megan could almost imagine him reading the newspaper while Fiona verbally cut him up.

Fiona started in again. "And you expect me to run errands for you at the drop of a hat. I have a life and it doesn't include 'fetch this, fetch that, Fiona' like I'm some sort of maid. If you wanted a servant then why didn't you add that to your list of marriage criteria—or get a dog."

Megan shook her head and started up again at a fast trot. She'd mention the gate later. For certain, Fiona wouldn't end any fight until she had an unquestionable victory.

Megan rounded the corner of Fiona's house and almost toppled over someone. "I'm sorry," she muttered, "but what the devil are you doing here?"

"I . . . there was . . ."

"The argument is pretty hard to miss, but that doesn't mean you have the right to come on private property." She looked him over—tall, thin to the point of being gaunt; the unappealing sort, as old Jeannie would have said.

"No. I—never mind," he muttered, not looking at her and hurried away.

She watched the skinny man disappear. There was something about his eyes. They were…well… squinty. It crossed her mind that she didn't like his attitude and briefly wondered why he seemed so cagey then half-scolded herself for fostering paranoia about men. Most likely the guy wanted a job working on Richard's coach house. Frightened off by marital discord she chuckled. Perspiration sliding down her cheek made her run off thinking of a shower.

CHAPTER 3

Fiona Kendall hurled open the doors of *Laberge et Cohen Architectes*. Her swollen rage erupted like a mad dog as she stomped down the steps. "Fuck architects and fuck Richard!" She knew it was a dramatic bid to shock, but there was no one around to scandalize. Besides that, she felt premenstrual and fat; even the Dior suit and Gucci purse didn't help. She had stopped here as a result of Richard nagging 'to get only the earliest prints' and, of course, the blasted firm was closed. *'De retour dans dix minutes'*. Well, she didn't have *dix minutes* to hang around at their convenience.

She checked her watch. Enough time to pick up some American cash for the trip to New York; she would be nice to Richard then. Around the corner from the coffee shop, Fiona hesitated to enter the currency exchange; the tasteless mahogany veneer and fake marble made her consider waiting for the bank to open, but as the place was empty, she decided to go in. Another seeming victim of PMS stared out from behind thick plate glass as Fiona shoved a wad of Canadian bills towards her. "I'd like this in American dollars."

"How much is it?"

"About four thousand, I think."

The girl replied critically, "You should know exactly before handing the amount to me." Without really looking at Fiona, the girl bent her head to count.

Fiona, not wanting to be overly harsh to a woman who spent her day behind a glass barrier, bit back a slicing retort. Besides she knew the mood. Behind them, the door opened, but even the twinge of self-satisfaction at being first didn't soften her wide-ranging irritation.

Suddenly, a male voice shouted behind her. "Don't move or I'll shoot!"

Startled, and carried by a surge temper, her mind screamed— Who's this moron? The voice commanded. "Put your hands up!"

Fiona saw the cashier freeze then hoped someone was pushing an alarm in the back.

The voice ordered sharply. "Give me your purse! Don't do anything funny or I'll shoot."

He means me? A dim-witted disbelief crept over Fiona's face as her hands went up and she turned around. He hadn't seemed real as a voice from behind. Now the stark reality was before her— tall and thin to the point of being scrawny. A wool cap was stuck on top of a nylon stocking that had been jerked over his face leaving one ear, awkwardly bent, protruding sideways through the mesh; his mouth was a wet, nylon circle. The result was ridiculously unnerving.

He jostled closer as if agitated. Her eyes fell on the gun. She fixated on the weapon because he was waving the barrel erratically and didn't seem to have a good grip on the thing. In no mood to deal with a fool, Fiona spoke coldly. "She has my money." She glanced aristocratically back at the pale icicle behind the armoured window.

"Give me... your... purse!" he spat menacingly, moved even closer and made a grab for her arm. Fiona stepped back from the chin hair poking through the nylon and shifted the purse behind her with one hand. He reached towards her again and managed to clench a fistful of Dior jacket. His voice pitched to an odd treble. "Give me your purse or I'll shoot, bitch!"

Fiona's mind blitzed in outrage— period or no period, life or no life, I will not be treated like this. With reflexive speed she tore his sweaty hand off her lapel. Her eyes smouldered with a venomous glare and she lashed out, "Go ahead! Fucking make my day."

Nylon looked startled. He held his stance for a second.

All she could make out was three stretched circles staring at her through chiselled, cheap mesh. She stuck her free hand forward and shoved him back; at the same time she managed to grab the barrel of his gun. Surprisingly, he lost hold of the grip. Idiot, she thought. The hilt hung freely in mid air with her fingers folded tightly around the cylinder. Madly, she shoved the barrel in her mouth like a hotdog, blubbering, "Goo-ahead...dew-wit."

The wet-mouthed nylon made a frantic attempt to grab the gun back. She hit him on the side of the head with her purse. He bent sideways swiping at the gun. She whacked him again, but he still got hold of the hilt. He twisted away as she walloped his head again and lost her grip on the purse. The bag went flying, hit the wall and bounced back. Nylon fell sideways banging his hand on the window. The gun went off.

The small blast sounded much different than she would have thought, like a distant pop. Suddenly weak and numb she fell against the wall and slid to the floor as the gun dropped. Everything started to float in slow motion. The nylon head moved in erratic panic as her eyes drifted over to the gun, but he seemed to be reaching towards her. She couldn't make a quick move if she wanted to. One of his hands closed over her purse, the other stuffed the gun in his jeans. He stumbled out the glass door while tearing the nylon off his head.

Her eyes blinked blankly as she patted her chest then checked her shaking fingers for blood. They were clean. She looked sideways. Some shattered gyp-rock surrounded a small hole in the wall. The bullet had just missed. Slumped in a quivering mass of sobs, she smeared a fist through her mascara in time to see Megan pass the door. She was staring straight ahead as if watching the fugitive who had just run out. Fiona's mouth opened in a screech. "Megan!"

Megan watched Fiona guide a rather shaky cup of coffee to her lips. Luckily the taut Westmount chignon suited her face, giving her a delicately elegant and vulnerable look in the worst of times. They had ended up at the Police Station to look at computer-stored mug shots and, due to some construction, the electricity in that section had been temporarily disrupted so Megan had decided to bring her to the station's coffee shop. The dingy little café was crammed with cops coming and going, but they managed to find a deserted table by the window. The dug-up parking lot outside did nothing to change their mood.

Megan mentioned that she'd left a message for Detective Ménard to join them if he had a few moments. Fiona nodded absently then finally, as if coming to some sort of decision, she drained her cup and got up, announcing that she needed to phone Richard. Fiona's cell, calling card, and small change all went with the purse so she was reduced to borrowing coins from Megan. Watching Fiona glide with long-suffering grace over to the pay phone, Megan wondered if Richard would give the sensitive support she would need at a time like this. Her thoughts were interrupted by a deep male voice with a French accent.

"Hello, Megan. I got your message. Is your friend all right?"

She looked up into the concerned eyes of Daniel Ménard. Somehow she hadn't wanted to meet like this, with him standing above her. She almost regretted leaving the impulsive message, but it was too late. Before she could answer, a noisy truck pulled up outside and started unloading gravel. The grating thunder made speaking impossible. She found herself smiling foolishly waiting for the racket to stop. He glanced at the table taking in Fiona's empty cup, and then pointed to another chair, inquiring with his eyes if he could sit. Megan nodded. He smoothly pulled up a chair, raised his eyebrows at the noise, smiled and sat down easily across from her. Finally the rumbling truck drove off.

Vividly aware she'd never returned his call from a month ago, a sliver of guilt prodded her to apologise, but she decided to keep it simple and just answer his question, "My friend wasn't hurt, but she's a bit shook up." The need to say something else persisted. Good manners called for her to do so and she knew it. She added, "I'm glad you had the time to stop by."

Ménard smiled in a way that made his blue eyes sparkle and said, "I was a bit surprised to hear from you," then fixed his face more seriously, "but extremely pleased."

Unease kept crowding her, but she managed to respond, "It's always good to have a friend in a police station."

She had no time to say more because Fiona, who seemed to have survived her talk with Richard, broke in, 'Why don't you introduce me to your handsome friend?"

Ménard immediately stood up and, tilting his head with a sincere smile, said, "I'm Daniel Ménard. Most people call me Danny."

"*Enchanté.*" Fiona replied demurely and sat down in the chair closest to Ménard.

Megan tried to overlook Fiona's tendency to exude her impeccably well-bred Westmount charm. She had seen Fiona break into this charismatic mode when she wanted to make a particularly good impression. Megan, having avoided giving Ménard any wrong messages, was almost certain matchmaking Fiona would think he was perfect for her, and start mindlessly feeding a fire that she didn't want lit. Also, Fiona had no knowledge of how she had met up with Ménard. Memories of the trial glared in her mind. She hoped he wouldn't mention anything about the ordeal and began an awkward introduction. "I met Detective Ménard a while ago… I thought maybe he could help us out…" Her voice trailed off as she felt a blush coming on.

Ménard broke the silence smoothly with, "*C'était une plaisir de vous aider,*" while flashing his amazing eyes at Megan, then added, "But first, there is something that concerns me. I spoke to the investigating officer about the circumstances of your assault. The facts seem to indicate that this was not a routine hold-up."

Fiona cried out with quarrelsome hurt, "Of course it wasn't! I don't think anyone experiencing such a thing would consider it routine." Tears welled up in her eyes.

At once Ménard leaned towards Fiona and put his hand compassionately on her shoulder, adding earnestly, "I must apologise. Please forgive me. I in no way wanted to minimise the trauma of your experience. It's just that...it seems that you may have been targeted."

Fiona looked astonished and stammered, "I... don't understand."

"The assailant only focused on you and your purse. He did not ask for money even though there was a pretty easy take on the cashier's desk. It even seems that you pointed this fact out to him and he still focused on your purse. So, we could hypothesize, unless he was excessively stupid, that it was not the money he was after. Did he ask for your jewellery or at any time turn his attention on the cashier?"

Fiona shook her head as a frown formed on her forehead.

He gently persisted. "Was there anything important in your purse other than the normal personal effects? Papers? Addresses? I know it must seem silly to have me ask, but in such circumstances, some people forget the most obvious and significant items."

Seemingly prompted by his encouraging smile, Fiona replied, "This all seems preposterous. I mean, why me? I only had the usual credit cards, cell, make-up... keys. I really can't think of a thing."

"Well, if you do come up with anything let us know, because little can be done unless the mug shots reveal a suspect," Ménard checked his watch, "I hate to make a hasty exit, I must get back to work. You have probably already realised this, but it will be necessary for you to change your locks as soon as possible." He turned to Megan and smiled sincerely. "I would like to give you a call."

Megan, feeling oddly ambivalent that he had focused mainly on Fiona, nodded slightly and stuttered over her reply, "Well, I... I mean..."

Ignoring her obvious flap, he responded smoothly with his French-Canadian charm, "*Bon*. Then perhaps on the weekend or before, if I hear any more details on your case." He stood with an elegant broad-shouldered and confident style, smiled once more, and walked away.

"How did your call to Richard go?" Megan asked, trying to draw Fiona's gaze off of Ménard's retreating physique.

"Oh, he wasn't there. I called the architects though, to ensure they send the prints via registered mail. That will take a few days longer and I felt vindictive enough to do it since Richard didn't have the sensitivity to be there in my hour of need."

None of the criminals on file seemed to fit, so they left the station leaving the police to follow up on the investigation. Megan avoided Fiona's lure onto the topic of dating given that Detective Ménard was so 'debonair', the word rolled whimsically off Fiona's tongue. Using any trick she could to evade the subject, Megan finally pulled her old SUV up in front of Fiona's home. Across the street, she noticed Karl Treiger walk briskly out of his home and climb into the passenger seat of his black Mercedes. His casual, but rugged looking attire made him appear even younger than Deirdre's estimate. The distraction didn't make her feel any easier because of the strange incident on the mountain. Fiona stopped talking and joined her preoccupied stare.

The older brother, Hans, was driving. Megan had met Hans briefly a few times and found out he had a hobby farm in the south of the province. He maintained a small apiary there and occasionally, after their introduction, he sent some honey over to her. Mostly, though, she'd hardly seen any of the Treigers.

They both watched as Hans drove slowly by their vehicle. Megan waved. Hans gave a smile, which made finely etched wrinkles lighten his sombre expression, but she couldn't help glancing at Karl Treiger, who as if sensing her look, cast a penetrating stare at her. Their eyes locked for a brief second. The impact was startling; a profound emotional reaction suffused her body, as if he had walked right into her soul. The Mercedes drove off, but her heart was pumping rapidly, leaving her strangely excited.

Fiona, unaware of Megan's reaction, remarked, "Will you look at that. Hans's wife was peeking through the front window and as soon as she saw me look her way, she dropped the curtain. At least, she could have waved. They are so secretive. That younger one, Karl, looks a bit uptight, but he's strikingly good looking, that is, whenever one catches a glimpse of him." Fiona got a mischievous glint in her eye, "Megan! I don't believe it. Are you blushing?"

This second disturbing encounter provoked her defences. "I'm not ready to deal with any kind of male relationship at this point whether its detective or neighbour, so let's get back on track, since you didn't speak with Richard earlier, you better prepare yourself for that."

"Sorry Meg. I didn't mean to meddle. I guess I'm pretty shook up. I was just trying to side-track myself from a wretched day," Fiona said, looking remorseful.

Knowing how sensitive Fiona was, Megan softened. "It's true. You've had a tough time. Listen, I'll call later and make sure you're alright."

CHAPTER 4

Rio de Janeiro, Brazil

Karl Treiger hung his leather knapsack over his shoulder and exited Air Varig's First Class compartment. In fluent Portuguese, he negotiated a fare with an off-license cab driver. As the taxi passed Ipanema Beach, Treiger spoke briefly on his cell phone. He had been waiting a very long time for this and by tomorrow, if all went according to plan, his worries would be over. Rio's beaches ended in majestic slabs of sandstone, forcing the road up in a hairpin route where dense jungle separated the road from the ocean. Soon Treiger had the driver pull over, paid the full fare, and climbed out. He watched the cabbie drive off before opening his pack for two items— a narrow key-type prong, which he attached inside the cuff of his linen jacket, and a small pouch that went into his pocket. A steamy jungle path led him to a massive fence hidden by thick foliage. With a brief search, he uncovered a bark shard lodged in the vines. Scored on the underside were symbols which when translated meant: *eleven tonight bay*. Good.

Not far away, he came upon a solid gate protected by electronic security and punched in his entry code. Further on, the foliage cleared, giving way to a four-story mansion pressed between the jungle and the crashing ocean. The locals referred to this place as a ghost castle because they could only see the structure from the water. The shadowy over-growth and jutting cliffs did make the setting mysterious, yet Treiger walked confidently because he knew its secrets. Having overseen the building's construction, he happened to include a few covert options; options that he meticulously concealed from everyone. Those devices were on tonight's agenda. Treiger walked up to the front entry. A day early. Just as planned.

A tall, young man whom Treiger knew as Edvard opened the front door, and using a well groomed, but terse tone, outlined, "Your call was necessary. We expected you tomorrow."

"Yes, I wanted a little leisure time here. Is there any problem with my being early?"

"As you know, strict security is upheld here at all times…for your benefit, of course."

Treiger found Edvard's stiff self-importance irritating. In all these years he had never got used to this typically distasteful attitude they all seemed to have. He replied smartly, "I want no one to know of my stopover."

"Of course, sir. I have assigned myself to look after your needs. The case you requested is in the office. Please, follow me."

Treiger unlocked the private door with his own key-card, entered alone, and crossed to the windows. The view overlooked a private beach surrounded by steep stacks of sandstone cliffs. Twenty years ago, under Joao's instruction, he had been foolhardy enough to dive off the highest lip into the raging surf, but it was a dangerous practice. On other sections of the coast local youths had died in the attempt. They never tried here because of the sentries. More pointedly, no cameras monitored the bullet-proof glass, but a guard on the cliffs might see in. He closed the drapes and turned to survey the spacious room. Same as always.

The wall perpendicular to the window was lined with a built-in bookcase filled with never used encyclopaedias. In front of the bookcase was a mahogany desk facing into the room. At the other end, an oil painting of German soldiers overlooked a conference table surrounded by imposing leather chairs. Along the adjacent wall was a heavy cabinet holding decanters and glasses. The furniture, including an oversized philodendron planter near the window rested on a silk carpet. This office was the confidential enclave for conducting Gau affairs, a sanctuary for Gau decisions. Gau, German for district counsel, had long ago been selected as the ideal name for the organization.

Edvard had left a silver-coloured case on the desk. Normally only core Gau members could enter on their own. Apparently things had changed. Edvard had obviously been elevated to some sort of special status. Arrogant runt. Treiger picked up the metal case and set it near the far end of the bookshelves. He shoved the end volumes aside, then using the tine from inside his cuff, inserted the point into the back corner of the shelf. The section in front of him swung inward, activating overhead lighting in a hidden room. A top-end SUN computer sat on a simple table at the back. Organized on each wall was a compact collection of weaponry— plastic explosives, detonators, timed explosives, grenades and ammunition.

Treiger packed the case carefully before crossing to the soldier painting, swinging it aside to reveal a wall safe, which he opened. A brief exam of the papers within made him frown. Decoys? He had been expecting a disc. Something wasn't kosher. Treiger stood back and had a good look. Ah. Same combination. Different safe. Someone had made changes in his absence. The workmanship was nearly undetectable, done to an admirable standard, but, nonetheless, he had not been informed. He required any repairs reported directly to him; a safety precaution to minimize discovery of his own secret. Perhaps Occam's razor applied here; simple explanations were more probable than complex ones unless given reason to think otherwise. The original had been in need of repair; a necessary substitution not worthy of his attention. But with the same combination? Treiger frowned again. Occam and the Gau didn't mix.

He circled the inside tapping, then roved his hand around the inner rim of the vault. There was a small hole and hoping he had a chance, inserted his little key. Surprisingly, the narrow prong slid into the slot without difficulty. Someone didn't cover all the bases. Treiger was used to that; he'd never met anyone except Hans who was more meticulous than he was. He gave his little devise a twist and the false back of the safe released, revealing a green envelope marked *NIPL* on the top corner. Stoltz's handiwork. Treiger had seen the acronym before, translated from Portuguese the words meant East Island Paradise, one of Stoltz's business ventures, sideline entertainment while he waited for the Gau to 'get things going'. A month ago, Treiger had tried to check the company out in case it was more than a dalliance for Stoltz, but the operation had recently shut down. Not surprising, now that Stoltz was fully involved in the central interests of the Gau. Born in the late sixties, Stoltz never posed a threat until he achieved membership in the Gau and became Treiger's biggest challenge.

Typical of his manner, Stoltz's name was scrawled haughtily across the front; emblazoned as if he was sole owner of the contents. Treiger returned to his secret room and, given the effort that had been put into hiding the envelope, examined the bookshelf to see if anyone had been prying about. Nothing. From the onset of his plan, vigilance had been his codeword, but, just in case, he set his mental alarm on caution.

With the help of an anti-marking spray, he gently extracted a disc from the envelope and flicked on his computer. For Gau purposes, Treiger had conveniently feigned computer illiteracy. The ruse had been useful in relaxing Stoltz's guard, but still, obtaining anything like an access code had been painstakingly difficult. Seemingly intrigued by Treiger's inept interest in codes and computers, Stoltz toyed with him by divulging bits of information. Treiger had managed to extract three possible codes from the exercise. He hoped one would work, but had no guarantees. He tried the first code. No go. He reversed the sequence to make sure it was useless. Another no go. Steadily he did the same with the second code. No luck. The third — dead-end.

Treiger tapped his fingers in rhythm. He needed to crack the code. He started again, this time breaking the ciphers apart and using a different sort of sequencing. Stoltz had alluded to this intricate technique the last time they had a cat and mouse discussion, giving Treiger an obscure, complex chain of numbers. Stoltz usually walked the edge in a discussion, taunting the intellect of others. Damn. It was just another piece of Stoltz's techno-trickery. Perhaps he was trying too hard. As Treiger took another deep breath, his eyes fell on the empty envelope. He picked it up and had a good look, then took a pencil to make some simple calculations. Satisfied with the result, he typed: 14091612. Success. A list of files flashed on the screen. Sometimes Occam's razor did apply. One of the simplest codes in the book.

Treiger hesitated, contemplating whether to examine the information or not, but time was a factor, especially with Edvard invigilating outside the door. A look would have to wait and, hopefully, after tonight the disc would be obsolete. Once copied, he resealed the original in its envelope and left the hideout pulling a small lever that caused the bookshelf to slide silently back in place. Seconds later, Stoltz's disc was back in its secret compartment, and he hid the decoy papers under the carpet near to the drapes. Realizing enough time had passed for Edvard to be suspicious, he swirled a shot of single malt in his mouth, and then emptied a good portion into the planter and left the decanter on the desk with the swivel chair moved out of position.

Carrying the briefcase, Treiger casually opened the door where Edvard stood as expected. Breathing into the young man's face, he gave a slight slur to his words, "Just removed a few papers from the safe," and slapped Edvard on the back.

Edvard smiled tolerantly and let him pass. Treiger suspected the blonde sneak would go directly to the safe and check what was missing. Good for him.

In his usual room on the top floor, his knapsack had been deposited untouched. Treiger waited to be called for a session of *capoeira*, the Brazilian form of martial art. That would limber up his muscles and followed by a hot-spray massage and a rest, he'd be prepared for the night ahead. Soon the phone rang with a stiff update from Edvard. "As per your request, the trainer is being escorted to the gymnasium."

Taking the metal case with him, Treiger descended to the gym where a sombre-faced Yanomamö stood waiting. The bronze-skinned man was clad in a string-like thong encircling the hips with the genitals secured flatly on the pubis. He looked perfectly at ease.

Treiger vaguely nodded, then removed his robe before circling his trainer with slow deep strides, dipping his pelvis and feeling the stretch in his hamstrings and the contraction of his quadriceps. His arms moved in a flowing motion that looked effortless, except that sweat started shining on his muscles as they warmed to the rhythm of his body. When positioned behind the trainer's back, he made his move – a quick heel slice to sweep the Yanomamö off his feet.

Before impact, the instructor leapt from standing to three feet in the air; at the apex he swung his body around, raising his legs to grapple Treiger by the neck. Treiger whipped his head back, narrowly missing the projectile legs causing the Yano to twist, landing on his feet, but bent over. Treiger catapulted towards the Amazonian, but the charge was interrupted as the native pivoted with a raised foot hitting Treiger's sternum. The amazing force thrust him away. Treiger found himself spinning over the floor. He leapt to his feet, quickly balancing himself into another strike position. He circled Joao trying to distract him with, "How did you do that Joao?"

"New move," grunted the native with a slight tone of satisfaction. Treiger feigned a light sway to the right, but instantaneously pirouetted around to Joao's left. The Yanomamö was ready. After several minutes struggle, they broke apart, breathing heavily.

"Bet you thought I was going to give in." Treiger scoffed. "You need to show me your new technique." Without replying, Joao started to demonstrate.

As the two competitors continued, miniature cameras recorded the workout. Not far away in a small room sat Edvard. He felt like laughing as he watched them gyrate, flip, somersault and, almost dance around the floor. He would have laughed, but antithetically, there was something very sensual about how the men moved. He loved the way their bodies glistened and how their svelte muscles reflected in the light. Two predators, well matched, who could choose to kill if they wanted. He watched for a while before suspending his attention to make a call.

"Commandant Higler: Treiger arrived early." Listening to Higler fire off questions, Edvard replied as rapidly as they came. "He said he's here to relax, but he took papers from the safe.... Yes, the ones you expected him to…the disc is still there. Yes, I'm certain…No, no communication with anyone, but he's in the gym with that Yanomamö…Yes, I am aware the Indian is his friend, but they have not spoken…only a few irrelevant words…You can trust me, sir. I have him under surveillance…Delay your flight to Montreal? Yes, sir. Should I send your shipments ahead as arranged?… Of course, sir and certainly, I will notify you of any further developments." The phone clicked off, leaving Edvard to fasten himself back on the workout.

After the session, an armed guard escorted Joao to the exit, while Treiger, metal case in hand, headed for the Vichy massage room. Finding Edvard waiting to assist him, Treiger set the case in eye view, requested the water set at full force, handed the blonde man his robe, then lay facedown on the padded table, ending with, "Turn it on and leave."

Steaming needles of wet heat pummelled every contour of his body, washing the tension away. Alone, he could focus on what lay ahead. Would the peace he searched for appear when the mission was over? At this point, he wasn't sure after all the years he had spent surviving the symbiotic union he had with the Gau. But, he was certain of one thing— after half a century, his time had come.

Back in his room, Treiger examined his bag, which clearly had been searched. Going over the room he didn't find any bugging devices. Thankfully, there was no evidence of cameras, but he'd made certain in the building's construction that this top floor would be next to impossible to survey. State of the art technology was rapidly making his built-in insurances outdated. The search meant that someone, probably Stoltz's watchdog, Higler, was alert to something. Higler had been around once when Treiger showed an interest in Stoltz's access code and had reacted badly, vehemently cautioning Stoltz to be serious. Evidently, the odds were now even; Treiger had got what he wanted and Higler had put him under surveillance. Even if he'd missed some auditory bugs, it didn't matter. He wouldn't be using the room for long.

A knock on the door interrupted his thoughts. The steak and salad he ordered had arrived. Edvard rolled the trolley in and went about arranging the table. Afterwards, he stood waiting.

Treiger glanced at him, "You're finished aren't you? Go."

In a bold fashion, tilting his chin up before opening his mouth, Edvard spoke, "I understand you are one of the Gau leaders... and the main donor to the A-G project."

Treiger, somewhat interested, waved his hand for Edvard to continue.

"I was wondering who might next be selected into the Gau centre?"

Treiger eyed him before deciding to respond, "There are about twenty of your rare breed. Is that correct?"

"I am the youngest, but there are twenty-two including Commandants Stoltz and Higler."

"Why mention them especially?"

"They, of course, are the only two who are already members of the Gau elite."

Rankled by Edvard's smug reply, Treiger poked about. "What do you know of the Gau?"

"They have the potential to influence powerful nations. The Gau kept Adolph Hitler's dream alive so that the world would have a better quality of human race."

Treiger smiled wryly, "How passionately you describe us. Gau, a simple word used by the Nazi Party to brand districts under their control. However the concept was extended beyond Europe and the war because our ingenious, albeit deceased, Dr. Buch constructed a new model based on Nietzsche's Utopia."

"We all know the Paraguay scheme failed."

"True, but Hitler enshrined Nietzsche's ideal, and demanded that her work in Paraguay not be lost. Hence, the creation of a faction mandated to produce top quality humans but, of course, that is all changed now."

"Changed? I was always led to believe that I...we had genetic advantage and I was told you were our father, so to speak."

"Ironically, I ended up being a major part of the project... my duty to the Gau, but as far as I am concerned, Josef Buch was your real creator. Where Nietzsche failed, Buch's genetics succeeded. He produced you by *in vitro* fertilisation and used surrogate mothers for a natural birth. Of course, unlike the blond, blue-eyed, inbred, disease-ridden specimens in Paraguay, Higler and Stoltz were the first to fit Buch's ideal. The Gau finally realised the process took far too long so when Buch died, no one else preserved his vision."

"If more human beings like us can be created, why not do it?"

"As I already said we decided with our great Gau wisdom that creating dominance competing specimens like you was passé."

Edvard's eyes narrowed slightly. "You sound disillusioned with the Gau."

"Do I, Edvard? Others say the same of me. However, my gruffness is how I get things done. I have waited many years for...a new beginning...for the perfect time." Piqued by the cadet's inept interrogation and now, certain he had untrustworthy motives, Treiger gave a cursory flick of his hand, adding, "Don't bother waiting outside my door. Let's just continue this talk on the beach patio at... say, eleven."

Edvard eyes widened, but he nodded and left.

Treiger set his watch knowing he needed some shuteye before things got underway. He awoke refreshed and began to empty the contents of the metal case into his knapsack. Next, he placed the copied disc into the waterproof packet from his jacket pocket and stuck the adhesive sided package under his arm. After changing to more rugged attire, he buckled on a commando-type belt housing his hand knife and few other items he would need.

At the right time, he carried his pack down the hall to an emergency exit and released an obscure metal lid. The security system covering the building and grounds was embedded in the sub-basement from where everything below the top floor was monitored. Let them figure this one out. Treiger punched in a code to over-ride the surveillance system. One of his little secrets. The system was temporarily neutralized both inside and out. Treiger confidently made his way out to a raised coastal patio protected by a seawall and a barbed-wire fence, which separated the building from the private beach. Sea access was through a locked gate. Edvard was looking in the patio windows at the opposite end of the walkway, obviously waiting for him.

"I'm glad you're punctual, Edvard."

Edvard swung around, "Wha...?"

"Sorry to startle you. I designed this place so I know a few short cuts."

"...Of...course, sir."

"I think a boat ride is in order."

"No launch is ready, sir. And security has to unlock the beach-gate. I'm not prepared."

"Edvard, there is a problem with being too perfect. So, for the moment, why don't we just rely on fate?" Treiger headed for the metal gate. Beside the heavy barrier, he opened a small hatch enclosing a computerized locking system and pressed a code. The door swung open.

Edvard's jaw dropped, "How...."

"A privilege of being a member of the elite, dear boy. Please note Edvard, I have been tolerant of your questions so far, but they are now tedious." Figuring it was Edvard's duty to follow him, Treiger headed for the beachside cliffs where massive slabs of layered rock cut into the surf. Treiger saw the periodic glow of a cigarette as he neared the base of the cliff. When they emerged out of the night shadows, Treiger addressed the figure, "*Boom note*, Joao."

Joao grunted his reply, looking piercingly at Edvard. He turned on his heel towards a motorized dinghy beached at the surf's edge. In the moonlight, his body glistened with smooth moves that contrasted with his curt affect and the sinewy muscles. Across his back was a stingray skin harness holding a Bowie knife. The knife, a gift from Treiger, was a constant companion and seemed to be part of him. With little effort, Joao had the dinghy floating and held it in place for Treiger and Edvard.

Meanwhile, Treiger kept his eyes on Edvard's face. As if he'd figured out an exit from his dilemma, Edvard tried, "I will be shirking my duties at the estate if I board, sir."

"You disappoint me Edvard, I thought your duty was to me."

"It is, sir, but..."

"But you would prefer to sneak behind my back rather than obey my orders."

Edvard looked shocked, "Sir, I am following orders."

"Whose orders?"

"Commandant Higler, sir."

Treiger got tough. "You, of course, realise that I rank higher than Higler."

"Yes, sir!" Edvard barked, but his eyes sizzled rebellion.

"Enough! Get in the boat." Treiger commanded, roughly shoving him into the dinghy.

With the help of the outboard, Joao expertly manoeuvred through the ocean swells. After exiting the cove, he followed the cliff-lined coast for a while before pointing out to sea. Soon after, Treiger tapped Joao on the shoulder. In response he shut off the motor, then sat back.

Treiger looked at Edvard and said, "There is nothing personal in what will happen next. Unfortunately you happen to be an enthusiastic misfit who could endanger my plans..."

He didn't have a chance to finish. Edvard thrashed out his foot, pounding the heel into Treiger's gut, then leapt across the dinghy in a grab for Treiger's throat.

With a huge gulp of air, Treiger dodged, lunging against the side catching the young athlete with a hook kick. The young man swivelled sideways, but fell over Treiger, knocking them overboard. Treiger deep rolled under the surface and came up on top holding Edvard submerged until there was only weak movement, then pulled him up sputtering and beaten. He pushed the young loser aside, letting him flounder in the waves, while he swam for the boat.

Treiger grunted as he heaved himself into the dinghy, "Strong bastard, but it's a long swim to shore if he makes it."

Joao looked at Treiger. "You talk too much," he said and started the motor.

Within an hour they beached on the narrow shore of a deserted off-coast island. Joao sped up a steep path and waited at the top until Treiger arrived. Before Treiger could catch his breath, the Amazonian lit an oil-soaked torch and entered a tunnel at a fast trot. Treiger followed feeling his second wind kicking in. Before long, the tunnel ended. The interior of the island had a natural plain several thousand feet long surrounded by mountainous rocky walls, forming a hidden runway. Near them stood a two-man military jet.

From his knapsack, Treiger extracted a sausage-shaped length of Semtex, a white putty-like substance that when combined with a detonator, created a destructive explosion. He taped it to the side of his chest before donning a pair of khaki coveralls and some leather gloves. Almost as an after thought, he tucked his favourite weapon, a silenced Rugar pistol, in his pocket before climbing into the pilot's seat. Treiger checked the gauges, and observing Joao had put on his headset in the rear seat, said into his intercom. "Pronto? We're headed for the Jurau River. Hope you don't mind a visit home." Treiger knew Joao's taciturn grunt meant he had mixed feelings about going back.

Within minutes Treiger headed northwest, high over the endless rainforest and tortuous Amazon. He started a mental rundown of his plan. Just after dawn, he radioed his destination. Minutes passed with no reply. Treiger kept repeating his ID and waited. Finally static-y German broke the silence, "Receiving you... Treiger. Your request?"

" ETA: thirty minutes. Prepare runway for landing."

Again there was a delay before the radio crackled again, "Acknowledged." At this point Treiger started instructions to Joao, ending as they circled a fairly large compound carved into the shadowy jungle. As jet glided to a stop, Treiger saw Wolffe and some soldiers waiting for him at the side of the runway. Wolffe, the Gau's 2-I-C in title only, was now an aged, flabby man dressed in a military-type uniform, looking a shell of what he used to be.

Not far off stood a series of large buildings connected to each other. One was a simple, but sophisticated laboratory linked to a building that was an office complex for Gau members. The adjoining section was a warehouse with several satellite dishes perched on the roof. Scattered about were other hut-like structures. Nearby stood two helicopters, a grey one belonged to Wolffe, and a khaki green Rooivalk.

The old General stepped forward, grasping Treiger's hand and rambling out in German. "Good to see you early rather than not at all. We also are ahead of schedule."

An obscure comment. Wolffe was hard to read and the delay for landing approval meant some discussion had gone on about his arrival. Treiger decided to keep light-hearted and see what he could find out. He smiled back, "Such a positive reception is unexpected, Wolffe."

"You're a driving force but, unlike the others, I do not have any regrets that you became a Gau member," Wolffe guffawed amiably, but the effort sent him into a coughing fit.

"Cigarettes should have killed you long before now. I guess an old goat like you holds onto life like a leech latching onto flesh." Treiger slapped his gloves impatiently across his palm.

The old General got his spasm under control and smiled weakly, "As you know, I plan to live for a very long time and with no more secrets. We are so close to our goal that I can taste it. In the end it will be worth enduring this God-forsaken jungle and the endless wait!'

Treiger broke in, "My time is limited. Have the meeting we set for tomorrow moved up to today, as early as possible."

"Didn't Stoltz notify you? The meeting has been cancelled."

"What do you mean cancelled?" Treiger demanded as shock blasted through him.

Wolffe frowned and said, "Stoltz arranged everything. I thought you knew."

"Knew what, old man!"

"Kleis told me Stoltz said you had approved the change. But there's no problem, everything is going as planned...only earlier. As usual, Karl, you're too fastidious. And don't be jealous of the younger members. They are our future. They understand what we strive for. Besides, success is now at hand." Wolffe stopped talking as his cough took over.

Treiger pressed his lips together until the paroxysm stopped, then peppered his words. "I wanted to see Kleis immediately. Make sure the Gau is assembled when I am through."

"Alright. Check the lab and be warned, I doubt he'll welcome your untimely arrival."

As if ignoring the comment, Treiger gave an offhand nod towards Joao who was hanging about off to the side. Joao looked blankly ahead, but slipped Treiger's knapsack over his shoulder and moved towards some nearby sheds past the soldiers guarding the area. One soldier attempted to delay him, but Treiger gave Wolffe a bored look of impatience. Wolffe growled a short command to leave the native be.

Treiger skirted the rainforest in a stiff stride towards the lab. Stoltz was tricky. Either he was simply vying for dominance, or this scheme was in jeopardy. One thing was certain; Higler was having him watched. Appreciating that more evidence was needed, he decided not to over- react as he entered Kleis's domain. Inside the entry, he surveyed four young men, all sunny-haired and tall, suited in loose overalls. They concentrated on their computers amidst rows of test tubes in glass-sided incubators. The picture of an Aryan dream, but he'd expected to see a beehive of activity in here. Treiger addressed one of the studious blondes. "Where is Kleis?"

The sharp looking technician turned away from his work in a snappy straight salute, stating formally, "Doctor Kleis is in his office."

Treiger ignored the salute and made his way through the lab benches to a sparsely furnished room where Kleis, hunched over his desk, looked up. His expression darkened when he saw Treiger, but he stated simply, "We expected you tomorrow."

"You know me, I don't like to arrive at the last minute. It seems pretty quiet around here. I see you're keeping some of Buch's handiwork busy on your production line. Where are the rest of the troops?" Treiger said, trying to sound casual.

"After Stoltz worked out the final target details, we only needed skeleton crew here."

"Stoltz didn't inform me about this. I suspected he and Higler had completed the shipment sites and checked in Rio. The information I obtained wasn't easily accessible. In fact I damn near had to steal it."

The wizened-faced old man stood up and moved closer, "I don't think it was necessary for you to come only to check on things. Stoltz has done a superior job. Unlike you, he was anxious to get things moving and is now ahead of schedule."

"I haven't lived through all of this to have the whole scheme fucked up by a purebred maniac. It's my right to know exactly what is going on." Treiger watched carefully for Kleis's response, hoping anger would shake the aging scientist out of his condescension.

It didn't work. The reply was cold. "You know, Treiger, I've never really felt good about you, but you were Volker Braun's protégé, and you've been around long enough. Well, you've been accepted, so since you're insisting, I'll show you the set up." Kleis walked out of his office. As he crossed the lab, the technician who Treiger had interrupted minutes before was in the process of taking a small, unlabelled bottle of water from a box. He twisted off its odd green cap and started to drink. Kleis growled at him. "Get that out of here. There is work to be done." The young man jerked to a salute and then carried the whole box away.

Kleis opened another official looking container lined with fluid-filled, plastic pouches. His lips pursed in a proud appraisal. "They look so innocuous don't they? What you see here is the last we have since Stoltz shipped out the rest earlier this week."

Treiger's body tightened. "Stoltz what? That's a breach in protocol. Why was that done?"

"You'll have to ask Higler. Stoltz left several days ago along with the full cargo."

Stoltz's presence was critical to his plan plus the entire shipment had already left. Control was now out of his own hands. By the end of today his wait was to be over; the plot executed, done with, finished. Could Stoltz have been aware of his intentions? He shuddered to think of it, but the warning was there in Rio. A twist of fate. The game now had to be played with new rules.

Kleis, as if prompted by the silence, explained, "Stoltz felt it was dangerous for the entire shipment to be in one place. I told him of your arrangement to transport small amounts to Quebec for 'so called' security. He took offence to that and I don't blame him. You've always acted like you are the highest authority. I've put up with you over the years because of Volker. Believe me, trusting you didn't come easily, but you know, Treiger, I don't think Stoltz ever will. In any case, Stoltz already told me you had agreed with these arrangements."

"I did no such thing. I was never given the opportunity." Treiger bristled. Stoltz had come to Montreal a few months back, but he'd considered it an immature power play. However, Stoltz may have been manipulating everyone. Perhaps that was an advantage. Time was tight, but it had become necessary to put his head on the chopping block for a short time. He continued, adding a note of severity to his voice, "Stoltz doesn't trust anyone except Higler, one of his own kind. You'd better keep that in mind, Kleis. My concern is what he's done with the shipments. Since he didn't choose to inform me, did he tell you?"

"Of course. I'm not a fool! They were sent to the target areas and Stoltz took some to Berlin for safekeeping. With the schedule in place, select personnel accompanied each lot. In any case, it doesn't matter whether you had a chance to disagree. You were out-voted. All the rest of us, even Volker, approved Stoltz's arrangements."

Treiger was seething. He stared Kleis down while he built up to something Kleis would react to— authoritative indignation. "Why was I not consulted? Do you realise what this could mean if some of this stuff gets into the wrong hands? We'd all be at risk, you imbecile!"

It worked. Kleis, obviously taken back, defended the decision self-righteously, "Stoltz assured me he'd been in contact with you. He is beyond reproach, Treiger. Besides, he and I have been working on something special; an exceptional development that will bring the Gau overwhelming global recognition sooner than anyone planned, even you."

Treiger let the full force of his voice carry his message. "Even if we are all visionaries of a new world order, not one of us is beyond reproach, not even you, Kleis! To allow Stoltz to convince you of such a decision in my absence was wrong. We could lose control of the project through such reckless actions."

Kleis's brow creased with uncertainty, but he shrugged as if worry was needless. "But why would you want to control the outcome, Treiger? The Gau triumph is their inheritance now. As for myself, I have been working on stage two. My legacy will be ensuring our young scientists to follow in my footsteps. With this new upshot from the latest results, there will be no stopping them. But, if you wish, we can discuss your dispute with the group."

"Wolffe offered to convene the remaining Gau immediately." Treiger turned away and left without another word. At least Kleis was showing signs of reservation. He'd done what he'd intended, planted a kernel of ambiguity. Now, he had to let Joao know of the hold up. He went outside and saw his comrade saunter out from behind the hangar. When Treiger gave his signal to delay, Joao tilted his head in an unusual indication of dismay then nodded curtly. Treiger understood. His friend would do what he could.

Treiger walked towards the conference room knowing that with both Stoltz and Volker Braun absent this would not completely end today. Braun was never really a problem. The aging leader had returned to Berlin for health treatments about two years ago. Before that Braun had been the Gau's kingpin since his brilliant transfer of their core outfit from Germany to South America in 1945. Recently communiqués on Braun's failing health eliminated him as a potential threat— a figurehead with everyone awaiting his death. Stoltz, on the other hand, would be a lethal opponent and there were precious few moments to find out where he could be found.

Treiger put on his gloves while deliberating on who would be in the room— the old guard: Wolffe, Kleis and Walther Bergermeyer. No problems there. But the remaining member, Egon Higler, was a worry. Higler was significantly younger and had come through the ranks superior in all fields including combat. His quick mind and strong body almost matched that of Stoltz. One failing was his exacting focus on the fine points, which distracted him from the larger picture. Higler was the one to concentrate on. The element of surprise would be a key part of his combination play. He would need to execute the match with the skill of a grandmaster.

Outside the conference room stood two guards who gave him a straight-armed salute. He ordered that under no circumstances was the meeting to be interrupted. Treiger paused before entering, reminding himself to 'get in' and 'get out', then crossed the threshold and bolted the door. He approached the conference table with a stony face, observing the collection of perturbed expressions. Higler sat somewhat apart from the others. Behind him was the back exit, but a set of metal shelves made a direct line to the door difficult.

Treiger felt confident of his opening move. The person not at the table was the person who could bear the brunt of suspicion. The sternness on his face softened to serious concern, but he let a sneer flicker on his upper lip as he glanced at Higler. He clicked his heels with a snappy salute mostly to benefit Wolffe and Bergermeyer who liked to be reminded of past triumphs. The gesture did create a dramatic cohesive effect when all, but Higler responded in kind. For the moment, he needed those other three on his side.

Before making his critical move, he wanted Stoltz's exact location, but Higler was not going to be easily bluffed. The two had a close bond and, unquestionably, Higler would feel the need to protect Stoltz. Getting him to reveal the information would require cunning. The stage had to be set just right. He removed his gloves, threw them down on the table then leaned on the flat surface, putting the pressure of his body on his fists, whitening his knuckles. Time to begin.

"Gentlemen. My reason for calling this meeting is extremely serious— a saboteur gnaws at the core of the Gau's mission." He paused, looked grimly at each of them, before deliberately adding, "Why is Stoltz not here?" Treiger turned his penetrating gaze on Higler and waited.

It was Kleis who broke the silence. "Stoltz sent a message that he would not be coming and cancelled the meeting. It all seemed logical given that events were moving more quickly."

"How very convenient for him that I was out of his way," Treiger replied with a glint of sarcasm, but reverted to a solemn tone. "Perhaps it might seem that I am over reacting. However, for all our sakes it is imperative that you hear out my concern. After all, we are all on the brink of success…or ruin. All of us are sticking our necks out for the cause. All except for Stoltz who is not here. Have we come this far to have a Judas in our midst?"

Higler broke in, "Impossible. Ernst is committed to our cause. He is more determined to make our success inevitable than anyone at this table."

"If I am wrong to malign Commander Stoltz, please accept my apologies." Treiger paused before continuing more intensely, "My dear comrades, do you not comprehend the nature of this current predicament? We need to proceed with the utmost secrecy. We have devised ways to complete our mission in each target country. Germany was not one of those countries. Our fatherland was only going to be involved because of fallout from other countries. Stoltz's maverick effort of taking a shipment to our homeland has greatly compromised us. There are seven of us in the

Gau, six of us were to congregate here in the Amazon, while *Reichsführer* Braun convalesces for what may be his final days in Berlin."

Higler interrupted again. "Braun agreed with Stoltz's move. He felt you would manage the North American phase, and that it was not necessary for so many members of the Gau to be present at this point."

Without hesitation Treiger replied. "Perhaps Stoltz was acting under some deluded orders from Braun. We have no way of knowing because he is not here. No one can be above suspicion, not even Stoltz. Because of the imminent time frame, we must start with the most obvious." Treiger swung his eyes deliberately on Luthor Kleis because he was the one who had first spoken of Stoltz's communication, but Higler had the answer. "Where is Stoltz now?"

As Kleis replied, his eyes slowly strayed to look at Higler, "I'm afraid I don't know. Higler only relayed the information that Stoltz had left ahead of time."

"Stoltz was with *Reichsführer* Braun," Higler blurted, "He checked on *Führer* Braun's health and informed..."

"That is an insignificant excuse." Treiger interrupted. Higler used the past tense, meaning Stoltz was probably no longer in Germany. More pressure, more doubt was needed, so he jabbed. "The Gau has always existed as a unified force. Even his stay with Braun should have gone through our internal process. Stoltz has gravely misjudged us."

Treiger watched Higler note both Bergermeyer and Wolffe nod with concern.

The blonde-haired Aryan made a cutting reply. "You've manipulated the whole plan to suit some other cause. I know it! Montreal was the wrong place to initiate the operation."

Treiger's eyes widened, his words razor sharp, "Really. You know very well that Quebec was chosen as the initial North American distribution centre for very important reasons. It is a western site with sufficient population along with possibility of political volatility, but without significant military organisation. Even with the United States close by, politicking for military support would take time. In other words, there is the option of a scapegoat if it becomes necessary to continue operating incognito; keeping our real powerhouse here in South America anonymous even if our Canadian operations were discovered."

Higler looked spitting mad, but his voice was confidently powerful, "We've never trusted your fondness for Quebec. You make it sound so ideal for our purposes, but you've kept us all at bay. What's really going on there?"

Treiger felt his anger rising. Higler was wasting precious time, but if he didn't reply to this challenge adroitly, he could loose the support of the others. Treiger toned his response as if admonishing a small child. "There is historical sympathy to our cause in Quebec. Some of their people enabled us to set up in the early years after the war because their hatred of the so-called 'English oppression'— a loathing that runs deep. The radicals believe in racial domination just as we do. Currently leverage has switched from the political ideology of a Franco-Quebecois race to one of economic feasibility. We, therefore, will have the advantage of being able to fund their dreams. Perhaps Kleis could even work on other projects to suit their needs. However, I digress. Such a milieu will indeed further our goals, but without contaminating the

Fatherland directly. A shipment should never have gone to Germany. Neither should any have been sent to our target sites. All we need is the stuff floating around the U.S., Middle East, Israel and now Europe ahead of time. It is essential, as General Wolffe has repeatedly asserted, that every action feed our cause. There was to be the final meeting before any plan of action was activated on our predetermined locations around the world. Such a meeting, I shouldn't have to remind you, is very much like putting the final piece in a puzzle."

Higler began to interrupt, but Wolffe gave a sharp wave of his hand for Higler to be still.

Treiger continued. "We are at a pivotal stage of our mission and such flagrant unilateral action could set us back... very far back, perhaps irrevocably. Designing the release sequence was left up to Stoltz and our Mr. Higler here. However, I have had no valid explanation as to why Stoltz rushed to implement his plans without prior unanimous approval by all of us. Preparation, precision and timing have always been paramount. Is our protocol now just a sham? Should not Stoltz be called to answer for this?"

Higler's voice coolly broke into Treiger's impassioned speech. "I find it strange that Stoltz is being accused when he left orders for me to have your every move monitored." With that, all eyes turned on the exquisite looking Aryan. Higler sat with cool composure, his hands flat on the table as if certain of his strategy.

The force of Higler's move to pin him down produced fleeting alarm. Perhaps it was a mistake to focus on Stoltz. The next words out of that blonde Aryan's mouth could destroy his attempt to undermine Stoltz. He couldn't think of a Houdini-like way out of this one. He would have to break the pin by force. "Why, then, is he not at this table?" sneered Treiger, "Stoltz has many desires. His most ambitious is to be the new *Führer* when Braun dies. He is arrogant, self-aggrandising and condescending. Are these noble qualities for leadership? I suggest not. Such character flaws are failings, which culminate in fatal judgement. The fatal judgement of not being here at this table!"

With a flushed face, Higler lashed out. "You are jealous of him. You are not better than he is. We are the most unadulterated Aryans ever born. We are the essence of your dreams. Humans bred to excel and cleanse the world. Ernst is absolutely loyal to our crusade. It is his dream that we are living. We will live it, while you...you..." he sputtered, "are an old relic who thinks only of wielding power." Higler arrogantly looked the group over with an icy stare stopping at Treiger and deridingly continued, "Look at your old, wrinkled carcasses." He stopped as if to regain control before flinging his jaw up. "Once the mission is a success, it is our generation that will live in triumph, while you lay as dust in your graves."

Treiger laughed hollowly, "If you say Stoltz is so superior, then how is it that your dear comrade is donating his sperm to impregnate all the virgins in Brazil? I've heard they are very willing. How pure will your race be? Does he have time left for you, my poor deceived Higler?"

"Enough!" Wolffe ordered gruffly. "We know Commandant Treiger is furious and rightly so. The issue of a saboteur is devastatingly serious, but we must not lower ourselves to derision. However, I still don't feel there has been a serious breach. After all, Stoltz has demonstrated his commitment, even if he has been over zealous."

Treiger swore to himself. He had been playing rook to king's knight, but now felt he had to castle. He began in a more accommodating tone. "Of course you are right, General. Let me explain. We of the old guard have taken risks, persisted with Kleis's genius and used our limitless monetary resources to operationalize our plan. I may have become eccentrically persistent, which is part of my German heritage, but if this is to proceed we must trust each other and work as a team. To have a wild card like Stoltz is exceedingly dangerous. If there is one lesson I have learned as an old decrepit commandant," he looked deliberately at Higler, "is not to leave the most critical elements of a plan to rebels. A lesson I suggest you all adopt if this mission is to survive."

Higler's voice edged with triumph. "What about the secret samples you took to Quebec?"

Treiger surveyed the others. Their eyes were back on him, digesting Higler's words with serious contemplation. He'd almost had them eating out of his hand, pushovers swayed by rhetoric, but now this stabbing accusation hung in the air. He coughed slightly and frowned as if hurt, replying softly, "You simply needed to ask me."

All eyes relaxed, except for Higler, who was holding back, taking up more vital time. He gave Higler the briefest condescending look and continued without flinching, seemingly considering the facts. "We have come so far with so much success under the greatest odds. We have lived to create a far greater vision than even Hitler could have imagined. I now fear that on the eve of our great renaissance, there is the risk that all could be lost. Our original plan was that, through me, the mission would begin in Quebec. I have been working very hard to ensure that the strike would not only be a tremendous success, but also a template for the following onslaughts. For that reason I took samples north for pre-testing. By doing this, I have taken greater risks of exposure than anyone here has in this room or elsewhere. Did I alter the whole shape of our plan by doing this? Of course not! But Stoltz has. He has changed the final key steps of our game plan, making us vulnerable to mistakes. Any mishap could create a perilous setback. We must stick together."

At this point, three heads were vigorously nodding in agreement. Higler had lost face. Would that mean more defiance, more time? Treiger's jaw tightened. He could not proceed without the answer, so he tried again with an appeasing tone. "Is Stoltz still in Germany?" Somehow the general change in mood and brevity of this statement seemed to work.

Higler replied simply, "No, his plans are to join me in Montreal, while the rest set up their individual operations."

Treiger gave a broad smile. "I will then take responsibility of notifying Braun of the situation. It will be useful for me to know when Stoltz will arrive in Montreal. I think we all should be aware of each other's whereabouts until this matter is settled. Is everyone agreed?"

The general murmur of approval was lost on Higler who sat even and still with his eyes glaring at Treiger. There was no sign of defeat in his eyes, only piercing hatred.

Time forced Treiger to push on; using the same tone of reason, he continued. "Alright then, at this point we can proceed no further until there is a guarantee of our success without any form of treason. However, I see no reason to delay the initial phase if we are in contact with Stoltz. Are we agreed? Good. Now Commander Higler, if you would be so kind as to inform me of Commander Stoltz's agenda? I want to deal with this as expediently as possible."

Higler looked around the table slowly, then as if the information was of no consequence, said easily, "Stoltz is due to arrive in Florida for an overnight stay at the island before proceeding to Montreal. I am to meet him there to commence stage one of the project."

A warning light flashed in Treiger's brain. Higler wasn't really knocking over his king in defeat. He was only going through the motions. This was the second time Higler had referred to the Quebec operation without including him. Such an assured slip most likely meant the two bastards had already planned to take over the whole enterprise. Killing him was probably high on their agenda. This match had taken time, but he'd found out what he needed to know. Certainly well worth the risk. Treiger smiled slowly. He saw everyone around the table relax.

Clearing his throat as if wanting to speak again, he paused and casually put his hand in his pocket, letting his fingers mold over the cold steel of his Rugar. Tightening his biceps, he whipped out the gun in a direct aim at Higler's temple and pulled the trigger.

The Aryan super-humanly evaded the shock attack with a lightening dodge to the left. The bullet only grazed his uniform. Higler rolled towards his brief case and probably a weapon. Treiger fired rapidly into the leather case knocking it away. Higler ducked behind the steel shelf and re-routed with jackal-like speed through the rear exit.

Bergermeyer, the most agile of the three, gave a shocked jump up, knocking over his chair. He lunged across the table, his eyes stretched wide with rage.

Treiger was ready for him. He reached out his free hand and encircled Walther Bergermeyer's throat with a lion's grip and twisted him down on the table. Bergermeyer gagged in disbelieving surprise. His hands clawed at Treiger's wrist, but the hold continued like the clenched bite of a starving lion. He remained helplessly pinned to the table gasping for breath.

Having temporarily disabled one, Treiger swung his gun towards a stunned looking Kleis who was on his feet. Still wearing his lab coat, he stood as if deciding whether to help Bergermeyer or bolt for the door. The effect made him remain paralysed staring straight into the barrel of Treiger's gun. The gun executed a perfectly centred shot into his forehead. Kleis slumped to the ground like a puppet. Treiger placed the gun to Bergermeyer's head. As he struggled and choked to move away, his eyes searched in vain for answers on Treiger's face. When he saw Treiger point the gun at him, his eyes reverted to a look of scornful loathing. That look reminded Treiger of the night in Berlin when he had knocked on Bergermeyer's door. Treiger didn't hesitate. He fired.

Letting the sagging body go, he reached for Wolffe who hadn't even managed to move from his chair. Only seconds had elapsed, but his one slip-up, Higler, could be fatal. Higler, like Stoltz, would be a vicious opponent.

Treiger's mind raced, powered by the adrenaline pumping through his veins. With Higler on the loose, he might need a blind. Wolffe wouldn't be perfect, but he was all he had at the moment. Treiger dragged the protesting general through the back entry and proceeded cautiously down the hallway. Higler went either outside and into the jungle, or into the adjacent hanger. Treiger heard the door to the conference room smash open, followed by pounding footsteps and shouted orders.

Treiger spoke shortly in Wolffe's ear. "One word and you're dead." He pressed the gun painfully against Wolffe's lower spine as the general started hacking. Two soldiers from the main entrance bounded towards them. Treiger gave an enraged bellow, "Get Higler! He's gone mad. General Wolffe is wounded. I'll look after him." The soldiers reacted with skilled exactitude and, without a word, divided their forces. One slipped through the door into the storage hangar, while the other called into his walkie-talkie for reinforcements before carefully stealing outside.

Treiger pushed Wolffe back to the conference room. He edged carefully through the doorway shoving Wolffe's reluctant form in front. Their entrance surprised the four young scientists gawking at the bloody corpses of Bergermeyer and Kleis.

Treiger barked at them, "Get out of here. Act quickly. Higler planted explosives in the lab!" His eyes grasped the one he'd encountered earlier. "We must find and disarm that bomb immediately. The computer programs and remaining shipment must be saved!"

One in the group blurted in dispute, "But sir!"

Treiger's knife-sharp glance slashed him to a stop. He wrenched his gun into Wolffe's back making him stagger and yelp with pain. Treiger yelled out, "Can't you see General Wolffe is wounded. Do as I say! NOW! I will try to save the General's life." The four raced back through the hallway into the lab as Treiger forced Wolffe to the exit. The old general stumbled painfully as he was jostled through the door.

Joao, dutifully waiting near the plane, suddenly darted forward, crossing the distance in seconds. Treiger shoved the old man towards Joao. "Take him, and if anyone asks, say he must be flown out for medical attention. I must deal with the unfinished details. You get ready for take-off."

Joao nodded and held the coughing general securely.

Treiger slammed another clip in his gun before entering the lab and bolting the door. He had to get the latest research data to Hans.

"We cannot find a bomb!" said the one scientist he had addressed earlier, who now assumed a stance of authority. "Sir, the other three are no longer needed. I can save the computer programs if it is still necessary. I request permission for them to depart."

"What is your name?"

"Hebner, sir!"

Treiger saluted them all and spoke very clearly. "I'm afraid your request won't be possible. Your bravery, however, is noted." Treiger levelled his Rugar at the closest. A spit fired from the silencer then angled rapidly to the right, firing again before pivoting a final shot into the temple of the third. All three fell sequentially without one having a chance to react. Treiger took a quick stride to Hebner, the only one left standing, and said to the shaken young man, "Hebner, do as I say and then I may consider allowing you to live."

Relief leaked into Hebner's eyes. "Thank you Commandant. I will not disappoint you."

Speaking slowly and calmly, Treiger said, "You have approximately one and a half minutes to send Kleis's work to this e-mail, then delete the whole operation here." With one hand, he typed the location, while his other hand kept the gun trained on his captive. A pounding on the door made Hebner's head swivel to the side as a harsh German command rang through from the other side. "Open the door!"

Treiger placed the silencer to Hebner's head, and replied. "We've found the bomb that Commandant Higler planted. Leave us. Wait! Before you go do you know where Higler is?"

"He set off into the rainforest by helicopter. Do you have further orders?"

"Leave us and go after him. We need to disarm this bomb!" The only reply was the light clatter of Hebner's typing echoing through the lab, which stopped seconds later when Hebner raised his head. "It's been sent, Sir."

Treiger numbed himself before pulling the trigger. The body slumped over the console smearing the keyboard with crimson blood. Treiger glanced down at the young man who seemed no older than he was when he started his plan in Montreal. He regretted the killing, but no loose ends could be left in this place.

A blast sounded from outside. Treiger ripped open his shirt and stripped off the packet of Semtex from his chest. He pressed the mass under the main console and attached a detonator, then flung himself from the building knowing only seconds remained. Wolffe's grey helicopter was in the midst of take-off. The noise and the dust added to the confusion. Treiger was acutely aware that even though the lab was about to explode, Joao's diversion was more of a problem. The compound was now peppered with more bombs, all timed to go off in sequence. His time was stretched to the limit.

A soldier came from nowhere, running near him. Treiger swerved to make contact screaming, "Save yourself!" while grabbing the knife from his belt. Aiming between the fourth and fifth ribs, he collided with the soldier, piercing the left ventricle. The soldier convulsed as the heart muscle fibrillated uncontrollably. Time was up and the lab too close. A thundering explosion spewed forth in searing red and white. The erupting mass shot projectiles in a smothering cloud. Treiger let the soldier's carcass fall over his torso as shards of metal and glass impaled the body on top of him.

A second later it was over and he pushed the dead weight away. More deafening blasts sent reverberations shuddering along the ground as other bombs detonated further away. Amidst the pandemonium, more soldiers ran towards him. Knowing how well the Gau-trained breed responded to authority, he shouted a command to search for survivors.

Explosions continued to rumble under his feet almost knocking him off balance. The distance to the plane seemed almost unreachable. With shear gut force he staggered forward, reaching the jet breathlessly just as the runway hangar jettisoned into an inferno.

Joao wordlessly shoved a parachute on Treiger's back and hoisted him up to the pilot's seat. Wolffe, now unconscious, was stuffed into the rear seat. Treiger readied for take-off hoping Joao would cram himself on top of Wolffe ASAP. Thought became reality as Joao's voice crackled on the intercom. "Time to go, Boss. Runway blasts next."

CHAPTER 5

Fiona Kendall undid her skimpy lace bra and discarded the silky under-thing on the Italian-ceramic floor. She delicately leaned over to test the temperature of the bubbling Jacuzzi. *What a day. Arduous and cruel. And where's bloody Richard!* Not wanting aggravation to completely win over her vulnerable state, she took a large sip of French Chardonnay, allowing the soothing mouthful to swirl in her mouth before swallowing. Her thumb looped under an edge of thong panty, sliding the string off, and she approvingly examined her slender legs before gliding them into the softly undulating water. The heady scent of Stephanotis bath essence engulfed her as foaming suds covered her body. *Ooo, so good.* Her eyelids drooped as the elixir of bath and booze blotted out the day.

Sharp rings from the bedroom phone bit into her softening mood, but she groggily relaxed when the answering machine clicked on. "Hi, It's Meg. Just checking to see if you're OK. Call me soon. Bye."

Her hands lazily stroked through the water and she sighed, as her mind dictated *'don't fall asleep'*, so she toted herself out of the water pulling a huge towel around her. During her soak, the sun had gone down. The entire house, upstairs and down, was totally dark, but she didn't care and let the towel slide away as she wandered gingerly into the bedroom. A floorboard under the plush carpet creaked as she reached for Richard's mahogany dresser. Crossing her furniture-studded minefield would be too much of a challenge. Finally she dropped under their king-size duvet and fell immediately into a sweet state of oblivion.

Her eyes flew open. She'd been asleep, but for how long, she didn't know, and wasn't sure why she woke. *Another nightmare?* Anyhow, she hated waking up tense and afraid. Deathly quiet kicked her mind into action. *Is Richard home? No. Too quiet. It can't be him.* She looked into the blackness where grotesque shapes of nothingness reflected back; fear made her wooden in the paralysing stillness. She opened her lips, inhaling carefully; taut chest muscles controlled each breath. A looming panic threatened her judgement, shaping itself into a strange sense of terror that taunted her senses. She could feel an alien presence in the house. Her eyes remained targeted towards the door; her ears peaked, listening through the eternity of another minute. Nothing happened, so she forced her head back on the pillow. *I'm just shaken up. My mind's playing tricks.*

The next thing she knew her head jumped again. *What's that! A creak. The stairs did creak. I know I heard something that time.* She kept still and waited. *It's nothing, silly! Just an over-active imagination. After all, this is an old house.* She shook her head to clear her mind of the tyrannical fear, but then tilted it towards the door. *Or is there something?* Now she could vaguely see through the half-opened door. *What is it? Wait? Did that shadow move? Come on! It's only the hallstand. What if it isn't?* Suddenly, the duvet didn't feel thick any more. A fine film of moisture covered her body making the cotton fibres cling to her bare skin. She quivered as goose bumps spread down her arms and over her breasts. Her eyes strained to see through the dark.

Please, God. Please, let it be nothing. Richard, come home! She thought she saw a narrow beam of light play in the hallway then disappear. *Shit, something's in the house! Oh, God. What do I do now?* She wanted desperately to pinch herself out of this dream, but didn't dare move.

Suddenly, a barely audible scrape cut the silence. Spasms of helplessness made every breath an echo. Convinced she saw light scurry over the doorframe, Fiona carefully slid her head off the pillow and under the duvet. There was a little slit between the cover and the bed giving her a narrow angle view. Straining her eyes, she could see the doorframe. Suddenly the little light skittered again, but vanished as the slit almost closed from the weight of the cover. *Maybe a stray cat got in the house or I'm going nuts.* The suffocating feather dome forced her to let another desperate breath seep in, each second endless until something slid over the carpet. *It's not real. Stay out! Stay out! Stay out!* She scrunched her eyes shut. *Don't move! Oh God! Jesus in heaven! It's coming in!*

She heard a click. Swamped with fright, she forced her eyes open to little more than a sliver of light. An awful dread took over when thudding, confident footsteps came close. They stopped. Her mind jolted. Thoughts scrambled madly making her want to make a run for it until a vague instinct of survival crawled into her consciousness hoping to depend on clear thinking. She made a valiant effort to pull herself together. *Sounds like a man...why did he stop? God, please don't let him notice me!* Desperation made her throat constrict. She listened carefully trying to track his whereabouts. Her mind fuzzily remembered bits of the room, like the duck-head bookends on the bedside table. The floorboards creaked under the carpet. *Toward the end of the bed? Yes, but past the end...towards Richard's bureau.* A drawer opened. She heard the muted scuffle of clothes being shoved around. Another drawer slid open, followed by a dull thud. Time floundered as she heard each drawer recklessly opened, violated, then left as if the contents meant nothing. She winced, imagining him kicking through the clothes in a haphazard search. *The bastard's robbing us!*

With random steps pacing near then far, she compelled every cell to lay deathly still, but shivers rambled over her naked skin. The thick air under the duvet made each breath a labour and her tongue stuck to the roof of her mouth as she swallowed.

A distant floorboard creaked. *He's leaving!*

But the footsteps halted and a fast tramping made its way back into the room.

The bed! He's thinking he missed the bed. Her lungs turned to stone as she felt X-ray vision exposing her— a breath away the tiny slit suddenly turned jean blue as his thigh brushed the sheet. *This is it!* Her ballooning lungs burst into a noisy inward suck just as the duvet sheared off her head.

She blinked into the bright room. No one was there.

Suddenly she saw a hand clutching the duvet with its body crouched under the bed. Without willing it, a primal defence gathered like a black cloud. Her eyes sped to a brass bookend beside the phone. She inhaled and swooped up the weighed duck-head with all her might as the face jerked into view. The bookend came down on the three round circles that she had seen covered with nylon mesh that morning, only this time they had a nose, cheeks and thin brown hair. He plunked with dough-like consistency to the floor. Red seeped from a gash on his brow.

Did I kill him? Quivering, Fiona gathered the duvet around her dragging the feather-filled sac to the bureau. She rescued some panties from the edge of a drawer, awkwardly slipped into them, and then hooked on her robe, tying it firmly closed. As if in a trance, she trod over to the still form, surveying him warily. A penlight was sliding out of his jeans' pocket with one of her diamond rings caught on the shaft. *Thieving bugger!*

Giving a quick look back and forth, she eyed her nail kit lying open amongst the ransacked drawers and used the scissors to hack a drape cord free. Triumphantly, she stomped over to his flat form and nudged him with her toe. *Still breathing.* She tied both hands before pushing his legs up closer to his body and pulling the rope taught around the ankles, frenetically finishing with a barrage of overlapping knots. Her hog-tying didn't seem finished. She looked about quickly, glancing back at him in fear that he might try to lunge at her like a mad dog. She hastily rummaged through the mess and found some black leotards. *Perfect.* She pulled the stockings over his head trying to be careful of the congealing blood, but making sure to get a thick wad of the black elastic over his eyes.

"Arghhh!"

The ugly sound thrashed up her fear. Slowly, she backed away, closer to the hallway door. He tried to move his hands up, but she hadn't left enough cord from hands to feet. He tugged at the rope again as if trying to figure out why he couldn't move them.

"Ugh...ugh."

"Don't move!" she said redundantly.

"Take this thing off my eyes," he said groggily, "Ow...my head. What happened? Where am I?" His head made a pathetic struggle to rise up, but as if that was too painful replaced itself gently back on the floor. He lay there and moaned.

"Shut up."

"Take these ropes off me and this damn blindfold, too. I'm OK now."

"Well, I'm not OK. You stole my ring and scared me to death!" Fiona glared wide-eyed at his ludicrously trussed body. He looked so thin, a stark disparity from what she imagined under the duvet.

He bent his hands towards his head until they yanked to a stop, causing the rope to pull his feet upward. He rolled back and forth in an odd unbalanced way trying to sit before falling back to his original position. "Fuck that hurts!" he yelped. His hands kept up a tug of war with the rope as his arms jerked with resistance. That seemed to clear his head. "Shit! You're not supposed to be home."

"Who in God's name do you think you are? You bastard! You nearly killed me this morning. Now you vandalize my home! You're going to be sorry when my hus..." The thought of Richard threw her off a rant. She had no idea when Richard would arrive. Momentarily confused, thoughts stumbled over each other until she managed to say, "Just look at the mess you've made," sweeping her hand broadly to include the scattered garments around the blindfolded man.

"I can't see," he said simply.

"It doesn't matter if you can see or not. I'm calling the police."

"Please, don't do that."

More confusion invaded her phoney self-confidence. She wanted someone with her. INSTANTLY. Shuffling distrustfully around him to the phone, her finger stabbed memory two. As each ring finished, tears rimmed her eyes. When the answering machine finally clicked on Fiona screamed, "Megan, where are you?" and started sobbing her story onto the recorder.

All of a sudden Megan's voice came on. "Fiona! I'm sorry I was painting and couldn't get to the phone in time. You said someone broke in! Are you alright?"

"It's the thief from this morning. He's tied up…in our bedroom." The man started to speak. Fiona momentarily turned from the phone to say. "Shut up." but immediately turned back to the receiver with, "I need help! NOW!"

"I'll be right over, but in the meantime call the police. They'll give you advice and send someone to help. Keep your distance from that man until I get there."

CHAPTER 6

Berlin, 1943

Karl Treiger snuck carefully down the grid stairway. The abysmal echo from each rung made good sense question his bravado. He knew there was probably time to retrace his steps before the guard upstairs returned, but he desperately wanted to piece together the mystery. By the last step, he defeated caution with some boyish convincing that he'd not get caught and stole along the corridor passed metal-covered doors. Single light bulbs hooded with tin covers cast pallid umbrellas of light along his route. This labyrinth of rooms, dubbed 'the bunker', was hidden underneath the Chancery. Rumour had it that this steel foxhole was targeted for a special project, that is, until Hitler returned from Prussia. Trailing the fingers of one hand along the curved wall, he looked back; the stairway was no longer visible. Silence strained from behind each door until, after taking a few more dissatisfied steps, he heard something.

Following a momentary pause, he decided risk had taken over his life two years ago after Walther Bergermeyer notified the Gestapo of his whereabouts. At the time he'd expected to be executed like his parents. Certainly, he would have been disposed of if the interrogation had worked. Since then he had grown taller than some adults around him and more often than not, everyone presumed him to be much older. That along with his striking blue eyes and blonde hair made him attractive to the eye. Girls, even women, often turned their heads as he walked by, but he ignored them, wanting no distraction from his objective. Descending into the bunker was simply another step towards his goal.

His luck he attributed to an astute sense of observation, but his survival was ironically due to an SS officer named Volker Braun. Bergermeyer, the smarmy squealer slipped up, revealing that Karl had turned himself in. This information had greatly interested *Reichsführer* Braun. Fortunately, Braun's interest had targeted Karl's strengths, one of which turned out to be a genius with numbers. That quality made him more useful than most other Hitler Youths; some of who had recently been sent to fight in the Ardennes, but Braun had arranged a special job for Karl here in the Reichstag. Regrettably, Walther Bergermeyer had similar aptitudes and had been placed in the same office, but today he had stayed away with the flu. Walther was blonde too, but his eyes were grey and his body fleshy.

At times Walther could be a fertile source of hearsay so Karl tolerated him, but he would never forget the interrogation chamber; cold concrete with damp walls, the clanging iron door…or the smell of old urine choked over with bleach. He remembered too, the central wooden chair and gooseneck spotlight; the small desk and chair with a light bulb suspended above— a lone yellow glow making the room blend into the pasty grey uniforms of two guards. But it was the emptiness that wailed despair.

After being pushed around and yelled at, one of the officers tied Karl's hands around the chair-back. Faced away from the door, he kept telling himself not to fear the monsters, but part of him wished he would die like his parents. He stared blankly at the guards. A glimmer of satisfaction surfaced when his stare seemed to irritate them. Finally one of the guards grabbed a dirty rag from the floor and tied it around Karl's eyes, leaving him only the miserable sound of footsteps pacing about the room.

Suddenly, the lock scraped and hinges screamed resistance; the guards' heels clicked and he imagined them snapping to raised-arm attention when they barked, 'Heil Hitler'. A chair rasped along the floor, the desk drawer squeaked and papers shuffled. Karl could only wait.

He felt the person who had entered watching him, deliberately keeping silent. Karl's head was hanging down, but he raised it when boots moved close. His head jerked to the side as a blistering slap blazed across his jaw. He didn't cry out at the unexpected assault, but was glad that the blindfold soaked up the burning tears that sprung to his eyes. Karl hated the harsh sting that lingered on his cheek, but the taste of fresh blood in his mouth made him feel alive. He knew then that he had to survive, if only to hate.

"At least you don't snivel at a small cuff on the cheek."

The shrill words seared his brain— this was the cold-blooded killer of his parents. A steel shroud enclosed his heart, suspending time; he felt numb with the icy void of hatred. Suddenly the blindfold was torn off. Before Karl could blink, the hand struck again, followed with, "I don't like to repeat myself. What is your name?"

Having only seen the facial profile when hidden in his secret tunnel, he looked swiftly down hoping there was no sign of recognition on his face and saw, as if to confirm that this creature murdered his parents, the ring with the same death's head insignia and the same diamonds. The hand lifted to strike again, but fell away when Karl raised his head and looked straight in the tyrant's eyes, saying, "Karl Peiter Treiger."

He watched the murderer's contoured jaw form a tight smile. The blue eyes were eagle sharp, but the voice, smoothly placating. "Thank you. Since we will be getting to know each other very well, I will introduce myself. *SS-Reichsführer* Volker Braun. However, you will address me as Sir."

Over the next expanse of time, Karl played a treacherous game of snakes and ladders with the black uniformed Braun. Karl tested when to look enthralled with Braun's authority, when to look contrite, and when to look indignant revealing a sense of unfairness. But, most importantly, he had to calculate when to give specific facts. Persistently during the interrogation, Braun probed Karl for meeting places used in the 'illegal removal of Jewish orphans' from Germany. Several times one of the other officers switched on the blazing spotlight, making it difficult for Karl to see anything, but a grey blur. When the hot beam was shut off he felt almost blind. The repetition of burning light followed with the pall of cold dimness wore at his energy.

Braun left the cell only once and one guard took this opportunity to land a punch in his stomach. Karl didn't cry out, but left his mouth open breathing heavily and drooling. When Braun returned, he cursorily admonished the guards for hitting him, but without any pauses, continued his repetitive questioning. At some point Karl lost the sense of time. Desperate to appear co-operative, he tried to figure out what to say.

Karl somehow reckoned that the secret transport of children couldn't be continued after his parents' deaths. Surely the underground conspirators would have to disband making old dates and times safe to give. He rambled on with volumes of irrelevant detail ending with, "My parents lied to me. They told me I was doing a great deed for the *Führer*."

Braun shrieked for the guard to transcribe every syllable and then he turned on Karl again; "Every piece of information is different. How am I to believe you?"

"I never used the same route. There wasn't any pattern to what I did."

"Well, your parents weren't all that smart. They've put you in grave danger. You are here, enduring this unpleasantness because of them. Your parents are traitors and they will be severely punished!"

A lump formed in Karl's throat. If only it was true. If only his parents were still alive and this evil man dead. If only this were an awful nightmare. Karl remained mute rather than betray the renewed grief he felt. He twisted his mind away from despair and, deep within, began conjuring a vigorous will to despise and deceive.

Braun regarded him with his piercing blue stare. "Who are your parents working with? Who are their friends?"

It was true. He did know the identity of some organizers. A sweat broke out on his brow and he forced himself to forget the faces he had seen from his secret hiding place. Lies were tricky because they were detectable. He began by putting hesitant confidence into his voice as if he was really trying to help. "Really, sir, I would help you if I could. My parents didn't let me know anything. I admit I did escort the children, but they had me convinced the work was for Hitler. I thought if I did what they told me to I could become one of the Hitler Youth." Desperately he doled out a fabricated tale about how his parents held him back from joining the Youth brigade on the pretence that he was too young. He even threw in envy towards Hans for joining against his parents' wishes and finished by blurting out, "My brother always gets the lucky breaks because he's older."

"Well, perhaps this time the tables will turn for you," Braun said, sounding sly. "Now, forget your family. Tell me once more about the children you…um, escorted."

Karl looked at Braun trying to gauge how much further he could go with the lies. He had held his muscles taut for so long that they felt drained; fatigue consumed every cell in his body. He couldn't count the hours that had already passed going over and over the details with haranguing demands for more and more information. He wondered how much longer he could go on, so when he couldn't read from Braun's cold expression how he should react, he asked, "What do you want to know?"

Braun exploded "You know bloody well what I want to know! The truth! Don't act stupid. You are much brighter than that. You demean yourself and me!" He raised his hand as if to strike.

Karl wished Braun did hit him again. He wanted something to make the relentless fatigue go away. On the brink of crying like a baby if he didn't think of something to tell them, he managed to drag out a sliver of energy from deep within, and started to talk, slowly at first, choosing his words carefully. He finally realised he could safely pour out lengthy descriptions of the children, also adding that his parents felt he was only capable as a guide. Besides, Karl argued, they weren't that certain how much he could be trusted, especially since they forced him to co-operate. He continued, even when his mouth was parched and his desiccated tongue clicked on his palate. Braun frequently sipped from a glass of water. Finally food was brought in. The guards ate in front of him with taunting satisfaction. Braun ate nothing. At first, Karl tried to look away, but his stomached gnawed with hunger so he decided to stare because focusing on the hunger was so much more bearable than the thirst, but still, he talked until he could think no more.

Finally, Braun smiled and said, "That's more like it. Now we need to switch to a more personal topic— that of your parents."

Karl looked at him hollowly. He thought he had no energy left, but this man seemed to invoke an unfathomable torrent of hatred as fuel. He used the heart-rending energy from his parents' massacre, weaving the memory into words of loathing. A critical element was to think of them as still alive; hinting any knowledge of their death would be lethal. Karl churned out his words with as much spite as he could muster, "My parents are weak— more like children than parents. I cannot rely on them. Only at school did I begin to realise that the secrecy they demand of me is wrong. I see now that they despise our wonderful *Führer* Hitler. I am ashamed to be their son." He scathed them with unmerciful lies. Words flowed out maliciously, particularly about his father. "My father is wretched and useless. He never stands up for his family so how can he ever stand up for anything as great as the *Führer*. He deceived me— used me for his own sinful purposes. A father should never ask such a thing of his son as mine did of me. ...And my mother, she follows him like a...a sheep. They can't be trusted." Karl cursed loudly that he never wanted to see them again, crying out to the *Reichsführer*, "Protect me, sir. Protect me from their shame. They are evil." With this blast, Karl knew his daring to convince was ebbing and stopped, hoping it had sounded believable.

Braun started pacing with his hands grasped behind his back. With each step Karl felt tension building. Every muscle in his body screamed for release from the timeless pressure as he waited each slow drip of a second for the verdict. Braun seemed to brood, giving an occasional intense stare. Exhaustion bleated for a final judgement. One more question would be unbearable.

Suddenly, the pacing stopped. Braun eyed him warily before bringing his snout right in front of Karl's face, the words spat out just like before his parents were slaughtered. A question, the question he feared most hit like a boxer's punch. "Why, my dear young friend, did you and your brother not go against your parents wishes earlier and report them? Are you both cowards or just good liars?" Braun's fist came smashing down on the stand beside Karl's chair. The gooseneck lamp smashed on the floor.

The steel vice around Karl's heart turned colder and started to squeeze. He knew that he sat on the sharp edge of a sword. If he said anything wrong, it could mean death for both Hans and himself. Hiding his fear with hard eyes, he tried for candid arrogance. "My brother is an idiot! If you had talked to him you would know. I never know what he is doing. Why, it was only yesterday that I found out that he had joined the Hitler Youth. He did what I dreamt of doing. I made a mistake. All the time he was out of the house I thought he was fucking girls! Go find him and ask him. I'm tired of this."

Braun scrutinized him again for an endless minute. More damp formed along

Karl's hairline and his heart thundered. Finally Braun, seeming to have come to a decision, replied, "As a matter of fact I have spoken to your brother and you are right. He is intelligent like you, but he is merely a follower." He slapped his black leather gloves sharply in his palm while again looking at Karl. He leaned over to the guard and gave instructions in an undertone then left.

Karl shifted uneasily in his chair, speculating over what decision Braun had made and he was dying to ask about Hans. Had he been treated like this? Hans, for sure, would have broken down. But he didn't know anything. He couldn't have betrayed them. Perhaps the *Reichsführer* was lying again. Perhaps he had assassinated Hans like he had his parents. A shiver ran through him. For the first time, the exhaustion left him feeling small and alone, but he knew he had done his best.

He was untied and hustled to another part of the building where he was shoved into a small room set up with a few furnishings, sink and toilet. His tired mind almost disbelieved the inquisition was over. A hot meal sat on a stool by the cot. He eyed the food with envy. It seemed like days had passed since his last meal, but he didn't touch anything or move too far into the room until the door was completely shut. He ran to the sink and turned the tap, slurping hungrily until some of the water snuffed up his nose. Cold, pressured pain across his forehead reminded him that he had to stay in control. He looked back to the bedside table and made himself slowly walk to the bed and sit down. Only then did he pick up the metal tin filled with watery stew. He thought he'd never smelled anything so good. He gobbled down the contents then cleaned the sides with his fingers, licking each one clean. His belly ached with satisfaction, but he knew he could never satisfy the hungry hatred inside. He looked at the locked door and then slumped across the bed in a deep sleep.

The sound of the lock being turned snapped him awake. An SS-guard, not seeming to care if Karl was awake, tossed a stack of folded clothes on the floor and tersely told him to get cleaned up. Using the sink, he did the best he could with the scratchy towel provided, before going over to the uniform. Emblazoned on the front left pocket was a death's head insignia. This was a Hitler*jugend* uniform. He couldn't think of a better way to survive and quickly put on the black pants, brown shirt with its special cuff band and a Boy Scout type necktie. He went back to the mirror and, wanting to make a good impression, ran his hands through his hair drawing the strands straight back so as to let the hair part centrally. Satisfied with the effect, he walked to the door and tried the handle. It was unlocked. The guard escorted Karl for evaluation, which eventually brought him to the Chancery where he listed funds and funnelled the results to Braun.

Two years in the office upstairs had given Karl some understanding about the Chancery and the workings of the Reich. He was considered an efficient, trustworthy nothing. Nothing, Karl thought, because the *Führer* only acknowledged the Hitler Youth who were courageously fighting and dying for the fatherland. And nothing because he preferred to be that way. He had fashioned himself into a self-made spy. Braun made certain that Karl got an education and special training in-between his paperwork. Only recently Karl had realised that the figures he dealt with were the finances of a very special branch of the Reich administered by Braun.

Braun had also arranged for special training in martial arts. Karl loved the discipline the sessions required. He often lived for those hours of concentration, learning to fight in an exacting manner, but overall avoided friendships and he kept to himself. Braun seemed to like the fact that he remained aloof from others. It irked Karl that he was apparently being prepared for something, but was not privy to the purpose. He learned to be innocuously observant yet, all the while, he eavesdropped and lip-read, trying to glean any scrap of information that would solve the bunker mystery. Braun dryly informed Karl that patience was part of his preparation and any further probing was immediately silenced. So for months Karl sat obediently at his desk day in and day out until today. Today was his first chance to sneak down to the bunker without Walther looking over his shoulder. Today was a day for action.

Earlier, Karl had seen a group of blond, well-muscled young men march past his office and disappear through the door to the bunker. That was not unusual having happened frequently over the past weeks, but they were trailed by Braun and some other men, one of whom he knew as Doctor Buch and another kindly military man called General Wolffe. Most important was Martin Bormann, Hitler's right hand man. Something was cooking. The urge to follow hunkered in his mind as he tried to concentrate. Forty minutes later the slick, blond specimens returned along the corridor. He wished he had been part of the select few and got the inside story, but being irrelevant in the intricate workings of the Reich had its advantages; he could sneak about unnoticed.

As the moments ticked by, impetuous curiosity prodded his courage. Finally the guard left his post. Karl had noticed different guards do this and disappear for quite long periods. He supposed security wasn't very strict because Hitler was seldom at the Chancery, spending most of his time at his headquarters in East Prussia. In fact, Karl had caught a glimpse of the *Führer* only once. The awe that the man's powerful presence had on others astonished Karl. After Hitler left, he wondered how such a short, almost insignificant figure of a man could have such an overwhelming effect.

Moments ago, it had been so easy to stand up from his paperwork and stretch as if he needed a break, then to put his hands in his pockets before strolling into the hall where, through the windows of nearby offices, he made sure everyone was busily occupied before disappearing down here. Patience and observation were the ultimate tools in his spy kit.

Muffled words became clearer as Karl stepped lightly up to one door. He laid his ear against the metal covering to get a fix on the mix of voices. Almost immediately the talking stopped. He stayed motionless.

In the same instant he realised his mistake, the door swung open. He lost his balance and sprawled into the room.

CHAPTER 7

Northern Amazon

Treiger started taxiing down the jungle-sided runway as more blasts ripped across the compound. Every second counted. While he had been dealing with the Gau, Joao had peppered the area with timed explosives, including the runway. Somehow he had to get this jet in the air before those detonated. He advanced the throttle.

Without warning, a thundering blast rammed him against the cockpit. Behind the jet, concrete erupted in a perpendicular hulk. He spoke into his headset, "Guess the meeting took too long, Joao!"

The words were barely out of his mouth when a second explosion shook them, crashing tarmac across the windshield. The wheels jolted over cracked asphalt. Treiger braced as waves of another blast shocked them. A dangerous slab of concrete slammed down metres in front. Swerving was out. There'd be only one chance. With barely enough speed for take-off, he wrenched the throttle back. The nose lifted, but their load was too heavy. The rear wheels crunched on the concrete hunk, whip-lashing them as the wings tilted perilously. Suddenly the powerful impact of another blast from the rear riveted through them. The jet hurled forward, heading up at a sharp angle. Treiger glanced back. The runway was completely decimated and probably the landing gear was wrecked. There was no turning back.

Over the intercom came a rare Yanomamö quip, which roughly translated as, "Good timing, Boss." Joao also added that he'd seen the quarry heading north.

Most likely, Higler had already radioed the second helicopter knocking it out as an ally. Both helicopters had missile capacity, but the jet outmatched them in firepower. However, with their manoeuvrability, they could set him up as a target along the zigzagging river bends. They were above the Abacaxis tributary of the Amazon, Yanomamö territory. He flew low, scanning the horizon. Wolffe's Aerospatiale would be easier to sight than Higler's camouflage-green Rooivalk. Treiger looked over the vast meandering river with its elongated elbow curves, and in the distance saw the grey Aerospatiale. And right in front, barely visible, was Higler, heading back towards home base. As if spotting the jet, both veered sharply around a bend and disappeared.

Treiger dipped the jet's nose in rapid descent, keeping his eyes on the riverbank. Higler was very good at evasive tactics and time was short. He wanted to eliminate Higler from the equation, but had to leave enough juice to make his way to Florida and Stoltz. He scanned below as he relayed his plans to Joao, wanting his friend to consider his own options. Florida would not be on Joao's agenda.

Risking the time, Treiger descended to the river surface, figuring that the jet's wingspan would fit between the walls of rainforest lining the river's edge. His aircraft could easily take out the two helicopters; he just had to find them. He estimated the place where they disappeared, then directed the plane to follow the river. The old tributary had long tortuous stretches of brown water broken up with huge hairpin bends, making his flight tricky. On the first bend he misjudged the distance and the left wing sliced through tips of the thick foliage. He needed more of a tilt on the turns even if the risk of hitting water was greater. The innocent-looking tributary would rip a wing right off if it contacted the surface, but at a higher altitude they might miss the copters. The jet shot over the murky waters. Treiger judged the turns well until, up ahead, he saw a wall of lifeless husks of trees shooting high out of the water. A dead flood pool. Reacting with split-second timing, he zoomed the nose skyward. Hell. No time for second chances.

Static crackled over the intercom. "Passing them. Well hidden." Joao's sharp eyes had caught the gleam of a rotor. A nice piece of luck. Higler was dangerous to leave alive, but not as critically threatening as Stoltz. He could cut his losses and head for Florida, but fate had given him a chance to dispose of this menace. He flew a wide circle and aimed for the bend with the protruding deadheads. His missiles were ready.

As soon as Treiger saw the exposed rotary spindle, he fired. A heat-seeker shot out from under the wing, streaking across the water. Blind impact. Chunks of grey wreckage, smoke and fire flared hundreds of feet in the sky. Raging debris ripped through the dense green background with mutilating fury. Fuel tanks must have been full. Treiger scrutinized the wreck on a return fly over. No evidence of Higler's Rooivalk. An annoyed growl escaped from his throat. He'd been duped. Wolffe's Aerospatiale was a decoy. Higler was heading towards Venezuela, the unexpected direction, instead of south towards the base. He should have expected that—never choose the most obvious option in guerrilla combat. In any case, his next destination was north.

Soon the khaki green helicopter appeared in the distance, flying higher than Treiger expected. Treiger closed in for the kill.

Without warning, the Rooivalk exploded in mid-air. Treiger savagely looked round for another aircraft. The sky was clear. Damn Occam. More than likely it was one of Higler's crafty survival tactics, knowing he couldn't outrun the jet. Treiger scanned the territory below. A camouflaged parachute was floating down over the huge expanse of green, soon to disappear into the vast rainforest.

By now they had flown northeast far enough to be close to the Padauiri River and home of the Yanima. Of all the tribes in Brazil, the Yanima were known to be the most ferociously territorial. If anyone trespassed on their domain, the intruder was stalked and captured by the roving bands of Yanomamö braves— the ultimate rite of passage into manhood: vigilant, fearless, not to mention barbaric defence of their land. Higler was taking a major survival risk by invading their terrain. Treiger circled to get a fix on where the Aryan would land. "Joao, we're right in the middle of your hometown. I guess our friend Higler has decided he can outwit your countrymen."

Joao replied with a few curt words, "Possible for him to miss Yano hunter if smart, fast and silent, but difficult to survive in snake-infested rainforest...probably die." He spoke while adjusting his parachute and when he was finished, asked simply, "Take him," meaning the General.

Joao could easily dispose of Wolffe given that the old general wasn't wearing a parachute. Treiger, who couldn't help but give a wry smile at the economy of his expressions, replied, "No. That will be my job." Then asked without really knowing why, "Will you go after the German?"

"Maybe." Joao prevented any further conversation by removing his helmet with the communication module. He placed the headset on the General's head before pressing the automatic hatch release to exit the plane. The force of air buffeted the general who groaned, but continued his oblivious sag after the lid closed. Treiger figured his friend would dog Higler to the end. And nodding a salute in Joao's direction, he adjusted his course, estimating there was just enough fuel to reach the Florida coast.

He flew tirelessly through the night keeping the plane low and, feeling lucky that the weather over the Caribbean was dead calm, set his mind on his next steps. The plane was nearing the Florida coast when a low moaning voice came over the earphones. "What is happening? Who are you?"

He returned almost pleasantly with, "You're awake, Herr General."

"Treiger!" the General's astonished, shaky voice radioed back, "Are you insane?"

"Absurdly, you could be right. However, I've always considered you and the rest of the Gau to be the mad ones."

A confused voice crackled into the cockpit. "Is it true that Bergermeyer and Kleis are dead? I find it impossible... a nightmare! We have survived so long, worked so hard, to give the world a valuable future. Why, Karl? Why are you trying to destroy us? At least that is all I can suppose by your actions. Is it because you, who have never wanted power wanted it all along...have you tricked us all? That is it, isn't it? You want to lead the Gau Reich to its glory, but you know it's not possible. Younger Aryans like Stoltz will never submit to your authority."

The fuel gauge was flashing madly, but perhaps some explanation was due for old time's sake. Besides, one never knows what twists of fate lie in the future. He certainly hadn't planned to be en route to Florida in search of Stoltz. Treiger chose his words carefully. "Power is a seductive phenomenon, with a forceful potential to corrupt, but obtaining that kind of power means nothing to me. Hitler's Third Reich resulted, at least in part, from his strangely charismatic personality convincing others that the ideals of racial supremacy were justified. The Third Reich became a moral death camp for depraved, greedy monsters inflated with their own superiority. Unlike you, I never accepted the Gau as more evolved. However, you are quite right in noting that my whole life has appeared devoted to the cause. My actions must seem confusing. Let me assure you, I want to see the Gau's radical vision reach its proper destiny.

Indeed Wolffe, you are to be commended. All the money and brains you secreted out of Germany was a triumph. Your ability to conceal the whole operation allowed the Gau to flourish, dispersing us, like a tumour, cut out of the heart of Germany, and seeding itself in the Brazilian rainforest. Perhaps not a very appealing analogy, but it is the only one I can think of at the moment. Your ingenuity disabled several governments' attempts to detect the mushrooming Gau, and the manner in which you set up the organisation made my job all that more lengthy. At times I wondered if I could succeed, but thankfully I continued to believe in tenacious persistence. My own victory is near, but here's my destination and where I leave you to your destiny."

"But Treiger, you still didn't tell me why you're intent on destroying us?"

Treiger added sharply, "The Reich exterminated innumerable souls who didn't know why they came to their fate, but I don't believe where you are going, knowing will matter. The automatic guidance system will direct you towards the Bermuda Triangle—a fitting burial site." He looked down at the offshore island he'd been looking for and knowing the small runway at the far end was useless to him, he pushed eject and whooshed out into the tropical night with only minutes of fuel left. The chute opened with a sharp tug of reality. The jet flew into the dark, slowly rising to a higher elevation. The sound of the engine began to fade. He wondered if the American radar monitors would see a small blip on the screen. It would be indecipherable and, if search planes were sent, by the time they reached the area they would find nothing.

The ocean was ink black, but the island was well lit at one end. He steered his chute towards the beacon of lights until finally splashing into the water. The oblong landmass he swam towards was attached to the mainland by a private causeway and referred to by the Gau as 'the island'. Some guests used their own jets landing on the private runway on the other side of the island. The Gau often flew people in for their own purposes. Others used the causeway, but had to pass inspection at the bridge. The cost of a sojourn depended on who you were. Wealthy guests paid astronomical prices to come to this secret hideaway. Those whose background was questionable, but needed asylum, or possibly a quiet place to rejuvenate from their exploits, paid according to their means. Anyone who would bring notoriety from the press was excluded, particularly movie stars.

Treiger looked at his watch. Badly in need of a rest, he would wait until morning. The short swim beached him near the base of the causeway. He quickly secreted himself in a grove of palm trees and stretched out in the warm air, planning to rise before dawn.

Chapter 8

Westmount

Megan replaced the receiver, frowning. Fiona copped a thief. There's more to this than meets the eye. She patted her hip pocket where, since her assault two years ago, she kept a small switchblade and rushed down the lower stairs of the tiered deck. A sensor flashed over the gate between the two properties, but as Megan approached Fiona's back door, the light above the frame didn't work. Her moccasins crunched on broken glass as she climbed the steps, and even though she had Fiona's spare key, the door just pushed open. In spite of Danny Ménard's caution, Fiona mustn't have activated her alarm system. Careless girl.

Megan left the houselights off. Just in case. Keeping alert for sounds, she hurried through the kitchen, but instead of taking the exit to the hall stairway, she went into the drawing room. Hearing nothing, she rapidly traversed the perimeter moving through to the dining room and then into an immense living room. Streetlight filtered through the neon curtains showing the coast was clear, so she exited into the wide hallway and crossed over, peeking in Richard's office on the other side. The room was a shambles, overturned drawers and papers everywhere. She wondered what interest a thief might have in Richard's stodgy affairs. Now, reassured there were no more prowlers, she called out. "Fiona, its Megan."

Almost instantly an upstairs light switched on with Fiona appearing at the landing, one hand strangled the top of her robe shut as she huffed, "Thank God. I thought I'd die waiting."

"Did you call the police?"

"I called Detective Ménard!"

The statement struck Megan like a baseball bat, zapping her mind back to the desperate night of her own arrest. Blood hotly flushed her face as she climbed the stairs two at a time while tightly enunciating, "He's in homicide. This isn't his type of case."

Fiona rambled out, "Well, I didn't really speak with Daniel. I left the message with a polite Constable who said he would send someone right away."

Megan topped the stairs and softened as she took in Fiona's white face trumped up with courage. "You are brave. I didn't think you had it in you to catch a thief." She gave Fiona a quick hug hoping to prop up her nerve and said, "I'll guard him. You wait for the police. And turn on all the lights."

"I promised him he could have something to eat."

"I beg your pardon?"

"He looks cadaverous! I feel sorry for him. A bit of food won't hurt. Once the police get their hands on him, the man could go hungry for hours."

Megan took a deep breath. Fiona was indulgence personified—with a core of marshmallow. "Well, I'll have a look at him first. Then we'll see."

"I'm going with you," Fiona said, slipping her arm through Megan's.

On her way to the bedroom Megan weirdly felt this wasn't going to be a surprise and the moment she set eyes on the intruder she knew why, even with his head half swathed in black leotard and dried blood streaking down his face. "It's you."

The man's head tilted at the sound of her voice, but he said nothing.

"You saw him too!" squeaked Fiona.

"Just to be certain…" Megan walked over and pulled. The blindfold popped off.

"Ow!" The man blinked his squinty eyes.

"He was outside your house this morning, Fiona."

The man said again nothing, but Fiona exclaimed, "And he's the same one who stole my purse!"

His mouth opened to speak. They both waited. He dithered then twisted his jaw. "I thought she said I could have some food. I haven't eaten all day."

Megan crouched down. Such arrogant confidence. "You're lucky my friend is kind hearted, but remember the police are on their way." She patted his pockets and retrieved Fiona's ring. "Is this all you took?"

His lips pinched before he replied with, "That was all I had time for."

"By the looks of this room and the office downstairs you had plenty of time. What did you really want?"

"Money."

Megan didn't believe him. Ménard had suspected some other motive too. "This morning you had a gun. Where is it now?"

He shrugged his shoulders. "Got rid of it after robbing her."

Megan looked at Fiona. "The gun isn't in his pockets so I think we could risk taking him downstairs." Thinking her switchblade might upset Fiona, she decided not to use it and started untying the knotted cord around his ankles. He winced almost too convincingly as she pulled. The cord was tight, but his work boots protected his skin from the biting fibre. She decided to check and shoved up his pant leg.

He pulled his legs back. "What are you doing?"

"Just making certain I don't have anything to worry about." Megan stuck her fingers down the inside of one boot. The bulky leather hid the gun well. She bent her fingers around the handle and extracted the weapon. Fiona gasped. Megan looked at him carefully. His hands were tied in front, so with his feet freed, he might have been able to reach it. He looked frail, but was obviously more dangerous than she would have guessed. Her words came out angrily, "You lied to me."

He actually laughed. "What duh you expect? I want outta' here."

The tension broke with a pounding on the front door and a stern shout: 'POLICE'.

Fiona rushed away and in under a minute two officers marched in with Fiona insisting, as only Fiona could, that the man should be fed. Before Megan knew what was happening, all of them were in the kitchen. One of the officers was halfway through a wedge of lemon pie and the intruder was sitting at the counter awkwardly downing a big sandwich. Megan blinked. This is nuts. The doorbell rang. What next? Backup for pie.

"Can you get the door, Megan?" Fiona asked as she tipped a second slice from the Pyrex dish onto a plate, handing it to the officer beside the intruder.

"I don't think you should be interfering like this, Fiona," Megan muttered, but Fiona took no notice. The robber whined his sandwich had dropped because of the ropes. One officer pulled out handcuffs. Good move. She left.

Megan hurried to the front door, opening it without checking the peephole. She wished she had. Ménard's six-foot height towered before her. His lips were pressed together, but he managed to flash a concerned smile. She had half-hoped he would be off duty. A familiar anxiety filled her throat as she stood silently feeling his eyes on her. A dog barked in the distance.

He seemed to be waiting for her to say something, however finally opened with, "How extraordinary that I get to see you so soon, but a second incident in one day worries me. I see the police are here so I gather the situation is under control?"

Words finally shuffled out. "Yes, two policemen are already here. I expected more officers just now, but it was you... I mean, Fiona said she'd left a message for you, but I thought you might not get it. Not being your department and all." To show appreciation, she added, "It's a relief to see a familiar face." Feeling clogged with first date jitters, she awkwardly motioned him to follow, adding, "Our prisoner is in the kitchen, eating. Fiona thought he looked half starved and..."

A loud crash stopped her. Fiona screamed. A gun fired.

Ménard took her roughly by the shoulders and shoved her into a room off the hall. "Stay here!" he ordered before bolting towards the uproar. All her instincts screamed to follow, but she stayed listening as his steps pounded towards the kitchen.

Ménard blasted into the kitchen to see Fiona cowering against the fridge and one officer unconscious on the floor with blood from his head seeping through shards of glass and yellow slop. The back door hung open. "Call an ambulance," he commanded while dashing out the door. Sensor lights flashed along the garden wall, fleetingly revealing the other officer who then vanished behind some shrubs. Ménard followed, but high bushes blocked his view. He heard grunting gasps before a shrill order rang out. "Stop or I'll kill him!"

Ménard dared to take another step forward. The skinny thief was using his handcuffed wrists to pincer the policeman's neck in a strangle hold. Ménard raised his gun, but the strangler violently twisted the garrotted policeman upward as a body shield and then unleashed his vicious hold, shoving the choking officer against Ménard. They both fell back into the bushes. The sagging officer managed to gurgle, "*Ca va...vas y!*"

Ménard disentangled himself and scrambled onto the perimeter wall bounding towards the back with a better view. Motion-sensors flashed sequentially until he reached a square granite building along the ravine barrier. He hopped off the ledge and walked cautiously up the side, picking his way around some large stones. He raised his gun and gave a quick glance around the corner just as the last wall sensor switched off. There was only moonlight and no man. He listened, heard nothing, then slid along the dark facade and checked the door. It was padlocked. Possibly the perp had climbed over the wall on the other side. Ménard moved slowly forward around some construction material, barely missing a wheelbarrow by stepping on some rope. Suddenly, his foot caught and the rope yanked tight, snaring his foot in a noose.

He stumbled, and twisting to keep his balance, his hand hit the wheelbarrow. His gun clattered away as he landed face down on the path, barely missing a large stone with his head. Scraping footsteps came from behind. *Ca va pas bien.*

He lunged for the gun only managing to grab the barrel and roll over before a knee landed on his stomach, squeezing his guts and knocking his wind out. His left arm was pinned under him and another knee had rammed his gun arm, down forcing him to drop the nozzle. Above him, squinty eyes stared down. The handcuffed squinter grabbed clumsily for the gun, but only managed to whack the hilt away.

At least neither of us has a gun, Ménard thought as he struggled to heave the straddling man off his abdomen. A light flashed on, he wasn't sure from where, but he wished he couldn't see what was happening.

A large stone was suspended above his head ready to smash down. Powerlessly, he saw the resolve on the squinting face. Oddly, the squint worsened as the stone dropped. Instinctively, Ménard wrenched his head sideways, but the searing crush of stone on bone was inescapable. As if in a dream he heard his name called.

Megan waited less than thirty seconds before disobeying Ménard. She helped Fiona dial for an ambulance before going in search of him, but only found the stunned and choking officer pointing in a panic towards the back. She took out her switchblade and moved cautiously towards the carriage-house. Near the structure, she triggered a sensor. The area flooded with light. Lordy! Ménard's head was about to be smashed in. Gut instinct made her take aim and fling the knife. The blade hit the dropper's forearm, but the stone fell nonetheless. Shivers goosed down her spine. Rash. Stupid. So what! She sprinted forward. It was dark again. Ménard! Her voice sounded high. She heard fast steps and scuffing. She nearly tripped over Ménard's body. He was alone.

His face was so still. She wouldn't even admit to handsome. She cushioned his head in her lap. A nasty scrape, but not much blood. His eyes opened. He smiled a little and snuggled his head in her lap. Time to be firm. "Lie still. I think you're going to be OK." He groggily lifted his hand to the sticky wound, obviously sensitive because he hissed, "*Oie.*"

"You certainly have something to say ouch about. Though I think you're lucky. It looks like you've got a slight concussion and a mean looking scratch on your temple. When I saw that rock fall I didn't know what to expect."

"*Moi aussi.* I thought '*C'est fini*' ...now my eyes open to an '*ange*'. An angel. It could be heaven, but I don't think one gets pain like this up there."

Uh-oh. Discomfort crept along her neck. She'd never known how to handle flirting. Don't overreact. It's just the typical macho response of the wounded male in the face of female observation: the best tactic— change the subject. She was an expert at that. "The man escaped."

"*Merde!*" He tensed to lift his head, but fell back.

"Hey, be careful. You're alive. Let's keep it that way. I figured it was better than having you dead and him captured."

"How do you figure that?" he questioned, wincing, and gingerly reaching up to explore the damage.

Megan gently pushed his hand away, "Leave your head alone. You might start the bleeding again." She paused and took a deep breath in preparation for his reaction. "Well, it looked like he was going to kill you so...instead of aiming my knife to bring him down, I aimed it at his arm. I figured the way to save you was to shift his aim."

"*Non*! How could you put yourself at such risk? I told you to staa...ohh!" He stopped and made another move towards his head, grimacing in pain.

Witness for the defence. "I did what I had to do! Fiona started screaming for me after you ran through the kitchen so I had to go to her. The other two cops were in no condition to help. I figure you should thank me for having a good aim."

He looked about to retort when the paramedics, led by Fiona, came running with their stretcher. Ménard sighed and said with finality, "We'll discuss this later," then closed his eyes.

Megan stepped out of the way as the pros prepared to wheel Ménard away. She was momentarily distracted by Fiona's voice, whimpering to the officer nearest her, "He was so thin and looked so hungry that I thought some food would do him good. The thought that he would use the pie as a vicious weapon never entered my mind. It's all too unbearable. I wish my husband was here." A rush of tears followed her woeful tale as Fiona ingenuously worked up a whole scene of pathos. The officer put a consoling arm around Fiona's shoulders and guided her towards the house. Megan thought of Ménard. Care-giving just isn't my field. And made herself fade into the shadows.

Natural curiosity led her to the mausoleum-like building where Ménard had been attacked. She noted the construction mess and the locked door, remembering Fiona had mentioned that Richard had become fanatical about doing his own renovations. Megan moved past a police spotlight and wanting to poke around, she hopped over the wall. The other side was pitch black, so she pulled out her key ring with its pin-light end and used the cold wall to steady herself. Fiona had once mentioned that the original stone wall had been put in place when the area was first settled as a protection from Indian raiders, but as time passed another wall had been built on top of the old one. The present wall's purpose was to reinforce the structural integrity of the property to keep it from falling into the ravine. Some of the wall was also on the Ogilvy estate. Edging along, Megan noticed that the soil was much looser in one section than the other and flashed her light over it. It looked like someone had been digging near the wall. Suddenly, a light flashed in her eyes.

"*Mon Dieu! Mademoiselle! C'est vous!*" A police officer, half-slung over the wall, began haranguing her in French. Megan missed a few of the rapidly fired phrases, but got the gist— 'she was foolish', 'he thought she was the thief', 'what would Detective Ménard say', and something about 'his *fesse* being... fried'. Making sure her face had chastened written all over it, she returned to the other side of the fence, thanking the officer for his concern. She decided to keep her speculation about the digging to herself. Besides it was probably Richard checking if the wall needed further support. Megan marched away from the irate officer and headed back to the house.

As soon as her hand hit the doorknob, she heard Richard's voice giving his rather cold British appraisal of the situation. "How do you get yourself into these absurd disasters, Fiona? This is absolutely ridiculous! If the police weren't here it would be a preposterous story. Dear woman, this morning you went out on a simple errand which you completely botched, you've involved yourself in two distasteful altercations with some sort of reprehensible character and I come home to a house full of slain policemen, and, by God, the reprobate escaped. A comedy of errors if you ask me."

Megan slipped into the kitchen. Fiona's face was splotched and she was giving the 'coup de grace' to a tear-drenched Kleenex as if it were Richard, but still looked emotionally torn to shreds.

Seething, Megan tried to keep her voice steady. "I don't believe anyone has asked you to be so totally insensitive. If you don't mind Richard, we've all had a very trying time. The police have graciously allowed us to finish our statements tomorrow, so, perhaps, our time would be best spent getting a good night's sleep. Fiona, don't worry about a thing, just go up to bed. Richard and I can clean up."

Richard, looking a bit sheepish, immediately changed tactics. "How right you are Megan. Fiona, my sweet, we should do as Megan says. I should have known better. It must all be very upsetting."

Fiona stood up with a brilliantly defiant stance, uttered, "Oh, Richard!" Then collapsed in a heap of sobs. Richard scooped her up and carried her upstairs.

Megan looked after them, shook her head, and began to put some order to the overturned chairs and mess on the floor. She had just wiped up the worst of the pie when Richard peeked his head in from the drawing room.

"Would you like a night-cap, Megan? If you don't mind my saying so, you look like you could use one. Leave all that. The housekeeper will see to it in the morning." He had put on a short relaxing robe over his trousers, and sported a pair of suede slippers. The outfit gave him a lean look of self-satisfaction. Standing at the polished sideboard, he turned his head to her and asked, "Drambuie?" pouring a substantial portion from the Waterford decanter.

Megan walked over and took the glass from his hand. She turned away and moved over to sit on the settee before taking a large gulp, letting the searing strength of the alcohol engulf her taste buds. So great to have a 'wee nip' in the aftermath of such bedlam. She felt Richard's eyes on her and looked at him out of the corner of her eye. His gaze seemed to rove over her body, finally stopping to linger just below her neckline. Megan crossed her legs and shifted her eyes onto her glass.

He finished his Scotch and poured another before saying, "Drambuie, the drink of the Scots. Most women don't like it, but then again you are a Scot aren't you. In fact, you are a strange mix. What is it? Cree and Scottish?"

She took a deep breath and replied factually and asexually, "Mohawk and Scot. It's not so unusual in Quebec. Some of the early immigrants intermixed with Indians."

"But its not so common now-a-days, is it? Especially for someone as obviously well bred as you."

He strolled over and stood in front of her, looking down, his breathing audibly heavier. She was fumingly uncomfortable and took another sip, trying to keep herself at ease. An impulse to just get up and leave was thwarted by the fact that she would have to ask him to move out of the way. She hated his smug, waspish, puritanical air of superiority. Richard usually had a point, and Megan didn't like where this one was going.

As she expected, he continued. "Usually Indian girls have quite a high libido or is it just a myth? You know, I don't believe I've seen you with a boyfriend. I admire discretion. Is it Scottish breeding that makes you that way?"

The words triggered her to her feet. He was unbearably close and smelled heavily of alcohol. Her hand struck full force across his cheek making him spill his drink and almost fall backwards. "You're drunk," she said, disgusted, "Think of Fiona you...sodden slug!" Megan knew she had to get out of the house before she added something she might regret. In these situations, the less said the better. She marched towards the door.

Richard fell back on the settee. "No, don't go. Fiona said you were out near the carriage house. I do need to talk to you."

"Well, you certainly aren't going about it in the right manner. I suggest you sleep it off and try this discussion at another time."

In her haste she almost missed his slurred mumble, "Did you see anything?"

She stopped in her tracks. She had seen something and turned to challenge him, "Should I have seen anything?"

The cut of her words caused a dramatic change in his demeanour and his eyes seemed to hood over before he spoke. "I don't know what you mean and I certainly don't need to explain to you. Furthermore, I don't like your tone of voice."

Megan bit her tongue, and made a fast exit.

Chapter 9

Waves collapsed gently along the sandy shore as dawn peeked over the Florida Keys. Treiger awoke refreshed and thankfully dry. For him, each morning's light was a reliable certainty. At times that certainty had been the only thing that kept him striving towards his goal. And now the unforeseen events in Brazil had hotted things up.

Using the foliage for cover, he made his way to the base of the private causeway connecting the island to the coast of Florida and waited amongst the pylons. The bridge stretched for about a mile across the ocean. Just above were quarters for the armed sentry who inspected each vehicle crossing the expanse. In need of a lift to the island's inner sanctum, he climbed up the incline beside the concrete supports in time to see a bus speeding across. The shuttle would arrive whether there were any passengers or not; a regular route that maintained the look of normalcy, but from here on a limo conveyed visitors to the resort. Guests bringing their own vehicles had to be vetted beforehand.

Treiger crouched behind the sentry's hut just as a navy mini-bus with dark windows pulled to a stop. No one got off, but the sentry motioned the bus driver into his office. Treiger kept low and followed. The door was ajar, but he knocked anyway, pushing the door open at the same time. The driver swivelled around, spilling his coffee, while the startled sentry pulled his gun.

Treiger began head on. "I expected a more organized welcome than this."

The sentry poked his gun with each word, "You weren't on the bus."

"That is of no consequence. I have an open reservation. My name is Karl Treiger. Call Rory. Have him send a limousine. Oh, yes, and some shoes. Dockers…size twelve."

The tight-lipped sentry kept his gun level, but signalled the driver to make the call.

Minutes later, Treiger climbed into a black limousine.

Their route skirted a coastline road before turning onto a more secluded track that cut through the heart of the island towards the opposite coast. The driver wove his way through dense growth, finally arriving at a formidable set of gates with an intricate symbol of the Greek gamma woven through the steel bars. The resort, referred to as 'the island', was very familiar to Treiger who had made annual visits for years. Those in the know regarded it as one of the most exclusive and confidential resorts in the world, combining Western technology with the exotic philosophy of the Asian spas to please everyone's tastes. Clientele could make eccentric requests even with respect to paid companions. More importantly, the extensive sports complex, above and beyond the regular activities, could handle requests for sparring in most martial arts.

Of course, the complex had been built and paid for by the Gau to serve as an elite Club for certain types wanting to completely disappear for a time. Part of the Gau principle was, if you need to vanish, then why not do so in luxury. An exorbitant fee was solely there to deter their kind of undesirables and ensured the restricted nature of the club. If the Gau felt it appropriate; that is, the person was valuable to their cause, there was no fee at all. Naturally, the whole operation served the Gau's own purposes.

The vehicle passed hidden villas only evident by glimpses of a roof edge until finally they reached whitewashed walls of the huge sports complex with its backdrop of sailing vessels docked in the small harbour. Next, the main building, a magnificent structure, came into view. The striking entry was lined with white columns towering above a Romanesque-style tiled patio surrounded by massive pots of broad-leafed ferns. The architecture created an air of luxurious simplicity.

When the limousine pulled up to the entrance, Treiger headed straight to reception where a man with slick dark hair and a white linen suit was overly busy behind the desk. Treiger was affable, but direct. "Hello Rory, I want to go to the vault."

"Very well, Mr. Treiger. After you're settled in your villa, we can arrange a visit."

"No, I want to look after things now. As well, it is my understanding that there is someone here who might compromise my affairs. I want to verify this confidentially."

"Certainly...with the proper authorization."

"You know I have it," Treiger replied sternly then flashed a co-operative smile. "Rory, if I didn't know better, I might think you were trying to hold me up."

Rory flinched out a "follow me," and led him to a high security section where he unlocked an office outfitted with a computer. Treiger shut the door leaving Rory outside and sat down at the computer, typed in his access code and set up a search for Stoltz, which included aliases he often used. When nothing came up, it crossed his mind that Higler might have sent a warning to Stoltz, but since he was on the run somewhere in the Amazon that possibility was unlikely. Treiger smiled. You might be ingenious, Stoltz, but superhuman, you're not. You've got a weakness. Everyone does. He brought up the sports schedules on the monitor and scanned for martial arts. Bingo! A two-hour session of *cipecut silat*—Ernie Stoltz's favourite.

Cipecut silat, the little-known Indonesian form of lethal combat where any flexible-type weapon such as belt or a length of fabric was turned into a deadly whip. The session was set for six a.m. until eight and it was already seven-thirty. Preparing for a confrontation with Stoltz wasn't going to be easy. Furthermore, he had some other business to take care of first. Treiger picked up the phone. In a moment there was a light rap and Rory entered. "Did you find who you were looking for, sir?"

Treiger lied in a pleasant voice, "No. That means I may have to cut my stay shorter than I thought. Therefore, Rory, I would like access to my safety deposit box."

Rory frowned ever so slightly, then smiled, "Just give me a moment to finish...."

Treiger cut in harshly. "My time is very valuable."

Rory almost saluted, "Of course, sir." He led Treiger to the main vault where, behind bars, a guard sat before a security system lined with monitors. Rory nodded to the guard who unlocked the door electronically. Treiger said, "Wait here, Rory."

Somewhat fidgety, Rory whined, "All guests are accompanied until their box is removed to the outside station."

Treiger spat out his next words, "Are you aware of my status?"

Rory's expression snapped to attention, "Yes sir!"

Treiger kept a severe look on his face. "I have always enjoyed the special privileges that entails! I will enter on my own. It is your job to ensure my privacy. Tell the guard to give me the key." Rory was a sweaty, little ferret. Treiger slammed the gate shut, locking himself in with the guard who looked at Rory for instruction. The ferret frowned, but gave the nod for him to cooperate.

After obtaining the universal key, Treiger casually struck the guard's temple. As his body slumped to the floor, Treiger pulled the surveillance connections loose and made his point to the astonished Rory. "It doesn't pay to irritate me. Here's something to occupy yourself with while I'm in the vault."

Once inside, he quickly found his numbered box. Slipping his finger to the inside of his belt, he extracted his own key. Inside were documents, money, and an expensive ring case. He selected the velvet case. Inside was a beautiful ring set with a flawless two-carat diamond. Beside that was Volker Braun's ring from the war years. Braun had given both to him long ago and Treiger devised a fitting use for the jewels. He loosened the casing holding the rings and another safety deposit box key slid out. Years ago he'd secretly obtained an extra box as backup— hiding places could be useful in times like these. He crouched to the bottom section and opened a second box before reaching inside his shirt and removing the waterproof package from his skin, wincing as fine hairs ripped away with the tape. After depositing the disc in the unregistered drawer, he relocked it and managed to quickly stand and replace the second key back under the ring casing just as Rory burst into the vault.

Treiger looked at him calmly, then glanced admiringly back at the rings before snapping the lid shut. "What's the matter, Rory? You look upset."

"As I said, your privileges don't include unmonitored entry in the vault."

"Oh dear. Well, in that case you'd better stay and observe me." Treiger collected another passport and two packets of American cash before he shoved the box in place then slammed the door securely shut. He then stripped off a couple of thousands from one wad of cash and shoved them in Rory's pocket. "I know you have other important things to attend to, but, as I said, my stay here could be short. Arrange a Vichy massage for me immediately, and prepare a selection of suitable clothes for me to wear."

Rory looked at him sceptically, "Ahh...um, there have been some repairs to the plumbing. I don't believe those massage rooms are functioning at the moment."

Treiger looked at his watch and tapped his fingers. "How annoying...well, I'm sure you could get one of them running by... say, nine o'clock. In the meantime I'll stroll along the beach to my villa. See that the clothes are in my room when I arrive."

Rory seemed distracted. "So you'll be leaving soon, sir?"

"You'll find that out when it happens." Treiger walked dismissively passed Rory and through the now-open security gate. He had only gone a few feet when he turned unexpectedly and flicked the borrowed key back. Rory missed his catch.

Treiger strolled through the spacious atrium to the ocean-side exit, aware that Rory was watching. Once on the beach, he ambled out of sight, and headed to the rear of the sports complex, where he slipped through the service entry. One hallway angled towards the front entrance to the complex, while the opposite hall accessed doors to individual martial arts training rooms. Above all the doors were ventilation windows for those who preferred to practice without air-conditioning. Strewn along the empty hallway were bins of soiled towels and racks of clean linen.

Treiger cautiously passed several chambers until he heard the laboured gasps of two opponents competing intensely. There was a lid-topped bin beside the door. He carefully climbed up near the vented window and peered in.

The room was oblong and about twenty feet wide. In the centre, Stoltz's well-muscled body was gleaming with sweat, carotids pulsating, as he stealthily stepped in a sideways circle. He watched as Stoltz easily parried his target, a short, stocky Asian, precisely calculating the strike of his thickly woven whip. The Asian looked harried, as if waiting for the session to end. Treiger knew the only thing Stoltz didn't like about a workout was that he could not complete the final act. Stoltz enjoyed the limpness of life extinguished from the body, like twisting the neck of a bird.

Treiger saw both fighters pause momentarily, then engage once more. He had been impressed with Stoltz's adroitness with *cipecut silat* although he had only seen him in action once before when Stoltz had used a weapon studded with tacks. Today, the belt did not appear to have the pain-inflicting additions. The sound of the pseudo-whip whistled through the air when an agitated thumping on the entry door interfered. Treiger ducked down, but not before he heard a yelp of unexpected pain from the Asian.

Stoltz's scorched voice lashed out, "*Sheis...Kommen-sie!*" And the knocker entered with Stoltz immediately accusing, "Idiot! You made me break Uyan's wrist. The session will have to end. Leave us, Uyan!" Once Uyan had disposed of himself, Stoltz's annoyance was obvious. "Well, what is it you want?"

The intruder sounded nervous and half stuttered, "I...I know you said not to interrupt, but I thought you should know. Treiger's here."

At least the little snitch broke Stoltz's concentration. Rory was vapidly deceitful, but he performed predictably. For the moment, all Treiger could do was rest against the wall and listen.

Stoltz's tone became more reflective. "Hmm...he's arrived much sooner than expected. Where's the vermin now?"

"Walking the beach."

"Fool! You let him out of your sight."

"Don't worry. He doesn't seem suspicious, just surly. The beach route is the long way to his villa, so he won't be there for a while."

"Presumably he gave no indication of his plans to someone of your calibre. What makes you say he suspects nothing?"

Rory didn't reply immediately, evidently thinking hard. "He was looking for someone. Didn't give a name. Used the island's colony list, but got nada."

"I will fill in the blanks. He is looking for me and I'm not on the system."

"He went into the vault."

"You stupid moron! How did that happen?"

"I had no choice, sir, but..." Rory stammered.

"Fuck the excuses. What did he do?"

"That's just it, not much. He only got a passport and money." Rory was very casual with the facts, implying he had been present the whole time.

Stoltz seemed to contemplate before replying. "I had the forethought to check his box and found nothing of consequence. Still, you never know with Treiger."

"Umm...he insisted on booking a Vichy. I thought that might interfere with..."

Stoltz broke in. "Don't think. Just keep a close eye on him. See that he makes it safely for his massage."

After Rory was dismissed, Treiger silently extracted himself from his perch and made his way back to the beach. Apparently Stoltz was expecting him and would, predictably, set up an ambush. He frowned. How could a message have been sent now that Higler was out of the picture? Again, there was no time to consider unknowns, he needed to plan his counter-strike and headed in a jog to his villa.

He entered the deluxe suite and went straight to the bedroom. Laid out on the bed was an assortment of clothes. Studying the selection, Treiger mused that Rory was either stupidly efficient or playing both sides; perhaps both— the kind who hedges his bets, switching hands to favour the odds. A precarious way to survive. Treiger chose his clothes. Luckily, a lightweight jacket was cased in a small knapsack. Keeping his hand-blade aside, Treiger packed the most suitable garments and his belt into the pack.

Rory called. The Vichy was scheduled for nine as requested. He threw off his crumpled attire and donned a jock strap, then a thick terrycloth robe. His knife went into the breast pocket engraved with the island insignia and he slung the knapsack over his shoulder. Speeding up his agenda, he turned on the stereo. A tolerable version of La Traviata was playing. He switched the air-conditioning on high, then turned on the bathroom shower. Satisfied that the villa appeared occupied, he left through the back patio doors, rapidly passing behind similar lodges as he headed for the treatment spa. Stoltz would try to strike at the most vulnerable moment.

He entered the aesthetics centre and casually greeted the slender, Norwegian-looking receptionist. "Hi there, I'm afraid I'm early, but I've been looking forward to this massage. Treiger's the name."

"Why, of course, Mr. Treiger. We do anything we can to please our clients."

He smiled. "Rory said they might be doing some repairs."

"Well, not that I know of, but there's no problem starting ahead of time. Go down the hall and turn left. Salon 2."

"Wonderful. If you can, make sure it's in a secluded spot." He twisted a hundred-dollar bill around his fingers and she smiled.

"Well," She looked at her roster, "I guess Salon 6 would be better."

"My lucky number. A girl as pretty as you deserves some flowers. Do you think you could arrange that too?" He slid the bill under the edge of the reservation book, then leaned closer. "Listen, a young friend of mine, about six-three, blonde hair, blue eyes, looks like a movie star, might show up if he got up in time. We've got some pretty high-powered business deals floating. But I don't like surprises. Is there any way you can notify me if he arrives?"

"Why, yes. Every room has a special red flasher to notify personnel that a client is on the way. It's by the door and fairly noticeable. I could use that."

"Why, thank you. By the way, I don't want my friend to know I'm way ahead of him," Treiger added, jovially tucking another note under the book.

"Certainly, Mr. Treiger." Her eyes sparkled.

He found the assigned room, the last before a stairway to the second floor.

Someone had forgotten a bucket and mop in the corner. Treiger took hold of the U-shaped door handle to Salon 6 and entered the dimly lit room. An assistant was folding towels on a small table near the water pressure and temperature dials on the wall. Flexible water pipes extruded from the wall console and travelled in an upward angle and arched parallel, about three feet above the massage table. Treiger made his request to be alone. After the assistant politely left, he went to work setting the thermostat to maximum and log-rolled several towels on the table. Next he set the tiny jets of water to run at the highest pressure. Steam quickly filled the air. As the room clouded, the towel-shaped mass on the table took on the look of a body. He hung his robe and knapsack on a hook near the door, dimmed the lights to an eerie low, and crouched off to the side, knife in hand, and waited.

Ernst Stoltz had mistrusted Treiger as far back as he could remember. He flexed his biceps as he considered how to corner the bastard. He would make it a fast, calculated strike. Optimally Stoltz wanted him incapacitated, but alive. He'd received confirmation that Treiger was targeting him, but hadn't foreseen the early arrival. However, it simply meant less of a wait. Although Stoltz hated Treiger, the man was one of the few ordinary humans to whom he bore a grudging respect. He'd never seen Treiger make a mistake. Hence, Stoltz considered him more like himself. Stoltz was immensely proud of his heritage, having proven himself to be exceptional in body and mind, and believed his acceptance of this as a strength. He feared no man. In fact, he couldn't think of anything on earth he feared. The main source of irritation he experienced was the stupidity and moral weakness of the average human.

Stoltz remembered being conscious of his own existence from the first year onward. He had been given the best education and performed beyond all expectations. He often laughed at the idea that others thought he excelled when in fact he found everything so easy. Life was a game and he anticipated winning the highest stakes in the name of the Gau. His closest confidant, if he could be called that, was Egon Higler. Someday soon they would have major world powers under their control. But at the moment he had to look after the wild card that had arrived in search of him. He chuckled to himself. This visit to the island would be the first mistake Treiger had made.

Early on he'd become aware of Treiger's cold disdain for the Gau as if appraising everyone, particularly the youth, as targets. Stoltz remembered, at age twelve, when he dared to stare back, Treiger's expression hardened. Thinking that Treiger was playing a game of chicken, Stoltz held eye contact until Higler, not knowing what was happening in the unspoken moment, recklessly interrupted them, forcing Stoltz to look away. Stoltz had been furious with Higler, but never forgot that moment, nor did he look away again when he realized that Treiger, who seemed to intimidate others, did not intimidate him. Succumbing to intimidation was a form of weakness and Stoltz, who had prepared all his life to lead, would not accept weakness in himself or in others. He walked brusquely through the door of the Spa feeling blood pumping through every vein in his body. Now was the time to rid the world of Karl Treiger.

The receptionist glanced up and flushed with recognition. She had noticed the obviously wealthy, bronzed blonde yesterday on the beach. He was the last person she thought Mr. Treiger had referred to, but the one she would have hoped for. His electric blue eyes fell on her and her heart beat faster. She'd never seen a more handsome man.

He paused at the desk only to demand, "Where is Treiger?"

She breathlessly replied, "In Salon 6...at...at the end of the hall and to your left."

He didn't smile, but his eyes seemed to tilt down to the low cleavage of her white silk shirt. She blushed, thinking how important the meeting must be. That's how rich, high-powered men did things; they made the most critical decisions while playing squash, having a sauna, or carousing at expensive parties. She didn't want to make any mistakes. Perhaps things would improve in her life if she were savvy with their egos. She watched his buttocks, gripped in skin-tight spandex, contract tightly down the hall.

Treiger flexed his muscles and wiped the sweat from his face with a towel. A dense fog obscured the massage table and the minimal light gave the room the distorted illusion of sinister Baskerville murkiness. His heart pounded and perspiration cloaked his body. Stoltz would be at more of a disadvantage not having adjusted to the intense heat. Near the door a red flash blinked briefly. Seconds later the door eased open.

The muscular leg of Stoltz entered first then, as his body moved forward, a sarong length of material in his raised hand eclipsed a fatal shot for the knife. There was a millisecond of incredible stillness when Stoltz's physique poised like a marble gladiator. But before the door closed, Stoltz made an unnervingly swift snap with his twisted sarong. The whip hit the immobile form on the table with enough power to crush the spinal column and paralyse the lower body— torture would be inescapable; the victim, an immobile puppet of torment. When Stoltz looked fleetingly nonplussed as his whip tore away towels, Treiger launched himself through the air targeting Stoltz's neck, his blade aimed for a lethal stab. Stoltz ducked a fraction of a second before being impaled and collided with Treiger's torso.

Treiger took advantage of the impact and slid through the jets of steaming water landing on the massage table, only to roll off grabbing the edge of the table to slide underneath. Stoltz's deadly lash whistled through the steam, splitting the mattress cover. Treiger didn't have time to get his knife hand out of the way. The end of the weapon caught his knuckles, jerking the blade away.

Thrashing his leg out from under the table, Treiger stabbed his toes into Stoltz's right kneecap. The Aryan toppled, giving Treiger enough leeway to catapult out from under the table. But Stoltz recovered quickly. Treiger felt the rush of the sarong through the steam. Instinctively, he put his hand up a split second before the wet strap encircled his neck, striking with a force that would have collapsed his windpipe had he not restrained it. He felt a searing slice across his palm. The sarong was laced with razor blades. The next second was his last if he allowed Stoltz to twist this death cord.

He shoved backwards, ramming Stoltz against the taps on the wall. Stoltz gave a distressed grunt, but his grip on the sarong was relentless. Treiger slumped down then pushed up with all his might, brutally trapping Stoltz against the console of dials. Finally he felt a slight loosening of Stoltz's hold. With his free hand, he clawed the wall for something, anything he could use. His hand hit the steam tube. He tore the hose from its joint and angled the scorching stream towards Stoltz, blasting a blistering hiss over his upper chest and arms. There was no scream of pain, but the noose fell limp as Stoltz made a frantic swipe to protect his face.

With an injured hand and no weapon, Treiger knew this was a fight he couldn't win. Leaping to the door, he grabbed his knapsack and lunged into the hall. Looking frantically about, he seized the nearby mop and shoved the length of it through the handle of his salon and the one next to it, making a temporary bolt. Grabbing a clean robe from a nearby stack, he thrust it on and headed round the corner nearly colliding with the aide. He used firm persuasion. "My friend's very upset with the noise upstairs, but he will stay longer if you see to the problem."

The assistant frowned, but replied, "Of course, sir," and scurried up the stairs.

Treiger hastened to the receptionist's counter and smiled at the friendly blonde. "My friend commandeered Salon 6. See that he's left undisturbed as long as possible, would you?"

She smiled back and replied smoothly, "Certainly, Mr. Treiger."

"I'm in a rush. Please call the main gate and request a limousine for me."

The distant sound of pounding became more audible. She looked uncertainly down the hallway.

"I mean now!" he rebuked acidly.

Her cheeks flushed red as her hand flew to the phone.

The shortest route to either the gate or the harbour passed his villa so he took the risk of returning there. As he arrived on the run, Rory was just coming out the front door. He seemed startled, but recovered with a quick excuse, "I just came to check...."

Treiger put a strangle hold on his neck and dragged him back inside. Rory had tossed the place into a shambles. At that moment Rory's cell phone rang. Treiger tightened his hold and said menacingly, "Tell him you haven't seen me."

Rory answered, listened briefly, and said "Not here." Stoltz must have slammed his phone down because Rory jerked his head away from the earpiece. Treiger snapped his flexed grip sharply sideways. Rory wilted lifelessly to the floor. A precarious end.

Ripping open his knapsack, he got dressed, and while wrapping a cloth around his hand, exited again via the patio and used the most secluded paths through the grounds. Stoltz would be hot on his trail. He'd meant the request for the limousine as a decoy, thinking to try for one of the speedboats— dicey because the quay was open area and well guarded, but it might provide the fastest escape.

Suddenly, a familiar figure came strolling down the path towards him. The lanky, balding man was Steibert Dubler. Treiger had run into him on a previous visit a few years before. Dubler preferred to be thought of as a South African playboy, but made his money as a professional assassin. He looked rested and tanned. Treiger called out to him, "Bertie, are you in the mood to do an old friend a favour?"

Bertie stopped whistling and took a wary stance, then relaxed. "Well, you old dog, since when were we ever friends," he said moving forward and slapping Treiger on the back. His eyes widened when he saw Treiger's bleeding hand. "Fuck, mate. You do need help, but is it something I would want to be involved in?"

"Your choice, Bert. I need a private lift out of here."

"What the hell. I still owe you for showing me that Brazilian dance shit you call fighting."

Westmount

Megan followed Fiona into her kitchen just as the phone rang. Fiona stopped her protracted reaction to the previous night's events to answer, while instructing Megan to make tea. Megan absently listened to the one-sided phone chatter as she filled the kettle. "You must be kidding! You didn't send it yesterday? Dr. Kendall will be livid... Are those the only copies? ...Archives at McGill University...hmm." She hung up abruptly and without a pause continued, "The architect's office was ransacked last night and now they can't find the maps or plans or whatever it is Richard wants. In fact, they think it is the only thing missing. Ha! That company has about as much accountability as a tart with the clap." She giggled with the glint of a naughty schoolgirl.

Megan eyed her thoughtfully. "Didn't you say you had just been to the architects office just before you were mugged yesterday?"

"Yes, but they weren't in."

"But someone watching might not have known that. Could anyone have known you were going there?"

"Probably everyone within a half mile. At breakfast Richard and I had a massive row because he was incessantly reminding me to pick the bloody things up. I remember he was embarrassed that the conservatory windows were open. But who would care anyhow? It's only a bunch of old prints."

Meg ignored Fiona's pshaw, adding, "It seems to me that thief probably thought you had the plans...or maybe, when he found you didn't, he came here to look for them, then after escaping us, robbed the architects' office...that means..."

"Enough with the 'or maybes'. I really don't care. I hope the police catch him and all this jazz will be over. Is the tea ready?"

"You said McGill Archives, didn't you?"

"Meg, I know what's on your mind. Can't I refuse to go? I want my tea!" she said petulantly, following Megan out the door.

Chapter 10

Brazil, 1944

Braun had protectively hung his arm across Karl's shoulders after they stepped off the Polish lifeboat. They were meant to look like father and son, but Karl felt old, as if a lifetime had passed since he'd found out about the Gau Group. The day that Braun had pulled open that door in the underground bunker, Karl fell in, sprawling on the floor. The men sitting around a large table all got up to stare at him. Beside the tall, blonde Volker Braun were the four others he'd seen accompany Braun earlier— the shorter, fat General Wolffe; a wiry, shrewd-faced Doctor Luthor Kleis; a soft-mannered, plump doctor with small round glasses called Josef Buch; and, Hitler's closest confident, Martin Bormann— all looking startled as if it was they who had been caught. At least, that was Karl's impression, but he was the one who would have to invent a fast explanation about why he was snooping at the door.

Braun saved him the trouble. Amused by his indelicate entry, he had chuckled, "My inquisitive young protégé, let me introduce you to our elite group. We've just christened ourselves as the Gau." The knot of conniving Nazis seemed to trust Braun's judgement in revealing their title, but at that point, Karl discovered nothing more about the secret group. After the introduction, Braun cursorily dismissed Karl, saying that later someone would come to collect him.

That evening an SS officer drove him to an apartment building and escorted him to the third floor. They topped the stairs just as a door opened and a messily dressed girl, younger than Karl, staggered out. She looked distraught and tried to cover her face, but not before Karl noticed a trickle of blood at the corner of her mouth. The officer rapped on the same door and when Braun answered, the SS officer saluted and left.

Karl had felt awkward as he entered what he supposed was the Commandant's home. The first thing he noticed was a gold-coloured, self-playing harp already plunking a tune. The salon was crowded with dark velour-covered couches, shaded lamps and scary sculptures draped with leather whips. His head automatically turned back and forth. When his eyes stopped on a door at the far end of the room, the commandant said, "That's the bedroom."

Karl had stood uneasily by the settee. He watched Braun go over to wind up the harp before approaching a table with a squat brandy bottle. He painfully remembered it was the same kind his father and mother drank on special occasions. Braun poured some liquor into two snifters. He handed one to Karl and then, after swirling his own and inhaling the aroma, asked, "Is this your first drink?"

Karl nodded, "*Ja, Commandant.*"

"Then chug it down, and sip the next one. And in the future, when we are alone like this, call me Volker."

Karl choked down the brandy, ending in a coughing fit. Braun laughed and refilled his glass. With an odd smirk on his face, Braun said, "Ever since I first saw you I wanted you to be prepared, your intellect sharpened and your body ready. I did not want it to be too early, but after today's display of clumsiness, your education needs refinement. Braun had Karl drink more brandy before bringing up one hand to caress his cheek. His other hand strayed over Karl's chest and then down around to his buttocks. Braun's intentions were confusing, but he'd heard of such things in the barracks. Karl felt a desperate urge to pull away, but didn't. Feeling stupid, he blinked in surprise trying to think. Clearly, beyond the initial abhorrence, this was the first time he'd had a bargaining chip. The brandy made him feel heady and brave. Remembering that on occasion Braun had encouraged him to use a haughty, superior attitude, he began with an air of authority. "Before I allow you to go further, I want you to arrange for the safe release of my brother, Hans. I want him taken out of Germany along with his girlfriend, Luisa Weiss."

Braun's hand sharply walloped his cheek. "You impudent whelp. You dare to make demands. You should be begging." His voice was cross, but there was a crooked smile on his face.

Karl knew then that he had chosen the right tactic. Blood seeped across his tongue from the slap; the warm flavour helped him keep calm.

Braun put his hand at the back of Karl's neck and pulled him face-to-face, whispering, "We'll see what demands you can make after I've made my demands of you."

Karl had no idea what to expect. He'd never had any inclination towards men in his fantasies. His only knowledge about these types of situations consisted of crude jokes and bizarre stories he'd overheard. Braun drew Karl even closer then held his head with his hands before harshly pressing his smooth lips on Karl's. The force of a man's probing tongue in his mouth was absurd, almost shocking. He felt the waves of Braun's desire as the commandant's hands again slid down his body and over his buttocks, pushing their groins together. Braun was violently erect. He tore Karl's shirt out from his pants and panted breathily, "Get undressed."

The simple words axed through what Karl thought was the most mortifying silence he'd ever experienced. Karl looked down and sheepishly started a careful process of undoing each button. By the time he reached the last one, Braun, already disrobed, was displaying his desire like a prize bull. He impatiently pulled Karl's belt open.

"Take off everything," he said.

When they stood naked, Karl felt his face flush as Braun grabbed him between the legs and started to massage his limp scrotum. Braun didn't seem disappointed when nothing happened, mumbling that Karl needed to relax and gave him another passionate kiss. Karl wanted to run from the room, but knew that in order to make a pact with this devil, he had to stay.

Braun demanded that Karl wash him with his tongue. The thought of using his mouth in such a way was appalling. Stunned by the revolting thought of oral sex with a man, he couldn't even imagine what to do. He asked for some more brandy because his mouth was dry. After swallowing the burning liquid, Karl got down on his knees. Braun steadied himself by placing his hands on Karl's head, while Karl did his best to use his tongue hoping he would not throw up. The whole process seemed endless.

Finally, Braun whispered a hissing, "Stop."

He moved around behind Karl roving his strong hands over his buttocks, roughly squeezing the muscles. The final debasement came when Braun penetrated his anus. The pain was unexpected and indescribable, like being pierced with a hot iron pipe. Karl held back the tears, holding his body rigid. The harp kept playing as Braun grunted and slavered the expression of his lust. Karl knew he had to put on the best performance of his life. Not an ounce of disgust or revulsion could show. Ever since seeing his parents murdered, he had understood there would never be a normal life for him. And Braun's violation became a symbol to never turn back.

Upon reflection, Karl considered that the physical defilement had been tempered at first, because Braun liked orchestrating violence and pain as well as sex. He later found out that Braun didn't mind if his attendants were male or female, as long as they were young. As time passed, the violations became increasingly strenuous. Karl alternated between acting like a doting puppy and a distant, hard-to-get lover, but he never got used to the physical part. Several times Braun made reference to Karl being with women, as if taunting him. Karl knew it was senseless to ask why; he would be informed of Braun's meaning when Braun wanted him to know. He also knew it was one of Braun's little psychological games to see if Karl would ask, so every time Braun alluded to his chances with women, Karl just nodded his acknowledgement as if he accepted this information, but had little interest.

In fact, it was quite the opposite. The more he was with Braun, the more intrigued he became about what sex with a woman would be like. He remembered seeing his brother touch Luisa's full breasts and feel between her legs. When he was younger the sight seemed comical, but now he constantly dreamt about touching and smelling a girl. Whenever he was with Braun, he fantasized as much as he could about women. Somehow, imagining things that way made the violence and violation more tolerable. Often, after being with Braun, he needed a hot shower to scrub himself clean, keeping in mind that his future success depended on enduring this relationship with Volker Braun.

Three months after Braun had initiated Karl into the alien sexual practices, Walther Bergermeyer, who shared a small office with Karl, divulged a rumour— Karl was supposed to be part of a special project in the bunker. Karl took in what he had to say, but didn't reply, virtually ignoring Bergermeyer who was panting for more information. Over the past several weeks, Bergermeyer had been trying to befriend Karl, obviously envious of Braun's preference. Karl always remained aloof; Bergermeyer could never be any kind of friend he would want.

A few days later, Karl saw Braun sweep out from the bunker entry. Wildly volatile, he blasted into their office, shrieking at Bergermeyer to get out. After his fat body scuttled from the room, Braun had slammed the door before beginning in terse, measured words. "I told them you were not suitable for this project, but Buch insists you meet the requirements."

Having no idea what Braun was talking about, Karl wisely said nothing. For some reason the Gau must have decided that his education, whatever that meant, should continue in spite of Braun's protests. Braun had ended by telling Karl to come to his apartment that evening and later, the usual sort of black limousine arrived to pick Karl up. Dressed in a clean Hitler Youth uniform and his overcoat, he climbed into the back, surprised to see Braun sitting there. Karl, Braun announced, was in for a surprise and without a further word the limo glided into the night and out of the city. After a time, the driver stopped at a deserted railway station.

Braun said, "Now you will see how good I am to you."

Karl squinted into the dark, scanning a dimly lit wooden platform and made out two soldiers, before noticing two other people huddled together.

"Go on. Get out of the car." Braun ordered.

Karl obeyed and went to the platform for a better look. One of the two bent heads looked up; the face caught in the diffuse light. Karl bit his lip fighting back the tears. The young man was Hans; he was sure of it. The other frightened figure had to be Luisa.

Unable to hold back, Karl bounded onto the platform, breathlessly calling Hans's name. His brother turned towards him looking stunned. Karl grabbed him and gave such a bear hug that the impact nearly made Hans keel over. Karl steadied his brother, noticing the fragile thinness; his body a ghost of what Hans, the swaggerer, had been. He smiled at Luisa, noticing her pale loveliness, but couldn't resist keeping his eyes on his brother. Karl almost didn't know where to begin. "My God Hans, where have you been? What has been done to you, you're so…thin."

"I'm more surprised to be here than you. I truly thought this was going to be the night I was executed." He glanced uneasily at the guards and continued. "They kept me …interned at Buchenwald as a dissident. My treatment was better than most…because I'm German. I managed to survive. It…it was terrible…the beatings…the hunger…the…" He began to silently cry, but then straightened up, looked at Luisa and said, "They brought Luisa to me just before you arrived. We are to leave Germany tonight. I don't know where we are to go."

Luisa, barely managing a weak smile, fidgeted beside Hans. Hans seemed to energize and spoke quickly, "What about you, Karl? You look great. Where have you… that uniform?" The pause said it all until he added fearfully, "Karl...be careful."

A grey train engine pulling battered boxcars chugged noisily into the station, cutting off further words. The rails sounded like they were screaming from the weight of the dark load dragging over them. Finally the cars grated to a stop. Great clouds of smoky steam surrounded them like a shroud. The guards moved menacingly through the mist towards the little group. A shrill whistle for departure blasted over them. With only a moment left Karl whispered to Hans, "When this insanity is over, we will find each other. Count on me and don't worry, I will be fine…take care of yourself and Luisa."

The train whistle shrieked once more. Karl hugged Hans again until the guards forced them to part. The two fugitives were hustled to one of the boxcars where guards and all, they disappeared into its black cavity. The heavy door seemed to slide shut on its own. The train noisily expelled more steam and pulled out of the station leaving a choking smell of burnt oil. Karl kept waving as the worm-like procession rolled heavily away. He watched until he could no longer see the last car and the misty fog around him had faded. When there was nothing left to look at, he slowly returned to the automobile and climbed inside. Without turning his head towards Braun, he asked, "Where will they go?"

"To the north coast of France and then onto a steamer to England. They should be safe enough with the forged documents we've given them. They have letters from relatives in Montreal, connections we have there, of course. Had time permitted I would have entertained her like I do you, perhaps both of you together. In any event, your brother has contaminated her. They are both *sheis*. My hands are washed of them."

Karl's mind was spinning. At least Hans was still alive.

Braun dropped him off at his barracks, which was a thankful anomaly, but Karl wondered what prompted Braun to fulfill his request for Hans's release. He lay in his bed restless and barely sleeping, wondering about Braun's next scheme.

Karl arrived at the Chancery early and was told to join a group of muscled young men down in the bunker. Since his first risky escapade, security had been tightened, and he'd not been back. The group assembled in a room filled with benches facing a stern-faced officer who told them to sit and then made crude drawings on a blackboard, tersely outlining what they were required to do. A wave of muted snickers passed through the room. Karl was stunned. Apparently, copulation was the object of the exercise.

They were given instruction on the sexual act and told that each must copulate with whomever was in the assigned room. He supposed the 'whomever' was female because the unisex body drawn on the board indicated that there was an orifice that wasn't contained in the male body called the vagina. The thought of making love to a woman he didn't know both excited and repelled him. He couldn't fathom why on earth he was being asked to do such a thing, but the thought of being with a woman was fascinating.

Near the end of the instruction, Braun, looking impatient, entered the room. He was dressed in full uniform, complete with his sharp brimmed Commandant's hat, and held a short whip in his hand. When the last word was spoken, Braun strode up to the instructor, tapping the whip in one of his palms, obviously giving orders and gesturing his head in Karl's direction. When the instructor clicked his heels with a straight-armed salute, Braun suddenly smiled and whisked out of the room without another glance at Karl. Finally, they were all told to wait and the instructor left the room. Everyone broke ranks to guffaw and chatter except for Karl who sat waiting.

Presently, the instructor returned and had them all march into the corridor where he allocated a numbered room to each of them. They all lined up outside their respective doors and were told to strip. At that moment, it didn't seem too peculiar seeing himself and the others lined up naked outside the closed doors. Later he realised how bizarre it must have looked. Before Karl entered, the instructor strode up to him giving a brusque order not to come out unless he was finished.

His first encounter was a shock. Sitting on a cot was what appeared to be a woman with a vacant stare and no hair, not on her head, nor between her legs. It had been shaved off. She looked to be old with hollow cheeks and an abdomen that drooped down; breasts that sagged flatly; and skin that hung on her like a desiccated, plucked chicken. He moved closer, and changed his opinion; she was younger than he had first thought. The moment she saw him move forward, she lay back on the mattress and spread her legs. He knew what he had to do.

Karl walked over and tried to look at her tenderly. She kept her head turned away. He climbed on the cot feeling the course texture of the starched sheet. He wasn't certain how to position himself and ended up kneeling between her legs. She didn't move. He thought he should touch her breasts, but he couldn't bring himself to do it. Instead, he leaned forward and put his hands on either side of her body. He was surprised he had an erection because the situation seemed so sordid. He pushed forward. He could barely find her hole and had to guide himself with one hand. He shoved again and she winced as if in pain. Once he was fully inside, the pulsing movement of his body came easily, but an endless amount of time passed before he came. He had tried to be gentle and quick, but he was fumbling and ashamed. Leaving the room without even looking at her, he took with him a tenacious smear of self-hate that he knew he could never wash away. He felt like he had made love to his own mother and knew that was what Braun had intended.

Every week after that, now and then two or three times a week, he went through the same routine; sometimes the cots had sheets, but they were softer when they didn't; sometimes being with the same woman again after a long interval. However, there was only one female he would never forget— a young girl about his own age, with full cheeks, rounded breasts and red, luscious lips. Her image, at first, reminded him of his brother's girlfriend, Luisa. This copular offering was the only one who ever spoke to him. She broke the barrier of anonymity he had placed around these unclean acts. He always remembered her embarrassment, trying pathetically and inadequately to hide her breasts and pubis with her small hands. She had nervously told him how she had been commanded not to speak, but she would, if he didn't mind. He had spent more time with her because she was a virgin and he had hurt her. Her name was Sophya.

He dreamt of being with her again, and sooner than with any others he walked into his assigned room and saw her huddled on the sheetless cot with her hands grasped around her flexed legs. She began crying and ran over to hug him. After he calmed her, she said after being with him, she'd been kept in a cell and fed well until she had a miscarriage. They never let her talk to anyone and doctors who looked like soldiers had kept examining her between her legs. It hurt sometimes. She hated the probing and felt humiliated that her body was treated with such deadpan disrespect.

He stroked her head. A half-inch of raven black hair had grown back, creating an odd ebony halo around her head that contrasted with her soft white skin. He wanted to protect her, and then grew hard wanting her, wanting to make her feel good. He started to kiss her neck, her ears, her eyes. Then he moved down to her breasts. They were soft, warm, round mounds. He thought he had never tasted anything so succulent as her nipples became hard and dark in response to his tongue. He suddenly became desperate to taste her just to have the experience. He moved his head further down, over her flat stomach, and then made a move to go further. She grasped his head to stop him, "No", she said apprehensively.

He lifted his head and smiled tenderly, "Don't be afraid", then cupped his hand over the smoothly shaven skin between her legs. He started to massage her gently, finally letting his finger open her genital lips and feel her thick moisture. He heard her gasp then moan. Her pleasure excited him further and he lowered his head again. There was no resistance. She spread her thighs wider and her breath became shallow, panting. After thoroughly exploring her silky flesh with his tongue, he knew he could wait no longer. He moved his body over her. He felt the heat from her beckoning him. As he moved to penetrate, she moved up to join him in a primal communion that made him want to drive deeper and deeper. For a few joyous moments they were bound in ecstasy, moving in a rhythm that became more and more frenzied until they both culminated in a mindless delirious bliss.

Karl lay on top of her exhausted, and finally had to shake his head to make sure what had just happened was real. Afterwards, she lay cradled in his arms until there was a sharp rap on the door. Their time was up.

Moments later, all the women, including Sophya, were herded down the hall. There had been nothing to wipe away semen, so she had to walk out with the opaque juices wetly dripping down her thighs. Karl didn't know where she was taken. He knew enough not to ask questions. If Braun found out about her, he would definitely never see Sophya again.

Some weeks later, he was summoned to a laboratory where samples were taken of all body fluids, including sperm, and a skin biopsy. Any inquiries he made received the non-committal reply that everything was routine, although he had to come back weekly for sperm samples whereas, as far as he knew, none of the others had to do so.

Karl continued his usual schedule with the women. Every time he entered a cubicle, his first glance was to see if the shaved head might be hers, but it was only another faceless body with the vacant stare, each head different, but none belonged to his vibrant, glowing Sophya. He tried to be kind and respectful to all the women. However, the message conveyed through the limp body posture wore away at his feelings. All the women communicated a functional acceptance of what was happening, but it was heavily laden with an air of barely tolerable contact. He realised that for them the act was a feudal-type business transaction. Knowing they all reviled the mere touch of his body against theirs, Karl started to treat his times in the cubicle the same as he did everything else; he found most of the women respected the cool, efficient approach.

Many months later, he entered his cubicle. Her head was turned away, but the shadow on the wall was distinctive— the shape of her head, the curve of her nose and the delicate long neck. His whole body gave a start: "Sophya!"

The head turned to him with a vacant stare. He rushed over and knelt before her. "Sophya, what have they done to you?"

As if that gentle move of human compassion was more than she could bear, tears began to flow in an endless quiet stream down her face. She told him in broken sobs, how, after their last time, she had again got pregnant and then miscarried. Once that had been established, she was given to many men. She didn't know how many. After weeks of being had by faceless violators, she was taken to a room. They siphoned water up her and then had taken the baby. Sometime later, she didn't know how long, she was brought back here. It had been a glimmer of hope that she would be with him, but that was swept away. They put her with someone else and she had become pregnant again. She was shipped out to the brothels for weeks until they brought her back to the laboratory and took her baby again. She had been kept in solitary confinement until today. Sophya looked at him, then lay back on the bed and spread her legs.

"No, I will not do this to you," Karl said protectively, determined that he would not contribute again to her defilement.

She looked back with that sickening, disembodied stare. "You must do it. They will check, and if you haven't, I will be punished. It happened before. One of the men came before he could get himself in me. I tried to stuff some in, but it didn't work."

He knew she was telling the truth and started to stroke her, to try to arouse her, but she pushed his hand away and said, "No. Just do it." Afterwards she just got up and left. That was the last he ever saw of her.

Karl felt haunted for ages after that last meeting and secretly tried to find Sophya, even to the point of asking the other boys if they had been with her. When Karl lost hope of seeing her again, he told Braun he never wanted to return to the bunker. Braun noncommittally put him to work on a special assignment with Bergermeyer.

Sophya lingered forever in his mind and he wondered how he could forgive himself for doing nothing to help her. Finally Karl stepped on his guilt, deciding that the Gau would vilely use anyone or anything for their own purposes. Living with the despicable fate of Sophya helped him to remember to stay on track; someday he would settle the score. Karl started asking Braun questions about the Gau along with withholding sexual favours; in reply sometimes Braun beat him, sometimes taunted him, but once, after too much brandy, Braun became maudlin, weeping over how, at last, thanks to Karl they had made a breakthrough, and that was all.

Still Karl believed he was onto something and pitched himself into the new project with Bergermeyer. Together, they were responsible for laundering money through the Swiss Banks and a vast amount was transferred to South America. Wolffe was the one who amassed the funds from the wet work of the SS. He seemed to like Karl, and although not impressed, Karl decided to cultivate the relationship. When gossip started that the Reich was in trouble, Bergermeyer came up with the creative idea of using Jewish names in the Swiss accounts, explaining they wouldn't link back to the Reich. The scheme worked out fabulously, and after the war the Gau was extremely well funded.

When more rumours of defeat flowed into the Chancery, Braun absented himself for several weeks, but essentially nothing changed until Karl heard Hitler was to move into the bunker. Braun sent Karl a note instructing him to go that evening to *Bahnhof Freidrickstraße,* Berlin's central train station, dressed in ordinary clothing. Karl arrived at the appointed time and paced, listening to the sound of his soles slapping on the pavement. Finally a limousine drew up to the curb and Braun stepped out. Immaculately dressed although not in uniform, he smiled at Karl and said. "For the next while you and I are going to be father and son."

A few minutes later Karl found himself in a first class compartment with cracked leather seats and grimy windows. Braun selected the side facing the direction of the train and left Karl to sit opposite. When the train jerked out of the station into the dark obscurity of the countryside, Braun sank into a surly silence so Karl let the muted clack of the wheels lull him to sleep. He was wakened twice as they passed into Switzerland then Italy. Border guards stomped in and asked for their papers, but gave them no trouble. With the train compartment remaining blacked out, Karl again dozed off.

All of a sudden, he awakened to high-pitched whistling sounds coming from the black void outside. He saw flashes in the distance, closely followed by thundering explosions. The pounding rapidly became louder, as if chasing the moving train. Powerful tremors coursed through their carriage. Finally, a bomb exploded so close that Karl closed his eyes from the blinding light. Their compartment shook violently. In the strobed flare of further explosions, Karl could see Braun calmly watching him and suddenly realised what Braun already had: as long as the train kept going they were safe. He accustomed himself to the shuddering blasts by listening to the continuous noise of the wheels against the rails. He knew that whatever happened he didn't want to become separated from Braun. He would stay with him until the last dog was hung. Then as suddenly as the barrage began, the bombing stopped and the train continued on as if nothing had happened.

They travelled all night. Braun never seemed to shut his eyes. When the grey mist of dawn appeared, Karl started to see vague shapes of houses through the mud-spattered windows and not long after, the train grated to a halt. French-speaking officers boarded, demanding to see their papers. Three uniforms crowded into the compartment and one, obviously the leader, grabbed Braun's documents barely before he managed to extract them from his billfold. The ill-mannered officer, his uniform tight over his plump belly, stood scrutinizing them. He spat out French demands focusing on Braun, but occasionally looking at Karl with his beady eyes. Braun replied to everything in well-educated Parisian French. Karl knew Braun would keep his cool, even show a degree of humility, because the situation required that he do so. Karl studied Braun's finesse for dramatic cynicism offset by creating just the opposite impression; observations that became well-learned lessons. The officer finally threw the papers back at Braun; barked exit commands to the other two, then left, seemingly satisfied.

When they pulled out of that station, Braun shut his eyes and fell into a deep sleep. Karl didn't feel tired anymore. In about an hour, the coast came into view; the turquoise of the ocean contrasted strangely with the bombed wreckage strewn along the countryside. They finally stopped in a small village on the south coast.

Braun brought them to an inn where the innkeeper, old with balding grey hair, gave Braun a hard time before grudgingly accepting a bribe to let one of his rooms. Braun demanded that the innkeeper provide them with something to eat. The churlish man walked slowly to the back of the dining room calling for 'Marie', disappearing through a doorway marked '*Privé*'. A thin, elderly woman came out and glanced at them furtively. After a short time, the old man resentfully presented them with soup plates containing a watery stew of broth with bits of stringy meat, but mostly cabbage. Karl ate ravenously, but Braun only picked at his food. After eating, Braun left Karl at the inn, instructing him not to wander about. Karl stayed in his room only coming down to the dining room for supper. Karl saw nothing of the innkeeper's wife, but the innkeeper slapped a container half-filled with mouldy bread and soggy boiled potatoes in front of him. Finally, Karl went to bed, but lay awake waiting.

In the middle of the night, Karl heard a truck pull up outside, followed by a pounding on the door downstairs along with Braun's sharp commanding voice. Karl decided to find out what was going on. He made his way quietly to the head of the stairs when he heard a single gun shot. Unmistakably, the innkeeper started to cry out his wife's name, but the voice stopped abruptly after a second shot. Karl quickly leapt down the stairs two at a time, and saw Braun come out of the back room. Braun was straight faced, and gestured for Karl to leave the deathly silent inn. A sickening rage flared inside him, but he obediently climbed in the truck beside Braun.

They drove to a small seaport, dark because the quay lights were out. Dawn was straining to heave over the horizon allowing a poor view of a few docked ships. They parked near one vessel, which Braun briefly referred to as theirs. The barely visible name on the side was in Polish. They climbed out of the car and Braun told him to wait while he checked on things. Loud splashes of water drew him over to the side of the steamer. Through the moonlight he made out bodies being dumped over the side, each giving one resounding splash as if they were weighted. In any event, none returned to the surface.

After an irritated summons from Braun, he returned to the car where Braun was in discussion with an officer Karl had seen occasionally at the Chancery. The officer led them up a wooden ramp onto the quiet vessel. Karl figured the rest of the crew were still busy on the other side of the ship. When he asked about the bodies, Braun's reply was bluntly sarcastic; "It wouldn't be very intelligent of us to run off in German U-boats would it?" He then handed Karl a Polish passport under the name of Ugo Lipski. The journey was arduous since Braun used his pent up energies playing sex games in their claustrophobic bunkroom. Karl's only other task was to learn Polish.

Four barely tolerable weeks passed with Braun never mentioning where they were headed. When land was sighted, Karl ran up to the deck. Brazil, he figured, deducing it from the South American monetary transactions made in Berlin. The scenery helped him to put the past weeks out of his mind. The sun was shining with only a few dark clouds in the distance. When he peered over the railing, the fascinating clarity of the water looked like he was seeing down hundreds of feet.

He stood at the bow, watching as the Polish freighter brought them closer to the coast. Karl studied the distant horizon, making out a coastal city that a passing deckhand called Rio de Janeiro. Scattered out from the coast were several patches of mountainous islands, lined with more pristinely clean sand. Karl had never been on a beach and couldn't wait to run along one and jump in the waves. Vultures, large and black with thick feathers encircling their throats, circled overhead and then flew back to the coast, rising high to orbit two skyrocketing columns of rock that towered out from the green, thousands of feet into the air. Strangely, the almost smooth-sided rock mountains seemed to be guarding the land. Karl wondered if he would be considered friend or foe in this new country.

"A new life for us, Karl." Braun's voice seemed to drift out of nowhere, carving into Karl's private thoughts. How typical of Braun to bring a sinister mood to what, a moment before, had been a special event in his life. Braun, seemingly oblivious to Karl's wish to be alone, continued, "We will carry on the Reich's work here. Bormann has stayed in Germany to look after the *Führer* who is…ill and may not survive, so we will establish ourselves in South America until the time is right for a safe return. As you know the war was not going in our favour. One has to accept that such setbacks occur. However, I feel we will take Hitler's vision far beyond what mankind can imagine, thanks to you, my boy," he chuckled and patted Karl's cheek with his sleek, white fingers, "but then you have little idea of what I am talking about. I have time and power at my feet…and I will include you in whatever rewards come our way. The world will someday come crawling to us on their knees! But it will take time and a lot of work." He gave Karl an affectionate squeeze on the shoulder also informing him with a special glint in his eye that their journey was not over yet.

"Will we go as far as Argentina?" Karl asked.

"I don't know if we will need to go that far," Braun answered with his usual evasive certainty, then added, "Wolffe is suspect that those going to Argentina will have problems and I trust his judgement." Braun seemed to feel the conversation had ended and headed down the deck.

Karl, again having no idea when the journey would be over, noticed that the sky was quickly clouding over while the waves became high heaves, shifting the angle of the deck. Still, he wandered unsteadily from fore to aft watching the blue ocean transform to an angry grey-black. The way Braun had spoken to him stuck in his mind. Braun enjoyed games of vagary, yet Karl had picked up an odd energy, perhaps excitement, in his voice. He paced the deck contemplating what Braun's plans might be, absently keeping track of the rising waves. Suddenly, in the distance, he noticed a dark grey hulk standing out against the waves and wondered if he had seen a whale. He stood and watched. Finally, as they cut through the heaving swells, he saw the form again. This time he identified the low-lying surface con of a U-boat riding above the waves. He couldn't tell if the submarine was following their boat or chasing them. Since all the crew on the Polish freighter was travelling incognito, the U-boat could mistakenly consider them the enemy. He figured either some frantic radio signals were leaving the transmission room, or perhaps this was another of Braun's schemes. He half expected Braun to return with a life jacket in his hand.

As if reading his mind, the surrounding crew's energy shifted urgently; everyone started hurrying along the deck looking serious, tying ropes, turning wheels, and calling orders. Braun reappeared wearing an inflated lifejacket, and handed one to Karl saying only, "You'd better put this on." Karl looked astonished, which seemed to please Braun, but Karl's surprise lay in the fact that his erudite guess had been correct.

"What are your plans for that?" Karl looked directly at Braun, but was pointing at the U-boat.

Braun appeared somewhat impressed that Karl had noticed the vessel and said, "Remember, he who sees first has won. That sub has orders to overhaul us. The next few hours will bring us to our destination, but there are a few details to look after first. Come with me." Braun turned and hurried with purpose up the metal stairs.

Karl watched from the glass windows on the bridge as the German U-boat came closer and charged up parallel to the steamer. He could see the commander, another officer and the gunner on the con. The gunner aimed his 20-mm gun and fired across their bow challenging them to 'Halt!'

Braun, standing beside Karl, didn't seem perturbed and nodded to the captain who then barked at the signalman to send out an SOS. Karl watched as both officers reacted simultaneously. The signalman immediately started to transmit while the captain left the cabin as if he'd already got his orders secretly. Karl felt some warmth on his cheek as the sun reappeared through the bridge window, but outside the waves were still high. Braun laughed and said, "Luck is on our side. Now all I need is calm seas." Then hurried off. Karl, knowing to stay close, pursued him down the metal stairs to the foredeck, but kept watch on the submarine's con.

The commander of the submarine was angry when his signaller reported the SOS. The situation smelled of treachery, he had a nose for it. Only a week before, he had been refuelling from a supply ship in the North Atlantic when he received a high order command to leave for Brazil. He thought that the orders were odd, but the Americans had doubled their efforts to rid the German forces of their elite U-boats, so he was glad to head south. A day hadn't gone by without depth charges being used by warships or aircraft to thunderously shake their vessel well beneath the surface. Sometimes they'd had to settle on the bottom in maximum silence waiting for the coast to be clear, emerging only at night. He'd had several close calls even though the submarines were supposed to be safer with the newly constructed *schnorkel*, a special curved, meshed pipe allowing air exchange while they were submerged.

Along with the original command came sealed orders to be opened at his destination. He had done exactly that, opening them several days ago. The orders specified that he wait until the Polish steamer, *Barchot*, arrived within reach of Rio de Janeiro; then use standard procedure to stop the merchant vessel and destroy it. The orders also included the unusual information that the vessel's crew would be co-operative; that stopping the boat would be uncomplicated, the crew was to be spared, but the boat was to be destroyed nonetheless. When they arrived, there were no Brazilian warships in the vicinity, and he convinced himself the exercise would be clear sailing. For once he had wanted a cushy, safe mission, but at this point, he was certain that wasn't on the cards.

Ordinarily the procedure would have been to inspect the Polish steamer under water at close quarters to determine the vessel type, real nationality, weaponry or any suspicious structures. He decided to skip this one step because he recognised the silhouette of the ship from the information he had received. The commander, as per protocol, had two torpedoes ready for immediate launching if resistance occurred from the merchant steamer. In this case, he hadn't thought there would be any need, but past experience made him follow the procedure. As usual, for the overtaking of a merchant vessel, he had remained on the surface. Speed was essential and surface attack would normally suffice to sink the ship; above water they could attain the maximum speed of seventeen point seven knots.

Everything was allowable until they sent out an SOS. Now his ship would be high and dry if enemy aircraft were sent to 'recon' the area. Brazil was now known to be militarily unsympathetic to Germany. Not only that, the sun and the calming surface made the water transparent and the track of their propeller more visible—they were sitting ducks.

He was angrier with himself than anyone or anything else. He had gone against his gut feeling that the orders were suspect, and broken his own rule to respect caution, telling himself that orders were orders. Surviving five years as commander of a submarine had taught him to live by his audacious wits. He wished he had used those wits before starting on this venture. Now that the SOS had been sent, he had no choice. The name and position of the Polish freighter had gone out in the emergency call, so he had to expect an aerial attack. Submerging sooner rather than later could save their lives. He ordered everyone off the con double time. Once the hatch was shut, he gave the command to dive to periscope depth. He shifted his weight at the base of the periscope. There was very little space to move about, because everywhere one turned there were pipes, chains, wheels for releasing air or controls to pump out water, spare torpedoes and personal equipment. He wished he could spit his tobacco on the floor as he tried to think of a fast way to follow orders and still get out of this mess.

Through the scope he saw the steamer had come to a stop. The original plan had been to board the ship and detonate a bundle of cartridges. Normally this would be done in the hold and in the engine room, breaching large spaces for maximum flooding to sink the ship quickly. Since orders demanded that the crew disembark, he planned to use the gunnery and a few carefully planted cartridges on the vessel to achieve a slow sink, so all the crew would escape. Now he had to forget all that and act quickly.

First he had to manoeuvre his boat to a ninety-degree angle optimizing his firing power. He needed just one perfectly aimed torpedo fired at *fangschuss*, point blank range, to sink the vessel. He commanded the ship into firing position; meanwhile, he took a sharp look skyward and along the horizon for aircraft. Only a few minutes before the darkened skies would have camouflaged them from enemy aircraft. Why in the devil had the SOS been sent out? He chewed on his tobacco and glanced at the clock as the alert sounded: "Torpedo tubes ready to fire!"

He was just about to shout the launch order when the sub resonated from a distant shock wave. He fixed the periscope on the central region of the steamer. Smoke was pouring out. A wide-angle view showed no evidence of what caused the explosion, but the ocean surface was scattered with floating lifeboats. He didn't take time to consider the matter; he had top brass orders to sink the sucker. He shouted his directives, "Ready to fire torpedo tube one. Fire." Relief came a second later when the torpedo hit the steamer— he wanted to shout with joy, a direct hit amidships; the steamer's back was broken, the mission accomplished. Now they could get the fuck out of there. Whenever they got to port he would get his crew drunk as a reward. He took one more look before ordering quickly periscope down. His fears had been real.

Fighter planes were zeroing in on the area. He bellowed for descent at full speed away from the sinking ship. The fact that all the crew on the Polish steamer had bothered to abandon ship before the situation called for it irked him, but he kept his mind on the crash dive hoping to save their own hides.

Karl had easily shimmied down the side of the boat into the life raft where there was room for six men, but Braun only allowed the radio operator and the captain to join them. The captain moved to the far end of the boat to sit beside the radio operator. The sky had cleared and the waves lulling as other survivors climbed into the remaining life rafts or clung to the sides. Karl turned to watch the activity, wondering why Braun refused to help. When he looked back, the radio operator was absent and a life jacket was floating away from their raft. Obviously, he was expected not to notice.

Braun went about the business of getting the raft steered as far away as possible from the steamer. When they had gone about twenty metres from the ship, a huge explosion ripped through the centre of the steamer. Large billows of black smoke poured out just aft of the bridge. One of the men in the next lifeboat pointed down and shouted. Karl heard a hiss in the water and caught a glimpse of a torpedo tracking beneath the surface. A second later, it blasted a cruel hole just below the water line. The ship, already listing helplessly on one side, began to rapidly submerge. After that Braun started assisting others into their boat until it was almost overflowing.

Karl looked up towards a droning noise overhead; four fighter planes were rapidly closing the distance from shore. The ocean was now calmer than before the squall had started. The sun poured down on the shimmering aquamarine ocean as the planes commenced a barrage of gunfire, creating foaming spray lines on both sides of the sinking ship. There was a deafening buzz as they swooped to circle the area, then split apart with two diving in a strafing run several thousand feet away. Karl watched as the remaining two followed suit, dropping a series of missiles. After the run, they all circled again. There was a pause as if even the planes were waiting for something to happen.

Suddenly thumping resonations, one after the other, shook the sea around them. Finally, several thousand metres away, a colossal upsurge of air and water erupted before the sub blasted through the mass. The bow was half blown away. The con hatch burst open and several bodies spewed forth before the boat slammed down. One body caught on the railing around the con and hung there for a second before water started pouring through the cavity, preventing anyone else from escaping.

The group on Karl's raft all scrambled in a tight grab for the sides as a shock of waves flooded over them. They sat awash with the salty water, watching the sub sink in a matter of seconds, while odd bits of debris started to litter the ocean surface, along with the floating bodies of the dead. There were no survivors.

The water gradually settled; the ocean seemed to lie back after the destructive human strike, letting nature take its course. Seagulls started flying overhead, squawking, while the larger black vultures he had seen earlier circled in a frenzy.

Braun relaxed against the side of the lifeboat looking self-satisfied. Karl wanted a confirmation so he ventured, "That first explosion wasn't caused by a torpedo."

"No, it wasn't." Braun kept the smug smile on his face.

"But that was a German submarine they sank," Karl probed, hoping for more.

"Sometimes sacrifices have to be made. We need evidence and a valid alibi in order to be accepted as refugees in Brazil. From now on you will speak only Polish until you learn Portuguese." Braun cut the interchange short by directing the rowers to head for the rescue ship headed in their direction.

Chapter 11

Northern Amazon

Joao fell away in a rush of freedom as Treiger's jet soared off. Like a bird of prey he pressed his arms along his sides in a dive towards the vast green below, his eyes fixed on Higler's disappearing parachute. Below him, the Paduairi River, an arm of the great Amazon, wound like a huge snake slithering through the enormous landmass. The sun was high in the sky, but in the distance monsoon clouds were advancing fast.

Not wanting to stray far from Higler, Joao pulled the ripcord and used the parachute straps to steer his body. As the air-filled canopy carried him over the terrain, Joao considered killing Higler an honour; he wanted to help Treiger, who had befriended him in a time of need— a debt to repay. He wondered if this was the right time. Time and place had meaning in the language of survival. The sense of awe he had for this land was built out of a deep respect that had soaked into every cell of his being. The sense of belonging here was more tenuous. Returning to his home territory could be a double-edged sword. He had gone back to his tribe only once since his youth and that had been once too often.

Below him was Yanomamö territory, a ten thousand year old ancestral home spreading over a rainforest-covered mountain range dividing the tributaries of the upper Orinoco River from those that flow south to the greater Amazon. Some tribes had been in direct, regular contact with the outside world since the beginning of the nineteenth century when fortune hunters, especially those seeking to mine gold, were the most common trespassers to invade their territory. However, first contacts with the Yanima, the most ferocious sect and the one to which Joao belonged, came late, but for Joao the contact was extremely important. Joao was only half Yanima.

His mother, a German nurse, was taken prisoner by a Yanima hunting party and had become the unwilling consort of the chief. Joao was the result of that union. His carved features, a combination of a muscular German physique, overlaid with the bronzed skin and dark hair of the Yanima, made him stand out, and as well, the Yanima medicine man, called the shaman, was certain that outsiders brought evil forest spirits, which in turn brought death. The shaman's influence made Joao and his mother virtual outcasts. Socially isolated, he often watched other boys out of the corner of his eye or sometimes defiantly in front of them and, deep down, even though he was son of the chief, knew that belonging was not part of his destiny.

It was during the *wither,* the rites of passage to become a warrior, that he found he did not truly belong. First, he'd been bitten by a viper as sabotage and then, the shaman who wanted to preserve his tribe, had given him an overdose of ground *yakowana,* a natural hallucinogen. Joao had survived, but the message was clear. The time had come for him and his mother to leave. They stole away one night and, after a few days, met up with some traders. But a Yanima tracking party caught up with their group and killed one of the traders. In the ensuing clash a Yanima was accidentally killed. Joao and his mother escaped with the lead trader called Riotur who brought them first to Manaus then Rio. But his mother died soon after. He buried her with the help of the monks at Mosteiro Sao Bento, the Benedictine monastery, high on a hill in the centre of Rio.

Joao learned to bargain for trade, went with Riotur into the rainforest and learned many tribal dialects. After a year or two Joao became a well-respected *sertanista*, a jungle-native contact man, taking those wanting to exploit the riches of the rainforests to interface with the native tribes. He soon found that in this new life where everything had a price, the novelty and excitement faded into disappointment. In the rainforest, every leaf, branch and root thronged with life. In the civilized world, even though everything was crowded together densely like the rainforest, the variations of pasty colours looked artificial and there was no evidence of life behind their walled-in existence. The people, textures and the size of the buildings varied, but as he turned each corner there was such sameness to all he saw. The Yanima, not having a concept of the future, only one of survival, had taught him to live as one with the environment and so he would disappear into the wilderness for months, and then suddenly find himself longing to go back to the city. He always returned to work with Riotur, resuming his routine of busy transactions in the marketplace mixed with the smell of cooking food and decomposing garbage.

One day he discovered *capoeira*. Through the centuries, native tribes combined combat techniques derived from black slaves into their own war rituals, first between tribes then to fight against slavers who sought to bring them into bondage for mining. For a few southern tribes it became a religion, but for Joao the attraction was the mental and physical discipline. He found the dance-like movements hypnotic, and thirsting to test his prowess, he began moving from tribe to tribe challenging their fighters to compete, refining his techniques and inventing new ones. By the time he was twenty, he found himself walking a sharp edge between both worlds, a nomad without a home. Then he met Karl Treiger.

On that particular day, Joao was in a Rio favela. This one was a real rat's nest compared with some of the other slums he'd fought in. The sun was beating down. The baking heat made it seem as if the burning ball of fire had moved closer to earth. Brown dust from the dry ground was settling around the form of a young man on his knees struggling to stand. Joao normally enjoyed his *capoeira* matches with favela gangs. Gang members lived only through survival instinct and could often be ingenious fighters. Joao loved the tough competition, but the way this match was ending concerned him.

Blood was streaming from his opponent's nose, but Joao didn't think his last kick had broken the cartilage. He went over to help the youth up because, as far as he was concerned, the competition was over. He had won fairly. The boy, about nineteen, hit Joao's hand away and spat out a call to his comrades. Figuring he'd better distance himself fast, Joao left the loser to his pals, but felt their eyes burning into his back as he left. The defeated gang leader, named Alves, had lost face. That kind of low-life always felt a bitter need to regain his position of authority. He had probably never lost a fight, having most likely scrapped like a snarling animal to get to the top. Joao had seen packs of starving dogs in the city and they could be vicious. Something in the look of the conquered gang leader's eyes reminded him of those dogs.

Anxious to leave, Joao cut through the clusters of misshapen huts thrown together with tin and cardboard. He was not familiar with this particular favela, but knew law and order stopped at the entry to any of these slums, the only rules being see nothing, hear nothing, ask no questions and keep your mouth shut. Luckily 'carnival' had started because most people all over the city, even in the favelas, were in a party mood. Carnival was the holiday of the poor. Hopefully, with the promise of a wild night of debauchery, this gang would forget about losing an ordinary fight.

In Europe, during the Middle Ages, carnival was a raging, lewd feast until squelched by Christianity. But even the sober church of the Inquisition could not purge carnival in the Portuguese colony of Brazil. Just as there are no legal rules in a favela, there are no moral rules for the carnival. Sex, booze and money pervade weeks of erotic, surreal parades of pastie-titted women of all ages, some ravishingly beautiful, and others more like grandmothers flaunting themselves in skimpy lingerie. All of them dance and dare to expose the most private parts of themselves in a decadent competition. Breasts and bottoms are exhibited in Kandinski fashion splattered with tattoos, paint and bits of fishnet coverings. Prices for everything from taxis to food to beds skyrocket along with car accidents and murders. Elaborately costumed, gold-glittered and silver-painted bodies include every variation of human sexuality. Caught up in the madness, ordinary people offer themselves as displays, or more, if you're willing to pay.

Just the night before, a corpulent woman plunged her huge bare breasts in front of Joao's face, offering him a long suck, languidly shaking the smoothly hanging melons. Bare breasts were not new to him, but an adult sucking them on the city street was not something he had come across before, so he declined with a shake of his head and walked on while another passer-by was accosted. Riotur saw it all and caught up with Joao telling him the woman was really a man. Joao smiled. The illusion seemed to fit the lunacy in the city. After that he headed back home to rest before the next day's competition.

The heat didn't bother Joao as he walked out of the hostile favela. Luckily, within a few minutes, he saw a tram headed in the direction of the city centre where he could catch a connection to the port. He waved and the driver slid to a stop, letting Joao climb in the rear entrance. This Sunday, the tram was crammed with people, some dressed for carnival, some dressed for church, and a few were just dressed. The more exotically attired were probably heading for the other side of the city to street dance. Some urban areas would be completely deserted while others, near tourist beaches like Cococabaña and Ipanema, would be packed with slithering, hot-blooded revellers, high on whatever they could get there hands on— booze, asses or tits were just appetizers.

Before the tram pulled away, two of the gang members climbed on and held the door open. Joao squeezed his way to the front. There was no place to fight on the packed tram, but a knife could easily be slipped between his ribs if any of the followers got close. He looked to the back again. The beaten gang leader, Alves, had been the last to enter. Still with a bloodied face, he arrogantly stared at Joao then let his eyes stray to the dirty windows. The rest of the gang was clinging to the outside. Joao looked dispassionately at them. Human packs were the worst kind of foe. The sun heated up the cabin mercilessly, and the noise of the tram mixed with the drone of talk and hot wafts from a few grimy windows that some people had managed to open. Joao and Alves stood crushed at either end of the sardine can.

Joao kept track of the pack, only occasionally glancing outside the driver's front window waiting to see the central depot, an unpaved expanse of dirt where dozens of buses and trams were routed every few minutes. During carnival, the depot would be teaming with partygoers, but he vaguely recalled that the surrounding streets were a hodgepodge of small half blocks and dead-ends. He would have to be careful, but he had a good chance of escaping if he was fast. He knew where he would go. The monastery where his mother was buried was in the district. He just had to find it. The tram neared the wide open-end station and Joao could see scads of people milling about.

Alves let the blood dry on his face. The cracking blackened smear was a symbol of revenge. He watched Joao from the back of the bus. This one had fought like he didn't care whether he lived or died. Alves had never met anyone like this before and was jealous of the ultra-cool indifference Joao exuded. He also envied Joao's manner of fighting; for a jungle-boy, a Yano no less, the guy seemed to improvise continuously. Alves had killed about twenty people in his life— mostly people who threatened his leadership in the favela; a few had been people he just didn't like. In fact, he was quite lazy and looked forward to a much different life in a few years. He was planning on becoming a gang leader, covering several favelas so he could get others to do the fighting for him. He wanted to be part of the black-market cartel. He'd heard that once you showed an ability to organize others, there was a chance at the big time. Alves continued to watch Joao; spiteful of the way the Yano glanced out the open windows then back at him and his boys as if he could see right through them. There was a plan cooking in that brain and Alves wanted to be ready for whatever happened. He checked the position of his compatriots. The tram was nearing the depot and he knew the surrounding area like the back of his hand. When he looked back, Joao was gone.

Joao waited until the tram was close to stopping, then slid quickly to floor level and skimmed like a serpent to the conductor's feet. With one hand, he pushed the driver's brake foot and with the other, he reached up and flung the door lever open. Everyone in the tram lurched helplessly forward; some women screamed and children started to cry. The tram driver tried to grab him, but Joao was out the door in a split second. From the corner of his eye, he saw that the boys hanging outside had been ruthlessly pitched several feet away from the car. They floundered against waiting travellers, shoving and swearing at them, while those inside the tram were gridlocked by the pandemonium. Joao pushed his way through a horde of sweating bodies.

Alves didn't have to see Joao; the Yano was fast and probably out of the tram. He dived over the masses and crammed his lean body out the closest window, making Joao out near the edge of the depot. He began the chase, whistling as he ran to alert his gang, barely keeping the Yano in sight, while his band scattered in different directions.

Joao zigzagged through the muddled streets. The pavement was empty of life, but littered with garbage. All the able people were either at church or the carnival and the old ones were stashed inside, out of the heat. He looked up above the rooftops for the towers of the Monastery, worried that he'd taken a wrong turn, but he couldn't be sure. If he were on the right track, around the next corner, only a short distance from his sanctuary, he'd enter a central square. He ran with all his might, hearing, in the still air, the pounding feet of the others. The pounding stopped. He wasn't sure why.

Karl Treiger had got up that hot Sunday morning wanting a peaceful distraction and decided on the Gregorian chant at the Mosteiro Sao Bento. He left his apartment near Leblon beach. The flat allowed him to carve out some privacy for himself, away from the Gau, but at carnival time there was very little peace in the surrounding streets. His off-license cab rolled through the city centre passing vacant streets of concrete buildings, while he listened to Allegri's *Miserere Mei Deus* on his Walkman. Tranquillity was what he wanted. He shifted in the seat to make himself more comfortable. His gun, a Rugar, was pressing against his rib cage under his light linen jacket. The gun was a necessity when travelling through a sparsely habited area of Rio.

Alves knew his crew and felt that he could take his time while his boys rounded the bugger up. They all had a route to follow avoiding any of the dead end streets. Alves chose his way past houses that were little more than shacks. Some had undergone renovation, making the rest look more sordid than they already were. When he ruled the favelas, he would live in one of the mansions on the other side of town with all the wealthy people. His feet left small clouds of dust as he jogged. He couldn't wait to see the Yano draw his last breath. He kept his pace even, not wanting to tire himself out in the heat. He would save his energy for the big triumphal moment when he cut the Yano's head off. The victory would make him famous throughout the favelas.

The taxi let Treiger off in front of the nondescript-looking Benedictine façade, such a contrast to the Baroque interior, which Treiger considered vastly overdone; too much gold ornamentation, too many dark religious statues painted garish colours in a darkly lit space along with the elaborate nave with its gilt ceiling. He knew he would just shut his eyes and allow the monks' perfectly modulated chanting to sooth him. A major turn of events had taken place and he could now further his plan.

Joao rounded the corner, relieved to see the small square he was looking for, but before he could cross to the other side, two gang members armed with knives barred his way. He turned to take another side street before realizing his mistake. Two more youths from the favela appeared. Joao watched as the gang collected around him like a pack of starving dogs. But ravenous dogs could be forgiven because at the earliest opportunity they used the killing bite. On the other hand, the kind of humans that lived on the low side of a favela didn't have the instinctual law of the jungle as a guide. The cruelty caused by scrounging for food while watching those who had lavishly more ate out their souls. They lived for revenge, for looting, and to see that others suffered more than they did. He watched their eyes. These types were lusting to see some pain and suffering. The earlier competition had only served to build a craving for torment in their blood. They wanted more. Their appetites were wet.

Treiger was annoyed. Halfway through the Gregorian chanting, a busload of tourists arrived, shuffling inside the church porch with low murmurs, disturbing the serenity. Today in particular, he was in no mood for people, having just been notified of his promotion to the Gau. He wanted to work out his strategy. Making his way through the crowd, he departed through the church courtyard, taking the secluded winding road down from the monastery. Even though his route was sided by a curving granite wall, trees massed with soft white, lemon yellow or deep pink blossoms overhung the walls. Under the cool shade of the walls, he could smell the heady scent of Jasmine and Bougainvillaea. He switched on his Walkman softening his mood with Tomas Tallis's *Agnus Dei*, and strolled deep in thought. There was not a breath of wind, so each leaf hung in the air as if suspended in time.

Joao tensed his muscles, and then relaxed them. Waiting for the first attack to come, he dispassionately assessed the slavering gang. All he could do was react to whatever came his way. The combat began. One of the group took a dash at him. Joao leapt into the air and hit him in the face with the flat of his foot. The boy's head whipped back as he squealed in pain. Joao turned to look at the others waiting for the next one to attack.

Treiger turned a corner into the square and warily eyed the crowd of boys. The music blocked out any of the commotion. The small square should have been empty on a Sunday morning, but the area was filled with dirty favela youths clamouring around what used to be a Yanomamö native. They had him cornered on the other side of the clearing. The young man was striving single-handedly to fend off the mob, fighting bravely even though his face look like bloodied pulp. Treiger was amazed that such a battered human being was able to stand and fight while maintaining an impressive amount of skilled precision. He'd seen the *capoeira* executed before, but never so eloquently.

Joao's second wind was just about finished as he grappled with another of the pack. He grabbed his attacker by the throat and scrotum ready to fling his body away when he felt a sharp, piercing pain in his lower back as another fist struck a blow from behind. With a surge of energy, he heaved the body towards the jeering watchers and turned on the attacker behind him. As he twisted around, the coward ran back to the surrounding group. They had been playing this game with him for a while. As he fought with one, another would dash in and punch him in the kidneys or the side of his head. Each of the gang had obviously been taking turns tiring him out, like a bull in the ring. He looked up to see the two towers of the Mosteiro Sao Bento, thinking that perhaps he would be joining his mother soon. When he lowered his eyes to meet the next assailant, he caught sight of a tall man watching him from the other side of the square.

As Treiger watched, a glint caught his eye. One of the attackers was handing a large, curved machete to another youth whose face was marked with blood; he took the knife as if pretending to be a gladiator. Treiger supposed that this was the leader. He also knew the tactic. The knife would be used to slowly inflict gashes, increase blood loss and tire the victim; each cut would be a little slice of death leaving the brave fighter without a chance in hell of surviving.

Alves loved the feel of the machete in his hand. His boys had been teasing the Yano for about twenty minutes, until in the last two jousts the bastard had slowed down. Alves grinned; his turn had come. He would use the blade to slowly hack at this loser's body until he was just a bloodied hulk on the ground. He couldn't wait until his victim was unrecognisable, then he would slash right through his neck. He would raise the head by the hair in one hand and the machete in the other. He would then turn to the crowd with his trophy. The vision glared like fire in his mind.

Joao had another boy's throat in his hand when he heard a whooshing sound, the sound of a swinging machete. He'd used one in the rainforest many times cutting a way for Riotur. Joao was so pumped up with adrenaline that he didn't feel the first cut and ignored the blood that spattered on the youth he was holding, even though he knew the blood was his own. He used all the strength he could muster to squeeze the consciousness out of the boy in his clutches and drop him. Then in one smooth motion he swung his leg around, using the other to propel himself off the ground. He felt as if he was moving in slow motion until his foot made contact. A crack of bone shattered through the air and as if in suspended animation he saw the machete fall and Alves' arm drop to his side with a narrow shaft of bone protruding through the skin of his forearm. Alves seemed to slowly scoop up his broken arm. The others stood in a gasp of surprise until Alves began screeching high-pitched orders.

Treiger watched from the side of the square. After the first cut with the machete, the valiant combatant showed no reaction save to follow through with an elegant springing kick to the leader's arm. He had gracefully landed, but instead of placing a killing blow, or even grabbing the knife, the Yanomamö stood slightly swaying as if he was ready to drop. In response to the fallen leader's slang Portuguese, a follower rushed to pick up the scythe-like blade, raising his hand high as if to slice across the fighter's neck. Without a second thought, Treiger reached for the Rugar. He aimed and fired. The first bullet hit the machete with such force that it was wrenched out of the boy's hand. He fired a second and third bullet into the ground at the feet of the now jittery group. Some turned to look at him; others didn't bother as they broke up in a frenzied burst of surprised fear. The broken-armed leader hunkered pathetically behind his fleeing tribe. The Yanomamö boy fell to the ground unconscious.

Joao remembered his first real look at Treiger. He awoke in a small modestly appointed apartment. He was alone. The door clicked open and the tall man he had seen in the square walked in. He looked not old, but not young either. His hair was sunny blonde and he carried himself with such ease that Joao almost felt reassured by the movement. The man looked at Joao and noticed he was awake, but made no effort to go near him or to talk. This was unusual. Joao had always found white people, even his mother, had a need to talk. They often spoke without even thinking and expected others to speak back. This man went to the counter and emptied some food out of a sac, mostly fruit— some melons, mangoes and kiwis. He suddenly felt very hungry. Almost as if the man had read his mind, he came over to the bed carrying some fruit and a knife. He set them down on the bedside table. Joao felt the man was very trusting to put a knife beside a stranger. Joao knew he was as weak as a newborn monkey and couldn't have used the knife if he wanted too. The man picked the jug of water up and walked back to the sink to refill it. Joao reached for a kiwi and consumed the whole thing, skin and all, in two bites. Sweet juice dripped down his chin. He reached for another and soon had demolished four of them in the same manner, then licked his fingers and fell into a satisfied sleep.

Later when Joao awakened, the man re-bandaged the wounds on his face and arm, and brought him more food. After several days, Joao started to feel better when the water that passed from his body flowed clear without blood. The man came frequently to check on him. Once, Joao went to the door. It opened easily as if giving the message that he could leave if he wanted to. Whenever the man returned, they said little to each other, but Joao found out his name was Treiger; otherwise he respected the silence. When Joao was awake, he watched Treiger, wondering why a European stranger would bother with someone like him. When he was strong enough, he had his answer.

"I want you to teach me how to fight like you," was all Treiger said. He didn't add or imply 'because of what I did for you.'

Joao felt if he said 'no' and walked out Treiger would not have stopped him. It was because of this that he nodded his head. After that, a bond of understanding connected them. They never spoke of it or even tried to understand it. Treiger took him under his wing, so to speak, and taught him how to survive with civilised values. Joao in turn taught Treiger the capoeira and how to survive in the jungle. He came to see that even though Treiger was secretive, he was a man with a purpose. Joao learned from his deliberate, methodical ways and admired how physically adaptable Treiger was in learning the *capoeira*. After about two years, Treiger presented him with the opportunity to attend a special school to learn to read. The choice was not simple for Joao. In the end he decided that before he would take up Treiger's offer, the time had come to confront his past. Learning to read would be like leaving the Yanima culture behind without giving himself a chance to re-enter the tribe on his own terms.

He went to Manaus with Riotur. They followed their usual route, but when it was time to pass into Yanima territory, Joao sent Riotur back, saying his life was at risk to be seen with him. Riotur was reluctant at first, but knew he had never been able to influence the boy, so he headed back. Joao entered the tribe alone and went immediately to his half brother, the new chief. The stern chief had him taken prisoner because his warriors claimed that Joao had killed one of their own. The shaman, thin and old, stood looking at him inscrutably for a time, then turned to the chief. The result of their discussion was a choice: Joao could die a warrior's death, or accept the ritual of the *hekura duku*, a spiritual excommunication.

The *hekura duku* was a lethal rite carried out by the tribal shaman using hallucinogens. No one had been known to undergo the ordeal without becoming a member of the living dead, which they called the *duku ka miri amahiri*. Joao realised that he wanted to go back to his friend Treiger. The choice was simple; he accepted the *duku* rite. Once the hallucinogens had been administered, Joao began an endless nightmare of thrashing and convulsing. The tribe laid him in the rainforest and left him as an untouchable. The shaman was the only one with authority to watch over him, but the tribe could hear terrible shrieks, howling and horrific flailing noises from his paroxysms. No animals, snakes or vermin ventured near as he lay for days in his own excrement and vomit, sometimes in a paralysed trance, other times in horrendous nightmares of black half-beast half men reaching into his head and ripping out his brains or disembowelling him.

Suddenly, he awoke, weak and filthy beyond recognition. The shaman came and knelt before him in a trance. Finally he left and returned with two young warriors who were instructed to bath and feed Joao. When Joao was finally strong enough to walk back to the village, the whole tribe knelt before him. He had become a mythological figure for them because he had ascended to the state of *heku di mis*, the layer of the anaconda. He was considered half spirit-half man, one to be feared, loved and hated. Only Joao knew he was just an ordinary man. A few days later, when he had gained enough strength, he left the tribe and never returned to their territory until today.

As Joao swung through the Amazonian sky, swells of loyalty for his friend passed through his heart, but his eyes never left his descending target. Higler was aiming his chute near to the river's edge. In the distance he saw the ravaged clearing of the northern perimeter highway like a cadaver's body in the process of being gutted. Higler would be heading for that as the dirt road cut across the Paduairi further down stream just outside of Yanomamö territory. The monsoons were nearly over, but Joao noted how high the river had risen, in some places the level was half way up the towering tree trunks and in others, it had only covered the alluvial wash. From his height he could see regions of flooding along the winding tributary and places where chunks of the riverside had broken loose swirling down stream in the current. He swung his chute upstream of where Higler had been absorbed into the unlimited sweep of muddy green.

As Joao landed, he saw evidence of natives, probably a Yanima scouting party. If Higler ran into them, they would either capture or kill him. If they took him hostage then, Joao would have no say in whether they would allow Higler to survive or not. They might decide to trade him for something they wanted from the outside world. It had been a long time since the *duku* rite and he wondered how much influence that would have. It was unlikely that the Yanima would accept interference from the half-breed son of a dead chief who had deserted the tribal ways.

Freeing himself from his chute, Joao stripped down to his narrow leather thong and quickly dispatched all other paraphernalia, except for the harness holding his Bowie. He paused unmoving, immersing himself in the mystifying and veiled aura of his land. His body was taut and alert to sound, movement, and scent. He let the essence of the untouched wilderness seep back, cleansing his mind of rules from the civilised world and replacing them with instinctual guile and a feral sense of savagery. As his feet oozed into compost containing millenniums of decayed vegetation, flesh and bone, he felt his blood start to pump in rhythm with the current of the flooding river. Refocusing his eyes, he knew he should move quickly.

Upstream rains were causing the water level to rise rapidly. Clouds were moving in overhead as if they were gathering for a battle, a phenomenon signalling the end of the monsoons. The day would start off clear, and then in a matter of minutes, you couldn't even see in front of your eyes from the pelting torrents. The race to catch Higler would now be a competition between him and the rainforest. If the rain came soon, Joao figured that Higler would probably disappear in the alluvial mud. He had never met an outsider who could endure the persistent rain and survive a flood wash, but still, Higler was resourceful. Joao wanted to win. Higler would not plague Treiger any more.

Picking a high site along the riverside that was less muddy, Joao lashed together three short, dry posts from trees washed out in a previous year's flood. The raft mimicked other islands of floating land that had been liberated from the river's edges by the current. He climbed on, covering his body with leaf fronds, blending him naturally into his homemade barge, and pushed his floater out into the current using a branch as a pseudo-rudder. In the rainforest, moisture penetrated everything and most materials made by man became wretched and useless, particularly guns. Knives, on the other hand, were indispensable. He checked his Bowie to ensure the hilt was at the ready.

Before long Joao saw torn overhang, the sign of a single traveller in the water, but after rounding the next bend, Joao noted several worrisome prints on the bank. The scouting group he had identified earlier were on Higler's trail already. Even though Joao felt he could deal with them, it wouldn't be easy unless Higler was already dead. Joao moved his contrived rig out into the middle of the river to catch the faster current, stopping when he saw pocks in the sludge. Higler's boots forced him to use precious energy to pull out of the slime. Soon the Aryan would need to remove his footwear and expose his legs to the water snakes. The Amazon was rife with them at this time of year.

He steered to shore and instead of setting foot on the muck, he took hold of the enormous overhanging bough of an Anaxi tree, raised himself onto a massive sixty foot branch. He jogged to the trunk, then speedily, and silently climbed high amongst the foliage. The distant cloudburst was marching even closer. Rain would slow down the others and increase his chances of dealing with Higler first. Joao tensed expectantly at the close swish of moving brush. Directly underneath he saw Higler grasping branches of shrubbery to help drag himself onto the bank. His blonde hair was covered in mud turning his complexion into a haunting grey. His clothes, laden with black alluvial silt, stuck to his body. He looked like an enraged monster rising from the primeval ooze. He struggled to unplug each foot that imbedded itself deeply in the mud. Yet the determination of each move showed that Higler was not going to give in easily. Joao unsheathed the Bowie. He would have preferred that the downpour had reached them, but he couldn't wait. The risk of the hunting party intervening was too great. Joao prepared himself. This would be his kill.

He let go of his hold on the high branch, aiming to strike Higler's shoulders. His freefall cracked a small twig. Higler instantly rolled towards the trunk of the Anaxi and scrambled onto a huge branch piercing deep into the forest. Good survival instinct, Joao thought in a split second, but the move won't save you. Before reaching the ground, Joao grabbed some foliage and swung with ease back onto a long Anaxi arm above Higler. He leapt, using the graceful yet lethal intent of the capoeira in his movement, holding the Bowie ready to strike.

In mid-air his body arched with racking agony as a carved Yano spear impaled him. He dropped to the ground trying to fold into a protective roll. As his body hit the earth, the spear shaft cracked and broke off, pushing one end of it straight through his side. He floundered. The pain he could endure, but his body was reacting in shock. He scrounged with one hand for his fallen knife, but he was too late. Higler was crouched beside him, the Bowie clenched in his muddy hand and his sleek, blonde features distorted with scorn.

He watched the German surveying him and his injury. Joao could feel that the spear had penetrated his side, but not struck anything vital, however moving would be difficult and Higler had the upper hand. Joao decided to wait for his moment. Then Higler did the unexpected. He put his hand on the end of the spear protruding through his side and pushed on it, forcing Joao to grimace in agony. *"Treiger sheis!"* he hissed. He waved the knife slowly in front of Joao's eyes before expertly slicing the blade across his abdomen, exposing the sheath of membrane covering his intestines. The next slice would cut open his bowels letting him succumb in the stink and muck of an agonising death. There was a part of him that didn't mind. His friend Treiger was worth dying for.

Before Higler could begin the second slit of his ritual carving, a Yanima brave broke through the bush with his spear raised to kill. Higler flipped the Bowie's knife tip and flung it straight through the raging native's heart. He left Joao's side, retrieved the knife from the corpse as the next warrior came throttling through the trees. This one he grabbed by the neck, and held the Bowie to his carotid. Higler let out a harsh, German command, demanding the cowards show themselves. The natives did not understand and made no sound. Higler finally dragged his captive off into the undergrowth.

A few moments later, three Yanima ventured forth. They looked at their fallen comrade and at the sweating, unconscious body of Joao. One of them murmured *"heku di mis"*, spirit of the anaconda.

Chapter 12

McGill University, Montreal

A sign indicated the library archives were to the left. Deeply concerned over Fiona's creepy episodes, Megan led the way into a sea of tall shelves separated by narrow aisles. Silence haunted their footsteps as Fiona tiptoed behind. At the end of the stacks stood a solitary figure bent over a central desk

"Don't ask her!" Fiona blurted, but had already caught the attention of a gaunt librarian with a hawk nose and greying hair pulled severely back into a bun. Megan shrugged off Fiona's hold and marched up to the desk. "We need some information."

The stern face was unyielding. "Do you have a library card?"

"Well...ah..." Megan paused giving a quick desperate look at Fiona.

"I do!" Fiona responded and, avoiding eye contact, began scrounging in her purse, fumbling with the contents. A pen fell to the floor with a clatter and some receipts floated after. Fiona rifled through a handful of credit cards until a dog-eared certificate turned up.

The librarian scrutinized the worn paper briefly. "Your membership's expired."

Fiona pressed her lips together and stared at the woman for a minute before saying, "I must say you remind me of a nun that taught me years ago at Saint Marceline's school for girls, Sister Marie..."

"Arendt," the librarian interrupted sadly.

"Why yes! She looked so severe with that grey and white habit..." then with only a breath of hesitation Fiona added, "but she seemed kind once you got to know her."

"She was my eldest sister. She died last year...of cancer," the woman murmured, her eyes glazing with tears before she stiffened, asking, "Now, what is it you want?"

Megan watched Fiona swing into name-dropping action. "My husband, Doctor Richard Kendall belongs to McGill's Faculty of Medicine and is looking for the architectural prints to our property. According to our architects, Laberge and Cohen, of course, an old copy of it is kept here. Goodness, I had no idea that our house could be an historical monument or anything of that sort."

"Where do you live?"

"On Roxton Crescent, in Upper Westmount."

"How curious. I think I can help you." The librarian headed between the stacks towards a glassed-in office at the other end of the room.

Megan whispered to Fiona, "You're amazing. I thought we were just about to be booted out of here and now we're getting red carpet treatment."

"Always remember dear, it's whom you know; what you know only helps in achieving that. I got my degree in philosophy here, married the right pedigree even though that's old-fashioned, and am now living unhappily ever after. But, I am rich."

"What are you doing hanging around with me, then?"

"You exude charisma. Besides, you have breeding even though you try to hide it.

There's much more to you than meets the eye. Such mystery appeals to my sense of..."

"Come to my office, please." Librarian Arendt's voice drifted into Fiona's words.

"...drama," Fiona's sentence ended with an elegant drawl and a flamboyant twist of her head as she obediently tagged behind the librarian.

The ingenuous comment had crept into the private part of her life and she didn't like it one bit. Megan's return back to Canada from Scotland was meant as an escape for her and, at that time, her daughter. It was so damn painful. She reminded herself that Fiona's flippant comment was only a distraction and that she'd better stay hooked on what they were after. She followed Fiona into a crowded office stuffed with two desks and several filing cabinets. Covering the top of one desk was a very large bonded book.

The librarian walked over to the volume and said, "I'm not certain if these are the prints you are looking for, but they are the originals of that area. I don't have the reconstruction prints so I am surprised the architect sent you here. Ordinarily, we wouldn't have kept all these documents. However, you do live in an interesting historical area. A solitary group of priests made a settlement there, Jesuit probably—the history is old for Canada, dating back to the 1760's, but not well documented. Some of the monks had to protect themselves from the indigenous peoples and Jesuits were renowned as hard workers. The high ground near Mount Royal would have been considered a safer location for a primitive monastery. According to the diagram, there were some stone buildings connected by a set of covered arches, creating a...well...a sort of cloisters, I guess you would call it. As far as I know, nothing remains of that early site. These documents were last viewed in the 1950's by a professor from Religious Studies, Rolfe. He may have studied them and knows something more, but likely he will have retired."

"Could we get a copy of this?" Megan asked tentatively.

"That is impossible. Such rare, old papers are too fragile and should never be removed from here. In any case, special equipment would be necessary to copy this."

Megan ignored the cold, business tone and persisted, "Why was this map in your office?"

"In fact, someone already asked to see these prints earlier. My assistant had difficulty finding them and asked for advice, which was why I even knew about it. We then found this." The librarian put her hand protectively on the binding.

Megan gestured towards Fiona. "My friend's home was broken into last night and we think the thief was after papers like this. Without trying to sound mysterious, I would strongly suggest that you store this safely for the time being. Do you think your assistant could identify the man that asked to see these prints?"

"I believe the request was made by a woman. But really ladies, don't you think that if there's a problem you should go to the police?"

Fiona broke in, "Of course, you're absolutely right. My friend has an overactive imagination. Thank you so much, Miss Arendt, and I will remember to pay my fees."

Megan didn't have a chance to say another word before Fiona nudged her out of the room and busily hauled her down the stairs to the main floor.

Megan bristled, "Why did you rush me away, Fiona? This could be important and possibly dangerous. Look what has happened. You've been mugged, your home broken into and that architect's office ransacked. Now we find out someone else is looking for the same prints. How often do you think that such a document is asked for in one day?"

"Be quiet, silly!" Fiona whispered as they shuffled through the turnstile exit. "I just didn't feel like wasting time. I'll bet Rolfe is still at the Faculty of Religious Studies. No one retires at McGill; those professors stay in their offices until they join the great departed. Let's see if we can find out anything more before tea time is over!"

Megan entered the stately Religious Studies building. Fiona pointed it out as an example of Greek revival architecture and much preferable to the brutalist cut of the library. Inside, Megan was taken by the potent sense of spirituality that emanated from the darkly wooded walls and high ceilings, yet there was a strange detachment about the few people walking about. Fiona ineffectively asked one where they might find Professor Rolfe's office while Megan found his name on a plaque listing names. She rushed Fiona up a wide, elegant staircase just inside the foyer.

Megan found a receptionist who reported that Rolfe was not in and, no, she didn't expect him to show up at this point. Fiona's hopeful expression fell and she dejectedly turned to leave, but Megan decided to ask, "Did anyone else inquire about him today?"

"Why, as a matter of fact, yes," the receptionist replied.

"Would you be able to describe that person?" When a look of disapproval strained over the receptionist's face, Megan added quickly, "Please. It is very important."

"Well, I don't have much to tell you. She..."

"It was a woman, then?" The words rushed out, so Megan smiled sweetly trying to imitate Fiona's style.

The receptionist eyed her, "Well, yes. An elderly woman who said she was a relative of his."

"What did she look like?" Megan hoped she didn't sound like an interrogator.

The receptionist sighed, "She had faded white hair like she used to be a blonde. She wasn't tall, not overweight. Strangely she had a bit of an accent. German I think..."

"That must be Mother!" Fiona broke in and grabbed Megan's arm. "Well, it has to be her! Trust me."

Megan had no idea what Fiona intended, but silently watched her continue.

"We came into the city for a visit and lost her at some point. She's a bit senile you see. We thought she'd come here...to my uncle's office...her brother-in-law, Professor Rolfe, I mean. Silly of us, but we entirely expected him to be sitting at his desk."

Picking up on the idea, Megan added, "Could you give us his address? She may head there. She had the address in her purse, but I haven't a clue where he lives myself."

The receptionist frowned, "Funny, she asked about his address too, but she seemed to have all her faculties."

Fiona joined in, "Well, that's senility for you. Probably forgot it was right in her bag. Quite seriously though, we are worried and would like to find her quickly."

"Well, I really shouldn't give out his address," the receptionist wavered.

Megan increased her tone of concerned sincerity, "Of course, we shouldn't be asking you to break the rules, but she is our mother."

The receptionist had reluctantly produced an address in lower Westmount that wasn't all that far away from Roxton Crescent, and minutes later Megan was twisting her Land Rover onto Rolfe's street. They tramped up the front walk towards a large, gabled house in need of paint. Dead hydrangea blossoms leaned over the grounds, leaving a narrow width of uncut lawn between the thick cedar-crushed boundary and the house. Megan climbed the porch stairs with Fiona on her heels.

Fiona looked at her watch. "What I won't do for a cup of tea! Although it is running into drinkies time, and I could use a good strong shot of vodka. This place gives me the creeps. It looks haunted."

Feeling unsettled herself, Megan murmured, "Keep calm, we'll only be a moment." She rang the bell, continuing in a hushed voice, "I just can't figure out who that woman at the library could be. Why would anyone, but Richard be interested in the plans for your house? In any case, I thought for sure it would be that guy who attacked you," She pressed the doorbell again.

Fiona quickly responded, "In the last battle, I believe it was I who attacked him, but I won't argue the point. Life with you as a friend, Megan, will never be dull. I could be at home feeling sorry for myself and here I am running around town on a wild goose chase, all for Richard's sake, but if we find the stuff, he will be thrilled. He's always more amorous when he's thrilled...or," Fiona added in a pensive mutter, "drunk."

Shaking off memories of Richard's behaviour from the previous evening, Megan moved along the veranda windows, trying to peer in.

Fiona looked cautiously about. "Don't do that. Someone might see you."

But Megan reacted like a hound on the scent. "Wait here," she whispered, lithely hopping over the veranda rail and disappearing around the side of the house. Further along the side was a bay window, but the ground sloped down and a briar rose bush covered the wall, so that she couldn't easily reach the windowsill to have a look. She jumped up once trying to get a peek through the yellowed neon curtains and was certain something moved. A wave of fear passed through so fast that the feeling was gone before she landed on the ground. She decided to get back to Fiona.

Megan swivelled over the railing with a short report. "There seems to be some kind of office around the side. Even though I didn't get a good look, I think someone's inside. Rolfe's old, perhaps he's hard of hearing." The strange feeling that something was amiss stuck with her so she added, "Try the door."

"Listen, Meg. Don't you think this is going a bit to far?"

"No, I don't." Saying more wouldn't help because the peculiar vibes she was getting would only spook Fiona.

Fiona reached for the doorknob. "Really, Megan, I will die of embarrassment if someone sees me...Jesus! It's open!"

Megan jumped to her side and cautioned softly, "Wait out here. Stay at the door and be quiet until I call for you." She pushed the door open and stepped cautiously through the entrance.

A small foyer led to a long dark hallway sided by a set of stairs to the second floor. The light switch by the entry didn't work, but regardless, she started down the hall. Even though she tread lightly, the touch of each step seemed to echo through the musty quiet of the house. A creak sounded. She wasn't sure from where, upstairs or further down the hall. Then all was silent again. She took another step. The cold, shadowy stillness made for a strange eeriness. In an effort to be subjective, she questioned whether she had really seen movement in the window. Reluctant to trespass, but, still concerned that something was not right, she decided to break the silence. "I'm sorry if I'm disturbing you, Professor Rolfe," she called out loudly. Her voice travelled hollowly through the house, dispersing into thin air.

She took another step. One of the floorboards moaned, making her hesitate. A few steps further on, she passed the door to the living room and peered in. Frayed brocade drapes covered the windows on the other side of the room. A narrow crack of daylight strained through the small separation in the heavy hanging material. The room was amass with dusty books piled everywhere, except on the deeply dented seat cushion on the chair beside the couch. A tarnished brass floor lamp hovered over the chair. Further on was a small dining room made darker by a cumbersome, walnut-stained dining room set. Her foot hit another weak floorboard—screaming wood condemned her as a trespasser. She sprung ahead then got hold of herself. The hollow silence resumed as if the walls were holding their breath.

Nearing the end of the hall, a door was ever so slightly ajar. For a moment she stood outside listening. She resisted a strong urge to walk by and slowly raised her hand to the wood panel. Her fingertips trembled in reaction to the edgy atmosphere and, ashamed of her fear, she pushed on the door. It swung halfway revealing a small office. On one side of the dingy room was a messy bookshelf crammed with all sorts of books with worn covers. A number of them lay on the floor along with scattered papers. Across the room, the old man was sitting in a swivel chair at his desk. His head was slumped forward and one bent arm lay on the desktop. He was just asleep.

Megan stood still and, to awaken him, said gently, "Professor." She pushed the door further and stepped in carefully, hoping not to startle him. With a better view of the desk, she noticed an awkward angle to his neck and the way his right hand fell heavily over the arm of the chair. She sniffed the air, an Indian trick she learned as a child. She hated the sickening smell, but the scent was so faint she knew the death hadn't been long ago. She almost felt as if his spirit hadn't left the room.

She moved closer, but didn't touch him. Ropes wound around his ankles under the chair. His left arm had also been tied. The wrist was raw with rope burns. The twine that had held his right arm was on the floor as if it had been hurriedly dropped. The phone cord had been ripped out of the wall. Only when she bent to take a closer look did she sense another presence in the room, but it was too late.

Fingers seized her hair, pulling with such force that she thought the roots were being wrenched out of her head. Her body lurched helplessly backwards until her head crashed against the wall. Stunned beyond comprehension, her legs buckled to the floor. Distantly, she heard Fiona screaming her name. As blinding pain wracked her skull, she flung her hands up to ward off a frontal attack, but only glass crashed. She forced herself to stand and staggered forward, barely glimpsing a thin form leaping out of the window.

Fiona rushed in, her eyes went to Megan then the dead body; her hands went up to her throat as she screamed and, after taking a few gulping breaths, fainted. Megan felt like doing the same, but sternly told herself 'get help'. She fell to her knees and, trying to ignore the mean pain across her crown, she rummaged hazily through Fiona's bag, found a cell phone, and dialled Ménard's number. "Danny, please help us," Megan whimpered feeling pathetic and barely remembering the address. In her dazed state, she saw a paper that the man had dropped before his exit. She crawled over and without even looking at the contents, roughly folded it and shoved the sheet into her pocket. She hauled Fiona's head into her lap then slumped against the wall waiting for Ménard.

"You're certain that it was the same man that you saw at Mrs. Kendall's the other night?" Ménard asked Megan.

Fiona moved in, interjecting smoothly, "Please call me Fiona."

When Megan frowned, he couldn't figure out what she was reacting to, Fiona's interruption or his question, but her answer sounded sincere.

"I know I was stunned, but the stature was the same. Call it gut instinct, second sight or just plain connecting detail with detail, but I could swear my life on it."

"You almost did!" Ménard retorted. She had been confoundedly stupid to go into that house on her own and he wanted to tell her so; he wanted to take her by the shoulders and shake some sense into her, then grab her and kiss her. He hated feeling this way. It was distracting and dangerous for his work.

"You needn't sound so arrogant!"

Her sharp defence brought him back into focus— he tried to soften his concern into a plea. "Megan, how could you put yourself at so much risk? You are not prepared for involving yourself in this affair. This goes beyond 'helping a friend', as you put it."

"How was I to know he'd been murdered? What if he'd had a heart attack and I saved his life!" She was so defensive that he felt he wasn't getting anywhere.

Fiona added in a huff. "Well, I refuse to stand here and be ignored. Personally, I think we should all be thankful that Megan and I have come out of this unscathed and you should be thankful, Detective Ménard, that you have an eye witness to the murderer. I think that Megan has had just about enough. She probably should see someone about that bump on her head. Can't you take her statement later?"

Ménard was about to reply when his partner, Jerry Bullard, called out, "Hey, Danny, did you say something about the McGill library earlier? A call just came in. There's a fire in the archive section. Most likely arson!"

Ménard pressed his lips together, worried about Jerry showing up with Megan here, but she didn't seem to recognize the voice. To stay on track Ménard replied, "Luckily Megan, your charming friend has brought the right perspective to this situation. Both of you have, perhaps, touched on something we do not yet understand and confusion is setting in. In any case, it is serious and dangerous. *Comprenez-vous?*" Ménard tried to be soft and stern at the same time. "People are willing to kill for some reason and you must realise this puts you at risk. You should not be alone for the time being. So, as long as you're all right, go home. I will need to speak with you both later, once I have tied up the details here." He stopped speaking just as Jerry Bullard walked up behind Megan.

Megan saw Ménard's face narrow, but then understood when he uneasily said, "Jerry, you remember Megan Brodie don't you?"

The thought of facing him made her want to retch, but she shrugged Fiona's arm off her shoulders and, with the sourest of expressions, turned towards the fat detective. His receding hairline, so closely cropped that hair stood straight up from the top of his head, made his pudgy cheeks stand out. His cheap plaid jacket hung open; his shirt, carelessly tucked in across his fat abdomen, stretched apart near the navel, revealed hairy skin. It was worth facing him just for the look of surprised hatred hanging from Jerry Bullard's jaw. She looked him straight in the eye and said, "You must excuse us. We were just leaving."

Chapter 13

Gau Island, Florida Keys

Treiger accompanied Steibert Dubler through a thick grove of palms. "You're just what the doctor ordered," drawled Dubler. The Afrikaner was medium height, thick boned, well muscled and, on retreat after completing an assignment in Europe, was getting bored with the seclusion, or so he said. The dicey contract had forced him to go on the lam, so he came to the island. Connections, Dubler explained, made the US reasonably safe, as long as he kept a low profile. Treiger bore in mind that putting himself in the hands of a mercenary was rather like jumping rope with a rattlesnake, but getting off the island undetected required an unconventional rebel like Dubler. Trust was the tenuous element. However, depending on Dubler was a necessity, not a preference.

Dubler's villa was in a secluded spot nearby and his sports car was parked outside. He described the customized Jaguar as his statement of independence on this 'bloody island hellhole for milksops', adding as he reached in the glove compartment for a first-aid kit, "Odd how often this comes in handy." While Treiger tended to his hand, Dubler delved into the trunk, throwing out his golf clubs and removing the spare tire. "It'll be a tight spot, but sounds like you're in one anyway. Besides, I'd translate your request as 'let's get the fuck out of here!' "

Treiger crammed himself inside and Dubler slammed the lid shut with the finality of a coffin, vaguely reminding Treiger of a squeezed space behind a fireplace. For the first time in a long while, a brief memory of his parents filtered through his mind and now, after almost a lifetime of waiting, the stakes were escalating by the second.

The engine erupted and the car abruptly gunned in reverse. Treiger jerked against the back of the compartment, then his torso rammed in return as the jag took off at a fast clip. There was a bumpy protrusion pressing against his back and he slid his hand over the carpeted interior, finding the annoying culprit to be a small bar embedded in the wall. He grabbed hold as Dubler took several rough turns. A safe getaway seemed promising until the car squealed to a stop.

He heard Dubler's convivial tone rev up, "What's up mate?"

A terse, business-like reply followed. "All vehicles leaving the island must be inspected." Obviously Stoltz had lost no time ordering an island-wide alert.

Dubler continued in an accommodating, but slightly bothered tone, "Sure, but I'm late for a meeting off-island. Will this take long?"

"Not once I check your trunk."

"Go ahead, I'll pop it open...what the...bloody hell, the latch is busted. Haft' a use my keys. Fuckin' lemon this thing is!"

Treiger wondered what was on the South African's mind. Certainly Dubler wasn't going to risk his life for the sake of a vague associate. The car shifted as Dubler got out still drawling a rolling conversation, "You know before I left, I thought I should change my tire. I think there's a slow leak. You look like a decent chap. Think you could give me a hand? That way I won't have to worry about getting a flat and being really late for that appointment. It'll only take a few minutes." Footsteps stopped just outside the trunk.

Treiger, preparing to react, removed his hold on the supporting handle. The back wall shifted so he shoved backwards. Surprisingly the posterior wall pushed in and up, enabling him to slide onto the back seat while Dubler politely persisted and the guard clearly and repeatedly stated that he wouldn't help. Treiger rolled quietly onto the floor and shoved the back cushion down into place just as the trunk lid flipped open. Dubler, not missing a syllable or seeming at all perturbed, continued with, "You know I hate being late...hey! I'm shit out of luck! How do you like that? You pay through the arse for these cars and there's no spare."

Another car pulled up. Dubler kept on talking and Treiger pressed himself on the floor as Stoltz's harsh voice rang out, "Did you find him?" Dubler added more loudly, "Well, can I go, mate?" The guard stammered at the shouting voices, "No!" then "Yes." Dubler walked back along the side of the car talking up a stream of gratitude and climbed in the driver's seat. He gunned the engine and called out as he drove away. "I hope you find what you're looking for!"

Treiger waited until Dubler had crossed the causeway before angling himself into the front passenger seat. Thinking about the special reinforcements he had made to his own Mercedes in Montreal, Treiger asked the South African, "Bertie, how did you know I would find the access to the backseat?"

Dubler laughed gruffly. "I took a chance, mate. Only the latest models have the mechanism installed on request. You cheated me out of a good workout! I was up for a decent fight until that last guy arrived...recognised him as that German...what's his name...oh, yeah, Stoltz...nasty piece of business that bloke...not surprised you wanted to make yourself scarce...well, looked all red in the face he did, and his car teeming with chappies packing guns like a nest of vipers ready to sting. Letting a type like that stew can be much more satisfying than a fight. Besides, no matter how well you might dance with that damaged hand, we were out numbered. I like better odds than that." Dubler laughed again then asked, "Where to now?"

"I'm obliged, Bertie. The Miami airport will do fine."

The plane travelled through some nasty turbulence before breaking out into clear skies over Montreal. Treiger scanned the view below as the pilot announced that Quebec was probably experiencing the last day of Indian summer because the rough weather they had passed through was headed east. He'd used a Canadian passport and paid for the flight in cash, but it didn't really matter, since Stoltz would eventually head for Montreal. In the meantime, he had to get ready.

As the plane circled the city, Treiger could see the fading reds of the woods covering Mount Royal. A grid of the central streets below the steep mountain was laid out like a map. Sherbrooke Street was the most obvious, cutting a swath for miles along the lower edge of the island. Lower and parallel to Sherbrooke, were Ste. Catherine and René Levesque streets with Notre-Dame laid out in the old part of the city near the port. Other streets like Beaverhall Hill, University and Peel cut uphill perpendicularly until the mountain cut them off along Avenue des Pins.

As the plane aligned for a westerly landing, he scanned the length of Sherbrooke Street until he saw the glimmering white of the Olympic Stadium with the spectacular arching tower. The architectural outline captured the landscape. Cables splayed out from the top like a glistening spider's web lashing hold of the immense circular roof. When darkness fell, the image would be singularly dramatic with thousands of lights encircling the outer edges, illuminating the superstructure. The sun, now low on the horizon, made the stadium glow majestically, but in doing so outlined its fateful flaw. The stadium roof, constantly plagued with repairs, had huge iron beams straddled across the top of the tower holding repair scaffolding. A disembodied voice droned out the landing ritual reminding him of the time.

As soon as he exited the customs area, automatic doors opened to a hoard of summer-attired greeters crowded behind a rope barrier. Heading directly to a pay phone, Treiger made his call. No answer. Normally when Hans was at work, Luisa stayed in the house. He wondered if they were in the lab together. The cell phone didn't work there. His mind briefly flashed back to that unknown railway station just out of Berlin when he had watched Hans and Luisa disappear into the night. He cursed himself for not calling before he left Florida, but he'd barely made the plane as it was. His aching hand reminded him that without Dubler's help, he mightn't have escaped at all.

He rented a Lexus and after signing the forms, scanned the crowded corridor wondering how long it would be before Stoltz got here, then collected his papers and walked away veering around several people. He hated crowds, but they did afford some camouflage. Perhaps it was years of deception and secrecy that made him turn to look at the arrivals gate. He wasn't sure why, but he was taken aback. Higler strode tall and purposefully through the exit. Treiger glanced at the arrival screen: Caracas – arrived. Somehow he'd escaped Joao, probably headed for Boa Vista. Yes, with luck, he could have made the connections. Treiger slipped outside amongst several tourists; this was no time for a confrontation.

What Treiger failed to notice was a thin, brown-haired man sporting a day's growth of beard. The man was leaning against one of the supporting columns at the far side of the waiting area. He was there to meet Higler and might not have become aware of Treiger, but he stopped right alongside staring directly at the striking German.

Treiger lost no time in heading for the city bound expressway, but he was perturbed; surely Joao would have gone after Higler. On the other hand, he asserted, life is unpredictable and people even more so, mainly because he didn't want to consider the alternative. For the moment the past didn't matter, he was more concerned about Hans. There was barely enough time to get to Westmount and prepare for an inevitable confrontation. Higler would charge ahead with Stoltz close behind and, at all costs, would try to set the Gau mission in motion. Montreal had been his own responsibility, but instead he had brought the Gau forces dangerously close to Hans and Luisa. The situation was obviously precarious. Hans needed to finish the experiments. Damn, why hadn't one of them answered the phone? Snarling his doubt into submission, he knew what he had to do— finish off the Gau and their dream.

A black sedan had steadily moved up from behind and was now maintaining a regular distance. Treiger shrewdly moved into the centre lane, and bypassed his intended exit, heading for Old Montreal and its mishmash of narrow streets. As Treiger exited the highway, the sedan sped up narrowing the gap.

Treiger shifted in and out of the rush hour traffic along the flat pavement of Rue Notre Dame passing massive, stone office buildings lining both sides of the street. Long shadows fell from them obliterating the remaining sunlight. The haze of dusk could only help. He needed to get onto the older streets, but the traffic was too heavy. The dark sedan manoeuvred its way behind, gradually making headway by zigzagging inelegantly through the traffic until a bus cut the sedan off. Treiger lost sight of it for a second. Suddenly, the bus pulled into a stop and the sedan blasted up neck and neck with the Lexus. Treiger took a fast look sideways. Higler was in the passenger seat.

For a split second, their eyes locked with the sparking intensity of a lightening bolt. Treiger didn't let Higler's icy blue hate message distract him. He rammed the Lexus forward and cut in front of another city bus forcing it to swerve dangerously. A swearing horn followed. Treiger viciously wrenched the steering wheel and careened onto a narrow cobblestone street.

The sidewalk was littered with sauntering strollers saturated with café-au-lait or red wine. Indian summer had brought out a late afternoon crowd to enjoy the fading sun and balmy air. T-shirt clad onlookers, lolling on 17th century steps, shook their heads in irritated amazement as Treiger shot by irreverently, jolting over the uneven cobbles.

In his rear-view mirror, he saw the sedan swerve recklessly onto the side street. Treiger gunned over a deep groove and the undercarriage scraped noisily as he swerved onto Rue St. Paul, cutting close to an outdoor café packed with customers. A man rising from an unsteady table perched near the verge jumped back, barely avoiding a swipe by Treiger's raging vehicle. His empty wine carafe toppled, crashing onto the cobblestones. The surprised drinker cursed loudly and took a swing at the tail end of the car. Seemingly enraged that his energy was wasted on a receding taillight, the wine-soaked man jumped into the street, shaking his fist. His tirade of abuse made onlookers stare. A waiter came rushing out just as the black sedan flashed around the corner. The back end spun in a wide arc raising the fine dust on the street, and the tires screeched piercing the air with an acrid smell of burnt rubber.

The irate drunk swung around in surprise, swaying like he was a puppet dancing on the irregular surface. He was smack in the centre of the street. His arms flung up in a wild instinctual effort to stop the car.

The sedan's bumper came to a dead stop inches away from the infuriated drunk who stood dead still as if paralysed. He swayed again then with a huge belch emptied his stomach contents onto the hood of the car. Thick brown-red material, looking like a melange of red wine and onion soup, streamed over one of the headlights.

The sedan madly reversed then swerved around the staggering victim, through the shattered pieces of the wine carafe, and onto the sidewalk. Bystanders crowded in after the car, watching it disappear down the street. Some shouted indignantly for the police, while others helped the washed-out man into a chair.

Treiger, relieved to avoid an unprepared clash with Higler, sped away, weaving a circuitous route into upper Westmount and cut up onto a non-residential side street close to the mountain park. A spattering of rain started to fall on the windshield. The sky was almost completely dark. He stopped at the dead end, coasting his car into the brush. Feeling satisfied that the car was well hidden, he found a dirt path leading into the woods and climbed steadily in the dusky light. Damp leaves made the ground slippery. Moving swiftly, he disappeared behind a thicket of briars and cedar brush and pushed aside some musty camouflage netting, ideal for concealing the narrow black steel-plated door. The door was built into the side of the mountain slope behind the thicket. During the winter this particular entry would be impossible to use because of the snow. Unlocking the rusty, but well-oiled lock, he slipped inside.

    It took a minute of groping before he laid his hand on a kerosene-soaked torch lashed beside the doorframe. He lit the twisted rags. A wavering yellow glow led his way down the narrow, uneven stone stairway. The walls were wet and slick, as were the stairs. He put his hand up to the wall, steadying himself. The cold rock was slimy to the touch, and he could hear the trickle of water leaking in rivulets down the stairs, and in the distance, a mean rush of water. At the base, he followed a confined passage with uneven stone walls until he reached a good-sized ledge where the floor dropped away, revealing a treacherous looking underground river. Once across, he could check if Hans and Luisa were in the lab and safe.

CHAPTER 14

Rio de Janeiro, 1953

"Go then! Go find your fucking brother and get out of my sight." Volker Braun's fist smashed down on his desk. The resonating force tumbled the pencil caddy off the edge, sprawling its contents over the carpet with contrasting silence. Karl stood on the other side of the desk. The office was expensively outfitted and oversized, quite in keeping with Braun's ego. Karl, used to bearing the brunt of such rages, shrugged while mustering a barely respectable salute. Having got an agreement now was the time to leave before Braun changed his mind. As he neared the door, Luthor Kleis entered excitedly, a manila folder clenched in one hand. Kleis half pushed Karl out, and slammed the door so hard that the latch didn't catch.

Karl hesitated. He didn't want to miss an opportunity. The door hung slightly ajar and the crack partially showed the two men. Like a mole he persisted in spying on Gau operations whenever he could. There was some risk here. Braun had just caught him perusing papers on his desk. Being noticed so close and so soon might create difficulties. However, chances to get concrete information on their dealings were rare, and Kleis obviously had important business to discuss. Karl casually leaned against the wall, indifferently lit a cigarette, and let his eyes stray back to the door. Braun was behind his desk as before, but intently focused on Kleis. Karl heard paper shuffling and leaned forward. Kleis was showing Braun some sort of report. Intermittent strings of conversation filtered into the hall. "Volker, this is the way to go. Time is all we need."

Braun who held onto his disagreeable mood like a growling dog, argued, "Luthor, will you stop trying to change course in mid-stream. Once Buch has perfected his technique, we can start major production!"

"I warned you a long time ago, Volker. We can't operate with only one option. Continuation of the breeding program with artificial insemination is acceptable, but this route will never be effective. Humanity depends on diversity— look at the Nietzsche mess in Peru— completely useless. No, Volker, I must remain firm. Even Buch thinks I should go ahead and you know how loyal he is to A.I. There's enough money, so I don't understand why you don't agree! We can proceed with both projects."

Braun paced in and out of Karl's view, apparently deep in thought, but sounded calmer when he stopped to ask, "Do you know what you're playing with?"

Kleis replied intensely, "There is no doubt in my mind that this is the right direction to take. With what we already know about genetics, I believe our dreams can be realised. However I want the entire third floor converted into a laboratory. Of course, my infra-structure will extend into the rainforest."

Braun, looking sceptical, moved into Karl's line of vision. "And Buch agrees?"

Kleis glared back. "Listen, I admit my research has been circuitous and it's been nearly ten years since we began. Things have changed. Why, just the electron microscope alone has incredibly altered my research. The research will take time; nonetheless, I am convinced we can find a new frontier before we get too old. If you don't agree with me, we might as well use the money for our own comfort and forget the future."

Braun grudgingly sighed, "Then do what you have to do."

Kleis gave a tight-lipped smile. "Thank you. However, I need you to enlist the expertise required. Can you convince him?"

Braun's voice seemed to soften, "I don't need to let him know. From the reports..." Braun voice muffled as he paced out of hearing distance, but words quickly faded back in as he paced back, "...he does seem to show promise. Our recruit on site can train him. This should be interesting. I was beginning to be bored."

Suddenly Kleis stepped towards the door. There was no time to disappear into the stairwell. "What are you doing there?" Braun shrieked passed Kleis.

Karl was still leaning against the wall. In the midst of taking a slow draw on his cigarette, Karl turned his head. Kleis looked awkwardly back to Braun, saluted and excused himself, hurrying in long strides down the hall. Calmly extinguishing his cigarette with his fingertips, Karl re-entered Braun's office before answering, "You dismissed me without providing information about my brother's address."

"What makes you think I have the information?" Braun hissed.

Braun was no fool and knew Karl had seen the letter, but something had changed in his expression. The demand to find his brother had been a provocation only moments ago, but something Kleis said made the situation more acceptable. Using Braun's sweet tooth for flattery, Karl mused, "Because, you know everything."

Braun replied, "Don't be insubordinate with me," but strolled over to the door, and closed it firmly before turning to observe Karl. A sharp hint of anticipation glinted from behind his gaze. There was always a price to pay when he wanted something from Braun. Karl hoped to get the ordeal over here and now, but held back. Braun didn't like a hasty attitude. Lately, Karl had avoided these advances, knowing Braun had a fondness for younger victims, either male or female. Unfortunately, Braun seemed to feel an emotional bond with him. The hard line was that he had to keep in Braun's good graces.

Braun moved closer and looked intensely into Karl's eyes, "Why does it have to be like this? Since I first laid my eyes on you, I found I couldn't resist you. You are my slave, yet you treat me like one. " Braun's eyes smouldered as he leaned near to suck a kiss off Karl's neck, then whispered, "In the beginning I let you exist, and now, you reject me. Have I been so terrible? After your traitorous parents were found dead, I took you in and saved your brother." Braun placed both hands on the side of Karl's face, and then kissed him passionately. His hands slithered down Karl's body, letting his desire speak for itself, then suddenly stepped back. "No, I don't want it to be like this, fast and sluttish. Meet me this evening." As if accepting Karl's acquiescence as established, Braun went to his desk, giving the unmistakable indication that the audience was over.

Karl had always acknowledged the distasteful truth that getting what he wanted meant bowing to Braun's wishes. To make certain that this was not just a scheme to satisfy Braun's lust, Karl challenged, "When will I get the information about Hans?"

"After," was all Braun said without looking up from his work.

When evening came, Karl went through the motions while Braun resourcefully made the event last as long as possible. The contacts were the closest thing to physical intimacy that he experienced after the Bunker episode, but his mind was now made up. After tonight he would never tolerate another moment like this with Braun. Such a stance might hold if he made himself indispensable in some other way.

The sound of splashing water in the bathroom was accompanied by a few off-key chords; a German love melody crooned with half-forgotten words. This was just a case of Braun being petty and vindictive, knowing that Karl wanted to leave. Already dressed, he sat on the bed and tapped the end of a cigarette on the table before lighting it. Normally, once Braun was finished slacking his lust, Karl would have left, carrying with him a reviling disgust towards himself and Braun. Tonight, he had to wait. Karl suspected Braun's 'little shower' would involve a shave and various other toiletries for the sole purpose of taking time. A small-minded sort of revenge. He put the cigarette to his lips and inhaled, absently taking in the decor: purple satin sheets for the bed, velvet-tasselled light shades creating soft ambient lighting, thick black carpeting stretching from wall to wall. The bureau held Braun's customary brandy decanter, a style reflecting the wanton pursuits Braun indulged in. Karl breathed deeply and stretched one arm behind his head on the pillow, excited to think of seeing Hans.

A long time had passed since that last uncertain meeting on the train platform. At least Hans and Luisa were safe. A man called De L'église, apparently responsible for shadowing Hans and Luisa, had sent in a report. Both had made it to Canada, ending up in Montreal as Czech refugees. De L'église's underlying drift was a solicitation for more money. So if Braun had been willing to pay for someone to keep track of Hans, there had to be a good reason for it. One thing was certain; he would always despise Braun for keeping his brother's whereabouts a secret. And now, Kleis's project had sparked a change in Braun towards his reunion with Hans. Hopefully, he could pry out some details, but he would have to tread carefully.

Some gargling noises penetrated into the room. Karl sat up when the bathroom door opened.

"I thought you'd be at the door panting to leave, dear boy," said Braun, sauntering into the room with a silk paisley robe tied loosely around his lean torso.

Karl looked at Braun. "As a matter of fact, I was thinking about you."

"Blissful thoughts, no doubt?" Braun probed, lightly towel-drying his hair.

"Only the best, Volker. Remember, you saved my life."

Braun smiled warily. He tossed the damp towel on the bed and smoothed his hair back with one hand. He walked over to the bureau. "Brandy?" He asked, picking up the decanter and splashing his glass full to the brim.

"As a matter of fact, I will, since we have the matter of my brother to discuss."

Braun took a long draught of his brandy. "Oh, how I do love the cut and thrust of negotiation, after a bit of cut and thrusting," Braun smirked, then the muscles around his chin tightened. "I will not forbid you from leaving. There would be no point. You would only resent it, and over time such resentments grow, sometimes becoming destructive. You see, dear Karl, I can almost read that face of yours like a book. You would not hesitate to expose our existence if you had the opportunity."

Karl kept his eyes on Braun's face, but his chest tightened as he forced himself to maintain composure. Braun loved being the shrewd interrogator. Denial would be too obvious and Braun wouldn't believe him. Karl tilted his head as if disappointed that Braun didn't understand and breathed, "Volker, you are my mentor. I am young so I do have certain resentments. It is only natural. Besides, what good would revealing the Gau to the authorities do? It would only initiate my own ruin and possibly that of my brother."

"I'm glad you spoke so eloquently, Karl. I have to admit I was saving your brother as one of my few bargaining chips. Speaking from the heart, as they say, I do not want you to go, but I will allow it, for a short period. Remember, some contacts I have in Montreal will be watching you. I'm hoping that after you see to your brother's needs, you will be more content here. I do not like you avoiding me. As of late, I have not been happy. My satisfaction is somehow intertwined with you," Braun smiled tightly. "Don't mistake that little piece of sharing for sentimentality. If you in any way compromise the Gau and my cause, you and your brother will die. It is as simple as that."

Karl raised his tall physique from the bed, and within two strides was beside Braun. He picked up the brandy-filled glass. "Don't worry about me, Volker. My life is also intertwined, as you put it, with yours," he said, tossing back the drink in one gulp.

Braun set his glass down. "Now that we are on the matter, I dislike the fact that you were snooping in my private papers. It makes me feel I should distrust you."

Karl chose his words carefully, but used a very matter of fact tone. "My brother is the only connection I have to my heritage. You were not helpful in answering my questions. I'm surprised you expected any less of someone of my ability."

Braun reacted with a quiet laugh. "Only your arrogance, Karl, could possibly rival mine. Just see that it doesn't happen again." He paused as if considering something, "Since you are going to Canada, there is some business there that needs looking into. Given your predisposition to spy, I want you to keep me informed about a few things. You will be very well compensated. We have some rather valuable assets in Montreal that cannot be disposed without problems. Your brother's landlord has been helpful in arranging for their storage. I want you to look into their liquidation."

He needn't have been so paranoid; Braun had an assignment for him in Montreal. Still he left with no added detail on Kleis's project or Braun's sudden change of heart.

Hans took his coffee cup over to the sink and put it beside the other breakfast dishes. Karl was sitting behind him at the small kitchen table. When they arrived destitute and afraid into the port of Montreal, De L'église had vouched for them and agreed to let them this basement apartment with minimal rent, paying Luisa as his housekeeper. Hans brought in some money doing odd jobs, but felt beholden to the couple. Last fall, he finally had enough money to register at the university and had come at the top of his class. But Luisa was unhappy and tired of being poor even though she said nothing outright. University cost money. Now De L'église had made a business proposition. That was all he had told Karl.

This was Karl's fourth trip to Montreal in as many months. At this point Hans wasn't certain that he enjoyed the visits. Karl seemed to have money, but insisted on living with them in their small basement apartment. Every stay was the same. Karl would appear unexpectedly, stop over for an undisclosed time, and then disappear. The first visit was awkward, the second not much better, but, on the third, he had introduced Karl to his friend from the university, Theodore Rolfe. That stay had been more congenial and Karl was...well...almost likeable. This visit had reverted to the previous dour tone with Karl asking pointedly about De L'église or what Hans and Luisa did for him. Who did he know? Did they ever deliver messages for De L'église? Did anyone ask questions about their own past or about him?

In fact, De L'église asked many questions, but he didn't tell Karl, and now De L'église had proposed this business venture. Between Karl, De L'église and watching Luisa scrub her fingers to the bone, his own dreams of study seemed selfish. Luisa wanted more out of life than drudgery and both De L'église and his brother were vying to manipulate his future for their own purposes. He put his hands on the porcelain rim in front of him and squeezed the cold, hard surface. He probably didn't know enough about De L'église, but the man was offering him more than Karl ever had and the real point was, he knew even less about his own brother. Years had passed since the train platform. Now after his surprise reappearance, Karl was pushing him to accept the university education his parents wanted for him. Karl was dangling a carrot in front of him, but he didn't trust him. Not only that, Karl's secretiveness about his own life was upsetting Luisa, especially since he kept probing to know everything about theirs. They had a right to their own privacy; he didn't owe his brother anything; they had their own lives to live and he didn't want Karl interfering or even worse dictating what he should do and how he should live. This morning's conversation had taken that distinct direction. He shut his eyes in an attempt to close out the confusion and make a decision. Karl was hard to get along with and De L'église was proposing a secure future. University could wait until he could pay for any studies himself and not depend on Karl.

Still Karl's questioning made him feel guilty, like he was doing something wrong. He had to say something. He'd had enough of Karl's guarded inquisition, resenting the expectation that he discuss his plans with Karl. Luisa, being kind, didn't want him to cause friction; astutely pointing out Karl was the only family they had left. For that reason he decided to give Karl another chance to explain. He turned to speak, but the words didn't come out the way he wanted. "Its not like you're the most talkative person in the world, Karl. I never know what you're thinking."

"Most of the time, Hans, you wouldn't want to know what I am thinking." Karl's face was unreadable.

"All I asked is why you're ordering me to continue my studies? Luisa and I have put aside every extra cent since coming here. I do not want Luisa to live in hardship any longer. De L'église and I are planning to start an antique business. I always wanted to go to university, but that is out of the picture now." Hans started pacing back and forth. "It hasn't been easy for Luisa and I. Do you think we like living here as pseudo-servants to these people? I have my pride. I decided when we came here that I would devote my life to providing for Luisa. I have tried university, but now something more lucrative has evolved. I need to be practical. Luisa wants children."

"You will have no children."

"What? That is preposterous!" Hans couldn't believe his ears. He almost screamed get out, but instead, shoved his hands in his pockets holding back for Luisa's sake.

"Never question me Hans. You and Luisa survived because of me. I need you to do what I ask without question. When I can I will explain. For the matter of your living arrangement, I have been looking into that. Come with me, and bring Luisa."

The conversation ended so abruptly that Hans was left hanging like a gallows. Did Karl save their lives? At what price? He wondered if the truth mattered anymore and obediently went to get Luisa. He'd only managed to tell her that things had not gone well by the time Karl brought his car around.

Karl frowned. He hadn't expected such resistance, but Hans had been living in close contact with Braun's associates for five years. Hans seemed no different than he remembered, with no vision of the future beyond providing for Luisa, and still gullible, but starting a business with De L'église was dangerous. Today he needed to find out exactly how vulnerable Hans had become.

The drive took them on winding streets to a wealthy section of Westmount. Luisa, who was sitting in the back seat, leaned forward and whispered to Hans. She was obviously anxious about something. Karl told them both to relax, but Luisa fidgeted in the back. Finally he turned onto a stately crescent and stopped in front of an impressive mansion squeezed near the sloping mountain. He stated simply. "This is your new home."

Hans looked angry, but Luisa broke in, "Don't tease us, Karl."

Karl turned in his seat. "Luisa, I bought this house, but the name on the lease is Hans Treiger. The house now belongs to both of you."

She looked doubtful for a moment then speechlessly rushed from the car and up to the front stone steps. Both Hans and Karl followed her. She turned with tears in her eyes. "Karl, we could never afford this. If you tell me this is a joke, I will never forgive you."

"Didn't I mention it? I have been involved in some successful ventures. I also took the liberty of investing some capital in Hans's name."

Luisa ran back down the stone steps and with happy sobs, flung herself into his arms. Startled, he unexpectedly hugged her back. She looked up with her tear-streaked face and gave him a wet kiss, then turned to Hans and started laughing, kissing him and hitting him at the same time, "Why didn't you tell me!"

Hans, eyeing Karl guardedly, hugged Luisa warmly and swung her in a circle. "You know there's nothing I wouldn't do for you."

Karl added, "Luisa, I thought you might like to spend some time exploring the house. Hans and I have a few errands to run."

She ran over and hugged him again then sprinted back up the steps. Karl called to her. "Wait, you'll have to unlock the door!" He lobbed the key up. She turned her shiny blonde head and grabbed it out of midair, a huge smile radiating on her face. She was in the door before they had a chance to get back in the car.

Hans said tightly, "I guess we all love money. Where did you get yours?"

Karl, not wanting to be affected by Luisa's reaction and wanting to be very sure of Hans, replied tersely, "There are plenty of funds. We are headed to the bank to open an account in your name. The house is already paid for."

Obviously, Karl had no intention of telling more and his tough tone was daunting, but saying nothing would put him in a morose, fuming silence and besides he had had enough. "Why such a monstrously big home, especially if we aren't allowed to have children?"

He heard the determination in Karl's reply. "Trust me Hans, after the bank, we'll discuss what is necessary." But the fact was, Hans didn't trust Karl.

Karl had expected a different reaction now that Hans was financially secure, but Hans was still stewing in silence as they left the bank. Perhaps this business with De L'église had gone too far. Hans wasn't agreeing to go to university, which had always been his dream. He knew that the next step had to be taken before he could risk further explanation. Karl felt he should to break the silence. "This is good fortune Hans. I thought you'd be happy." When Hans gave no indication that he intended to reply, Karl continued, "I decided to buy the house after your friend Rolfe told that intriguing story about the monks."

"Fuck the small talk, Karl! You don't answer my questions so why should I answer yours?"

Karl cooled his smile. "Next stop is a warehouse. There, I think, answers will become evident without long explanations.

Hans wanted to have the last word. He wasn't going to let go of this. "I remember the uniform you wore in that railway station, Karl. Don't take me for a complete fool. Just who did you get into bed with!" It was more of a statement than a question, but Hans saw the dramatic effect it had on Karl. His brother's forehead creased and the eyes hollowed. The tormented look reminded him of his comrades in the Buchenwald camp, but there was a difference. Karl's eyes lacked the vacancy of absolute helplessness.

A profound silence fell between them.

The drive took them down to the east end of the city. Karl parked the car on a back street. He opened the trunk and extracted a crowbar then led Hans to an iron-grey storage building with boarded over windows. Hans followed behind, feeling more sullen as the moments passed. Once Luisa started asking questions, and she would definitely ask them, he would have to have some answers. He walked up the ramp to the sliding door and watched Karl unlock the bolts.

When Karl stood back drumming the tool on his opposite hand as if he was preparing to use the bar forcefully, Hans said, "You first," almost stuttering, and then felt foolish. How could he be afraid of his own brother? Then again, he recognised his resentment at Karl turning up like a ghost a few months ago. In fact, Karl did frighten him. On the other hand, he didn't know much more about De L'église. He felt wedged between the two of them. He took a deep breath and followed Karl into the warehouse.

The extensive space was lined with wooden crates sealed with flat metal strips. Some were stacked high, almost nearing the ceiling, and other smaller ones marked 'Fragile' were lined up in front of the higher lots. Off to the side were shelves holding other boxes. Hans stood uncertainly looking at the containers and then back at Karl.

Karl looked serious. "What do you think might be in these crates?"

Hans was dumbfounded, "I'm sure I have no idea." He walked over and examined the markings. "Some of these labels are written in German. Would these have anything to do with the war?" He was jumping to a conclusion, but the atmosphere in the storehouse reminded him of the war: the dark, dank wooden room, the uncertainty and the subtle intimidation of his brother. Karl was now eyeing him suspiciously and he didn't like the feeling. Not only that, there was a sharp edge to the tone of Karl's taut reply. "That's a good guess. I always thought you were smart enough to figure some of this out, especially since you seem to be so interested in antiques."

"Hell, Karl! I haven't figured anything out. Basically this place makes me feel edgy. Why don't you just tell me what is going on?"

Karl walked to one of the smaller wooden crates and started to lever the lid open. Once the top boards were loosened, he tore them away and lifted off the shaved wood packing. The first item was a carved mahogany box of considerable size.

Curious, Hans walked over and flipped up the lid. He gasped. It was filled to the brim with solid gold cutlery. The shining display was magnificent and, in his own mind, priceless. He gingerly fingered the costly pieces.

Meanwhile, Karl started levering open another crate. Inside was an exquisite French Renaissance vase. He continued wielding the lever unceasingly on box lids, all the time watching Hans follow from box to box, admiring, then frowning, handling items with wonder then shaking his head. Finally Hans backed away from the priceless articles. He straightened himself and swept dust from his suit, as if trying to compose himself.

Karl wondered how seduced Hans was by the wealth of expensive pieces. All of the crates had been secretly shipped here at the beginning of the war. De L'église also knew this address, but obviously he hadn't brought Hans here. Still Karl wanted an answer. No matter how much he cared for Hans, he knew where his loyalties had to lie. Still, he waited until Hans hesitated with a look of disbelief.

Then Hans let go. "You bastard! The Nazi's collected this loot during the war. You're one of them. You and your arrogant holier-than-thou attitude— you're not worth the spit coming from my mouth. I don't want any of this," he raged, sweeping his arm to indicate the hundreds of crates behind him. "The house has obviously come from the same effluent source, so don't expect me to set foot in it. You repulse me even more than this shameful pile of human treachery. You obviously think I am a greedy, heartless wretch." Hans gasped apoplectically, "This represents to me the dust of millions of incinerated lives! I've had enough of the war. I don't need to relive any memories linked to that horrid time. Luisa has put up with enough. We want to build a good, clean future."

"And you think you can do that with a man like De L'église?"

"As far as I know De L'église knows nothing about this. If it weren't for Luisa I would have nothing to do with the man. Nonetheless, he offered us an opportunity, while you want me to sell my soul." He followed through with a hard slap across Karl's cheek.

Karl's head jerked at the impact. In fact the sting on his skin was a relief. He began quietly. "I had to know, Hans. There was too much to risk if greed had gotten to you. The people you work for were Nazi sympathisers during the war."

Hans's voice was filled with resentment. "Do you think that is news to me, Karl! I may have had my suspicions about De L'église, but he never tried to seduce me like you are. I have taken advantage of what they offer because of Luisa. We had nothing and no one. We had to start somewhere. Let me tell you this, Luisa and I plan to leave anything to do with the war far behind and if that includes you, then so be it!"

Karl had heard a delicate hint of unforgiving hysteria in Hans's voice. He had to be careful, but Hans's outburst was exactly what he needed to hear. Trust was necessary before he could confide in Hans. This warehouse was not the right place to make Hans understand and, in Hans's current state, he might need some help. Karl nodded seriously and said, "I'm sorry to put you through the deception, but believe me, it was necessary. But don't be too certain about De L'église. He's putting you in a very risky position. Let's go and pick up Luisa. We need to find somewhere to talk this over."

All three walked into a small bar with dark brown booths lining each side. The smell of old cigarette smoke hung in the air. Karl selected a booth near the back and sat across from Hans and Luisa making sure that he had a view of the entry. Hans had been treating him distantly since their row at the warehouse. He didn't blame Hans, but now he needed some time to lay out what the future held for them all. Before starting, he called to the barman to send over some beer. He leaned forward and looked them both in the eye. "What I am going to say can change your lives forever. Are you willing to listen?"

Hans snapped back quickly, "Well, we're here, aren't we?"

Luisa looked distressed and frowned at Hans's clipped response.

Karl stopped while the bartender set three drafts on the table. Karl paid, then looked past Hans before he continued. Two men in suits had come into the bar. They chose a table in the centre of the room with a clear view of the booth. One lit a cigarette while the other called for double whiskeys. Karl couldn't help remembering that Braun warned him that they would be watched.

"I know I have been very guarded since I entered back into your lives, but there is a very important reason for my behaviour. If you had been indoctrinated by those still sympathetic to the Nazi philosophy then my problems would have been greater."

Hans slapped in an interruption, "From what I saw this afternoon you are very familiar with their philosophy."

"Yes, I work with them, but not for them. I need your help to destroy them."

"Who are ' they', Karl?" Hans demanded his face etched with scepticism.

"One is the man who took me to the train station near Buchenwald. His name is Volker Braun. He arranged for you to be removed from Germany. Hitler's second hand man, Bormann, recruited Braun and three others. Their project was shrouded in total secrecy. I'm not even certain if Hitler knew exactly what was going on, however, they were working on one of his favourite themes, the development of a master race. The project is continuing, but they are working on another angle, and I don't know what it is, except that their scheme involves genetics and their mission seems to be far reaching. For all I know, pockets of the organisation could exist throughout South America and who knows where else. Don't you see?" Karl looked imploringly at Hans, "I need to know their plans and how extensive their goals are before creating a strategy to destroy them. They even keep track of everything about you. I feel strongly that anything to do with De L'église is a ploy to influence you or control you. That way Braun could keep a hold over me, but de L'église has probably made a mistake by planning to use the contents of that warehouse. Greed does funny things to people."

"So that was why you asked all those questions, to see if I knew of the stolen valuables. Every time you visited, I felt you were interrogating me, especially when you revealed nothing of yourself. Now, I understand."

Karl motioned to Hans to stop talking. One of the men sitting at the table near the bar got up and walked passed their table. He took a look at the three of them and then walked over to the telephone to make a call. Luisa watched him pass and shrank back in her seat. She whispered, "Is that one of them?"

Karl took a sip of his beer then quietly replied, "We have to be careful of everyone. For certain, De L'église is watching you, so you need to get out from under his thumb as soon as possible. In any case we should leave this bar. I don't like the mood."

Hans said, "Wait, can't you tell us more? This is much too clandestine for me."

"It will remain that way too. I can't divulge too much for now. Secrecy is important for your protection and Luisa's."

"Yours too!" Hans sounded a touch defensive.

Karl looked at him with the directness that truth requires. "True, to some extent myself. But if those I am associated with find out about my intentions, then my life will be meaningless. Perhaps yours would be spared."

"How do you expect me to trust you?"

Karl hesitated, "I don't know how to answer that. All I can tell you is that they are moving ahead with the research, creating a private clinic and laboratory to experiment with genetic factors. In order to fight such an organisation, we have to be smarter than they are."

"Frankly, I don't see where the 'we' comes in." Hans broke in doubtfully.

"I need you to learn about the medical sciences, to become an expert in whatever area I find they are working on. They have an excellent university here. You need to learn about microbiology, biochemistry, whatever will help. You can never tell a living soul."

Hans looked at Karl, tears brimming his eyes, "I'm not sure I am up to the task."

Karl felt he should reach out and hold his brother, but he couldn't bring himself to make the contact. He swallowed, wanting to say something meaningful. All at once, the words came easily. "Hans, do not blame yourself for what happened to our parents. To me they are heroes. They died for what they believed in. They knew the risks and they were willing to die for their cause. We were too young. There was nothing we could do to counter such evil. But now, we have the opportunity. If a seed of the horror that happened in our homeland is growing, we must work to destroy it."

Hans bowed his head. With the back of his hand he wiped away a tear that strayed down his cheek. "I will do whatever you ask."

Luisa put her arm around Hans and hugged him. "I love you. I believe this is the right decision." She glanced back at the two men and leaned across the table to speak in a hushed voice. "What about Hans's agreement with De L'église?"

Karl looked at her seriously. "Don't worry. I believe I know exactly how to deal with someone of his sort."

She looked around again before asking, "Will you…will you have to…kill him?"

Karl was touched by her innocent reaction that was so close to the truth. He decided to soften things, "I suspect Volker Braun won't appreciate that De L'église had plans for those items Hans and I examined this afternoon."

Hans spoke up. "De L'église never mentioned the warehouse. I'm not certain he even knows about the place. "

How ingenuous Hans was. He had always been like this and that was why he would have to be very careful to protect him in the future. He tried to be clear, but gentle when he said, "My dear brother, I already know De L'église is well aware of the address. Whether he knew of the contents is irrelevant, but I suspect that was how he intended to establish this antique business. The organisation will let him go…in their own way."

Chapter 15

Montreal

"Treiger is long gone." Higler's German accent fell like hot tar in a slow drip. He looked at the skinny driver, who was craning his neck through the windshield in search of the Treiger's Lexus. What a wretched dog's body. Obviously no ability to predict instinct, a feature Higler considered crucial to success. Higler put his search-and-kill energy in check the moment the car halted inches from an imbecilic drunk. If he had been driving, the fetid lout would be stamped with tire tread. "Let's get out of here," he ordered, then pressed his lips together. *"Fucken-sie."* Higler sucked air between his teeth. Hunting here for the double-crossing bastard was now utterly useless. Future opportunities would arise, he told himself. He would make them.

Higler winced as the car lurched ahead. The man's mental capacity could fit on the head of a pin. He closed his eyes as the driver churned out words like a wimp.

"Chill out, man. It's been a busy day. I tracked down, uh, two copies of that map Mr. Stoltz asked for. It was tricky."

"You have them both, I hope." Higler said dryly, not ready to revise his opinion and noting the hesitation in the driver's voice.

"Well, not exactly. It's a long story." He said, swinging away from the old port.

"Fascinating. Why don't you run the details by me?" Higler controlled his sarcasm so he could filter out risks and possible leads from the dimwit's garble.

The driver began, "I got one from an really old guy, a professor, eh. Bugger's dead. Guess I got too tough, weak heart I suppose, then some bitch interrupted me...funny, I'd seen her earlier so I got outta' there."

Higler asked sharply, "You got rid of them?"

"Like I said, only the old man. I feel kind'a bad...but he didn't want to hand it over. Geez, why suffer? Good thing he kept glancing at the bookshelves. I found the papers just before the fuckin' bitch arrived. Knocked her senseless and got out by the skin of my teeth. That's when I saw the old Treiger woman outside. Don't know how they managed to follow me."

"I can't imagine how myself." Incompetent wretch.

"The old guy's copy was pieced together from an original kept in some library. I sent Bart, that's my brother, to look after things. Mr. Stoltz said he wanted all the details taken care of. Libraries are easy places to commit arson."

"How perspicacious of you."

Apparently the caustic tone in Higler's voice wasn't lost on the driver who retorted, "Look man, I'm doing this to help you out and I could be in big trouble. I'm not stupid, you know. Besides, without me you wouldn't have recruited my brother and, for sure, you need him. Not only that, my name is Durn. That's Mister Durn to you."

Higler coolly ignored the outburst, but he was concerned; this lowlife had left a dead body to be found and had been seen. Mistakes. And probably not the only ones.

Higler tersely asserted, "I need a place to set up my computer. Treiger will come later."

"Fuck," Durn grunted as if feeling unappreciated, "Guess my place will do."

At Durn's apartment, Higler pushed ahead and took a fast look around; worn clothes were strewn about and empty cartons of take-out food lay discarded on a table. He sniffed with discontent, hating disorder. Ernst considered this pig reliable, so he would stomach the subhuman riffraff. If he had been controlling the car, Treiger would be dead by now. The luck of spotting Treiger had been phenomenal. Stoltz would have approved of his effective disposal of the problem. Killing Treiger would indeed have been a triumph. Now they would have to start at the beginning. Even worse, Treiger knew they were in the city. But, Higler pacified himself, Treiger would have expected no less than an immediate reprisal to his treacherous acts and, given he'd sent the Yano after him, Treiger must have been shocked when they made eye contact. He laughed to himself recalling how he'd sliced open the sneaky native's guts. Treiger had overestimated the Yano freak. He laughed out loud hoping the death had been slow and painful; his amusement didn't stop his task of connecting up his laptop.

"What are you doing?" Durn interrupted.

"I have a little job to do for your employer," Higler replied condescendingly. He certainly wouldn't divulge any details to this imbecile. Higler's work was meticulous and rapid. Typing furiously, he hacked into Canadian Interpol telling them to expect an international liaison by the name of Claus Wirt in Montreal to confirm the recently reported existence of Nazi criminal Karl Treiger, alias Ugo Lipski. Also conveying that Wirt would not require assistance as he was only following a lead; the message was a matter of diplomatic etiquette. Next he switched discs and hewed his way into the personnel files of Interpol Paris, inserting Wirt as a liaison officer." Finally he detached the laptop connections with a smug, "As they say here— voila!"

"What's next?" Durn asked, yawning.

"Treiger's place needs to be checked even though he's too smart to have headed back there now. Still I need a lead. On the way I want to study those maps and soon Mr. Stoltz will need to be collected from the airport. Oh yes, I believe a meeting with your brother could be appropriately arranged at that time."

Higler got out of the sedan a block lower than Roxton Crescent, slamming the car door shut. Durn had only a copied piece of the old map. The most important part, which included the Treiger mansion, was missing and the fool had the library original burned. Angrily, he decided on his plan— visit Treiger's house; if nothing was happening there, search for entrances to the caves using landmarks from the scrap of map until it was time for that flunky to pick him up.

Megan looked critically at the canvas then dabbed some cerulean blue on her palette. When she and Fiona had arrived home, Deirdre insisted on tea and 'details'. Fiona accepted, but Megan had declined, pleading a need to unwind. She needed her own space. Even though her head had cleared after that stunning blow, the attack had been more than upsetting. Once away from everyone, she remembered to look at the papers from Rolfe's office. In the confusion, she'd forgotten to tell Ménard, but he had just called saying he was on his way over to take her statement.

She mixed a little more colour while reflecting on the two stray sheets of paper. One of the documents looked like the outline of tunnels. The second paper was a confirmation of this written by the professor. Beneath the monastic settlement, the monks had used tunnels linked to an underground river. Some passages were for sanitary purposes, others to escape from attacks by Indians. At one point, the monks were completely wiped out and the site was abandoned, until a land developer took it over in the early 1800's. This document was drawn up before he rebuilt over the area and evidently must be significant; she would have to show them to Ménard. She stepped back to survey her work, and then skilfully used her brush to highlight before glancing at her watch. Ménard would arrive soon. She collected her brushes and moved over to the sink.

The mirror on an angled wall of her apartment happened to reflect a view of the street and something in the intensity of the figure's stance made her stop to inspect him. His statuesque form was intriguing, but an eerie alarm overcame her. When she was growing up in Scotland, old Jeannie told Megan that 'for a wee bairn, she ha' an uncanny ken of the mysteries in tha' mist.' The back of her neck prickled. She hated the feeling. This was not going to turn into a waking vision. These strange and terrifying daydreams plagued her when she was young until she'd finally learned to ward them off. With a little concentration, the shivering stopped. She kept her eyes on the man. Megan was certain she was watching someone who didn't want to be noticed; then chided her distrust of, very probably, a simple situation. Just like a spaghetti western: Deirdre always on the watch, Hans's wife often peering out her window and now a mysterious stranger joins in. Even so, a serious splinter of unease remained.

Absently putting her brushes away, her eyes kept flitting to the mirror. Still there having a look around. Was he following Fiona, perhaps a hired spy of Richard's? Richard was always accusing Fiona of infidelity. Strangely, the man seemed to be watching the Treiger residence, not Fiona's. In any case, Fiona was upstairs drinking tea and hopefully safe until Ménard could figure out what was going on. Megan did feel over-protective of Fiona. Her friend was quick-witted, however, the intelligent accumulation of facts filtered through a quirky imagination. Fiona's ingenuous helplessness, albeit frustrating, brought out Megan's shielding spirit; whereas Megan could handle many different situations, Fiona would inevitably be inept. Megan smiled at herself as the thought 'maternal instinct' flashed into her mind. Unexpectedly, tears blurred her vision. She blinked them away. Sometimes it happened that way, a stray thought of Emma jabbed her no matter how hard she tried not to let the memories slip in. To avoid all that, she intensified her focus on the man in the mirror.

The figure extinguished his cigarette with his thumb and forefinger smoothly placing the remaining stub in his pocket—an automatic movement as if used to hiding evidence. He was too young to be a Westmount eccentric and too handsomely dressed to be loitering about without a reason. Megan chewed on her bottom lip and considered that she was letting her dramatic Scottish blood get the best of her.

Almost as if he became aware that someone was studying him, he looked directly in Megan's direction. Involuntarily, she jerked her head back. How silly. He couldn't see in the mirror. She looked again. He was gone. She ran to the window just in time to see him whisk like a shadow around the corner towards the mountain.

Without knowing exactly how, she felt strongly that this man was linked to all the mystery. Too bad that Ménard was taking so long to arrive. A strong urge made her not want to let the stranger disappear. She grabbed her jacket, promising to only see what direction he took, and hurried out the door towards her private trail; the shortcut would shave a few minutes off the unknown observer's head start. The scent of autumn air made her nostrils tingle. She had missed the heat of adventure, and felt sure-footed with her moccasins. As she pushed uphill, overhead clouds were closing in and darkening the fading light. A light rain began to fall.

Once she reached the main mountain track, the rain began falling more heavily. Half considering giving up, she decided to look for footprints, hiking several yards before finding a newly-smeared print in the mud—hiking boots with a deep tread; the print was uneven and fresh; the outline had to have been made, she judged, only moments before. There was no one else in sight so it must have been the handsome stranger. Inspired, she forged ahead. The rain started to pour down; mud sprayed her jeans and before she knew it, she could barely see in front of herself. The trail took a steep cut upwards and without even thinking, she headed up the slope clutching onto branches as the rain beat down.

Chasing a stranger in the pouring rain didn't seem like a smart judgement call, nonetheless, once on the go, she rarely gave up a hunt. So what if it ended up as a wet, wild goose chase. She pushed drenched tendrils of hair away from her eyes and made her way over the uphill rubble, using any outgrowth for traction, propelling every step. It was a Mohawk technique Uncle Dekanewidah had taught her as a child. She looked forward to reaching the top where there was a well used plateau frequented by joggers and it had lampposts. Any amount of light would help, because at this point the rain was blinding and she was soaked.

Topping the ridge, she peered through the rainy haze. There was no one in sight, not even the usual dog-walking sort in a raincoat. The rain slowed suddenly and seemed to stop. She crept into the lamplight and looked for fresh footprints; with some scrutiny she found a smeared depression in the soggy grass pointing towards the cedar-thicketed embankment to the left. Wondering if she was being foolish, she debated whether to follow. With all the time she'd taken, he was probably long gone; so, in fact, now that the rain had slacked off, it would be safe. She moved in between the trees, but couldn't really see her way because of the deep shadows. Disappointed, she turned back.

Suddenly, a strong push on her jacket shifted her forward; her legs flew out from under her. A strong forearm encircled her throat and twisted her backwards. She found herself being dragged powerlessly through the dripping thicket. The hold was choking her, only allowing a muted grunt. She lashed out with her feet, trying to get a grip with her heels, but the moccasins were useless on the wet ground. She writhed from side to side, struggling to loosen the vice-like hold. The wrenching arms dragged her several meters further into the dark. Thinking it was the stranger, but wanting to know for certain, she tried to get a glance at his clothes, but with this hold like steel, she couldn't angle her head; her only view a helpless look at the moon peaking through black clouds. Abruptly he stopped, and whipped her roughly onto her feet. His hold around her neck loosened. She shifted forward hoping to back-kick him in the groin when she heard rather than felt the crack of bone, her own skull. Everything went dark.

Chapter 16

Treiger stood by the edge of a rocky subterranean river, where rushing water echoed like rumbling thunder. Mist rose above the racing water and wandered through his flickering torch. He looked down at the white-capped torrent striking with all its might against jagged-edged slabs of limestone. Rocky points broke the surface like barbed stalagmites sending surging water up to splash on his feet. This was the only crossing point as there was a decent ledge on the other side. He exhaled heavily as if trying to blow away years of memory. The cave system, which he had found during one of his early visits to Montreal, had become his secret base.

The discovery came about after Hans introduced him to a friend, Theodore Rolfe. Rolfe had been completing his doctorate in theology and, on occasion, would drop by Hans's apartment to chat. On the afternoon they met, Treiger had been sitting at the kitchen table when Rolfe knocked on the door. Treiger watched quietly and, even though he expected Hans to be hospitable, was irritated when Rolfe accepted the offer to come in for a drink. Hans got out a bottle of cheap vodka and set three glasses on the small kitchen table. Treiger pushed his chair back near the wall to make room for Hans's guest.

Hans and Rolfe had carried the conversation for a while, when Rolfe, about halfway through his glass of vodka, began an interesting tale about local history. In the 17th century, Jesuit monks found an underground river buried beneath Mount Royal. Rolfe had discovered a map of where their settlement might have been located. He explained that the Jesuits were known for their ability to befriend Indian tribes and, in their efforts to convert the natives to Catholicism, became the earliest explorers of eastern Canada. The French government often used the Fathers' services to help with peace treaties and alliances because of the monk's acquaintance with native dialects. Then England challenged ownership of the land. The British understood the Jesuit danger; spreading religion and the French language amongst the Indians threatened the Commonwealth. To counter the menace, the English made allies of the Iroquois, placing a price on the head of any Jesuit priest they could eliminate. The Iroquois went about their duties with a vengeance, hideously torturing the missionary brothers. According to Rolfe, some monks, to escape the persecution, dug tunnels to a hidden river.

Rolfe drained his glass, which Hans quickly refilled. He next introduced a legend about Father Jean de Brébeuf, a Jesuit priest sacrificed by the Iroquois. After a lengthy swallow of vodka, Rolfe lay out in detail how the monk died; pointing out that each step of torture was designed to ensure a gruesome, lingering death. He spoke slowly. "Well, first a huge pyre of wood was set alight. Beating drums set the rhythm while the women and children incited their hot-blooded warriors with high-pitched shouts. Everyone in the tribe danced in a great circle about the blazing fire; noise and smoke thickened the air making the night fevered with hostility. They stripped Brébeuf and tied him to a post, close to the fire, of course. To start with, Brébeuf's hands were chopped off. This was a brutal symbol of their power over him.

Once that was taken care of, the Iroquois used spikes to pierce the monk's hot flesh. The punctures formed small streams of blood flowing down his body. The result must have been frightening—grotesque."

Rolfe looked at Hans to make certain that he had captured his attention. Treiger remained sitting back in the shadows. Satisfied with Hans's expression of rapt interest, Rolfe went on, "Some braves prepared red-hot Tomahawks, and suspended the searing iron around his neck. The scorching axes made every turn of his head an agony. I don't know how he stood the pain, but apparently he didn't even cry out. Natives have a particular respect for strength, but such endurance would make them proceed to even more cruel torture just to see how much Brébeuf could take. Their next device created a particularly punishing anguish. A belt composed of resin and pitch was tied around his waist. A warrior brandished a flaming torch in a frenzied dance, taunting the pain-riddled Father with his intent before setting the tar alight. The searing black muck melted on his skin. Unfortunately the heat staunched the flow of the blood dripping from his wounds, lessoning blood loss. At this point, Brébeuf let his voice rise above the cries of his tormentors and powerfully preached the word of God."

Rolfe took another long drink and set the glass down carefully on the table. His eyes looked off into a glazed distance as if in a trance and he began again, " '*God forgives your innocence*' this poor martyr cried. His voice began strong, but his might finally dwindled. Before long, he started praying in an incoherent gibberish of Latin and French. The natives reacted to his soulful lamentations by seizing blistering hot sticks from the fire and thrusting them into his mouth. When Brébeuf continued his garbled exhortation they rallied to drain him of his power. He was finally silenced when a youth, shining with sweat bulged muscles, hacked Brébeuf's lips away with a sharp knife. Brébeuf was a strong man and death still evaded him." Rolfe shook his head as if he had actually witnessed the tragic slaughter. He drained his glass and continued. "The mutilations, in all their severity, were such that they would neither kill nor render a strong man unconscious. Brébeuf only fell to his knees and bled. His persecutors continued their torture by flinging buckets of scalding water over his head in a mock baptism. They cut pieces of his flesh from his limbs and his trunk. Before his very eyes they roasted the raw chunks of bloody scarlet pulp in the fire and ate them. I always wondered if they did so with savage relish or if it was a symbolic gesture to devour his strength and endurance."

Hans, his face flushed from vodka, broke in, "How long did he last?"

Rolfe set his glass forward indicating with a pinch of his fingers for a drop more, and shook his head with a heaving sigh, "To be honest, I don't know, but I'd have to assume several hours were involved, perhaps the whole night. You see the peace of death finally came after they managed to amputate his feet and tear off his scalp. Not finished, the savages sizzled his mutilated body at the stake. A remaining missionary was left alive to tell the tale. That's why there is so much detail in the history books. Instead of fleeing from persecution, the Jesuits aimed at shielding themselves from Iroquois raids by seeking out escape routes and hiding places; to me, tunnels on Mount Royal are an example of their ingenuity."

Treiger was amused by Rolfe's ability to dramatize the facts, but fascinated by the idea of tunnels. He had also found Rolfe talked intelligently about war, death and torture and couldn't resist drawing the theologian into a debate on what constitutes human evil. He could have chosen a story from a vast number of historical cruelties, but he picked one that echoed his own past. Afterwards, he had to admit to himself that he did so because of Hans. Treiger outlined the story of Dr. Fabian von Schlabrendorff, a member of the German resistance against Hitler. Treiger detailed the protracted tortures this man endured at the Gestapo headquarters in Berlin. The torture, not just hours long, went on for days. Before he was captured, Schlabrendorff had already heard how relentless their tactics were. The Gestapo found starting with pain counterproductive, so they began a wearing down process of interrogation. A Gestapo interrogator named Habecker started off with the usual tricks – presenting a file with false evidence, threats to his family, the production of false affidavits. Schlabrendorff was taken from his cell any time of day or night. In between time, he was kept fettered both hand and foot in his cell. Stripped naked, he was given only inadequate amounts of rotten food; sometimes they filled his food bowl with his own excrement. Habecker included a girl in the team to demoralize his ego. The incessant questioning and shouts of abuse were endless, but Schlabrendorff used his skill as a lawyer to mentally brace himself. His apparent calm throughout days of this ordeal enraged Habecker, who moved to the next step, inflicting pain. Schlabrendorff's hands were chained behind his back and his fingers were inserted into a device that injected spikes into his fingertips. The SS team continued with the gooseneck spotlights and ruthless verbal assaults the whole time. In the ensuing days, after each successive torture, he would wake up in his cell covered in his own blood. When their entire array of pincer devices failed to work, Schlabrendorff was placed on a medieval rack. They stretched all four limbs in wrenching jerks until the bones were dislocated. His heart couldn't take the dehydration and constant strain. He collapsed with a heart attack, but still survived. When he was at the point of committing suicide rather than give in, he managed to invent a fantastical confession. The intense tortures stopped only because the Nazi's had got a simple piece of false paper that justified moving on to the next prisoner, yet kept this one alive in case they needed him for some other purpose. How could these men and women from modern times do this to another human being, Treiger asked Rolfe?

Hans sat at the table with his head hanging down. Treiger knew his brother must be recalling the slaughter of their parents and his internment at Buchenwald, but Treiger did not stop. He filled all their glasses with more vodka, then set forth the point that evil is rooted in narcissism and that narcissistic people lacked the capacity for empathy. Such people sought leadership for vain purposes. The most charismatic rulers, like Hitler, were able to convince others that their vision of power was to create a better life for their culture. He furthered his argument, hammering out that such egocentric leaders can blind in others the capacity for empathy. Their methods of using lies, intimidation, sarcasm and favouritism often resulted in individuals scapegoating others to improve their status or to take suspicion off themselves. He further proposed that followers of this type of leader lacked an inner self-discipline to stand alone in the name of justice, relying on the apparent superiority and self-discipline of the leaders. The sore point came when Treiger argued that no retribution or forgiveness could match the nature of their deeds.

Rolfe countered by stating that one cannot study a disease without the intention to heal it and, after a thoughtful pause, pointed out that the psychology of evil must be a healing psychology. A slight shiver passed through his spine when Treiger remembered how he had backed off from the discussion at that point. He did not want to hear what Rolfe had to say. He almost left the room. Rolfe must have recognised his extreme discomfort, because he abruptly suggested they go on a scavenger hunt to find the tunnels. Luisa came in from work just in time to join them. Treiger orienteered the group, leading them all on an energetic chase across Mount Royal. No tunnels were found, but those few hours held the most fun he'd had in his life.

On another private search, he discovered the entry he had just used. The door had rotted through and was knotted with vines and dirt, but the stone stairs were intact. His first difficulty was crossing the dangerous river, but over several return trips he was able to explore the whole system. Treiger figured the Jesuits, obviously no strangers to hard labour, must have taken years to dig and construct the connecting tunnels. The river, at one point, probably millions of years ago, was wide and deep, as if it had been created at the same time as the mountain, during the volcanic eruptions. The raging water carved a cavern through the underbelly of the mountain, searching for a way to survive the burning hot lava flows. Now the river was older and curved, but still fierce.

In all, he found four exits, each in a different location. One branched off from the river, leading to a sealed wall connected to his residence on Roxton Crescent. Along the river itself, across a dilapidated bridge, he found a large room-like cave with a high ceiling closed off by a rough wooden door sealed. For lack of a better name, he called this space the crypt and later set it up as a lab for Hans's work. Nearby he found an extra connecting tunnel parallel to the crypt route, but it was small and difficult to navigate. Both his home and the Kendall coach house replaced the remnants of the Jesuits primitive stone structures. An architect by the name of Crane had erected his home over one site, and had built a coach house over another entry. The coach house tunnel had also been sealed off sometime before Crane's death. Later the property was divided, and Roxton Crescent was created. The coach house ended up on the Kendall's property across the street. The third entry he had just used was built into the natural features of the mountain and furthest away from Roxton Crescent. The fourth entry was closer to the crypt.

Treiger didn't exactly know why the caves were abandoned, but construed that the Jesuits' long-held secret had captured Crane's imagination and after his death, the tunnels again became a mystery for someone else to discover. When Treiger purchased the house, he had an underground garage built adjacent to the house and reopened that entry. The tunnel across the street remained closed until Kendall had broken through a wall underneath his coach house. Luckily, he hadn't yet ventured further, and Treiger had hoped it wouldn't matter, that the business with the Gau would already be over and the lab obsolete. But now Kendall's breach created a risky problem. There were enough problems without being exposed by a bumbling explorer.

Treiger looked overhead for his transport, a thick rope with a pulley. Dowsing the torch in the water, he set the smouldering stick in a primitive holder carved into the rock wall. By cinching the roller system to his belt and encircled the cable with his legs, he crossed the raging water hand over hand and then hastened down the passage. Hans and Luisa were his next concern. Stoltz couldn't have already discovered the lab, but, on the other hand, Higler was hot on their trail.

So far they had survived through strict secrecy. Now their conspiracy had been blown wide open by the survival of Higler and Stoltz. They were no longer the hunters, but the hunted. The Jesuits didn't survive the Iroquois torture, but that kind of brutality could be expected if the Gau survivors captured Hans and Luisa. Two hundred years ago, torture was a matter of winning a war to gain more territory and power. The goal wasn't calculated genocide like the Nazi regime, but, like Brébeuf, many priests brutally lost their lives. The hidden passages had not saved the monks. He therefore shouldn't rely on the caves to save Hans and Luisa, nor himself. Still, history moves in mysterious ways. The ingenuity of these priests had allowed him to work secretly.

Soon Treiger crossed a bridge made of suspended rope railings and a base of wooden slates; there was another similar one just outside the crypt. He arrived at the bridging, disappointed that no light filtered around the crypt door where he'd expected Hans to be working. He crossed the swinging support and made his way to the door. All was silent and dark. Damn. Where were they? Anxiously, Treiger moved into the room. A slight movement caught his eye. He darted forward, and rolled into combat position as the light switched on.

"Thank God, it's you." Hans breathed. His face held an expression of stunned relief. He set down a knapsack that he had been holding over his head as if to fling the bulk in defence. His cracked voice continued excitedly. "We couldn't be sure if you had returned or someone else had found us. Luisa just came from Theodore Rolfe's place. He's dead! Murdered! Luisa's certain the killer got the tunnel plans. Does that mean you failed? When I didn't hear from you I knew something had happened." Hans looked gravely distressed. His wrinkled hand reached out protectively towards Luisa.

Treiger said shortly, "Calm down, Hans. Yes, something did happen. The worst of the Gau circle, Stoltz and Higler, escaped."

Hans drew Luisa closer. "My God, if they got a map of the tunnels we are dead."

Treiger added conviction to his words. "Even if they did get those old diagrams, it would take time to find the entrances. Rolfe never knew for certain that the caves existed, so he couldn't have given them any help."

Treiger turned to Luisa. "Are you sure they got the plans?"

"I think so. The man I saw leaving had papers in his hand."

"That means they haven't found us yet, but you're right, they could. And soon."

Luisa added hesitantly, "The two young women from across the street, Megan Brodie and Kendall's wife showed up at Rolfe's. They scared the killer off."

Treiger frowned. "Those women couldn't have known anything." He paused in thought before continuing, "We must stay focused. How is your work coming, Hans?"

Hans swallowed, then turned and asked Luisa to fetch some brandy in the storage cupboard. He looked seriously into Treiger's eyes. "Karl, the last sample you sent is designed perfectly, meaning that it will be damned hard to detect."

When Luisa came back with the brandy, Hans reached out and took a gulp from the bottle. He handed it towards Karl, who shook his head continuing to probe,

"Hans, have you got any further on the results?"

"Karl, you know I've been working day and night! I've covered the first step in identifying what we're after, but until I find out the exact process used, finding a treatment on my own could take another lifetime." He slumped forward, letting his head fall into his hands, "We are lost. I'm sorry, Karl. I have failed you."

Not wanting his brother to loose control, Treiger placed his hands on Hans shoulders and said, "Stop feeling sorry for yourself, old man. You are afraid of dying—of others dying. If you give up like this, then you are already dead and so are they." When Hans looked ambivalent, Treiger shook his shoulders. "Come on, snap out of it." He then let go and started pacing the uneven crypt floor. He could not let them feel that their lives were in vain. Hans and Luisa watched until finally, he raised his head, "Perhaps it is time that we revealed ourselves."

Luisa's eyes shone with concern, "No Karl! We'll be branded traitors."

Treiger took a deep breath, "I mean, we could reveal the scheme. The samples are our proof. Other scientists could help. What do you think Hans?"

Hans's voice sounded more hopeful. "Perhaps a team of us could make headway. I have not liked working in isolation and always feared we would come to this point. Trapped. But essentially you're right, however, I need to set my data up for transfer."

Treiger replied, "Then get to it and I'll try to ward off Higler and Stoltz."

Luisa stepped forward. "Perhaps I should go back to the house for supplies."

Treiger placed his hand on her shoulder. "No, Luisa. Higler and Stoltz are intent on stopping us. The house will no doubt be a target, but you could pick up what we need elsewhere. Use the mountain tunnel exit and take a flashlight."

Luisa nodded, then went silently over to Hans and gave him a kiss on the cheek and a little hug. "I won't be long." She left the crypt and started across the bridge. She had always hated the way the ropes swayed shakily and the boards creaked. Once across, there was a large flat surface. The surrounding walls were uneven and curved with huge gouged out indentations big enough for a person to hide. The obvious route to take was to follow the stable and fairly wide shelf along the river, but she walked straight across the widest part near to her and disappeared into the narrow crevasse. The fissure was lined with man-made granite blocks and stretched into a tunnel, ending with a stepladder bolted into the stone. She held tightly to the rungs and slowly climbed up.

At the top she shoved a small trapdoor open, then proceeded to crawl slowly through a small path cut through dense thicket and cedars. The branches were dripping wet. Her crouched march was awkward and made her feel short of breath. An ache started in her chest. She stopped. Not because of the pain, but she heard something. There was someone near, so she shut off her flashlight. The sound became louder. She already felt on edge, but now the fear of being discovered gripped her. Luckily the moon had reappeared after the rain. She made out a darkly dressed figure struggling with someone, and peered more closely. The Brodie woman was in a man's grip; he was raising a heavy stick. Luisa couldn't help herself, she screamed as the club came down on the Brodie woman.

The attacker let his prey sag down, and swung around as if zeroing in on her.

"Megan!" an accented voice cried out from further away.

With that call, the figure raced away across the wooded mountainside. Luisa ran over to the motionless body and felt the pulse in her neck. The girl was alive. She heard the sound of others coming. Going back to the tunnel was too risky. Her breathing became rapid as she scuttled away from Megan's prostrate body. She took a nearby path with a steep gradient and, as silently as possible, retreated as voices came closer. They would find the girl, she hoped. Her old ankles were unstable making her skid on the gravel and dirt. She clung to branches, finally reaching the bottom just near a street. Damp from rainwater and sweat, she slumped into some brush. The pressure in her chest started again. She took a pill from the prescription bottle in her pocket and slipped the small white tablet under her tongue.

As she rested, another figure came sauntering off the mountain not ten yards from her. She observed him carefully. He crossed the road and pulled out a cell phone. Before long, a black sedan pulled up and the driver's window opened. In an effort to hear, she shifted to her knees, but some twigs crunched.

"What's that?" said the blonde man, swinging his head in her direction.

"Probably a racoon. The mountain's infested with them," the driver replied, handing him a cigarette through the window. Before putting it in his mouth, the muscular blonde man curtly told the driver about Megan. The sound of the attacker's German accent sent shivers down Luisa's spine.

"If you hit her hard enough to give her a concussion, maybe she'll end up in a hospital. As you said, she's your only lead. If it's the same woman from this afternoon, she must have a hard head." The sound of an ambulance siren echoed across the terrain and sounding amused the driver said, "Bingo."

The blonde seemed to reflect out loud. "She must know something. Why else would she follow me? But first it is time to pick up Stoltz. Then we can get busy."

"Sure thing, Mister H. My brother will meet us at the airport."

Once they drove off, she stood in a brief panic, then raced as fast as she could to Roxton Crescent. Karl's warning rang in her ears, but the street was empty and the house dark. Outside the backdoor, she deactivated the security system, then made her way towards to the front entry in the dark. She knew she was there when she bumped into a darkly carved mahogany stand holding a French Renaissance vase. She carefully steadied the delicate porcelain. Nearby was a small brass elevator that took her to garage level. She then pressed the floor indicator buttons in a varied sequence, and the elevator moved further down. The only door opened after she pressed another series of numbers. As she stepped into the dark, the elevator door closed and moved automatically back up to the garage. She felt alone and cold. The pain in her chest started again, making her slip another nitro-glycerine pill under her tongue. This was the only tunnel with lighting, and she knew it well. Karl would be angry, but she flicked on the string of wired bulbs anyway. When she felt able, she walked through the passage to the underground stream, and followed the bank until she crossed again to the crypt.

Treiger came out as she reached the threshold. His eyes flared with concern and he said harshly, "We could hear you a mile away. Why did you go to the house?"

Luisa's spoke with an anxious pitch, "I'm sorry Karl. I had no choice. There was a man near the mountain entrance. He looked very much like the Stoltz that came to see you several months ago, but I found out it was Higler. He was very close!"

"This is serious. You're lucky to be alive."

"And Megan Brodie was there. He attacked her, but I don't think she's dead."

Treiger cut Luisa off. "Brodie again? Why would she be near the cave entrance, especially after being at Rolfe's that very afternoon?"

Luisa anxiously added, "They are going to track her down. We need to help her."

Treiger frowned. "You're not making sense, Luisa. There is nothing we can do."

With that, she sat down on a nearby bench, tears rolling down her face. She began to speak. "That woman saved my life, and more importantly, she saved this place from being discovered. I'm sure of it. She mustn't be left for them to slaughter."

Treiger was silent.

Hans, who had been standing by his compute, rushed to Luisa's side, "My dear," he consoled her, "there are some things we can do nothing about."

Luisa looked back and forth into both their eyes pleading for them to understand. "We are allowing that woman to have her life sacrificed so that we can save others. We will consciously allow that to happen in the name of what? Righteousness? I am afraid then we have become part of the evil that we have spent our lives fighting against." She thought for a moment, staring into space. "You two have important work to do. There is little I can do to help you but, perhaps, I can help that woman."

"Are you determined to do this?" Treiger asked.

She couldn't read what he was thinking, but through the years she'd learned Karl's thoughts were always racing ten steps ahead of everyone else. She looked back at him with as much determination as she could muster and nodded. She felt such conviction that her decision was the right one, but she couldn't explain the reason why she felt such a necessity to search for this woman.

"How do you intend to go about it?" Treiger inquired.

"I will call the hospitals and find out where she was taken, then go to her."

"If it is that simple then how do you know you will reach her ahead of Higler?"

"I don't know, but I must try."

"Luisa, are you certain of what you saw? Because I don't have time for mistakes and I don't want you putting yourself at risk."

"Karl, you don't need to worry about me."

Treiger looked at her with his impenetrable expression. "I'm not worried about you, Luisa. I'm worried about the Gau. There is much at stake here and already miscalculations have been made. Life is not that predictable. At the very least if you intend to proceed, take this cell phone with you, that way if we get separated I can keep track of you."

CHAPTER 17

Brazil, 1968

Luthor Kleis entered Buch's second floor office at Gau HQ. "I hope my time's not wasted! It's not a holiday resort in the rainforest. I have work to do."

Buch squinted through his round glasses. Being much shorter than Kleis, he made up for it through his waistline. "You know me, Luthor, I would only bring you back if I had succeeded."

"You old scoundrel! You mean we have a breakthrough? I don't believe it."

"You will soon. One of the greatest scientific developments yet to grace the technological frontier is within our grasp. But first, come with me. I have something to show you before we go up to the lab."

Buch quickly slipped a white coat and handed one to Kleis. They exited into Buch's domain; a pristine corridor laced with the smell of disinfectant and lined with patient rooms. Down the hall, near a solarium with large potted plants, stood a young woman accompanied by an inconspicuous man. As soon as the woman saw Buch leave his office, she touched the man's arm and they hurried over to him. The handsome woman, wearing a tailored grey suit tightly-fitted at the waist, extended her arm indicating that she wanted his attention. Even though her chestnut brown hair framed her face exquisitely, her eyes were a swollen red. A lace handkerchief was crumpled in her hand. "Dr. Buch?" she put forth, her voice meek and hesitant, "Do you have a moment?"

Buch laid his hand on Kleis's shoulder, signalling him to pause, and turned with a look of sincere interest towards the attractive woman; he also gave a brief glance of concern to the man standing beside her, hat grasped in his hand. The man would not meet his eyes, and Buch presumed there was a cloud of angry disappointment behind those hooded lids. Choosing a caring professional stance and speaking softly, he said, "Of course, Mrs. Routinberg, how can I be of assistance?"

"I'm sorry to bother you. You have been so good to Saul and me, helping us when we had nowhere else to go. I feel like such a failure." Tears slid down her cheeks. She reached up to wipe them away and mustered the control to continue. "You have already tried your procedure twice, I know and...and both times...my babies died. We were told today to go home...home with no baby...I mean...I...I know it is bold of me...perhaps it is too much for me to ask, but I must." She looked at Saul for support, but he kept his head lowered. With a deep breath, she blurted out her plea, "Couldn't you try one more time?"

Buch leaned forward respectfully. "My dear, you have done your best. You did not fail by trying. However there is the emotional aspect that must be dealt with. I thought I had arranged to have you see our psychologist before your departure."

He knew she already had finished her sessions, a service he offered to all investigational trials with positive results. The counselling avoided problems in the aftermath of his experiments. He usually tried to get at two confirmations from the same subject. He didn't want to get into an ethical squabble with the medical community and their sanctimonious standards. He did, however, randomly select some women for a third insemination resulting in a normal baby, doing it just enough times to give him a good reputation abroad. Fertility was a delicate political matter. However, he rarely did a third procedure on a Jew. He watched her shoulders chug up and down as she tried to stifle the sobs with her bit of lace.

Buch smiled consolingly, "It is now time for you to look after yourself and your husband. You must make your lives as God has determined for you. To try again would be dangerous for your own health."

Her tears didn't stop. Buch took one of the man's hands away from his hat and clasped it firmly in his own. The gesture made the man look into his eyes. Buch's whispered, "Your wife needs you now more than ever. Be there for her."

Saul's defiant look faltered with a film of tears. He bent towards his wife and put his arm around her shoulder. They both turned away and started a leaden march towards the end of the corridor. Buch and Kleis watched as the couple faded down the hallway.

"Your bedside manner never ceases to impress me, Buch. I can't believe your patience with those slagging Yids. The fact that you are the one to deal with them makes my time in the rainforest seem worthwhile just to avoid it." Kleis ended with a smirk.

Buch was still watching the couple and said offhandedly, "Pretty little thing, but two confirmations are the limit. I could have allowed a third pregnancy with a viable result, but I really didn't like that rat-faced husband of hers."

This was nothing new so Kleis, trying to maintain interest, asked, "So what's your total so far?"

"Including the early work in Berlin, we've had 4037 confirmations with 100% success."

"You mean to tell me that many foetuses have been aborted for your research? Astonishing. I hope your results were worth the effort." Kleis let a tinge of sarcasm leak into his response.

"That's nothing compared to what I have to show you. Our Doctor Schwartz has pulled through with a new discovery. Before that, you must indulge me. I want you to meet someone very special." Buch knocked briefly on the door beside him, opened it and walked through. A blonde woman with blue eyes sat in a pink chenille robe. Sun was shining through the window onto her and the bundled baby in her arms.

"Hello, Gerta. We came to check on the little one. How is he today?"

Gerta smiled brightly and replied, "He is fine and so strong." She looked down at the blue-eyed baby who turned his head towards her breast trying to suck her robe.

Buch patted her on the shoulder and smiled at the baby's urgency to get what he wanted. He spoke with finality, "Hungry as well, I see. We will spare nothing to enable him to reach his fullest potential."

As they left the room, Buch looked at Kleis and said, "The child's name has been chosen. He will be called Ernst Reinhard Stoltz." Buch started to laugh quietly and added, "Volker chose the name, of course. You'd think he was the proud father. However, it is an interesting title: Ernst in memory of the elite commander of the brown shirts, good old Ernie Rohm, that notorious homosexual. No surprise with that one. Reinhard, of course for Himmler's lackey Heydrick, that dashing blonde X-chief of SS Intelligence; a perfect Aryan: brilliant intellect, outstanding violinist and linguist, an expert fencer and skier. And, to boot, he had a virile taste for women. Fits Volker's odd tastes suitably, I'd say. The family name is from Volker's mother. You know how close he was to her. She died at Dresden. He never forgave the allies for that. So, our little Ernie has a lot to live up to. Well Luthor, what did you think?"

"To be honest, Buch, all babies look the same to me. Not my area. Is he special?"

"One never knows with this sort of thing, and we are genetic pioneers. I am the front-runner because I experiment on humans. Plus the work in Berlin was invaluable. The mainstream scientific community works on drosophilae for God's sake. Believe me, fruit flies are inconsequential when you can use mammals of the quality we have here. Ernie's brother is on the way. However, it is my hope that our Ernst here will be strong and intelligent, but most importantly, he will carry PAG's in his sperm."

"PAG's?"

"Pure Aryan Genes. That's what I labelled the gene sequences. Their designation has a nice ring to it, doesn't it? Believe me, finding them was quite a process. We made many mistakes. Some of the embryos were quite horrifying, yet fascinating. First you dissect out a gene. I'll show you that process in a moment. Then we implant the gene and you find there are legs growing where the eyes should be. Figuring how to dissect a gene out from a human chromosome took us twenty-three years; after the first one, though, it was easy. For my *Lebensborn* project, we select German women from pure stock and reward them handsomely. I have plans for more like strong little Ernst."

When Kleis rolled his eyes, Buch replied defensively, "Don't be smug. This isn't what you're here to see. Schwartz has made a lucky innovation on our joint project."

Buch took Kleis to a lab where long counters were scattered with all types of test tubes, experimental storage containers, small refrigerators and large microscopes. Buch passed some technicians and headed over to a particularly handsome scientist. Buch addressed the black-haired man with his striking dark eyes. "I know we're late, Schwartz, and you would rather be out on the beach chasing women, however, Doctor Kleis needs to know exactly what you have found."

Schwartz shrugged with a charming smile and opened the storage refrigerator beside his workstation. Buch started a clipped explanation of each step, which Kleis found irritating. The plump, bald scientist was looking old and some of the research on those foetuses was outrageous. Kleis thought of Mengele's concentration camp experiments— bizarre surgeries like making lampshades out of irradiated Jewish skin. At the moment, Kleis didn't need a doddering old eccentric interrupting his own work. He spoke up impatiently, "I thought Volker told you to give up on this baby business. It's too time consuming."

"Really Luthor, give me some credit. Its not all babies—Schwartz has done sterling work here and you can use it to your advantage."

"What do you mean?"

"I have tracked down a gene sequence that has specific Semitic traits and along with that mutant gene from Treiger's sperm, we could have something very special here."

"So what! You create a bunch of Germans who can't mate with Jews. Big deal. You've been talking about this for years."

"You're completely missing the point, Luthor. You can use this. My work is virtually finished. I'm going to continue perfecting what I've already discovered and produce some fine Aryans, perhaps creating a nice little family of true Aryans before I die. Now I can even use your sperm if you like." Buch smiled and bobbed his head in an excited way with an impish look on his round face. He said, "But you, Luthor, will be able make this next discovery so much more useful. Most certainly this gene had some over-riding ability to destroy a vital portion of the DNA within the fertilised egg of a Jew. In the next few minutes I am going to present you with hope. Success is possible!"

Kleis was now slightly interested, but he'd heard Buch get excited about this sort of thing before. He sighed and said, "Let's see what you've got."

Buch gestured towards the dark-haired scientist and said, "Schwartz here will show you. He was a good choice, since Treiger's brother failed to be of the quality we require. Schwartz's background in cell biology is superior, and he has gained considerable knowledge working with me in genetics. The two make a wonderful combination."

Schwartz stepped up confidently and proceeded with his demonstration. "This blue fluid contains cloned segments of the Y-chromosome Dr. Buch mentioned. I have added radioactive atoms to tag the segment. That way we can see the results on X-ray film." Using one of the tiny pipettes, Schwartz took some pink fluid from another test tube. Carefully exacting his view and guiding the pipette, he put some of the substance into the fluid containing DNA. The specific location of a particular gene is called its loci and in between these loci or gene clusters are long lengths of the bases that don't, as far as I can tell, do anything. So the goal here is to try and dissect out a particular segment of DNA that I want. I have added a restriction enzyme to this fluid containing DNA from the Y-chromosome of a male of Jewish descent. This particular DNA is a longer segment than I want. That is to say, I've added a small protein taken from a particular type of bacteria. The protein is very selective and can actually corral the segment I want away from the rest of the molecule.

You see DNA is DNA— all the different species arise from the same DNA. So I can add 'bacterial DNA' to 'human DNA' at this microscopic level and the both work effectively together. This very selective bacterial protein will extract out, or in other words, cut away the segment of this chromosome that I want. The pink fluid contains the special enzyme that will mix with the DNA to create the individual portions. I can then identify them with gel electrophoresis." Schwartz took the test-tube mixture to a piece of square glass coated with an agarose gel. "I just insert some of the DNA mixture in these tiny slots. Of course you can see nothing with the naked eye. Unfortunately we have to use X-ray plates to show us the results. I've been working on a technique using fluorescent tags, which would greatly speed up our work." The DNA slide fit snugly into the small machine standing on the counter beside his work area, and he flicked a switch.

Schwartz turned on a screen with X-ray negatives already clipped into place. "These are already finished. See how the fragments have separated out into lanes in the gel. This is the particular one I am interested in."

Impressed, Kleis peered at the X-rays and commented, "Fascinating. You've managed to cut away a section of the DNA fairly precisely."

"Not fairly. Exactly. As I showed you, the process is achieved with well-chosen restriction enzymes created from bacterial DNA. I have already started replicating the selected DNA segments in other molecular solutions so that there will always be significant amounts of this gene to work with. I've also been able to track down the location on some of the foetuses that were aborted. Now take a look at this. I just need to take some DNA from this bacterium and slice out a piece of it. Both these snippets of DNA have sticky ends. It seems to result from the slicing process. The two separate DNA pieces hook together. Now all I have to do is move it into a bacterium where it will duplicate it repeatedly."

Buch pulled Kleis away from the counter and flapped his hand at Schwartz saying. "Yes. Yes. Well that's enough of your showing off, Schwartz." He then put his head close to Kleis and said, "What you are looking at is the latest gene sequence we've discovered. I'm thinking of calling it the Jewish Determining Sequence. Find something that attacks that sequence and you will have complete control over the Semitic situation."

"Hold on, Buch. Do you know what you're saying?" Kleis found himself staring at his colleague in astonishment. Possibilities of what he could do with such a process were expanding exponentially in his mind. He felt slightly dizzy with excitement. "My God Buch. You're a genius."

"Don't tell me you've been in doubt." Buch chuckled. "However, I'm only slightly ahead of the game. Brilliant researchers are working elsewhere on this type of thing and will soon have the same biotechnology. I'm just giving you a head start."

Chapter 18

"Megan!" Her name crept through a thick void of nothingness. "Please wake-up!" penetrated like distant pounding. Somewhere in the fog, Megan recognized Fiona's relentless voice and struggled to reach the dream-like wisp of awareness. Finally, a vibration passed through her throat with slurry impatience, "Shu...ut up. I want to slee-ep!"

Fiona's barrage hammered on. "No! You can't sleep. You must wake up. It's very important. Wake up!"

After a half-hearted attempt to open her eyes, she decided a deep sigh was easier. "I mean it, Megan. Wake up!"

A bit of spittle splashed on her eyes. "Ugh...my head hurts."

Suddenly, tender arms encircled her shoulders with a warm hug. Rushed, almost tearful sentences followed. "I was so worried you wouldn't wake up. And Deirdre is distraught beyond belief! If that little dog of hers hadn't started barking, I would never have seen you bolting up the mountain path. Danny Ménard arrived just after that. He followed and luckily found you. You're at the Royal Victoria Hospital now...Danny's been marvellous, but very upset! We all are. In fact, we've been trying to find out if there is any family we should notify. Deirdre gave Danny an old address in Scotland..."

The words zapped like a cattle prod. Megan's eyes flew open. "You didn't call!"

Fiona looked startled. "Gosh, Danny took the address, but I…"

The headache worsened as she manage a few stilted words, "Listen, Fiona, my family...is my business. As far as you or anyone else is concerned...my friends are here ...nobody else matters."

Sounding hurt, Fiona said quietly, "Honestly Meg, I didn't do anything. Danny took the address and mumbled something about getting in touch if your condition worsened." And as if trying to dispel the tension, added in a happier tone, "Danny's so cute. He was so distraught when he found you. You know, I believe Danny thinks he's in love with you. Damsel in distress stuff works wonders with men like him. That's probably why he's in the police force."

Megan's fingers fidgeted with the edge of the sheets. If there was any chance her grandfather would be contacted, she had to stop it now. She threw back the covers and marshalled a speck of authority. "I have to get out of here. Please, get my clothes."

Before the words were out of her mouth, the door opened and Ménard's deep accent cut across the room. "I'm afraid, Miss Brodie, that you will be going nowhere. The doctor recommended that you stay overnight for observation. I intend to see that those orders are followed. I will post myself as guard outside your room if I have to." His words finished with a tone of finality as he walked across to the bed.

Megan drew the covers back over her legs and frowned. She hadn't missed the sensuous undertone in his threat, as if he wanted her to take him up on it. And if her head didn't ache so much, she would have argued back. She didn't want him to be worried about her, although the fact that the concern was there touched her. She sighed and said, "Oh, alright, I'll stay. No problem."

Ménard, looking disappointed, replied, "Well, in that case, *je n'ai plus rien a faire ici.*"

"Wait! We're not finished yet!" The oomph shot a pain though her skull. She put her hand protectively over what felt like a turban-type dressing and said with more control, "Don't you dare try to contact my grandfather."

He frowned slightly. "*Mais pourquoi pas, Chérie?* You have been badly hurt. You could have been killed. Why wouldn't you want your family to know about you in such circumstances?"

Megan was livid, but the angrier she got, the more her head throbbed. She tried to get a hold on her rage. Her Mohawk uncle, Dekanewidah, had told her that snapping the whip of anger means that the nerve of truth has been stung. The real truth lay in the fact that she was talking to a man who cared about family, cared about people, cared about her. Burning tears rimmed her eyes and she fought them back before saying, "Leave me alone... just…just leave."

Ménard shifted his weight awkwardly as if undecided, then made a move towards her, but Fiona put a hand on his arm and spoke gently, "She's very distressed and probably not thinking clearly anyway. Perhaps you should discuss this another time."

With a wave of sad defeat on his face, Ménard took his eyes off Megan. "*Comme toujours*, Madame Kendall, you speak wisely." When he turned back to Megan, his eyes masked his emotions. "I wish you a speedy recovery. Tomorrow morning, I will send someone to take your statement."

"Not you, Detective?" Fiona interjected quickly.

"Regretfully, I have other things to attend to." He smiled tightly and left.

Fiona looked at the vacant doorway and said lightly, "I just know he wanted to say something more. Men. What is there to understand? You can see right through them." She put her hand softly on Megan's shoulder.

Megan closed her eyes and let the tears fall. Confused, wretched feelings played against abject stupidity— stupid that she was always shooting herself in the foot— stupid that she was lying in a hospital bed with a patched-up gash in her head— stupid that she was pushing away a man that might genuinely care for her. Her stupid life was always filled with angst, no matter how hard she tried to avoid it. She felt weak and hated breaking down.

Fiona's hand pressed on her shoulder. "Don't worry, Meggie. I didn't let them cut any of your beautiful hair before they stitched you up. Well, the doctor didn't actually stitch, he glued the skin together."

The comment was so off base, Megan looked up.

Fiona had a big grin on her face, but she continued in a more serious tone, "Look, honey. You are my friend and I love you, so let me come straight out with it. This guy has his baggage. You have yours. And you both have the rest of your lives to work it out. You don't have to do it tonight. Tonight your job is to sleep and his job is to go out and find the bastard that did this to you. I have a feeling he intends to do that with ferocious intensity." Fiona gave Megan a warm kiss on her cheek. "By the way, I brought you some clean clothes, but forgot a jacket, so I'll leave your wet one here. Meanwhile, I must get home for my beauty sleep, wrestling with the painful truth that such a sensual hunk of a man is besotted, not with *moi*, but my best friend. Life just isn't fair."

Megan smiled, wishing she had the strength to pitch her pillow at Fiona's retreating figure, but instead she said, "On your way out, do me a favour and see if a nurse out there has something to kill this headache."

A few minutes later a rather petite nurse arrived wheeling a contraption for measuring blood pressure. She smiled kindly while she introduced herself, and asked a few specific questions. Somehow her soft hazel eyes made Megan feel more at ease. Her light brown ponytail and pastel pink uniform seemed to match her sensitive approach as she checked Megan's pupils with a penlight. She poured some water from the jug on the metal bedside table, then handed Megan a small, plastic cup containing two tablets and said, "Its only acetaminophen, I'm afraid. I'm sorry your prescription isn't stronger, but, even with a mild head injury like yours, something more potent might sedate you. But if the pills really don't work, just ring the bell, and I'll see what I can do." When Megan thanked her, the pretty nurse squeezed her hand reassuringly before leaving.

After that, she slipped into a fitful sleep until she heard the door to her hospital room open and tried to open her eyes. The lids seemed glued shut and, with the same throb in her head, she vaguely worried that she might have some brain damage because her body felt like a dead weight. Sweat seemed to cover her nakedness beneath the simple hospital gown, and pressure from the sheets became almost oppressive as someone pressed against the bedside. She still wanted to open her eyes, but couldn't. Feeling unbearably hot, she flung her arms out throwing off the covers.

The nurse said nothing, but oddly climbed onto the bed lying full-length over Megan's body, holding her motionless. A haunting fear gripped her throat. The pressure on her groin, the hard shape could only belong to a man. Panic paralysed her.

Suddenly and brutally his hands tore at her thighs, shoving them apart. A familiar pain of violation stabbed her. She felt like she was being cut open. The pain drove up the centre of her. She wanted to shout RAPE, but each time she tried to scream, hoarse air huffed out. Her arms were lead weights. If she could only cry out, the real nurse would come. Again, she tried to yell, but with no sound, and she realized her brain had been severely damaged. She felt him cruelly shoving himself into her again and again, each time more forcefully, as if he was ripping her apart from the inside. She thought she was going to die. Then, in the pitch-black stillness of impending death, her eyes finally opened to a visual haze of the great hulk heaving on top of her.

He was covered in blood. Red drips fell from his head onto her eyes then slid to her lips. When she again opened her mouth to holler, the sticky, thick globules got inside, tasting dreadfully salty. The crimson flood engulfed her as if trying to drown her in a hot avalanche. She tried frantically to push the body off. It didn't budge. Then she heard screaming from far away. Was it Emily's voice? She had to get to Emily...Emily needed her. The screaming continued. She had to get this body off. She tried to call to Emily...run...get away...but her voice still failed her. The absurdity of a scream belonging to Emily struck her. Emily was dead. A flashing insight — in a bizarre way, this foul molesting was part of the retribution she must pay for letting Emily die.

More helpless than any other time in her life, she stopped fighting the defiling assault and watched as if disembodied. She lay motionless staring into the black hate-filled eyes as his heavy, bloodied arm grabbed her bandaged head, slamming her skull mercilessly against the bed. Pain shot through her eyes. She knew she was looking death in the face, but the end didn't matter— all she cared about was Emily. Even if it was her last word she wanted to say it and finally forced out a croaked, "Emily."

"No, its Luisa! Luisa Treiger, your neighbour."

"What?" She blinked at the elderly woman shaking her shoulders. "Who in the devil are you?"

"I live across the street from Deirdre Ogilvy. My husband, Hans, brought you honey sometimes."

Megan shook her head, vaguely remembering Luisa Treiger's slight German accent. "Where am I? What time is it?"

"It's late and you're in the hospital. Listen, I don't have time to explain, but you are in terrible danger. If you stay here, you will be dead by morning."

Drenched in sweat, Megan spoke weakly, "I feel very confused...my head was injured...I think I should call the nurse."

Luisa replied impatiently, "No, it may be too late already. We can't alert anyone. We must leave or they may get to you again."

"What are you talking about? You need to explain." Megan felt unconvinced, but memories started to flash back about Rolfe's death and the strange man she followed. What could Luisa Treiger have to do with any of it?

Megan looked questioningly as the old woman whispered frantically. "Twice today I saw you in the wrong place at the wrong time. That man who attacked you on the mountain is very dangerous. Somehow you've got mixed up in our affairs. How did you end up at Rolfe's home and on the mountain, too? Do you know about the Gau?"

"The Gau?" Megan tried to fathom what the word meant.

"Never mind! First, I must get you out of here, but eventually I will have to find out how much you know." She shoved Megan's clothes onto the bed. "Put these on as quickly as you can. I'll check the hallway."

The white-haired woman's desperation compelled Megan to follow the instructions. Besides, after witnessing a murder, being brutally attacked and, now, dreaming murder, she figured nothing made sense anyhow, and quickly slipped on her jeans and T-shirt. Grabbing her still damp jacket, she joined Luisa Treiger on watch at the door.

Luisa turned her head back and hissed, "We'll go left passed the nurse's station. The hospitals are short staffed so there wasn't anyone in sight when I slipped by. I rearranged the names on the board listing patients' names. That could buy us time. Anyone seriously looking for you will go to another room first. At least, I hope so."

The alarm in Luisa's tone made Megan ask, "What makes you think they would try to find me in a hospital? What could I have done?"

Luisa's forehead creased with deep concern and her eyes narrowed as if in dread, but she replied coldly, "You have no idea who you are dealing with."

Luisa motioned for Megan to follow along the dimly lit hallway until they reached the central nursing station. As they crept stealthily into the light of the circular counter-console, Megan was surprised to see the nurse who had given the pain medication resting her head on the desk. She had seemed particularly conscientious and Megan didn't think they could sneak by without disturbing her. Luisa turned, mouthing the words, "She's dead. He's here. Be as quiet as possible."

As they passed, Megan was caught in the vacant stare of the lifeless body. Tears filled her eyes. Such casual disposal of a human life was incredible. She wanted to turn around and scream vengeance to the bastard that did this, but Luisa pulled her anxiously into the stairwell.

After descending several flights, Luisa took an exit opening into three dissecting hallways. Luisa took the centre one, whispering, "My cardiologist has his office in this department so I know my way around."

At the end of the corridor was an emergency exit. Luisa pushed her through the door onto a black iron balcony, obviously, a very old fire exit. A wrought iron ladder led directly down to the next level. Luisa motioned for Megan to go first. Circular metal bars arched around the ladder. Megan would have preferred they were not there, reminding her of the medieval hanging cage where prisoners were left to starve to death. At the next level down was another black landing with a spiral staircase leading to the ground. Moving swiftly, Megan landed on the lawn a good minute ahead of the older woman.

Her eyes raced back up the huge stone facade. Crow-stepped gables, dominating turrets and blackened lancet windows loomed down on her like a castle from the Dark Ages. The layers of black wrought iron that she had just descended crosshatched over the walls with thick meshed rails as if prisoners, not patients, would be led down their narrow rungs to face their doom. The massive slate roof made the fortress tower ominously over the sloping street in one vast shadow.

As Luisa stepped down beside her, Megan's instinct was to head away from the main entrance, but Luisa grabbed her arm. "Don't go that way. You'll just end up at the Allen Institute for the mentally ill." Luisa pulled her towards the parking area in front of the main entrance where one taxi stood at the curb. They ran through the shadows to a low wall surrounding the parking area and climbed over. Luisa pushed Megan past the taxi's sleeping driver towards the only other car, a Mercedes, parked near the exit. A man's head became visible. He had a gun aimed at them. She recognised the tall, dark figure. It was Karl Treiger.

The elderly woman seemed to panic and dragged Megan back to the taxi. She swung the door open, almost shoving Megan in the back, and commanded with German-accented French, "*Monsieur! Vite, vite, départez!*" Then hurried back over the wall surrounding the parking lot and disappeared. Megan could only think that Luisa was terrified to see Karl Treiger.

The engine started and a grumpy, thick accent wafted her way. Oblivious, Megan kept her eyes glued on the Mercedes. As the cab headed towards the exit, she saw Treiger squat into the shadows with his gun still levelled. She ducked her head and cowered on the seat praying, that he wouldn't shoot.

"Yur not excapin' frum dat Allen joint," the taxi driver broke in, sounding like he had just arrived from Bosnia and thrust a distrustful look in the rear-view mirror.

"Alenjont?" Megan said, distracted and still crouching.

"Yuno. Dat crazy place up de hill 'cause if y'are, yu go bek. T'other with yu luked weird tu." He turned onto the street.

It dawned on her he was talking about the psychiatric institute Luisa mentioned. Alarmed that he might take her back to the hospital, she sat up trying to look normal and said, "Nonsense, I just had some stitches in my head, and now I want to go..."

"Okay. Vher' yu go?"

Thoughts streamed madly through her mind. Was Karl Treiger trying to kill me? How did Luisa know Fiona and me were at Rolfe's? Did Luisa kill Rolfe?

The cabby's strongly accented voice forced her to pay attention. "Hey, lai-dee! Vher'yu go or ve turn bek!"

Megan's head was throbbing beyond belief. She felt some pressure at her side, and put her hand down. Fiona's cell phone lay neatly in Megan's pocket. The last number she dialled was Ménard's. Megan flipped the phone open and pressed redial. The ringing stopped with a groggy grunt. She had a hard time keeping panic out of her voice. "Danny, I must see you now!"

His voice was instantly awake. "*Mon Dieu*! Megan! I'll come to the hospital right away!"

"No, I'm on my way to your place. But send help to the hospital." She paused trying to figure out the most logical way to proceed. "Where do you live?"

Treiger aimed his Rugar on the shadowy figure. He held off firing while the cab swung passed. Against his better judgement, he decided to help Luisa deal with the Brodie woman. He had been vigilantly waiting until unpredictably they both appeared on the lawn above the parking lot. Both were unaware that someone was following. Good for Luisa, recognizing his warning and using the cab. The man in the shadows did not have the build of either Higler or even Stoltz. He was reedy, not muscular. Treiger hoped that this person was not a wild card with a personal vendetta against the Brodie girl. Still, he couldn't risk the chance this thin man wasn't in league with Stoltz and he didn't need another detail to attend to. He decided to wound the pursuer. At least that would slow him up. Treiger started to squeeze the trigger.

"I wouldn't do that if I were you."

Treiger froze. The calculated words chilled him to the bone. He recognised the all too familiar voice of Ernst Stoltz. Because of a slight scuffling sound, he instinctively knew Stoltz had Luisa with him and was sorry she hadn't climbed in the taxi too. Her capture was going to greatly complicate things.

"I have something you lost. Your precious sister-in-law was trying to sneak over to you behind the wall. She was so easy to trap."

A gurgling sound that made Treiger turn his head. Luisa's neck was snared in one of Stoltz's wire nooses. A silenced Glock rested against her temple. Her breathing was laboured in short gasps. Blind terror was the only light in her eyes.

"What harm does it do to let her breathe easily, Ernst?" Treiger spoke evenly without a hint of fear.

"It pleases me to torture small animals, especially if they belong to traitors." Stoltz gave a sneering smile. His sharp features took on the look of a gargoyle in the dim greyness that surrounded them.

"She is of no use to you."

"Shut up!" Stoltz cut him off, "I will decide what is of use and what isn't. You are in no position to tell me anything. Now, open the car door and get in."

Treiger pressed the remote entry key causing a subtle click, and moved to open the door to the driver's seat.

"Get in the back, Treiger! I have my own chauffeur." With that, the gangly co-conspirator joined them and grabbed the keys from Treiger's hand. Treiger now recognised him as the airport driver with Higler. Stoltz turned his aquiline profile towards his accomplice and said, "Call my friend. Let him know of our unexpected catch."

The thin man took his cell phone and dialled. He spoke only briefly before looking back at Stoltz. "He wants to know where to meet you."

"Tell him to stay where he is for now. I will call him once I have more details."

The thin man conveyed the information, but instead of hanging up he asked, "Hey, let me speak with my brother."

Stoltz didn't take his eyes off Treiger, and held Luisa close, as he snapped at his subordinate. "Make it short."

The thin man looked upset, but shrugged his shoulders and said, "Give me a call back in a few minutes Bart, we're busy right now. Ya', its 226-6600."

"Hang up, you fool! And watch Treiger while I get her into the back seat." Stoltz shoved Luisa, blue in the face and barely able to stand, into the back seat. He kept his hand holding the noose, but the Glock was now pointed at Treiger.

The would-be driver shoved the cell phone in his pocket. The man made a move to grab Treiger's arm, but Stoltz intervened, "Don't touch him Hector. That could cause problems. Just see that he gets into the back seat."

Treiger obeyed, keeping his eyes on Stoltz. Luisa sat with her eyes closed. Stoltz ignored her and said smugly, "Let me introduce you to our driver, Hector Durn, who has also been assisting me in other matters. I believe your dear sister-in-law was vaguely introduced this afternoon. Hector saw her watching them, what was he? A professor? The professor's house, but wisely decided not to follow her to save his own neck, didn't you, Hector?" Stoltz laughed hollowly, motioning his head at Durn to drive.

"I wouldn't have thought he was your type, Ernst." Treiger's words were salted with sarcasm. He wanted to irritate Stoltz, but such a tactic was risky. If he precariously triggered Stoltz, Luisa could be harmed. Still, he had to find a distraction.

Stoltz seemed to second-guess him. "Nice try, Treiger but, we aren't talking about me, we are talking about Luisa here. She seems to be not only a useful sister-in-law, but also a devoted one. She must have been quite attractive at one time. I must say I was surprised when she showed up at the hospital tonight. I took a chance that the stupid woman that followed Higler up the mountain was someone of use to you and under a little duress, would reveal your whereabouts. Now, instead, I have the ultimate prize— you and…" he tugged the nylon wire around Luisa's throat making her gag, "someone who will make you talk. It is always painful to see a loved one suffer, is it not?" The wire puckered her skin so deeply that a thin wet line of red appeared.

Treiger let his gaze fall blankly on Stoltz's face. He didn't dare show Stoltz any concern for Luisa. It would only make things worse. Curse you, Luisa, for going after that crazy Brodie woman. Soft hearts can be lethal. Luisa, he feared, was going to learn that lesson the hard way and there was little he could do at the moment to stop it. First he would have to escape, and he wanted to figure out a way to do so without endangering Luisa. It would be a delicate, patient process. First, he would have to try to draw Stoltz's attention away from Luisa. Treiger used a detached tone to say, "You can try to get something out of her, but essentially, she knows nothing."

Stoltz laughed sarcastically and said, "We'll see. However, I wonder how long you will last when you see what I have planned for her? Family is always a weakness. However, I don't want her to die before we get to that point." Stoltz loosened the snare around her neck. Her breathing became more normal. He sat back resting, partially turned against the door keeping hold of the loosened piano wire, but placing the Glock back in the holster secured across his chest. He casually looped his small finger through Luisa's gold hoop earring, and ripped the stud down through her ear. Some blood spurted and she whimpered as the thick scarlet trickled from the raggedly torn lobe. Stoltz chuckled at her reaction and smiled in a way that made his lips very thin. Treiger looked at him, controlling any reaction by reminding himself that his goal was the priority. Nothing else could matter or bar his route from that end. He spoke again in a dispassionate voice, "Stoltz, was that really necessary?"

Stoltz replied haughtily, "I simply wanted to see your reaction and hers. Need I tell you, dear Treiger, how incredibly inept you have been. The only thing I can't figure out is why you, of all people, are bent on destroying the Gau. You can't possibly stop us now. Instead, you've destroyed yourself and your family. Tragic really." Stoltz then used the thumb and forefinger of his free hand to remove an errant drop of Luisa's blood from his lip and then smeared his fingers together obliterating the offending blemish.

Treiger watched the outside scenery, knowing that the driver was headed for Roxton and there was a sharp curve up ahead. Treiger bided his time and tolerated Stoltz's dramatic arrogance. He hoped Stoltz's conceit would distract his vigilance. Stoltz pressed the cigarette lighter in back of the front seat with his free hand, then deftly slipped a cigarette out of his front pocket and positioned it at the corner of his mouth. Durn was slowing the Mercedes in order to turn onto the steep part of a street close to Roxton Crescent. Treiger noticed Stoltz turn his head slightly towards the front in a subconscious move to check why they had slowed.

Treiger let his hand slide into Luisa's pocket. At Treiger's touch, she shifted in a half faint against Stoltz. Her move made Treiger realise how smart and strong she really was. She was trying to help him in her own way.

Stoltz reacted immediately to her pressure and jerked on his thin wire making Luisa gag, and her eyes opened widely. The cigarette flipped up and down as Stoltz started to speak. "I warn you, Treiger, don't make any attempt to escape if you want this dear woman to live longer than thirty seconds. This wire is sharp enough to cut across her windpipe. I see it's already made a nice start on her white skin. That can't be very comfortable for her, can it?" He shoved Luisa back to an upright position.

Treiger left his hand where it was, but said, "Stoltz, what is it you want for me to do in order to let Luisa go? Let's negotiate." Meanwhile, he let his fingers slide over the digits on the cell phone in Luisa's pocket.

Stoltz laughed loudly then stopped abruptly and said, "I will enjoy torturing her and then you."

A second later, Durn's cell phone rang and he veered slightly as he flipped open the receiver. Stoltz's reaction was volatile. "If that is your fucking brother, hang up immediately. Higler is the only…"

Treiger grabbed the cigarette lighter with his right hand and shoved it onto the fingers holding Luisa's garrotte, at the same time raising his feet over the driver's seat to whacking Durn's head so forcefully that the car jolted, swerving wildly. Stoltz's hand had swung back to hit the window, but he recovered with a lightening grab for the Glock. As the car twisted out of control, Treiger shoved sideways past Luisa, deflected the gun barrel up, and flipped the door handle. The door flew open. Stoltz lost his balance, grasping frantically for a hold. Durn slammed on the brakes, but Treiger had made his exit. With a double rolled flip, he half protected himself, but his back skidded across the pavement and he lost balance twice before finally landing on his feet several yards behind the car. He leapt over a short hedge and around the closest corner before Stoltz could follow.

Treiger took short cuts across several front yards until he reached a narrow back track leading to the mountain park, where a series of paths headed towards the mountain summit. It was easy to get lost at night unless one knew the trails intimately. Still Durn might know the area. Hurrying desperately, Treiger neared the park entry. Suddenly, headlights swung around the corner. His heart sank wondering how they could have followed him so quickly. He calmed his pace immediately when he recognized the inactive red and blue lights on the car roof.

The car rolled towards him and came to a stop at his side. The female constable put the car window down. "*Monsieur, il est trop tard pour se promener sur la montagne.*"

"*Oui, mais,*" Treiger agreed sincerely, and then described how he had fallen on his walk earlier in the evening and lost his keys, explaining in eloquent French that his stroll had taken him near to this entrance to the mountain, so he felt sure they would be there. The officer nodded and wished him a good evening, then drove off towards the dead-end part of the street, obviously planning to turn around there. As soon as Treiger reached the park, he quickened his speed, then disappeared upwards into the brush. Just as he reached a rocky ledge with a good view of the street, the Mercedes speedily turned the corner.

The headlights hit the police car, forcing it to slow up, and coast by the entrance. Stoltz wouldn't risk stopping now. The policewoman pulled her vehicle over to the curb and let it idle as if watching them. The Mercedes picked up a little speed and turned at the end of the street, then drove back past the police car and the trail entrance. Stoltz seemingly had given up the chase or, at least, Treiger hoped that was so for the moment. He watched as the police car proceeded to follow Durn, Stoltz and Luisa. At the very least, that policewoman bought Luisa some time while he figured out if there was any way to save her, if not for his own sake, then for Hans's. They had always been his connection with the humane part of his existence.

CHAPTER 19

A glimpse of herself in the rear-view mirror made 'escaped convict' flash to mind. Megan shook her head. The effort only nudged her headache back to life. She hadn't been able to explain anything to Ménard on the phone because whatever had just transpired was too bizarre for her to understand, but she would have to— eventually. Now, here she was cringing in the back of this smelly Lincoln, while the driver plotted his route to Danny Ménard's condo way down in the old port area.

They skirted under gnarled branches clawing out from the rugged mountain rockface. This side of the street carved into the steeply sloping escarpment and, on the other side, dark high-rises overshadowed old mansions in long black veils, making them disappear in a void. The taxi seemed to strain in slow speed. Megan looked out the back window. Both sides of their route seemed to close in as if being sucked into a vacuum. She squeezed her eyes shut trying to think but, unable to concentrate, her eyes again strayed out the stained window to the well-defended Cuban consulate complete with fences and cameras. That was no comfort. The driver took a sharp elbow-curve down to a narrow, winding street, finally twisting onto a wider avenue. Her eyelids drooped with anvil weight exhaustion. Just get to Ménard's.

She stared doggedly out the window at short streets with dead ends. Along here the buildings were built into the side of a long cliff with their main entrances on the street above. She saw one of these short roads had a large desolate building locked in by a heavy iron grid fence and eerie looking spotlights. The dead end extinguished into a wide flight of concrete stairs fading murkily up into darkness. Oddly, the scene made her think of Treiger near the cross on Mount Royal. Suddenly, hairs prickled on her arms.

"Rawshun Cownsowlat".

"What? Oh, that's the Russian consulate," Megan said with toneless civility, which she hoped translated into Bosnian as 'No comments please'. Guess not. The driver nodded vigorously, and started in with his foggy accent. The cutting force of fatigue made her more pointed. "I'm in a hurry." Solid silence followed as he picked up speed, swerving through a yellow light onto Rue Peel. Heading steeply down, they soared across Sherbrooke near, in fact, to the university library, where the day's craziness had started. The dull ache in her head reminded her of the whole mess. Seconds later they turned onto a flashy, but deserted shopping area on Ste. Catherine. But the minutes seemed to stretch out endlessly as the driver wound down Beaver Hall Hill to the old city. Finally they turned onto a narrow street with buildings that looked like warehouses.

Ménard, outside and waiting under a streetlight, was dressed in grey trousers and a dark blue shirt with rolled-up sleeves, showing his muscular forearms. She wondered if she had done the right thing in calling him. Fiona's caption 'damsel in distress' came to mind. Somehow this broad-shouldered policeman seemed to fit the profile of a marshmallow whenever women were involved. Still, she couldn't help feeling a swell of contentment at the sight of him.

The spurt of relief seemed to dissolve the last of her energy, making her arms and legs weigh like dead branches. She wasn't even sure she had the strength to get out of the cab. As the vehicle pulled to a stop, she sat woodenly, leaning heavily against the door. The cabby bellowed back, sounding like he was hollering through a gas mask. All she did was stare at him blankly. He rudely jabbed the metal meter with his stubby forefinger; almost spitting out his words trying to make her understand. The frustrated pitch made the amount doubly indecipherable. She turned her head and looked up into Ménard's eyes, not giving a thought to the crazy turban bandage twisting her hair into a mess.

Seeming to realise she had no money, Ménard hurriedly stuck one hand in his back pocket taking his wallet out and flipping it open. Megan let her brain soften into the neutrality of being assisted. She didn't really notice that with his other hand he reached to open her door. As the latch released, the door disappeared into thin air. She couldn't right herself and tumbled out, falling helplessly towards the pavement.

Ménard reacted quickly, dipping down to encircle her torso with one arm. The impact made him stagger backwards. She felt his hold around her waist, but her breasts were squished awkwardly against his chest and her legs flailed out of control. Struggling to recover, she slung an arm around his neck. He jostled sideways and tilted back as if he was doing the Limbo, barely managing to keep a slippery hold on her. Sliding down his belly in incremental shifts, her feet kicked loosely above the ground, dragging her T-shirt up as her body dragged down. She managed to bind her legs around his thigh, stopping the slide. Ménard had already edged a twenty halfway out of his unfolded wallet and was shifting himself forward closer to the cab. Megan moved her other hand to help, sending him reeling backwards again. He recovered quickly and tottered forward unsteadily. He was still unable to extract the money all the way without dropping either the wallet or Megan. Suddenly, she felt herself propelled upward with a great heave. His hand landed on her buttocks, fixing tightly on the muscles. Using his teeth, Ménard pulled a faded green note out and kind of spat the bill into the cab, saying in French, "Keep the change."

The cabdriver's neck craned back. His arm snapped between the seats snatching up the money before it hit the dirty floor. He mumbled a barely audible sentence. The only clear word was tip. He stepped on the gas shooting down the street. The car door slammed, giving Megan a start before the rusty Lincoln squealed around the corner.

She felt both of Ménard's arms wrap around her protectively like an injured child, gently adjusting her into a cradled position with one arm around her back and the other supporting under her knees. She laid her head on his shoulder and closed her eyes. She felt him put his head down close to her and inhale deeply as if he was taking in her scent very intimately. She thought if the circumstances were different, he might have kissed her. She wasn't certain how she felt about that, but she did like the comfortable, secure warmth in the strength of his arms. Megan knew she had something important to tell him, but her thoughts turned fuzzy and mixed-up. She managed to mumble, "So much happened...I really don't understand what's going on...but it's serious. Did you...did you send someone to the hospital?" The throbbing started again and she felt very drowsy.

"Silence," he whispered with his intensely French accent.

He was pressing her so closely to his body that she could feel the pounding of his heart and smelt a soapy freshness to his skin. Shaken by the evening's tumultuous escape and unnerved by the overwhelming warmth and tenderness of being in his arms, Megan decided to follow his command just until they were safe in his apartment. Letting the fatigue overtake her, she left her head resting on his well-built shoulder.

She woke with a start. Wondering what the time was, she looked around. Ménard was sitting in an easy chair a few feet away, dozing. He must have put her in his bed. The disarming scent of his cologne and his masculinity surrounded her like the sheets. She rolled over and, suddenly reminded of her wound, groaned and pushed the binding turban off her hair.

In a flash, Ménard's eyes opened. *"Avez-vous mal?"* he asked, leaning towards her.

"It's OK. My head feels better without the pressure of the dressing," Suddenly, reality dawned. "How long have I been here? Did I tell you about the Treigers?"

"You have slept since the moment you arrived…a very much needed sleep, I think. But it is still the middle of the night. You have only been here for an hour or so. Rest now. Whatever it is can probably wait until...."

"Danny, you don't understand. This can't wait. Luisa Treiger is in danger. Something very strange is going on. I'm at a loss. You must help,"

Ménard smiled comfortably from his chair and said, "I can see sleep is no longer an option, so, of course, tell me what it is that brings you to my doorstep in such a state. Perhaps you should start by explaining who Luisa Treiger is." He laid his head back giving her the impression his complete attention was devoted to her.

Megan put her thoughts in order before speaking. "She is a neighbour who lives across the street from Fiona Kendall and my landlady, Deirdre Ogilvy. They own the third property on Roxton Crescent. I think Luisa Treiger was the old woman looking for Dr. Rolfe just before his murder. I'm here because she came to the hospital tonight. There was a murder…a nurse...murdered because of me. She…Luisa Treiger, I mean, said I was in danger," Megan knew she was rushing her sentences, but couldn't help it. "I think her brother-in-law is crazy. He came at us with a gun."

"Megan, you're injured and confused. Are you certain that you saw another person dead?" Before she could answer, Ménard's cell phone rang. He raised his hand for her to stop. "I'm sorry. I must answer this. It will be my partner."

She wondered what the truth was. It had all seemed real. Treiger's gun. The dead nurse. Was this another long, endless nightmare?

Ménard spoke tersely in the background. *"Qui! Ou? .... Quand...*Alright Jerry, I'll be there as soon as possible." He turned his eyes on her, and in a low and serious voice began. "Apparently your story is genuine. I hoped it was a dream because of your head. *Malheureusement*, a nurse was murdered tonight. Are you able to come with me back to the hospital? I need to hear the details of your story."

Ménard sped his Volvo through empty streets while Megan filled him in with facts of her escape, trying to pace her account so as not to sound frantic. For her, the most perplexing part of the story was Luisa's startled response to the gun-wielding Karl Treiger. She was just finishing when Ménard drove into the hospital parking lot. Police cars were randomly strewn about with their blue and red lights swirling strobe-like flashes. Some uniformed officers were milling around. Once Ménard stopped his car, Megan took a moment to point out where she and Luisa had crossed the grounds and where Karl Treiger had been located. She didn't notice Ménard's partner, Jerry Bullard, leaning near the hospital entrance.

As she got out of the passenger's side, Ménard came around the front of the car as if to join her. Hearing someone walking up to them, she turned around. Bullard was standing with coffee in a Styrofoam cup. The revolving lights behind him made his bulging plaid jacket turn a sort of odd purplish-orange.

Without any preliminaries and completely ignoring her, Bullard began filling Ménard in with the particulars. "The victim's been dead about three hours. Was found by the night supervisor. Must have been discovered within an hour of the murder. The only person or patient missing is her." He used his head to gesture towards Megan before actually turning to her. His affable expression while facing Ménard changed to sardonic contempt and his eyes turned to ice. He looked back at Ménard and said, "Looks like a professional job, very clean, fast, quiet." He turned his head back to Megan and in a hard voice said, "I'm afraid we are going to have to take you in, *Mizz* Brodie."

Alarmed, her eyes shot to Ménard. "But, I didn't do it! I only saw her after she was dead. I had to leave. I was afraid for my own life!"

Ménard broke in with a calm voice, "Megan, Jerry is only suggesting that it may be necessary to question you further. My partner thinks it is unusual for someone to leave the scene of such an unusual crime."

He next looked to Bullard and said, "Jerry, I know what you're thinking, but this murder is much more complicated than you think. Megan has already told me her story."

Bullard quickly became red in the face and said angrily. "Listen friend, I think you're messing with a big conflict of interests. This is the second murder this woman's been involved in today and we all know how capable she is in that area. If you want to get into her pants, in my book that's a justifiable reason for taking you off this case. Can't you see? She's playing you for a fool!"

"Enough! Not in front of her."

Ménard grabbed Bullard by his lapels and dragged him aside. Coffee spilled on Bullard's hand, making him swear. They began a heated discussion a few feet away while Megan waited uneasily beside the Volvo. Her heart contracted with Jerry Bullard's cold appraisal of her. His narrow little mind had classified her as a murderess two years ago. That is all he could or would ever see of her. She felt a snarl of scorn erupt as she watched them go at it. Two years ago she had been released in the clear, but in Bullard's meagre mind, she would always be the half-breed who got away with murder.

Within minutes Ménard returned with a fuming Bullard, who, acting like he was being hauled by the scruff of his neck, began brusquely, "I apologise for my behaviour, Miss Brodie." He looked at Ménard who nodded sternly, and without an ounce of sincerity carried on, "Detective Ménard has filled me in on the details. We shall proceed with the investigation under his direction." He turned and marched back to the hospital.

Ménard looked apologetic. "I'm sorry Megan. He's like that when there is an unsolved case."

Please change the subject. She stared ahead. "I'm troubled about the Treigers."

Ménard looked down at her with sincere concern. "I know. Jerry has already notified dispatch to send a patrol car to their place. In a few moments we'll be finished here. I can drop you at your home because my job is to investigate this myself. *D'accord?*" He put his hand on her elbow and steered her towards the entrance.

The Mercedes coasted off Roxton into the underground garage of the Treiger residence. There was space for several cars, but only an old van stood in the corner. Durn left the door open at Stoltz's request and parked the car near the domestic elevator. Stoltz told him to bring the woman. She was trembling and very weak as Durn half-dragged, half-carried her into the small lift.

"What's next?" Durn asked as he propped Luisa against the wall.

Stoltz pushed the button to the main floor. "Well Hector, between you, me and sweet Luisa, we will find Treiger and get rid of him."

Stoltz pursed his lips, savouring the idea. For so long he had hated the confident, silent, relentless Karl Treiger. Stoltz knew that Treiger had been the last initiate to the Gau's inner circle until he and Higler made the grade. As he was growing up, Treiger had at first been his idol. He had worshipped him as a brilliant, great man, admiring his towering frame as one would admire Michelangelo's statue of David. He had even imitated his movements. As he grew older, he realised how aloof Treiger was, to the point of complete disregard; eventually, never able to break through Treiger's cold exterior, his adoration transformed into a hard, unforgiving resentment. He'd always hated that humiliating indifference. Now he knew why. Treiger was no more than a traitorous, scheming bastard. At this point, he could barely accept the fact that he had ever been immature enough to want Treiger as his mentor. Treiger's death would be slow and painful and he would enjoy every minute of it. He looked down at the grey-faced Luisa. But first, he would warm up on her. It will be like foreplay, he laughed to himself.

The elevator came to a stop, and the door opened revealing the main foyer. A Ming vase stood on a carved walnut stand just beside the elevator door, seemingly placed to set off the ceramic floor and creating an aura of luxury and wealth. Other priceless objects were artistically located along the wide hall furthering the opulent effect. Stoltz let his eyes linger over the décor before commenting to Luisa. "Your brother-in-law has exquisite, old-world taste...but then, we all know where this came from."

Durn's interruption was impatient. "What do you want done with her?"

Stoltz's eyes rested on Luisa. "Take her to the kitchen. Surely enough utensils for my needs can be obtained there. Tie her in a sturdy chair. Once you're finished, start searching the house. Do it systematically. I want the entry to those bloody catacombs found. You will have your work cut out for you so don't fuck it up. I suggest you begin in the basement. But, in your obvious haste," Stoltz added, "don't concern yourself with accidental destruction of property," While he spoke he let his arm swing out, deliberately toppling the priceless vase off it's pedestal. Shards shattered across the ceramic with one large piece arcing through the air, piercing Luisa's ankle. She cried out sharply. Blood spilled out onto her shoe and the floor.

"Remove her!" Stoltz commanded and Durn dragged Luisa down the hall leaving a trail of wet blood. He was left to survey the valuable objects lining the hallway and knew many other exclusive items were littered about the house. Stoltz strolled into the drawing room, thinking of his first visit here a few months ago.

It was an unexpected expedition, planned because of a discussion with Luthor Kleis. He had been in Brazil finalising the plans of the Gau mission when Kleis informed him that for years Treiger had regularly been taking samples from his experiments to Canada. The moment Kleis revealed what he thought was an innocuous piece of data, alarm bells started ringing in Stoltz's head. His distrust for Treiger escalated exponentially and he knew he had to check out exactly what Treiger was up to in Montreal. Unfortunately, the visit had been useless and frustrating. He'd found nothing.

Of course, at that point he hadn't been in a position of power like he was now. The brother had answered the door. His hair was grey, unlike Treiger's blonde, and the old man appeared obsequious, even nervous, but then Stoltz had heard Hans Treiger was a useless hanger-on. "Karl will be home later," the brother had informed him, standing in the doorway as if at a loss of what to do. Stoltz had just pushed by. It was then that he first laid eyes on the incredible contents of the house. He had been brought up with the best education and knew quality when he saw it. Hans rushed after him and escorted him in here, the nearest room from the hall.

When he'd asked Hans about Treiger's business affairs, subtly hinting about the Gau, all he got for a response was a baffled stare. Stoltz reflected on Treiger's apparent brilliance and wondered how he could have a brother at the other end of the intelligence spectrum. In futility, Stoltz had given up his inquiries on Treiger and asked Hans about the priceless objects, hoping that this Neanderthal might reveal some detail to substantiate his suspicions. Once started, Hans didn't seem to mind talking. "It's quite a tale. All this will probably all be inherited by you someday, Herr Stoltz. Karl, nor myself, nor my wife, have any relatives, so I suspect Karl plans for all this to go to his comrades in 'business'. That's how he refers to you, but as he seldom speaks of anyone, I can only imagine that would be in his mind. Some old friend of Volker Braun's. Ribbontrop? Yes, I believe it was Ribbontrop. Mind's going," he chuckled pointing helplessly at his head, and continued, "was responsible for all this being sent over. Similar to how Luisa and I got here."

Stoltz had almost laughed in his face. What an inconsequential fool. His lifestyle was already extremely wealthy. However, he felt a surge of power at the thought of all Treiger's possessions belonging to him no matter what. The success of the Gau operation became vital once he understood the meaning of their undertaking. He'd always treated wealth as functional because the artful use of money created expediency and efficiency. He, therefore, had not allowed riches to affect his decisions. His only vices were sexual indulgences of all sorts and the occasional cigarette. However, the effect of knowing of these special objects— symbols of the history of the Gau and the sacred principles on which the Gau organisation was founded— gave substance to something that had only been a visionary quest. The hunger to possess these fabulous assets had begun that evening. The new appetite carved out a sense of urgency and excitement, but in the end he left Treiger's house infuriated.

While waiting for Treiger to arrive, he had impatiently watched Hans jostle his head back and forth as his tedious voice rambled, "...some are priceless paintings, look at this Raphael, 'Portrait of a Young Man' and, my favourite, 'The Rape of Europa'. We have all sorts of objects even more valuable... where was I? Oh yes, that was just before, I guess, about several months before, was it? Yes, several months..."

Stoltz sat in a high-backed leather chair and faced into the room, but he still had a side view of the door. The room, with a massive bookcase along one wall, was filled with infamous paintings that had been secreted for half a century. The demented commentary was contaminating the special feeling that had emerged in him for these invaluable spoils of an old war. The idiot brother droned on. "Once Karl moved to Canada, he made sure I was educated. What year was that now? In any case...."

"You flunked out, didn't you?" Treiger's entrance had made his brother utter a fast apology for being boring and made a move to leave. Hans sort of looked down in a cowed manner as he reached the doorway, and had to hesitate while Treiger moved out of the way. The memory was so etched in his mind. Treiger had looked almost amused as his brother left, but the look became the usual, steel-eyed critique when he turned to his visitor. Stoltz had stood up, not wanting to be at an inferior level. He recalled Treiger's laughing attempt at intimidation, his voice, scathingly sarcastic. "You must have a very good reason to give me the unexpected pleasure of your company, Ernst."

He had felt like a slingshot ready to snap and shot back. "You took some of Kleis's latest product! I demand to know where it is!"

Silence. Embarrassing silence was the reply, making him feel a fool. Stoltz remembered he had been on the brink of blurting out suppositions and demands. The memory renewed the stark rage he had for the man. He felt toyed with. In fact, it was almost a joke when Treiger then commanded that he, Ernst Stoltz, search the house. He, of course, had to decline as a matter of prudence. If he was wrong, such an impudent move could cause problems with the older members of the Gau. The humiliation of the indignant refusal made him remember how much he hated Treiger. After leaving that night, he went directly to a more seedy section of Ste. Catherine Street and picked up two young whores. The pimp charged him extravagantly to take the both of them. After that, he got his money's worth by cruelly slaking his lust so that both girls had to spend a few days in hospital. It mattered little to him that he had taken out his anger for Treiger on easy prey.

He began caressing a magnificent Bruges Madonna. "Now the last laugh is mine," he mused. Somewhat like Midas, everything he touched made him feel a sense of dictatorship. The vase he'd just destroyed was a sign of his discipline and power. What he owned he could destroy if he so wished. The only fortunate luck on that first trip was hiring Durn. If not for Durn he would not have found out about the caves.

Durn's voice broke in. "She's in the kitchen when you want her."

He now felt mentally prepared to fully enjoy his work, and briskly made his way to the kitchen. He entered the spacious room with its oak cupboards rising to the ceiling, and large counters around all the walls except for the three doorways. One exited to his left leading to an elaborate dining room, and the other at the end of the room led down a set of short stairs, which he supposed went to a rear exit. Beside an oversized table in the centre of the room was Luisa Treiger. Her wrists were tied to the arms of a chair and her ankles strapped to the front legs. A gag was tied tightly around her mouth. Only her eyes revealed her distraught emotions. The expression pleased Stoltz.

He walked slowly to her and spoke softly. "Well now, dear lady. You don't look like you are going to hold up very well under torture." Stoltz pulled out a pair of latex gloves from his pocket and slipped them on as if he was a surgeon. Durn had thrown a cleaver and a few carving knives on the table. He began examining the sharpness of each blade, making sure that Luisa could fully observe what he was doing. When he began again, his voice was soothing. "Ah. I see the fear in your eyes. No…don't try to hide it. Fear can be very useful. Fear makes a person say things. But they must be the right things. If you tell me what I ask, I won't prolong the pain. The longer you hold out, the more I get into my work and then I may not feel like stopping even if you do tell me." Sometimes he looked at her and sometimes not, but his explanation was matter of fact. He proceeded to look casually in several drawers near to her, selecting a sharp-pronged fork and a vegetable peeler, laying them carefully along with the other instruments on the counter. "I think the removal of a few fingernails is a good place to start. Hmm, there usually is a pair of pliers in the kitchen, a utility drawer like this. Aha! Here they are."

He smiled harshly while clamping and unclamping the pointed pliers in front of her face. "I will have to leave your mouth gagged. I don't want a lot of loud screaming. I hope Hector made you feel secure in that chair. I think he did. To me, it looks like there is absolutely no chance for escape. However, before I carry on, is there anything you would like to tell me? Just nod or shake your head. Remember, as I just said, once I get involved with what I am doing I may forget to ask you for awhile."

Stoltz took a deep breath letting his words sink in. The approach he took was calculated. Keep centred on the goal. Increase fear to the maximal degree before beginning. Fear was an extremely useful weapon, particularly with women. He had always found the 'inciting to fear' unusually easy. In the Western culture where feminism was rampant, intimidation only made them angry. Really, he thought, all it takes is a few well-chosen words to create the right image. Indeed, imagery is the way to go, he reflected. He would have his way with this old crone whether she liked it or not. Just the thought of mutilating her helped to salve some of the burning malice he felt for Treiger. Once he caught Treiger, he would bring the stinking traitor here to show him how proficiently he had worked on his sister-in-law.

He didn't want to waste any more time. The sooner he got started, the sooner she would talk. He took the pliers with their soft rubber-covered handles and shoved them under the nail of her right forefinger and yanked. She jerked back and gave a muffled scream, but he didn't bother to even look up at her face. If he wanted her to break soon, she needed to feel a lot of pain fast. If this didn't work, he would strip her and start working on the more vulnerable parts of her body with some of the sharper instruments.

Stoltz had been operating with methodical skill for only a few minutes when the doorbell chimed. Luisa was pale and sweating. Tears streamed down her face onto her gag. A pathetic moan filtered through her guttural breathing. Blood dripped from the raw fleshy fingertips of one hand. Stoltz lit a cigarette and said, "My, you are losing a lot of blood. Should I cauterize these?" Her eyes lit up in terror as he inhaled deeply so that the cigarette tip glowed brightly.

The doorbell continued to ring incessantly. Durn quickly checked with Stoltz in the kitchen and grimaced as he looked at the ashen-faced Luisa.

"You'd better take care of it," Stoltz replied, but cautioned him further, "Remember Karl Treiger is a man to watch out for. He is ingenious enough to send someone to the door to distract us. I hoped he would try to save his dear sister-in-law, however such an obvious ruse is beneath his style. I am not worried."

Constable Legault had been on the force three years. She was young and energetic. Normally the night shift was pretty easy in Westmount. They didn't have the same problems with low-life riffraff as they did in other precincts. The crime here took place at more discrete levels. Kingpins of the drug trade had their homes high on the mountain, as if displaying how untouchable they were from the local police. Sometimes there would be a multi-million dollar fraud or scam to fleece the rich, but very rarely a gangland-type murder. The crime was more just petty mugging of careless residents who decided to jog late at night, or an elderly person living alone. The other type of target included those who decided to walk their pedigree dogs after coming home late from a gala at Place des Arts. She drove her patrol car up the streets towards Roxton Crescent. She knew exactly where the crescent was as she patrolled every street in her district. Because of the low crime rate and cutbacks, she hadn't had a partner for six months, and now patrolled alone. She stopped her car in the driveway right in front of the Treiger mansion. Because it was Upper Westmount, she did not leave the lights on her vehicle flashing. A distraught complaint from the neighbours would not be helpful for promotion. In this kind of district everything counted, so you only wanted to be noticed for the good things.

She paused for a moment to look at the house. Lights were on at the front and at the back of the main floor. Someone was awake. The dispatcher had told her to wait until backup arrived, so she decided to have a quick glance around. She followed the curved driveway to a thick stone wall, which started to descend. Around the corner of the house, she saw the open garage. Leaving a garage door open at night was dangerous, so already something was out of place. She looked inside— a Mercedes and a utility vehicle were parked in the back, but no sign of movement. She headed back up to the main entrance, hoping this wasn't just another domestic problem. In this area, such intimate problems normally required a psychiatrist, not a police officer.

For her, wealth translated into discomfort. People with so much money made her feel ill at ease, especially the nouveaux riche who flaunted their affluence as some sort of power trip. The dispatcher had told her that Ménard and his partner would join her, so she waited by her car for a moment or two pacing back and forth. She felt a bit irritated at having to wait for the men to arrive. Waiting didn't allow her to show any initiative. She leaned inside the car and picked up the microphone letting the dispatcher know she had arrived and would call back in ten minutes.

Once her call was registered, she walked up the wide stone steps and noticed how well cared for the place was. She could never hope to come close to this kind of prosperity on her salary. Even the huge door looked like several months' worth of her paycheques. She rang the bell and waited a moment. No one came. She rang again. Sometimes, if the resident was elderly, they took time to get to the door. Nothing happened, so she decided to ring more persistently. She didn't want to give any indication that she hadn't been thorough, especially as the garage door was open and lights were on in the house. As her ex-partner used to say— you never know.

After several minutes, she definitely felt uneasy. Pounding on the door just wasn't done in this type of neighbourhood. However, if some aged scrooge had croaked then she didn't want to be accused of negligence. She rang again out of frustration. At last she heard a male voice ask through the door. "Who's there?" The voice didn't sound like an old person. More to bolster her own inadequacy rather than to intimidate, she used a tough voice, calling out loudly in French, "*Police! Ouvrez!*"

The man hesitated then spoke again, "Wait until I turn off the alarm."

She waited, hoping she hadn't interrupted some rich man in a middle of a late night tryst. That could be why the garage door was open. He had probably come home drunk. On the other hand, Ménard wouldn't be called in unless there was a murder or, in this case, probably a death threat, scaring the pants off the rich buggers. Finally, the door partially opened and she was surprised to see a stubble-faced, younger man dressed in jeans and a cheap cotton shirt. He seemed familiar to her and then she thought he looked very much like the driver of the Mercedes on the mountain. She didn't like the way this situation was turning out and centred herself on scrutinizing his demeanour. He had a controlled nervousness, but was not necessarily afraid. Because of his looks, it didn't take much instinct to tell her something *mauvais* was happening here. In any case, she was glad backup was on the way and that her walkie-talkie was hooked on her belt. She again used a professionally forceful tone, "*Bonsoir. Le détective Ménard m'envoie...*"

The man bristled and interrupted tersely, "I don't speak French." He kept the door open only as wide as necessary.

"I was ordered by Detective Ménard to check on this house." Legault looked the man straight in the eye. She also noticed some dirt on his clothing, making her wonder what was really going on. Instinctively, without asking, she pushed the door further open making him stumble back a step or two. That gave her a chance to look past him into the house. Her eyes fell on broken glass and a large smear of coagulating blood on the floor.

"Please step aside, sir," she said, putting her hand up to unhitch her holster.

The cheaply dressed man reacted quickly, saying. "I'm sorry officer, but there's just been a small accident. My grandmother tripped and broke a vase— uh, accidentally cut herself, I'm afraid. Not too badly. Really. We've just taken her to the kitchen to patch it up. I'm surprised someone called you. She didn't scream or anything."

Legault didn't believe a word. She eyed him again, then said, "I should have a look. She may need medical assistance."

He sort of twitched in response. "Really, there's no need."

"Let me put it this way. You don't have a choice. Step aside." She thought perhaps she should call this in, but she wanted to keep her hands free until she entered.

Durn could see she wasn't going to give him any leeway. He shrugged his shoulders and stepped back, opening the door wider. She moved deliberately until she saw the trail of blood leading down the hall. But he really didn't like it when she raised the walkie-talkie to her mouth. More cops would be a bit too much. He grabbed her right arm and wrenched her biceps down and back so hard he felt the shoulder joint dislocate. She grunted. Her hat fell as he swung away from the door, using his foot to slam it shut. Keeping his grasp tight, he held the back of her neck and rammed her head into the wall several times until she collapsed, then gave one last whack to make sure she was out cold. Blood trickled from the top of her head.

He reopened the front door. The crescent was dead silent with only a dim light from the big house across the street. Durn felt pleased with himself as he quickly undid her belt and gun. He put the holster on along with her hat and uniform jacket. The sleeves were too short, but he didn't really care. Durn figured with his slender build, if there was the slightest chance anyone had seen her go in, then, they wouldn't be able to discriminate the difference in the dark. He shut off the outside lights, entered the police car and drove the blue and white vehicle a few streets away. He quickly hiked back to Treiger's where the officer's body still lay just as he had left it. He took the constable's wrists and dragged her through the trail of drying blood down the hall to the kitchen.

Stoltz leaned against the counter, taking some time to finish his cigarette. Luisa had lost consciousness so he stopped the torture and was just planning to sharpen some knives. His head swung up as Durn towed his victim through the kitchen door.

"Fool!" He snapped when he saw the limp body, " Why didn't you just get rid of her! She would have notified her station that she came here and that means we have to act fast. There will only be moments before others arrive. Where is the police car?" he gestured towards the unconscious officer.

Durn looked vaguely perturbed, but replied simply, "I took care of it," and waited.

"Then get out of here. Use the back door. Go to Higler. I'll join you as soon as I can. And get rid of that coat and hat." He shook his head discontentedly. Unfortunately, Luisa Treiger was now dangerous to him. He selected an appropriate knife and moved behind her. The slice across her neck was fast and complete. With the slick skill of a professional, he removed the latex gloves and shoved them along with the cigarette butt in the garburator, disintegrating the evidence. He ran to the front of the house and quickly wiped off the statue he had touched. Through a neon-curtained window, he saw the lights of other police cars swing into the driveway. He ran back to the kitchen, then heard the front door opening. It was too late to escape. Taking the portable phone from its holder on the wall, he dialled 911. He knelt beside the prostrate officer just as a command came sharply from behind. "Police! Don't move!"

Stoltz made his body stiffen and said slowly, "I only have a phone in my hand. I am police too."

"Get up very slowly and put your hands on the wall. And I want ID because at the moment things aren't looking good for you."

Stoltz did as he was told and felt a gun push into the back of his neck. Stoltz kept it calm and simple. "Certainly, but you don't look like a police officer."

"I am Detective Ménard. Where's the ID?"

This Ménard sounded tough, but Stoltz wasn't the least bit intimidated by his bravado. How he hated these weak-minded minions hired to protect society. "Left pocket." Stoltz stared ahead as Ménard pulled out the folded leather holder and once he'd glanced inside, Stoltz added, "Claus Wirt, Interpol, at your service."

A couple of others, one in uniform and one in plaid, rushed in with their guns drawn. Ménard ordered, "We need an ambulance here. Officer down."

The uniform left quickly while the plaid jacket stood staring at the blood-covered body in the chair and whistled. "Bee-ewe-tee-full! What the fuck happened here?"

Ménard tossed the ID to him. "Have at look at this, Jerry."

The man caught the case and briefly glanced at the papers inside. "Looks legit. I'll have it checked out."

Ménard pulled his gun away and said warily, "Tell me how you came to be here?"

Stoltz turned around, purposefully leaving his hands up, but retaining a casual stance. "Two days ago we had a tip that Karl Treiger, a Nazi war criminal, was in Florida. He has a few aliases – one is Ugo Lipski. We tracked him down and nearly apprehended him, but he escaped. We figured he might come to Montreal. His brother owns this house. That's Hans Treiger's wife there," he said gesturing his head towards the bloody corpse. "I arrived in Montreal this evening and staked out his house. A car came about an hour ago and drove into the garage. Later that policewoman was let into the house. A few minutes after that, someone came out and drove the police car away. I didn't like the look of things and figured I would take a chance, so I came in to check it out. The front door was unlocked. I followed the blood in here and found this mess only a minute before you came through the door. I was trying to call for help before you came in."

"You saw no one else?"

Stoltz noted that Ménard seemed to believe his reply. "I didn't see anyone, but there was noise back there." He pointed towards the rear exit. "But I was more concerned about these two." Stoltz looked back towards the officer receiving medical attention and then at the slumped form of Luisa Treiger still tied to the chair.

Ménard glanced at the other detective, "Jerry, check out the back entrance." He then continued his questioning. "Did you see who moved the car? Was it Treiger or his brother? I'll assume it wasn't the officer who was attacked."

Stoltz thought lying was risky so responded vaguely, "Tall. I didn't get a good look because he had the police cap and coat on. I hoped it was Treiger, but I'm not sure."

At that moment a stunningly natural woman walked into the kitchen. It took him a second to recognise her without her head bandaged. So this was Megan Brodie. Hector Durn had found out her name by pretending to be an orderly. Stoltz had seen her with Luisa Treiger in the hospital parking lot. Her way of walking was so silent that Ménard didn't seem to notice her entry. Stoltz noted how she put her hand up on the wall to steady herself as her eyes fell on Luisa and then on the pliers lying on the floor. One of the ragged fingernails was sticking out between its pincers. She looked towards Ménard. She obviously knew him. Stoltz knew he would have to find out how she had ended up here with Ménard. Such eventualities disturbed him. He didn't believe in coincidence.

Ménard wasn't really certain that Claus Wirt was who he said he was, but he had identification and a plausible story. All of a sudden he caught a change in Wirt's expression. A look of concern? It was a slight enough nuance that he'd almost missed it. Obviously Wirt had seen something in the room that disturbed him. Ménard turned to look where Wirt's eyes had strayed. Megan was standing near the body of Luisa Treiger. He kept his anger in check and asked Wirt, "Do you recognise her?"

The Interpol agent remained silent, but frowned slightly, as if he had been caught off guard. Catching people unexpectedly was a good way to find out the truth, so Ménard repeated toughly, "I said, do you know her?"

Wirt shifted his weight and looked a bit sheepish, "Excuse me, Detective Ménard. This is really none of my business, but it struck me as odd that a woman would be here, that is, apparently not connected to the police, unless she is, as you would say, undercover."

Ménard took a second look at Megan. He then noticed how pale, small, and out of place she seemed, gazing at death. She murmured as if in a shocked daze, "What a senseless, perverse slaughter."

"You got that right, lady!" replied a policeman. "I gotta' get started on this before the forensic examiner arrives." He held a camera up to his eye and started flashing.

Ménard stepped in front of Luisa Treiger's lifeless body, blocking Megan's view. Before he could stop himself, he said harshly, "What the hell are you doing here? I told you to wait outside.", but he immediately wished he had kept his mouth shut rather than sound so sharp with her, especially in front of Wirt.

"I had to know what happened to Luisa, but I will leave now," was all she said, but a look of surprised hurt was in her eyes.

"I'll take you as far as the door." Ménard replied. He saw her blinking back tears and was even more sorry for his loss of control. He noticed how reluctant she looked for him to accompany her, but he felt he must, after his outburst. He said to Wirt, "You'd better stay with me." He didn't want to lose sight of this man from Interpol until his story could be verified. At the moment Wirt was his most intriguing problem and his only lead.

As they were walking down the hall towards the front door, Megan turned to the two men and asked, "Did either of you touch her?"

Ménard thought the question was a bit odd, but shrugged and said, "I'm afraid that would be out of the question for me. It would disturb the evidence."

He saw Megan's eyes narrow as she looked at Wirt and said, "You did then."

Wirt tilted his head as if insulted that she should address him so directly. He looked at her piercingly before replying. "We have not been introduced, but my name is Agent Wirt. I am with Interpol. In response to your rather odd question I did touch the victim briefly. When I ran into the kitchen, instinctively I knew she was dead, but I felt compelled to check."

His answer seemed to satisfy Megan because she nodded in acceptance as if somehow this made sense. Ménard's attention turned to his thickset partner who came barging over to them from a doorway at the far end of the kitchen. Bullard took a long scathing look at Megan, but before he could say anything, Ménard raised his eyebrows in a warning look. He also observed that Bullard's hostile reaction was not lost on Megan. He almost felt the humiliation radiating from her, but still, she would have to understand that murder investigations were intense. There would be a lot of pressure on them to solve the case as quickly as possible. He would explain it to her, but now wasn't the time. She would understand, he reassured himself. He would take the time to make sure she did. Besides, he couldn't let himself be distracted by her, no matter how he felt.

Ménard focused his attention on Bullard's cut and dried rundown of the evidence. "Well, Wirt was right. Our man went out the back door, probably as we were coming in the front. Whoever it was, was quick on his feet, but stupid. Threw Legault's hat, jacket and gun into the bushes. Should get some nice prints off of those." He looked at Wirt and smiled, "Now all we have to do is check with Interpol and I guess that'll let you off the hook."

"Was it only one person or two, Jerry?" Ménard asked.

"Definitely one."

Ménard next spoke to Wirt, "And you said that possibly Treiger came out the front of the house in disguise. You didn't say he came back, so how did he get to the back of the house and why?"

Ménard noted that Wirt hesitated before he replied saying, "The lighting was not good. As I said, it could have been Treiger. The man was tall perhaps thin."

Megan absently watched the conversation feeling noticeably left out and embarrassed. She should have realised what kind of a reception she'd get. Even when she tried to enter the house, one of the policemen sternly told her to leave. Fortunately another called out, "Its O.K She's with Danny." The first officer reluctantly let her past, muttering under his breath, "She'll probably keel over."

Megan had wanted to know what happened and now she did. So horrible. Luisa had looked like a trapped animal that chewed its paw off trying to escape. Only someone else had done the mutilation. Then, when they left the kitchen, she noticed that the smell of death did not leave. For her, it was just as strong as when she was near to Luisa. Now she had to stand with that scent hanging off Wirt. He couldn't help it. At least he tried to save her. But all in all what a typically insensitive bunch of macho...Wirt's words ended her thoughts— "...tall and thin." The whole day seemed to flash before her. She blurted out, "The same man that killed the professor!"

All three men turned to look at her. She felt herself trying to shrink into a small speck. Gathering some confidence, she attempted to continue. "I mean, from what I told you, Danny, about the hospital. I mean, I thought it was Treiger who was after me. When I saw her dead, I thought it was Treiger. Now, I wonder, perhaps there's someone else. That thin man is the key. First Fiona, then the professor, now the Treigers. Karl Treiger could have been protecting Luisa. The thin man is the link."

Wirt spoke up. "Do you always allow your girlfriends help break the case?"

Before Ménard could reply Jerry Bullard lashed out, "He's right, Danny. For God's sake, she shouldn't even be here!"

Ménard looked at her coolly. "Megan, it's been a long night. There is still much work left to be done. I will have one of the officers accompany you home. Later when you've had a rest, we will talk again." He turned away and called to one of the policewomen at the scene.

Megan didn't look at anyone. She fought back the tears and wished she was dead, but held her gaze steadily in front. Above all, no eye contact. She had been dismissed. Dismissal was not new to her. She knew very well how to behave in these circumstances having learned a few lessons about her place in the world in Scotland. At least that life had prepared her for this, she figured bitterly, marching away with her escort.

Stoltz watched her leave with a sense of satisfaction. He could tell from the moment he saw her she was trouble, and automatically knew he was going to do something about the bitch. The fact that she was attractive would make it entertaining, much more so than working on that old Treiger hag. He was glad he had humiliated this pesky creature in front of Ménard. The little statement he had made was presented so as not to antagonize, but to put enough of a derogatory slant on what this nasty little insect of a woman was saying. Her words could have taken the suspicion off Treiger. However, he felt he had handled the situation adequately. Implied sarcasm was a great form of put down, he thought. He turned and smiled at Ménard. He felt confident that Higler would have given him a solid cover. Higler was so precise about everything he did. Stoltz reminded himself that he did, however, have to arrange a reckoning with Durn. To leave evidence like the policewomen's paraphernalia in the open was unacceptable.

Chapter 20

A tight little hiss slipped through Higler's lips. "*Fucken-sie.*" His cheekbones slashed white across his cheeks in dramatic contrast to his granite blue eyes. He stood absolutely still in the kitchen doorway watching Hector Durn and detesting his wait in this slimy little apartment. There was a to lot do and he wanted to get busy, yet Stoltz had been adamant that all plans be delayed until the woman on the mountain was found. But Stoltz was taking much too long. Higler inhaled impatiently, and immediately regretted it when a pungent waft of old Chinese take-out desecrated his nostrils. A guttural snore cut through the air from Durn's brother, Bart, who lay prostrate on a frayed brown couch with several Stella Artois beer cans lolling on the floor. At the airport, Bart had officiously strutted up to them in his uniform as if expecting an introduction. Stoltz had promised both men a lot of money for their involvement, but so far Higler had yet to see evidence of the brother's contribution.

Once Stoltz heard about the unexplained girl in the hospital, he decided to go after her. Perhaps a precautionary detail, but much was at stake. Now Durn had come back on his own, recounting the whole botch-up. At least he'd found out the female's name— Megan Brodie.

"I thought you'd have a backup plan," Hector Durn said smugly over his shoulder while reaching into the fridge.

Higler surmised Durn's vulgar mind had reduced him to a haughty Kraut, stewing like he had a hot pipe up his ass— the only way a lowlife like Durn could think. A contemptuous leer replaced the anger on Higler's face as he baited, "How strange that you escaped leaving my partner to deal with the police."

Durn slammed the fridge shut and twisted round with a beer in his hand, waving it like a shield and angrily spitting, "I followed orders— he t-told me to leave!"

The slight quiver in Durn's voice made Higler regard him scornfully. "Shut-up! You could end up with a very long jail term if the authorities found out about you. In any case, if your inferior quality work causes more slip-ups, you may find out I am capable of doing." Higler pointed at the dead to the world hulk on the couch, "You seem fond of your brother. Things happen when you don't do your job properly."

Durn frowned. "Fuck off with the threats. You're lucky I even agreed to help you and that's because Mr. Stoltz asked."

It was irksome that Stoltz could develop such odd relationships with offensive and pathetic inferiors, but Stoltz thought finding use for those of lesser quality was akin to 'noblesse oblige'. Higler had no such creed. He would just as soon be rid of them all. However, he understood that he was only one person and there was only so much that one person could do. Not accustomed to waiting and because Stoltz was apparently indisposed, he felt compelled to get on with their objective. He stepped back and changed the subject, "I have some important business to take care of. You will stay here and wait for Stoltz to contact me. If he calls, tell him that I am out on our arranged errand."

Almost as if Durn saw this reaction as a sign of backing down, he lashed out sarcastically. "I'd better write that down since I'm not supposed to make any mistakes."

Higler stepped so quickly forward that Durn took a step back. He blasted right in Durn's face. "Do-not-bait-me, idiot! If my partner calls, I'm certain you can manage 'hello' und 'good-bye', but you had better remember what he says." Higler gave Durn a staggering slap across the face. Fed up, Higler slung a knapsack over his shoulder and left the mangy apartment leaving Durn to open his can of beer.

He had a cab drop him two blocks away from his real destination. His target had fairly heavy electronic security, but only one security guard. He walked down the side of the spread out building to a black metal door. The alarm system was no problem; within five minutes he was inside, walking down a deserted cement hallway. Heavy pipes over a foot in diameter were strung along each side of his way. In time, he passed several open pools of water surrounded by safety railings and monitored by a computerized kiosk. Following more pipes, he came to a set of concrete stairs and descended making his way to a waist-high cylinder rising out of the floor. A spider web was stretching from the ceiling to a round Plexiglas cover. He looked into the cavern. Now he needed access.

He backtracked until he found a raised slab of concrete, inlaid with heavy metal, and hoisted up the trapdoor. A cage of rounded metal bars served as a ladder down to the swirling water. Higler rolled up his sleeves then opened his pack. Inside were small plastic packages that barely covered the palm of his hand and some clear clamps that had miniature timing devices built into their hinge. He first examined the packages to ensure that they were intact. One side looked to be a hollow empty space inside a flexible plastic capsule; the other contained water. He attached a timer onto the liquid side and set it, leaving more than enough time for them to complete their work and leave the city. He stripped away a cellophane sheath covering a gummy back, and leaned as far as possible through the bars, sticking the device to the cistern wall below water level. The packet would be very difficult to detect even if someone were to try and find it. At the indicated time, the clamp would press down on the fluid side of the parcel, forcing the water into the hollow section. Once a critical size was reached, the container would burst.

Satisfied with his effort, he retraced his steps and left the building. No one even knew he had been there. He looked at his watch. The job took a matter of twenty minutes. Good. More than enough time to hit the other six sites on the island where he intended to complete the exact same procedure.

He finished just as the sun started to rise. Before heading back to the apartment, he stopped at the Ritz hotel and ordered a large breakfast a la carte. He took his time eating, while he contemplated his next moves. His part in the original scheme was now essentially complete, leaving only Treiger.

When he arrived back at the apartment, Durn was sitting half-sprawled across the small kitchen table, asleep. Durn's brother was still on the couch. Higler looked through the half-closed door to the left of the entry. Inside, a mess of clothes surrounded an unmade bed with dirty sheets. He went in, kicking some of the dirty laundry out of the way, threw the bedspread over the mattress, and lay on top, sleeping until late afternoon, only waking up once when he heard someone stagger to the bathroom to relieve himself. At four o'clock he got up and went to the bathroom to shower and shave.

When he came out, Durn's brother was eating leftover Chinese take-out and watching T.V. Durn was still at the kitchen table. He lifted his head and yawned. As he went to stretch his arms, he knocked over a half-empty beer can. Cursing under his breath, Durn pitched the dripping tin into the sink. He looked at Higler and shrugged his shoulders in a clear statement that there had been no calls.

Higler pursed his lips. "When Stoltz has a chance, he will contact me. For the moment his cover should be good enough. No doubt Treiger is in his tunnels, believing it is the safest place for him. He will most likely stay there until we smoke him out." He thought a moment then addressed Durn directly. "You mentioned someone else besides the Brodie woman."

Durn looked puzzled and offered, "Treiger's sister-in-law?"

"No, fool! Didn't you say there were two women at that professor's house?"

Durn's expression brightened. "Ya. It was the neighbour lady. When I broke into her house the other night, she caught me."

"No kidding." Higler barely managed to keep his reply to the two words.

Durn shot back indignantly, "It was dangerous, man! In no time they were all over me. I was lucky to escape."

"For a person like you, luck is a necessary commodity."

"What?"

Higler ignored Durn and went on. "So, there must be more than one entrance to these tunnels. One of them must be across the street. If I had a topographical map, I could compare it with the architect's plans."

Durn tapped his fingers then started rummaging about the kitchen. Higler started to pace about the filthy apartment like a caged tiger. He winced as he heard another can of beer snapping open.

Durn, reacted defensively, tossing off an irritated retort. "Hey, loosen up man—you're making me nervous."

Higler glared in disgust and muttered under his breath, "How Ernst hired such a piece of human effluence I can not fathom." He walked over, snatched the beer from Durn's hand, and dashed it against the wall. "I expected Stoltz to contact us by now. But never mind, we can proceed on our own." He stared into Durn's eyes trying to hold himself back from ripping his throat out. "What can you tell me about the tunnels?"

Durn having failed at looking defiant, ended up avoiding Higler's eyes. "I dunno' much. Your pal hired me to find out information is all."

"How did you find the plans?"

"Funny thing is, it was a fluke. The next-door bitch is married to a real piece of work. I was sittin' at a bar, wondering how to find get the plans and this guy, drunk as a skunk, starts talking to me about tunnels and such. Turns out he's Treiger's neighbour." Durn sniggered as he went on with his story. "I kinda' led the guy on, saying that I heard there was buried gold that had been hid from the Indians. You know the bugger bought the story. I could tell from the way he looked. He changed his story, but it was too late by then, he'd already told me the architects had arranged for him to have a copy of some old plans. I just needed to find out who the architect was."

"It seems like it should have been straight forward to obtain them."

Again Durn shifted his eyes. This time Higler didn't hesitate. He grabbed Durn by the throat, lifted him with one hand out of the seat and slammed his body against the wall. Durn sputtered, eyes wide with fear. Higler measured his diction and forced out every word so that his saliva dripped down Durn's cheek. "Tell me what you are hiding."

"Wha...what's in it for me?" Durn barely choked out his words.

"Your life." Higler replied with sneering finality.

"I.... I found the tunnel. Or I think I did. On that guy's property. I went there on my own and dug around at the back of the stone wall surrounding their place...but I only uncovered what I thought was a possible entry...I'm not even sure."

Higler rammed Durn's head once again against the wall. "Show me, fool!" was all he said, using most of his energy to restrain himself from exterminating the quivering mass in front of him.

A grunting cry of outrage made Higler whip around and using instinctive force, thrust the base of his palm into the face of his emotional assailant. Durn's brother fell to the floor, his nose bent at a crooked angle against his face. Blood poured out, running down his cheeks and pooling on the grimy floor.

"You've killed him." Durn cried out, lunging to his brother's side, and wiping blood from his floppy head. His brother moaned.

Higler looked down with cold disdain. "If I had my way he would be dead, but for now you both have extra motivation to be trustworthy. All that is required of your brother is that he do the right thing at the right time. The money will arrive after the job has been completed. However, it is getting dark and there's work to do."

Chapter 21

Megan splashed water on her tear-stained cheeks. A few fitful hours of sleep didn't make her feel much better. She gave her face a brisk wipe with a towel. After last evening's humiliation and the horror of Luisa Treiger's death, she wondered if she would be haunted by disaster wherever she went. She walked out of the bathroom and over to a feathered Mohawk headdress. The mass of feathers cascaded in layers down from an intricately-beaded headband of turquoise, emerald green and burnt charcoal. The headpiece hung on the wall across from her bed so that she would see the colours when she awoke. Her fingers danced lightly over short, fluffy white plumes edging the headband, reminding her of Uncle Dekanewidah's musical laughter. He had bequeathed the beautiful headdress to her, but she had never been told until she had returned to Canada. Dekanewidah had died while she was in Scotland and she would never forgive her grandfather for not letting her know. There were many things she would never forgive old Duncan Brodie for. There he was again. Just like old Brodie to show up when she didn't want him to. Deirdre even knew of him.

She refocused on one of the last times she had seen Dekanewidah. He had found her hidden in the shrubbery behind his home, alone, afraid, and in tears. Gently he sat beside her, but did not tell her to stop crying. Instead he asked her why she had put herself in a cage of sorrow. Megan told him how two young braves had ridiculed her, taunting her for being half-white, not a pure person like them. One had pulled at her dark hair, while the other threatened to cut a handful off, saying that she was born not only a female, but also stupid. Dekanewidah nodded thoughtfully and asked her if what they said was the truth. She looked at him as tears began falling once more and shook her head saying, "No, uncle. They have not spoken the truth, except that I am female." He laughed first, but then became gravely serious. He said, "It is not wise to listen to those that do not speak the truth." Megan remembered asking "But what is the truth? I may be stupid." He spoke so clearly that she always remembered what he had said, "Truth is the smile in your heart, the spear in your words and the free-flying bird in your soul. When others do not speak the truth then they are the ones that are caged. You, my little feather, will always fly free if you let truth be your guide."

Megan smiled thoughtfully wishing that the truth was more obvious. Well, at least her head didn't ache. Monzie sniffed consolingly at her ankles. She slipped on her jeans and frowned in the mirror. "Well Monzie, looks like your owner has to chalk up another loser on her list of 'people who have lived here'." She scooped up his taut little body. He snuggled his warm, pulsing softness against her and panted with his tongue hanging over his fuzzy chin, then gave an expectant little bark as if to say 'what's next'.

Megan looked at him with a scrunched nose. "Let's see if there's a drop of tea left in Deirdre's pot." She hiked upstairs and ambled into the conservatory. The sliding glass door was open just a crack, allowing a waft of fresh air into the room, and sun reflected in the glass-topped table where Deirdre sat. Monzie scampered past her legs and plunked himself in Deirdre's lap, making her chuckle and put down the morning paper. A wrought-iron armchair lined with plush cushions beckoned her to sit. Megan smiled sheepishly and said, "I've come to scavenge a morning cuppa'."

"Of course you have, my dear. You must need it after last night." Deirdre sort of pursed her lips together and raised her eyebrows, giving Megan a sly sidelong glance. Nonetheless, she smoothly filled a convenient teacup that was already on the table.

"I thought you'd be surprised that I'm here," Megan said, accepting the tea.

"Nonsense. I wouldn't have missed all the excitement for the world. My! What a ruckus! This street is normally so boring. Last night was thrilling, but I'm dying to know what actually happened. I admit I was very worried, until I saw you come home. Before that I just couldn't sleep. I was so shocked to hear you had ended up in the hospital, I decided to sit up. I was…uh reading, until I heard a car come up the road. I didn't see any headlights, which was strange, but I saw Luisa Treiger come home with those two men. Later, oh, I would say maybe a half an hour, a police car drives up and this policewoman starts looking around. One of the strange men answers the door and lets her in. Then he comes out— very mysteriously— and wearing, would you believe, her coat, and drives off in the police car. Was he an undercover cop? " She paused dramatically with her eyes glittering in anticipation.

"Wow. How did you manage to see all that?" Megan was astounded, but her mind raced over the details. "Wait a second. Did I hear you say there were two men?"

Deirdre responded with an astonished tilt to her head, "Of course, my dear. I pride myself on accuracy. Gossip, you know, has to be as exact as possible, otherwise it is a complete waste of time. There was one man driving, the other was sitting in the back seat with Mrs. Treiger."

Monzie leapt down onto the floor and started barking furiously towards the patio door. Fiona's head appeared over the top ridge of the deck. When she recognised Megan, she ran the rest of the distance and shoved the door open with a spastic greeting. "Megan! For God's sake! What are you doing here?" She took a second to glance at Deirdre, "I beg your pardon, Mrs. Ogilvy, I hope you don't mind my bursting in on you, but I'm so relieved to see Megan." Deirdre barely had time to smile before Fiona continued. "I called the hospital this morning and they said you'd left. That's why I'm here. I saw the patio door was open and thought I'd check. Besides, do you know what's going on? Richard said that there were police cars and ambulances over at the Treiger's last night. He said he saw you there too. I can't imagine how I didn't wake up." Fiona abruptly stopped speaking and looked at Megan expectantly. In fact, all of them, including Monzie, fixed their eyes on her as if she was an oracle.

Megan knew she was in the presence of two loveable, but voracious scandalmongers. It was going to be tough avoiding their inquisition, but she only wanted to tell the details once, and that had to be at the police station. More importantly, she didn't want to deal with their emotional reaction to Luisa Treiger's murder. That would be tough. She tried to avoid Fiona's prying stare by saying, "Fiona, I don't really understand what is going on, but I suspect it's a long story."

Fiona came over to Megan, leaning down to hug her. "I'm just glad you're OK. I knew I should have left that handsome man to watch over you," she teased.

Megan left the comment alone and asked as innocently as she could, "Fiona, can you describe the man who attacked you the other night? I want to refresh my memory."

Fiona settled into a chair. "Well, that's a quick change of topic. Hmm. Tall, maybe six-two, extraordinarily thin, gaunt cheeks and creepy eyes that contrasted with his brown hair. The colour softened his features giving him a pathetic, child-like appearance. That's why I felt sorry for him."

Deirdre interrupted her, "Yes, I would say that at least that stature fits the man I saw coming out of the Treiger's front door. At that point he had on the officer's hat and coat and drove off in the police car. Still, I got a pretty clear look at him."

"Are you sure? It is a fair distance." Megan asked, tilting her head and looking Deirdre straight in the eyes, knowing how active her imagination was.

Deirdre picked up a pair of high-magnification binoculars snuggled between her ample hips and the chair, pronouncing, "I used these."

Megan was taken aback and Fiona's eyes rolled over to the patio window as if to see how much of her own home was visible. Fiona followed up in a perturbed voice. "Why was he after me if he really wanted the house across the street?"

Megan got up and started pacing back and forth. Monzie decided to follow at her heels, letting his little nails lightly clatter on the purple ceramic. Thinking out loud, she began, "I think that man is our link. I thought the same thing last night, but now I'm more certain. I'd like to piece this together. Richard's doing some renovations and that man was interested in your house when I saw him the other morning after my run. You were attacked after you went to the architects' office. There must be a tie in because he broke into your house that night. He must have been looking for the architect's map. Somehow he must have found out about Rolfe somehow. The plans of the two houses must be connected. That's where we have to start looking!"

"Look for what?" Fiona asked.

"I don't know. There must be something," Megan mused.

The phone rang. Deirdre answered with a cheery 'good morning', listened briefly then handed the phone to Megan, "It's for you, dear. Someone called Detective Ménard."

She slowly took the phone and replied in monosyllables, "Fine. OK. Yes. No." then hung up.

Fiona looked like she had been hanging on every word; guessing the questions: How are you? Can you come to the station? Is right now convenient? Do you need a lift? "Well?" She said arching her eyebrows.

"He needs to complete his report." Megan answered shortly.

"I'm sure he just wants to see you!" Fiona whispered excitedly.

"I really couldn't care less, Fiona, and I wish you'd stop harping on my personal affairs." Megan hated cutting her friend off, but a nasty surge of emotion made her want to cry and she was determined not to show it.

Fiona reached across the table and squeezed Megan's hand. "I'm sorry, Meggie, but I can't help myself – such a hopeless romantic am I! Do you want me to go with you?"

"No thanks. It could take hours. I'd like to drop by your place later, though, if you're going to be home."

"Are you kidding? I'll stay home. I want to stay *au courant* with this intrigue."

Not long after, Megan found herself half-heartedly dragging her feet towards Danny Ménard's office. 'I'm guilty of nothing' she chided herself. Except, of course, of being in the wrong place at the wrong time. 'Stiff upper lip' she reminded herself, then rapped on the door with an opaque glass window bearing his name.

Her heart sank when Jerry Bullard opened it. He gave her a cursory stare then said blankly, "She's here." Bullard looked passed her in a disembodied manner as if she didn't exist, and barred her way in. She felt a burning flush rising up her neck and took a long deep breath to stop it before noticing Ménard talking in the background.

Finally Bullard let her step by him into a crowded looking office painted a sickly yellow. To her left was a half-windowed wall showing people crowded around desks and talking on the phone, all looking either angry or serious. Just at that moment, someone walked by, giving her a thorough up and down frisk. She turned away from the stare. Behind Ménard's desk, filing cabinets had books and files stacked on top. Being behind on paperwork probably kept everyone on edge. The all-encompassing focus was the desk complete with a computer, ashtrays and more papers. Old cigarette smoke hung in the air.

Bullard was still hovering beside her at the door. She suspected he remained there to stop her from bolting out. Perhaps he was more perceptive than she gave him credit for because that's exactly what she felt like doing. She kept her eyes on Ménard who was just hanging up the phone. He flashed a warm smile at her and said, "I'll be just a moment," motioning for her to take a seat in a lonely chair placed near the windowed wall. He looked at Bullard and gestured for him to close the door, revealing another occupant in the room, who she had missed because of Bullard' obstructive position. Sitting in a padded armchair was the Interpol agent, Wirt.

When the door clicked shut, Megan's discomfort deepened. She remained standing, feeling like she was being slowly strangled by her mere presence in this small office with three men. Bullard she was clear on. He hated her and at this point there was no way to change the way he felt. Ménard was more dangerous. There were definite signs that he was infatuated with her, yet to explore those feelings at any level would make her more vulnerable than she now felt. Last night was a brilliant reminder of that. Then there was Wirt – he was handsome like a stunning movie star. He seemed concerned and in control, but he definitely made her uncomfortable. Beneath those good looks were suspiciously sharp edges. Even though she knew she had to temper her paranoia about men with common sense, ultimately, there was no good reason to trust any of them.

Ménard spoke briefly to Wirt, "Interpol Ottawa has confirmed your story. They received information yesterday about your business. Of course, we will co-operate as much as possible. Since our ongoing investigation and yours appear to overlap, I don't see that there will be much problem." He turned to Megan. "Please sit."

She thought he must have noticed how tense she looked because he got up, and guided her to the chair. Ménard put his hands firmly on her shoulders. The touch made her swallow hard. He gently pressed her down. She wanted to protest because he was giving her the delicate female treatment, which she hated, and after what he said to her last night, she wasn't feeling all that forgiving. She looked into his eyes, and remained silent because both Bullard and Wirt were watching them. Ménard turned to Bullard. "Jerry, how about getting us some coffee." Then as if to get things started, he began, "I don't believe there was time for formal introductions last night. Agent Wirt, may I introduce Mademoiselle Megan Brodie," he said in his usual disarming manner. "Megan, I was hoping you could shed some light on yesterday's events for us."

Megan took her eyes off of Ménard and for the first time looked directly at Wirt. "I'm not sure that I feel comfortable discussing anything with this man present."

Ménard looked somewhat surprised. "You have nothing to worry about. As I said, we are working together and I've filled him in on what happened to you."

Megan shifted uncomfortably in the chair as both men looked at her expectantly. She decided to put her cards on the table. "I have a witness that saw two men driving with Luisa Treiger last night."

"You mean Fiona Kendall?" Ménard asked.

"No, it was the owner of the house I live in, Deirdre Ogilvy. She was able to clearly see two men in the car."

"Could she identify them?"

"She knew the skinny man for certain. But, for the second man, it seems to me that Mr. Interpol is the obvious one to ask."

Stoltz remain calm, restraining any outward sign of annoyance, but he felt a tremendous urge to step on this little bug. He put on a concerned expression and looked Ménard straight in the eye. "Mademoiselle Brodie's information is extremely important. From the angle I was standing, I was pretty certain there was only one man. I can't believe I was wrong, unless Treiger was suspicious that the house could be watched. Perhaps he ducked out of sight? We must indeed get more information from this Madame Ogilvy. Perhaps Treiger was hiding in the house all along. If I lost a perfectly good chance to apprehend him..." Stoltz finished with a frustrated huff, grinding his lower jaw as if disillusioned.

Ménard looked seriously at Megan and asked, "Do you think the second man could have been Karl Treiger?"

"I didn't think so from the way Deirdre, I mean Mrs. Ogilvy, was talking. Surely she would have recognised a neighbour of so many years and she was using binoculars. Besides I can't imagine Karl Treiger killing his sister-in-law so brutally."

Stoltz decided to interject some pertinent albeit counterfeit details. "Treiger is a survivor with an exceptionally wily character. He had a very malicious past. If you read the Interpol file, you would see that in his youth the most proficient elite SS Protection Units trained him. They were interrogators of the most vicious kind. Treiger was also involved in scientific experimentation on Jews. Some of the terrible crimes he committed are difficult to repeat."

"Well, he was at the hospital pointing a gun at us," Megan mused hesitantly. "The guy who murdered the nurse could have been that skinny guy. I don't know. Last night was pretty confusing."

Stoltz smiled inwardly. He knew he had won. Doubt had peeked into the room. He pressed his advantage, speaking with passion, "We are so close. I can almost taste it. It is imperative that we put an end to this insurgent murderer."

Ménard intervened, sounding terse. "Megan, let's start with yesterday afternoon after you left Professor Rolfe's house. How did you end up on the mountain?"

"Well, I needed some time to myself, so I decided to go to my part of the house. That's when I saw the man watching Treiger's house."

"What man? You never mentioned him before." Ménard's prodding sounded irritated as if he'd been caught off guard. Stoltz perked up his ears realising that his first impression about this pretty creature was precisely accurate. She was dangerous.

"Until now I had completely forgotten about him. He was standing on the street for a while and then went up onto the mountain. He was tall, good-looking, chiselled facial features, striking blonde hair...he almost looked like you, Agent Wirt."

"I'm glad you said good-looking," Stoltz made certain he smiled, but his mind was on an entirely different track. The fucking bitch saw Higler. She had to be gotten rid of and quickly. He kept his expression intent on the woman's face, thinking of her as a moth flying around a hot flickering candle flame.

Megan continued as if reliving the incident. "I felt there was something wrong about him. He seemed out of place. When he suddenly headed for the mountain path, I followed him. I don't really know why. It was foolish I guess, but I just felt I had to go. I suppose I thought it would help me make sense of that Professor's death."

Stoltz intervened again, trying to confuse her memory. "You're certain it wasn't the same man as you saw that afternoon, the thin man?"

"Definitely not. It wasn't at all like him. More like, as I already said, you."

"It's just as well I'm on the right side of the law then," Stoltz smiled and noticed her ingenuous reaction to him.

"Oh, no. For sure it wasn't you. But someone with similar features."

"Do you think it was this man that attacked you?" Ménard continued questioning, sounding even more irritated.

"I don't know. I didn't see him. The person who got hold of me was very strong."

"Could it have been Karl Treiger?" Ménard persisted.

Stoltz watched Ménard shift aggressively as if he wanted to control the questioning himself. So weak-willed with no self-control— the man was jealous. He would manoeuvre these two petty minds just the way he wanted.

Megan carried on, looking back and forth at the two of them. "I was following the stranger, but I'd lost him by the time I was attacked. It could have been anyone. Wait! It just came to me. I heard someone scream."

Ménard jumped in seriously with a startled reaction. "You mean it wasn't you who screamed? That was how we knew what direction to take to find you."

"No, there was a strangle hold around my neck," Megan responded slowly, and unconsciously put her hand up to touch the bruises at her throat, then added quickly as if her thoughts had come together. "Someone else screamed...perhaps it was Luisa Treiger! Perhaps she saw her brother-in-law attack me and that's why she came to warn me in the hospital!"

Stoltz broke in to moderate the suppositions to his advantage, "That makes more sense to me than some stranger wandering about. The stranger could have been a lost tourist, while we know Treiger is a dangerous man."

"We can't ignore any possibilities," Ménard said sternly as Bullard came in with the coffee. "Jerry, take Megan to the police artist to try and get her description of a new suspect on file. Meanwhile, I'm going to get a warrant to search Treiger's house."

He looked back at Megan with concern. "After that you can go home. Please don't put yourself in any more danger. I'm afraid you seem to attract it. Once I get the warrant, Detective Wirt and I will stop by to see you and Mrs. Ogilvy before going to Treiger's place."

Chapter 22

Megan parked her Rover in the Ogilvy garage, thinking the next hour was planned if Fiona agreed. She threw her jean jacket in the back seat and looped her thick tresses into a ponytail, wincing as hairs pulled over the glued gash on her crown. On her way to Fiona's back entrance, she looked down over the lay of land around the coach house. The stone fence stood as a firm boundary guiding her view. Friendships like boundaries had fine lines that once crossed could easily chip away trust and tolerance. Her relationship with Fiona was a bit one-sided because she listened and advised, but deliberately avoided confiding much about herself. Fiona had always accepted her reserve; even so, every friendship had its limits.

Megan climbed the stairs, but before she even knocked, Fiona opened the door with no welcome in sight. Her eyes were red from crying and her expression more serious than Fiona's usual reaction to distress, as she cried out, "Why didn't you tell me Luisa Treiger had been murdered! It's so horrible. I really can't believe its true."

Feeling ashamed, Megan began an awkward apology. "I'm sorry I didn't tell you this morning, Fiona, but I knew you would be very upset and that I would have to go to the police station. There wouldn't have been time to explain."

Without seeming to soften, Fiona smoothed her hand over her sleek, tied-back hair, frowned at Megan and still sounded harried. "I could have been killed the other night. I thought he was just a burglar. I'm so frightened. I've been attacked, you've been wounded and now Luisa Treiger is dead. What's happening?"

Megan gave Fiona's forearm a sincere squeeze. "It is all very strange and I don't really know why, but I have my own suspicions and the police do have some leads. The situation is not hopeless. That's why I came over here. I have a hunch that this all ties in with the coach house renovations. I don't want to upset Richard, but can I have a look."

Fiona stepped back, causing Megan's hand to drop away. She looked down, slowly picked a piece of lint off her Calvin Klein jeans, and said doubtfully, "I don't understand you, Megan. When you were in the hospital, Ménard mentioned that he met you after the death of your daughter...I mean...is this some leftover guilt from her being killed? You haven't ever really opened up to me, but I know losing her must have been pretty traumatic."

"I just feel that I can do something to help. I will never be a victim again."

Fiona looked more upset and her voice quivered as if she might cry. "Megan, your not making sense. You never act like a victim and furthermore, did Danny Ménard tell you to go ahead and investigate on your own? I'll bet he didn't. No doubt he told you not to interfere and would have said that for your own good."

Perhaps not letting Fiona know more of her past was a mistake, but it was too late to start now. She bit her tongue and tried to stay on track. "All I'm asking is to check around the coach house. I think there's either a cave or something important buried back there." Megan had tried to make her voice persuasive, but her tone was pushed. She didn't want Fiona to blockade her and she was determined that this was the right thing to do.

Fiona's voice became fractious. "But Megan— think! First you're looking for our map. Now you're going to search on your own without one. Even I can see something really dangerous is happening. Quite frankly, I'm scared. Aren't you? I mean, somebody's actually tried to murder you, and here you wander in asking— let me get this straight— if you can dig up my backyard to find some tunnels to find a person who wants to kill you." Fiona's stare was incredulous as she added, "My question is— what are you going to DO if you find him? Danny Ménard isn't going to just SHOW UP every time you need a heroic rescue."

Like a trigger, Megan fired back, "I can look after myself! It's my life! Listen Fiona, if I let someone else try to solve my problems, then I become the victim. Don't you see? I would rather die trying than let that happen."

"Well, I don't want to die! Go dig all you want, but don't expect me to help. If Richard finds out, you can deal with him. I don't want to know anything about it."

Megan backed down off the stairs, hurt and frustrated. If Fiona didn't understand, that was that. Still Fiona's opposition and lack of faith in her burned deep. She regretted the words before they were out of her mouth. "Thanks. All I really wanted was to let you know what I was doing. I know you wouldn't want to get your jeans dirty."

Fiona looked out the window as Megan made her way through the back garden. Guilt washed over her. The emotional pressure lasted a full thirty seconds before she walked into the drawing room and poured herself a stiff vodka tonic.

Megan surveyed the coach house. The rope Ménard had tripped was still on the ground along with the wheel-barrel and a shovel. On the door hung a huge padlock flashing in the sun like a neon sign blinking KEEP OUT. She wiped dust from a small side window and peered in, but it was too dark to see much of anything. Asking for the key would be too humiliating, but she then remembered to look under the stone pot. The hidden key slid nicely into the padlock making entry easy.

There were no renovations to speak of except for a new sliding bolt on the inside and a really bad patch-up job on the floor, half covered by an old tarpaulin, but there were lots of tools in a huge red toolbox on wheels. Megan was reluctant to disturb even a cobweb. First of all, it looked like there was nothing important here and secondly, Richard would be livid if she touched anything and she was in enough trouble with Fiona as it was. Her interest really lay on the other side of the wall outside. Richard or someone had been digging around there and she wanted to find out why.

She went back out, tossed the shovel over the wall, and then scrambled over. The steep ravine was littered with fallen limbs and boulders, but odd-shaped scrub trees were scattered along the escarpment. She went over to the pile of dirt she had seen two evenings before. There was a hole, about two feet deep, and a dark metal bar protruded from the dugout earth. Beside the hole, parts of what looked to be the original wall could be seen. Megan clambered down into the hollow and started digging. In no time the hole was two feet deeper and chunks of clay were slipping back into the hole as she tried to cast each shovel-full out. She was now about neck deep in the hole with a pile of loose dirt surrounding the edge. Sweat was pouring off her brow and her T-shirt was sticking to her back. She stooped to have a look. There was a definite line between the original wall and the restoration above. The more recent addition, at a guess, had been done a century ago and the monks had probably built the older part a century earlier.

On closer examination, she saw the edges of some upper granite blocks had been damaged. The previous digger had been trying to pry them loose. She reached her fingers around the edges, then realised only a lever of some kind would budge the weight of the stone. Obviously the person before had tried using an implement of some type. She popped her neck out of the hole and stretched for the bar she had seen earlier. She met with some resistance, but after a good yank extracted the whole piece. The rusty metal pike turned out to be a heavy crowbar. She positioned the straight end between two of the lower stones when a powerful shiver ran down her spine. Exhausted and slightly dizzy, she sat down in a cross-legged position.

When her head cleared she was lying flat, looking up the earthen walls out at the sky. The hole was different. The walls were far away. She felt pressure against her body and pushed to the side against what seemed to be another body. The person didn't move. Then she noticed there were many people lying in the hole with her. Some were criss-crossed under her and others squashed beside her, and then she realised some were pressing down on top of her. They were heavy and the weight was stopping her from breathing. She took a few gasps to revive herself then called for them to move…to let her out. They lay still. These weren't people— they were bodies. White, naked, shaven corpses strewn in endless layers, all stiff and paralysed. Stench. The smell filled her nostrils and seeped forcefully into her head until she thought her skull would burst. Her shivering became uncontrollable and she was cold, so cold. A sudden wave of nausea made her whole body convulse in a spasm of horrendous revulsion. She was afraid. Afraid of the bodies, afraid of herself, afraid to die. She started flailing crazily, reaching through the mass of iron-like limbs, trying to push away the clay-covered, mucky cadavers that confined her. Her nails broke and her hands were bleeding before futility and hopelessness overcame her. She lay back helplessly and started to sob. Strange, disembodied voices urgently called out. She couldn't make out what they were saying. All of a sudden a few clear words came into her mind. 'You are having a vision.'

With a deep breath and with a great amount of self-control, she found herself still sitting cross-legged at the bottom of the hole. That was a vision all right. She hadn't had one for a long time. At least she knew it was a vision. People who didn't, often ended up in mental institutions. The one she'd just had was downright soul eating. When she was ten, Dekanewidah brought up visions in one of his tales about Indian spirits. He said that only the very wise or the cursed were endowed with the ability. At the time, Megan knew she was too young to be wise and in her simple child-like way, she asked him if she was cursed. Normally he answered her questions with a philosophical teaching, but this time he questioned her back, inquiring why she would ask that. She didn't answer, but asked if the visions could be stopped. Dekanewidah then looked deeply at her with his piercing, earth-brown eyes. She had turned away, unable to hold his intense gaze. She felt bad and wrong for not telling him, and dreaded that he would question her further. He remained silent for such a long time that she wanted to squirm away, but couldn't. She held her tongue. Finally she understood. He wouldn't ask. It was up to her to tell him of her own free will. But she didn't, and the regret had lasted ever since. In the end, all he said was, "They can be ignored. But whoever has the vision then loses destiny's opportunity to release a soul: one's own soul or the soul of another... perhaps many others."

Taking another gulp of air, Megan got hold of herself. She shuddered before standing up. A second later, she set to work by placing the heavy crowbar between smaller stones and heaved down using the force of her body. She grunted with effort for a minute or two before one of the stones budged. She renewed her leverage with more fervour, until the smaller of the two blocks fell out. Like a hole in a dike, the earth and masonry between other stones started to crumble. She wedged and twisted the crowbar until she could reach in about a foot and a half. Strangely, all she felt was more stone. Somewhat disappointed, she inserted the crowbar like a pike and picked up a small flat piece of stone and whacked the crowbar until the sweat running down her forehead blinded her. She felt like giving up. Frustrated and bushed, she slammed the rock against the crowbar one last time. With that, she pitched forward as the crowbar gave way. The length of it slid through the hole and only kept from disappearing by snagging the hook end. A damp draft exited the opening.

Excitement spurred her on. She wedged the crowbar behind one of the large stones and heaved with all her might. Her effort was useless because her body wasn't a strong enough lever. She scrambled out of the hole and scavenged for a sizeable branch. Once the wooden arm was lodged in place, she sat at the edge of the hole. Using her feet, legs and body, she forced the top of the branch downwards. After three good shoves, the rock literally slid inside. The hole looked large enough for her to squeeze through. Reaching in, she felt some sort of plastering. With the crowbar, she hacked the rest away with little effort, and with a tight squeeze, she extruded herself through to the other side. Just enough light came through the break revealing a cavern of fair height, perhaps ten feet. Dusk had started to fall, but it was bright enough to make out a wooden torch leaning against the wall. She felt around for matches. A small waterproof container was neatly fit into a slit in the stone. The first match failed to light, but on the second try, a flame took hold. There was now enough yellowy light to explore the area.

In the shadows was a large wooden framework from floor to roof. At the top was a platform layered with stone. Scaffolding put in place deliberately, she thought, to stop anyone from easily accessing the cave from above. Her brow puckered. Did Richard find that someone had been digging around the coach house? Is that why he is guarded in talking to Fiona about what he is doing? She put her hand on one of the wooden supports and gave the structure a shove. The scaffolding was makeshift, but secure. She was tempted to climb up and make her way through the floor into the coach house, but decided to leave Richard's property alone as a wise precaution.

When she moved to the far end of the cavity, the smoke from her torch drifted further into the dark into a narrow opening near the floor. It was about three feet high and wide enough for a fairly large man to crawl through. She crouch-walked into a tunnel made from the same type of blocks used under the coach house. The height was just high enough for her to walk without hitting her head.

After several minutes travel, the tunnel looked like it came to an abrupt end, but she heard running water and walked further. Wall shadows obscured a link to another wider tunnel that had been carved out by a fast-flowing underground river. Figuring out her bearings, she thought she couldn't be too far from Treiger's house. The water looked very powerful, flowing in a smoothly dark way. A muggy mist pervaded the air, soon damping her T-shirt and jeans. She shivered. This wasn't a river that beckoned an over-heated body in for a swim.

A left turn would probably take her towards the Treiger residence. To the right was the unknown. She peered through the darkness. Perhaps the path led to an exit on the mountain. Remembering Ménard's caution and Fiona's admonishment, Megan decided that up stream, away from the house, was a safer bet. She didn't want to meet up with Treiger alone and in his own territory. Farther along she noticed the torchlight reflect on something along the ceiling. She looked more closely to see that intermittent lights had been wired along the top of the cave. Intrigued, she moved on to a junction where the water became more forceful. The torch illuminated another branch of the river with an entering torrent that caused a whirlpool effect where the current joined this main stream beside her. There was a rope bridge crossing over. The difficult lighting didn't allow her to get a good view of the other side, but the noise of the water indicated that this stream could be dangerous. She decided to follow the cave with the overhead lights. The wiring obviously led somewhere.

The current swirled along past the river edge where she walked, and she figured the depth must be somewhere over four feet deep, about chest high on her. As she moved on, the water seemed to become somewhat deeper. The river finally disappeared underground against another sleek-sided wall. Her path came to the end, but there was a second narrow rope bridge. The flickering torch made her feel that her eyes were playing tricks on her. She leaned forward, holding the torch over the water. Almost certainly there was a door carved into the wall.

Megan almost decided to turn back, but weakened with curiosity, she set the torch down and put her hands on the rope side rails. The bridge swayed awkwardly and the wood under her moccasins was slippery, but she crossed quickly and moved up a short path to the doorframe. She took out her switchblade and, suddenly feeling like a reckless fool, she turned away just as the door swung in.

A hand grasped her upper arm and wrenched her whole body backwards. The unopened knife dropped as she swerved to twist out of the clutches of her attacker. Helplessly she was jerked bodily through the doorway. She staggered in the dark, hollering, "Let go of me!"

A hand clasped around the back of her neck. Panicking, she remembered the attack on the mountain. His grasp was amazingly powerful, and he started to force her down towards the floor. She strained desperately against the pressure, but her foe already had both her arms restrained behind her. She grunted and pushed upwards with all her might, but he used his knee to press against the back of her knee-joints making them collapse. He used the hold on her neck to guide her down so that her shins didn't slam down on the rock. Unlike on the mountain, his hand only hurt when she resisted, still she made one more attempt to rise up. He pulled her arms upwards, causing just enough pain in her shoulders to make her whimper in surrender. In less than a minute, she lay helplessly pinioned with her face turned away from her assailant. She felt like a lamb wrestled into submission before slaughter. Perhaps her vision in the ravine had been right. She had walked into her own death.

Before she could take another breath, she felt her wrists being lashed behind her back. He seemed to miraculously noose them both with one hand firmly restraining them at the base of her spine. His other hand remained firmly on her neck. She began to kick her legs. His free-moving hand slid strongly over her buttocks, pushing down firmly. She resisted by shifting her hips to the side and trying again to kick him. His hand slid to the crease of her buttock where he pressed deeply in with his thumb and she felt temporarily paralysed as if he had used curare. His movement was efficient rather than sensual or violating, but she felt unnerved by the touch.

Again his hand moved downwards. The strength of his fingers passed down over her calf down to her ankle. Using the same rope as for her wrists, he noosed the one ankle before binding both together. Only when she was completely trussed did he release his hold on her neck. She refused to lay still and persisted to squirm until she was able to roll over for a look at her captor. She squinted in the dark. She felt his hands brush close to her and reacted instinctively by thrusting her chest forward to fight him off. Her move forced his palms to slide over her breasts, but they didn't stay there. The heels of each hand carefully slipped under her arms and easily lifted her into a sitting position against the hard stonewall. The posture wasn't exactly comfortable. She had to bend her knees to her chin to make the position more tolerable. His footsteps sounded like they were moving away. She almost panicked thinking he was going to leave her, tied up in this horrid, hidden cave, to die. She called out desperately, "Don't leave me here!" Her words were swallowed up into a black void of nothingness.

Overhead lights flashed on. She had to blink several times before her eyes could focus. It was now clearly evident who really killed Luisa Treiger. Up until this point she hadn't been sure whether it was the man she had seen on the street or Treiger. Now, she was face to face with the executioner of Luisa and, for all she knew, probably his own brother as well. He stood tall and formidably beside the wooden door through which he had so forcefully yanked her in. The expression on his face was thoughtful rather than callous, but she already knew what kind of person he was from the Interpol agent. Karl Treiger was a despicable slaughterer of human beings—cruel, heartless, and essentially a coward in hiding. The fear she felt at being left alone to die switched to anger. She had no respect for him and tried to let it show with sarcasm. "Are you going to kill me too?"

He looked at her as if considering the possibility. She writhed against the cold rock trying to free herself. She remembered Luisa had been tortured and started to feel indignantly enraged. How could he have killed her like that!

Seeming to ignore her frustration, he asked evenly, "How did you find your way here?"

"Let me go and I'll show you," she sneered scornfully.

He smiled, which she thought was odd, and said, "I won't let you escape, Miss Brodie. I want you to answer some questions."

"I don't talk to murderers and that's just what you are."

"And whom am I to have murdered?"

She almost shouted the name. "Luisa Treiger!"

Treiger's face hardened before his head turned away. She heard a stifled grunt, and for the first time noticed Hans Treiger standing next to some tables of equipment. Her sidelong glance took in more than his gaunt, bloodshot eyes and cowed stature. Behind him was a table and stool with some sort of high tech computer. Beyond was a strange, closed-in glass partition with lots of equipment. Hans Treiger stepped back into a shadow as if he was ashamed. The darkened features made his eyes looked hollowed out of his skull, giving a bizarre look to his grey hair that fell messily over his forehead.

She turned her head back towards Treiger. His expression had become clouded and was now touched with a fearful determination. Treiger was a disturbing man. She hated him for being a callous tyrant and she hated being so physically constrained in his presence, so she would fight back any way she could. Words spurted out. "Are you torturing him too? Am I next? You... you sadistic bastard!"

She heard Hans Treiger start to sob and looked back with pity. He was choking out a heartbreaking mumble, "Karl didn't...he didn't...kill her." His words finished feebly as tears streamed down his cheeks.

Treiger broke into the wretchedly emotional moment, sounding almost tender, "Get back to work, Hans. There's no time for that now. I will find out as much as I can."

Treiger had turned his attention back on her. She stiffened as he leaned down and planted his hands on her shoulders. She struggled away from his grasp, but he held her firmly and shook brusquely. His face was so close to hers that she couldn't look away as he spoke. "Many people's lives depend on what you tell me. First, are you the only one that knows of this place?"

She looked at him defiantly, yet felt completely confused. What she saw of Treiger before her, here with his brother, was different than what she knew about him. She kept her lips clamped shut. She would not give answers until she knew more. In reaction to her silence, his expression changed as if he was deciding what to do next. The fingers of his hands explored her shoulder joints. A second later his thumbs dug in between the ball and socket. The deep pain made her wince and pull back sharply. Her weak attempt was no good. She couldn't free herself from his hold. She knew he would not stop the drilling pressure until she spoke. She gasped out some fast sentences, "The police are after you. They've got Interpol involved. Now everyone knows what you are. Nothing more than a petty war criminal!" The pressure released as suddenly as it had begun. Strangely, there was no residual pain and she bet that she would have no bruises. She was grateful for the relief, but surprised when Treiger burst out laughing. The startling humour was momentary. His serious demeanour returned and he said, almost as if he was in deep reflection, "A war criminal. Well, I suppose there's some truth to that."

Puzzled by the jumble of facts in her mind and hoping to manipulate him into say more, she proffered, "I don't understand."

His expression was stonily grim. "It is not for you to understand. There is too little time. Now, what entrance did you use?"

Something about the circumstances— Treiger's seriousness, his strength, his subtle care in handling her even when he intended to inflict pain, or maybe Hans's presence— she wasn't certain what exactly made her feel compelled to tell him more. He remained silent, listening intently to her story. When she finished her brief description of what had happened to her over the past two days, Treiger swore under his breath. "If a little fool like you found an entrance, so will they."

He was still squatting so close that his breath warmed her cheeks. His hands had remained on her shoulders. They felt comfortingly warm through her damp T-shirt. Almost as if he suddenly realised he was touching her, he let go, leaving the empty feel of cold air to replace his contact. He moved away in a nimble, flowing motion as if every muscle in his body were under his domination. He only had to will the movement and they would perform like well-played music. He began to pace rhythmically in thought. Seemingly ignoring her, he said out loud, "Interpol is involved. I am listed as a Nazi criminal." He contemplated momentarily, "That has to be Higler's work. He was at the airport so it makes sense. Luisa's murder, though, was Stoltz's doing."

Megan had not taken her eyes off of him. The names were strange. She missed the first one, but grasped onto the second and asked quizzically, "Stoltz?"

He looked at her and answered simply, almost as if he trusted her with the information. "Yes, Ernst Reinhard Stoltz. He is an assassin along with his colleague, Egon Higler. Both were trained by an unusual group of Nazis. They are targeting Jewish peoples for a form of genocide. It was Stoltz who tried to kill you at the hospital. I imagine that was because you, for whatever reason, interfered."

A cutting rebuke flew out of her mouth. "You must be insane. You're making this up. At the hospital, you were the one pointing a gun at us." She watched Treiger warily. His movements were not sharply disjointed like a maniac bent on torture, but more like a worried man of stealth and purpose. He was a closed person, but Hans was here, vouching for him. Neither could she disregard the blond, blue-eyed man on the street or the thin man. Were they Higler and Stoltz? It was hard to fathom that real Nazis still exist. For heaven's sake, Nazis were got rid of fifty some odd years ago. No matter what disparity existed in her thoughts, for some reason, she thought she should help him. Her words came out spontaneously, "I could speak to the police on your behalf."

Treiger left his eyes on her. There was a simple sincerity in her offer. He had to laugh at the irony of the situation, but felt an urge to explain, "This began long ago. It is not something either your police or you could understand. It is a much too complex and insidious situation for that."

She snapped back in a not unexpected manner. He was getting a feel for her temperament. "What on earth do you mean? How can anyone help if you don't let them?"

Treiger narrowed his gaze, taking a closer look at her. The rich auburn hair was so deep in colour that it was almost black and the skin of her face was young and smooth. Her voice was quick, but not harsh. There was a slight accent that he couldn't place, giving the texture of her words a charming quality. He gave a clear reply. "I do not want anyone's help."

She had such rebellious determination when in a helpless posture. What struck him most profoundly was her innocence in the face of the unknown. That aspect of her vaguely reminded him of someone, but he had no time to think who it was. His memory of the young Jewish girl from the bunker was little more than vagueness in his mind. The bunker memory itself had become a locked door from shame, but the unusually natural beauty of this Megan Brodie disturbed him. He forced himself to focus on the present and his next move. "It is dark outside and I must risk covering up that entrance. At this point I need to buy time for Hans to finish his work."

It seemed natural to speak out loud in her presence. He did not consider her a danger, but a careless risk taker. He used that appraisal to help him ignore how acutely aware he was of his captive's confusing allure, but refused to allow any feelings of protectiveness to arise. She was, after all, the reason why they were now in peril. Luisa's legacy would be that she thought this woman Brodie was worth saving. Luisa's voice echoed through his mind, 'we become what they are'. He was tempted to wish his mission were over, that all the pain, intrigue, planning and waiting were ended.

Further conversation was not necessary. The time had come for action. He needed to make certain that the breach into the tunnels was covered up. Treiger figured that he had better be prepared. He walked over to the far wall and unhooked the smaller of two knapsacks hanging on a jagged outcrop. He hung the sack on his shoulder then passed Megan and disappeared through the tunnel door.

Megan felt forlorn and cold after he left so, to reassure herself, she craned her head around the stone corner. Hans was sitting on a stool using a computer, working intensely near what looked like a makeshift laboratory. She could see a metal table with a hood behind a glass shield. She wondered if it was airtight because the stainless steel cabinet with glass windows had gloves attached to round pots in the side. The other scientific equipment surrounding his workspace looked pretty sophisticated and his table, pushed up against the glass walled area, was next to a massive generator. Hans was a strange, aloof sort, somewhat like his younger brother. Megan had run into him a few times, but her longest meeting was on the sidewalk outside his house. He was carrying a jar of honey and, upon her inquiry, he mentioned that beekeeping was his pastime. He had a small hobby farm south of Montreal near the border to the United States. She had shown interest in his honey-making process and he seemed very grateful. After that, she'd found a jar of honey left on Deirdre's doorstep. Megan judged that he had always been kind and gentle in demeanour; perhaps he would take pity on her and let her go. She spoke hesitantly, "Do you think you could loosen these ropes around my wrists? They're awfully tight."

Hans ignored her. She watched him work. There was a peculiar sort of energy about him as his fingers clicked rapidly across the keyboard. Meanwhile, the damp seemed to seek out her bones, making her feel even more miserable. She snuffed her nose and started worrying the thongs around her wrists until her shoulders ached, so she gave up. She dozed off, and when she next opened her eyes, Hans was still hunched over the lab table, working furiously. Finally his head flew up and he cried out, "They've changed the bloody design again. Luisa, I've done my best, but I need more time."

Megan cleared her throat. He turned his head towards her as if remembering she was there. Tears ran one by one down his cheeks. Suddenly his head dropped as if avoiding her eyes. She saw him try to draw on some sort of inner strength to regain control. When he was calmer, Megan mustered her courage. "Don't you think it's about time you told me what you're doing? After all, it doesn't look like you or your brother intend to set me free. Just call it my last wish."

Hans walked over to her with his wooden stool and sat. "My dear, those of us that die sooner will be among the fortunate. Luisa is now part of that blessed group." His voice faltered only slightly as he went on in a convincing tone. "Life on earth brings us suffering, uncertainty and misery. To be past all that may be best for all of us. However, I have a few moments before Karl returns." He moistened his lips. "You are so young. Do you know anything about the Second World War?"

"About as much as anyone, I guess. Some maniac called Hitler tried to become a dictator over Europe and used genocide as part of his tactics."

"That's a very terse summary. And since you want to understand and I need a break, I will expand." He took a deep breath and smoothed his hand through his grey hair. "I suppose every generation has its own epidemics. For Germans the plague was not created by an illness, but by the spreading of an exceptionally virulent form of police state. In the nineteen thirties, Adolf Hitler became an extraordinarily dangerous ruler and ruthlessly eradicated Germany of civil freedom. I often wonder how he managed to be so persuasive. Were we as a German people too weak, too fearful, or just… mesmerized?" Hans stopped and his eyes drifted absently past her before picking up where he left off.

"No matter what the reason for the followers he had, Hitler managed to imprison most of the Western world in a vicious, terrorizing war. To think that before coming to power he was simply an irritating political agitator. However, when he took over the leadership of the Socialist Party, his influence became terrifying. Under his brutal direction they came to be known as the Nazi party. He reigned absolutely for twelve frightening years, massively expanding the borders of the German Reich to unite those who he considered belonged to true Germanic heritage. By nineteen forty-two he had scourged Europe and most of the Eastern block including a large part of Russia. His campaign cost the lives of over fifty million men, women, and children."

"That's an incredible number. I didn't realize so many lives were lost."

Hans looked tragically serious. "Yes. It was terrible. Some died through battle, but many died by mass-slaughter, starvation, and extermination in concentration camps."

Megan reacted spontaneously. "Concentration camps! That's what the vision meant." Hans looked bemused. Knowing she wouldn't be able to explain a waking dream and still have him think she was sane, she explained simply, "I dreamt about a concentration camp recently."

Hans nodded, and said, "Well, such dreams are disturbing. I know because I was held in Buchenwald for over two years. I didn't really understand the war at that time. But let me continue. Hitler's power stemmed largely from the creation of his highly organized and brutal police state, giving rise to two enforcement factions: the SS and the Gestapo. The SS was the secret police force, while the Gestapo oversaw political law enforcement. Both held Germany in a reign of terror. While the German army fought Hitler's battles outside their frontiers, the SS and Gestapo surreptitiously fouled every corner of the country with their insidious cruelty. The sinister evil that underlay Hitler's plans was his vision of a master race, meaning the racially superior would rule. Optimal rulers were to be the Nordic Aryan peoples leading to, of course, world domination by Germany. Eventually all those in power would be of Aryan stock. This vision became widespread in Hitler's regime. Hitler seemed to draw racist people to him who were willing to go to any length to fulfill the Nazi doctrine.

The Nazis functioned like a well-oiled machine, putting extreme value on regulation, bureaucracy, fear and intimidation. The fundamental Nazi infrastructure was organized in districts, each named as a specific Gau, and headed by a Gauleiter, meaning district leader. The Nazis use of such Gaus was thought to be dissolved along with their heinous regime, but that is false. A secret neo-Nazi Gau still exists. For years, only we monitored this small group. But now they have shaped themselves into a real threat to humanity."

Megan sucked in a big breath. "This is all very far-fetched. I mean, so much time has passed. How could such an organisation be a threat to the world now?"

He leaned forward with a wrinkled stare. "Believe me, the threat is closer than you think. But first you need to know more. A man called Martin Bormann became indispensable to the maniacal *Führer*. His agents were directors of the Gau districts, giving him control over the entire civilian war effort. In just over one year Bormann was screening all of Hitler's activities; what the *Führer* read, whom he saw, and as well, outline instructions for any interviews Hitler had. Bormann acquired immense power and soon had most of the Reich's international administration under his control. He managed to reassure the failing dictator that his vision of the *Völkisch* or Aryan culture was still possible. Hitler became a puppet to Bormann because, as the war turned against the forces of the Reich, Hitler became fanatically desperate to see his dream continue. Bormann orchestrated a new Gau under the leadership of an elite SS member, Volker Braun. This special Gau unit was comprised of a group of committed idealists who would work towards a master race called *Lebensborn*. The war finally ended with Hitler hiding in Berlin, master of a few square yards of territory. He committed suicide, but the Gau had been seeded elsewhere. That is where our story really begins."

Megan shifted uncomfortably. "But what could this organisation possibly be doing that is so horrible. I've never heard of the Gau, but I have heard of the genocide and insanity in Rwanda or even Kosovo. Well, I suppose there are those crazy suicide bombers. I guess that's a form of the same thing."

Hans nodded solemnly, "Let me explain further. Nazi ideology relied heavily on both American and German eugenic theory to propagate anti-Semitism and their subsequent genocide practices. Even before the war had started, the Nazis tried to build on Elizabeth Nietzsche's utopian experiments in Paraguay. Her brother, a philosopher, proposed a new society led by a breed of supermen whose "will to power" would set them above the great masses of inferior humanity. Nietzsche researched this racial doctrine, trying to control heredity factors through mating in an effort to create the ideal Aryan. Bormann decided that he would spearhead a satellite Gau organisation to explore ways to continue Nietzsche's work. He described it to Hitler as the salvation of the Reich and Hitler worshipped him for it. The new Gau included two scientists, a geneticist named Buch and Kleis, a microbiologist."

"So this organisation called the Gau got involved in human experimentation?"

"That's right. They began their experiments in a bunker in Berlin until they needed to secretly dissolve and escape to South America."

"I can't believe they still exist. They must be very old!" Megan broke in, trying to comprehend what this would mean so many decades later.

"Yes. Well, some of them. They expanded. Karl became a member of their group later on when they felt they could trust him and needed to bring in younger blood."

Suspicion emerged again. She wanted to hate Karl Treiger and this was a very good reason to do so, but somehow she wanted to understand why he would do such a thing. She gave what she thought was an encouraging look and said, "Go on."

"Well, at the time, in vitro reproduction was all they had to work with. The understanding of genetics was minimal, but still they struggled on. Struggle is a bit of a misnomer. They had abundant funds, so it was research and technology that held them back. Their Bunker experiments, just like Nietzsche, resulted in genetic anomalies. You know, the kind of unwanted traits caused by inbreeding. So to circumvent time, the Gau experts put all their efforts into genetic engineering."

Megan felt she had to break in. "Your brother said this was about anti-Semitism."

"You're absolutely right. The master race breeding program was paralleled by another genetic engineering project. Buch, the Gau geneticist I mentioned earlier, also used Jewish women in the early experimentation to try to determine the genes specific for Jewish traits. They experimented on foetuses produced by the union of their prime Aryan soldiers and the Jewish women. By breeding the same females over and over and extracting the foetuses they covered generations of work in only a few years. Using Jewish foetuses like lab rats, they found a random anomaly on a genetic segment of one Y-chromosome was causing non-viable foetuses. Even when this mutant Y-chromosome was discovered, they still didn't understand the particular genes involved. That was as far as they could proceed at the time when they had to evacuate the bunker. All work on the Jewish receptacles, as the women were termed, ceased and the survivors were gassed."

"So how did they continue all this time? Did they work in a cave like you seem to be doing?" Megan glanced towards the glass section built into the side of the cavern.

"No. Not like me. They created a technologically top-notch lab in South America, where it was far easier to conceal the nature of their work. The Nazi sense of moral turpitude continued amongst the formidable Gau elders. They were willing to take risks that no ethical scientists would consider. The first two human babies Buch let live are now very powerful in the Gau. Karl mentioned them earlier, Ernst Stoltz and Egon Higler. They are here in Montreal to destroy our work and that involves killing all of us."

Something started to make sense for her. "So it was one of these Gau super-types who attacked me on the mountain and Luisa saw him do it. That's why she came to help me. You say these two are on the loose in Montreal. Are there more?"

"They are only as super as perhaps a thoroughbred race horse might be. Remember their breeder, Buch, died in the early eighties. But, he did work with foetuses much the way our scientists study Drosophilae, the common fruit fly. He was ruthless with any of his failed Aryan babies, destroying any that didn't fit the Nazi specifications. But Buch's main contribution was discovering a form of gene splicing, which brings us to the gruesome Jewish factor. He was determined to use a special DNA sequence to kill Jews. In order to obtain co-operative maternal subjects, Buch set up an international fertility clinic in Brazil."

"This is bizarre. How did you ever think you could combat this mess on your own? You must let me go. I can get the police involved."

"I have to leave those decisions to Karl. He has already said no. For my part, I have really only existed to help him and even in that I have failed."

"But he is part of this Gau organisation and so he has contributed to whatever they are doing. He is a criminal just like them and just as evil!"

"Whether an action is evil or not is dictated by those who judge the action. Karl has now commenced the destruction of the group. He may have waited too long. If that is evil, then so be it. For my part, I like to view him as a thread that, when pulled, will unravel the evil of others."

Megan could see his eyes begin to water. To help him save face she asked, "Why was your brother so special to this organisation?"

"A few moments ago I mentioned a man named Braun...Volker Braun somehow felt responsible for Karl. Sort of a father-son thing, I think. In fact, I don't really know. Karl never mentions their relationship. However, Karl did not know what exactly the Gau were doing even when he became a new member. Buch and Kleis didn't trust him. That is how the Nazi structure works. They don't necessarily let the left hand know what the right is doing. Still, as the old boys aged, they became desperate. In the early 1970's their scientific exploration took a turn to a more expedient way of creating their so-called supermen. They decided to eliminate the competition."

"What do you mean 'eliminate the competition'?"

"Find a way to perfect genocide of inferior races, starting, of course, with Jews."

Her jaw dropped. "It sounds like the whole scheme has been a failure. I mean, producing a few gladiator types that can't be reproduced. But why work on the Jewish angle? All those innocent women and babies destroyed for nothing."

"Unfortunately that is not so. This is the blackest part of all. It wasn't just women and babies. When Kleis came on board, they seemed to be feeding off each other. A macabre pair. Kleis co-opted respite homes for destitute people in Jewish communities in Europe, using a fantastic scheme testing out his virus on people no one cared about."

Megan shook her head in a confused way. "You've lost me. What virus?"

"I'm sorry. I've got ahead of myself. Their expertise in genetic engineering had advanced to the point where biological warfare was an obvious next step. They wanted to produce a microbe designed to eradicate certain types of people depending on their genetic make-up. Given the history of the Reich, they wanted to start with the Jewish population. They seem to have discovered this avenue before anyone else. I've heard that several countries are now working on similar projects. Once the Gau have done their clinical trials on a global scale, they will move on to other races. They have their standards. The group they target would have to fit into their definition of subhuman. The Gau aim at resolving the over-population problem by creating their version of survival of the fittest. So, obviously, the first target host would be the Jewish race specifically. Of course there is a possibility the virus will attack anyone with Semitic genes, which massively increases the numbers of those who will die.

"How could this man Buch have discovered such a monstrous thing?"

"Well, Buch found a specific gene sequence, which he termed JDS, meaning Jewish Determining Sequence. He was convinced that these were genes that identified Jewish hereditary traits. This is now proven to have some validity. Using genetic analysis, male members of the Jewish priestly line, known as the Cohanim, have an unusual set of genetic markers on their Y-chromosome. This priesthood is three thousand years old. By keeping their communities so strictly together with little inter-racial marriage, the Jewish peoples may have written their own death warrant. You see, the other man I mentioned, Kleis, hooked onto this. He fanatically searched for a means to attack those specific genes. He chose a virus. Some viruses can be very difficult to detect and, even though billions of dollars have been spent on research, no treatment is yet effective for viral infections except preventive vaccines. Some vaccines have been developed for certain viruses like Hepatitis B and some of the flu viruses, but I can tell you, they are difficult to invent. Currently, Kleis's virus is targeted to infect only those with JDS. Kleis had been working the virus angle for years. We thought he would never succeed, but there was always a chance. He did come up with what I thought was the final result, but recently Karl brought me another sample. This virus is slightly different. I don't know if the virus mutated or what, but my work has been devastatingly set back, given that Stoltz and Higler could release their supplies almost immediately."

"So, what is your part in all of this?"

Hans nodded and sighed. "My job was to create the antidote. You see, the first rule in biological warfare is don't create a lethal weapon until you have a vaccine or other treatment for it. Meaning of course, if the weapon got into the wrong hands, the agent could be used against you. In this case, the Gau doesn't need an antidote for their virus because the thing has been created to kill very specifically. It is virtually safe for those with the *correct* genetic map. Any non-JDS person, like the elderly, the young or chronically ill who die from the non-activated virus, to the Gau, are simply weak specimens. They don't want an antidote and I haven't..." He lost eye contact with her and his voice drifted off.

Worried he might break down again, she tried to direct him back onto the Gau scheme. "But how could they effectively distribute a lethal virus? There are Jewish people all over the world."

Hans seemed to centre himself. "First of all, a virus has to spread from some place. In the scientific world it's called a reservoir. This particular virus thrives in water, so that the plan is to infect water supplies. Once the virus enters the human body, it will easily infiltrate human cells. But the major problem will be to eradicate such a minute and strange microbe. You see, the detection of a viral epidemic means that the scientists have to find the source where the virus lives. The first mistake that they will make is thinking that the usual aerosol route transmits this flu-like virus. Those that die will at first seem to be the unfortunate casualties of an unfortunate epidemic. When they realise that it is really a pandemic, the serious nature of the problem will take hold. Now the annual threat of a flu epidemic looms even with vaccines. Nothing approximates the death toll of the 1918 flu— not a natural catastrophe nor one created by man— that includes the trench warfare of WWI, the attempted genocide in WWII, even Stalin's scourges. In such a short time span none could compare, until now.

The Gau is manipulating a new kind of worldwide plague. I fear that the massive infiltration of their JDS virus will make it too late for many Semitic people. Let's say for the sake of estimation that there are fifteen million Jews dispersed worldwide. The major conglomerations are mainly in the United States and Israel with Europe and Canada following behind in lesser numbers. A vaccine can't be developed overnight. There is no recipe book on how to do it. It takes a particular type of genius and experience to know what ingredients will make the vaccine effective. In any case a vaccine is for prevention. For those who will have already been exposed, only prayer will help. The first step in eradicating the microbe will be finding the reservoirs. Without the exact location, such an endeavour will be almost impossible. You have to understand that viral packets will be distributed in critical sites throughout the Western world and the Middle East. By the time they even start to understand the extent of the problem, the damage will be done. Who knows how many Jews or others will survive."

"But won't the water purification systems eradicate it?"

"The Gau has been perfecting various aspects of genetic engineering for years. Creating a virus that could withstand both heat and chemical destruction became a simple challenge. They just had to make changes…as has already been done with fish."

"Fish?"

"It is possible to create fish that normally swim in warm ocean currents that can tolerate northern cold currents. The same is true for viruses. Just exchange the gene code for heat tolerance taken from a fish that tolerates the colder water. In this case, the JDS virus does just exactly what the Gau shaped the little beast to do. "

Megan wasn't sure she wanted to know the answer to the next question, but had to ask. "How does this virus…kill…?"

Hans frowned before he started to speak clinically like a doctor trying to achieve an extreme level of emotional detachment. "Viruses exist essentially to replicate. Some are cytotoxic. That means they kill the cell they reproduce in. Once consumed, the virus will create flu-like symptoms in just about anyone. But in a person with the JDS sequence, the virus infiltrates the cells irreversibly. For the prototype I was studying, when it attaches to the right genetic sequence the illness progresses like a haemorrhagic fever. The closest one to it is the Junin virus that causes the Argentinean haemorrhagic fever. At the onset of the illness, a person will experience fever and body aches. They'll gradually feel worse and worse, and after four or five days they will find it hard to keep moving – like one normally feels with the flu. Most people then seek out medical assistance. However, everyone knows there is little that the medical field can offer once the virus has entered the body. So the fever continues and flushing of the face, chest and back becomes so extreme the JDS person looks like he has severe sunburn. In the next day or two they would begin to develop subtle signs of bleeding, tiny haemorrhages in the skin advancing to huge areas of bruising.

When the replicated viruses burst from the infected cell, destroying it, they move on to infect other cells. The blood pressure drops indicating that haemorrhaging has begun internally, especially in the gastrointestinal tract. They will vomit blood in copious amounts. Often there is convulsion and coma before the person actually perishes."

Hans looked absently over towards his computer as if the dormant machine contained the whole story and continued. "Once the haemorrhaging begins, the end is inevitable. Very nasty. And before whoever has to deal with this problem figures it out, most of the Jews in North America, Europe and Israel will be dead. Many people will die because again, like the AIDS virus, it will take too much time to discover the antidote or even a vaccine. As I said, logically most scientists will attempt to study this as a virus and not the genetic weapon Kleis engineered."

"The first big launch is targeted for Montreal. In a few days, there is an International Jewish conference and diplomats from across the world will be there. Apparently their latest version of the virus is in transport. It may already be here. If the Montreal project becomes a success then the Gau has arranged to contaminate all major Jewish communities. But this conference is to be their head start, which will confound the whole scientific community. I have to say, Stoltz was ingenious. The plan is well co-ordinated, his rebels are strategically placed in Israel, North America and obvious other locations worldwide. Stoltz has the plan all laid out with dates and details."

"I still don't see how they got so far with this! Your brother should have done something before this."

"A few days ago when you saw me in the car with Karl, he was on his way to put an end to the Gau, their lab and the virus. He was only partly successful. The worst and most powerful are on the loose."

"You mean this man called Stoltz?"

"Yes. And Higler. It seems Stoltz became suspicious. Karl had been bringing me small quantities of the virus to work on a genetic vaccine. The task, under these conditions, was insurmountable even though I have been attempting to do so for years. I never received the final generation of virus until recently. It's mind boggling, and I'm so familiar with the bloody thing." He pointed over to some vials on the table. "Those all contain the previous samples, which I have been able to attenuate."

"Attenuate?"

"Weaken. The process requires some intricate genetic engineering. The whole time Kleis has been working, I have been trying to figure out ways to counteract whatever they devise. Karl couldn't find out the source of their work. The task has been overwhelming. I have prayed that they would never develop such a demon virus. Only they did succeed. That's why we're in our present predicament."

"It must have been difficult to do this on your own."

"Karl is the one. I am a mere shadow. My part, I have to admit, has been very frustrating yet fascinating. You see this virus is much like a living Lego set. It disassembles itself to get rid of useless bits, then reassembles itself using the genetic component of a cell. Perhaps I could show you."

Hans loosened the ties around her ankles and helped her to a standing position. He said kindly, "I'm afraid I will have to leave your hands secured, my dear. Karl would be very annoyed if I freed you. But don't worry, he has no intention of hurting you. He just needs time to finish his work." As they walked over to the computer, Hans continued his dissertation. "Of course the virus replicates most effectively in human cells."

"You mean you tried this out on humans!"

"In a manner of speaking. Luisa and I..." His voice faltered before he forced himself to go on. "We infected ourselves with the virus. It was no danger to us. Not having the JDS sequence."

"My God! You're infected?"

"No, I'm not a carrier. However, I had to look for antibody development."

Megan was still reacting to the risk he took. "Why didn't you try it on rats or mice?"

"My dear. We don't have the facilities for all that." Hans looked at Megan without saying more.

Silence was too heavy to bear after such a story, so Megan let words fathom what was going on. "So Karl's plan was to eradicate the Gau and the virus producing lab in one fell swoop. Since it was in the Amazon, no one would have been the wiser and the world would have gone on as if they never existed. And if he had succeeded, then your antidote wouldn't have been needed."

"Well, if I had completed the work, yes, it would be needed. As I said, other countries are not far off this type of biological genocide. Work is being done to create lethal viruses specific to their own particular targets. It doesn't mean the research I've done is completely useless. If this stuff ever gets released, my results will give a head start on combating the epidemic. Unfortunately, many people will die before a vaccine is finally developed. Here, let me show you."

Megan saw how honestly Hans spoke. But believing him made her judgement of Karl Treiger completely wrong. She was not going to accept that just yet and probed further, "How can you be so sure of your brother? Someone who has lived so long with those people, they must have influenced him. How do you know he's not just using you? How can you be so certain my neck isn't on the chopping block for knowing too much?"

"If Karl had wanted you dead, you wouldn't have lasted two seconds after touching that door," Hans said with finality, but his head turned abruptly to the door.

Megan noted his edginess. Perhaps the subject was becoming emotionally unpredictable. Deciding to switch to a less volatile topic, a strange contraption with an odd green screen caught her eye. "What's that?" she asked.

"Oh, it's an electron microscope. This cave is a perfect location for it. Almost a natural Faraday cage." He must have noticed the blank look on her face because he explained further, "Electron microscopes are invaluable in studying viruses. It creates an enormous magnification, but any small vibration or electromagnetic interference can completely distort accurate results. Most scientific units are placed on thick basement floors, surrounded by layers of copper mesh forming what is called a Faraday cage. The screen itself enables me to see the actual structure of these minute viruses. I could never have proceeded as far in my investigations without this equipment. The procedures to use it though are very complex. What was that?" He ended sharply, almost harshly.

Megan leaned against the computer table and looked around briefly. "I didn't hear anything. Perhaps your brother is returning?"

"No, it wasn't Karl. I would know." He listened again then seemed to relax, "Perhaps it was nothing." He clicked his mouse a few times and a low hum started to emanate from the machine. He went to work seeming to forget her.

An unusual echo filtered into the cage, but Hans was fiddling with a disc and ignored it. Now Megan felt jittery and unnerved, almost afraid. 'Mustn't let this oddball get to me' emitted from her brain almost convincing her this was only a surreal dream.

Hans seemed to finish what he was doing, and focused on the computer screen. Clicking rapidly with the mouse control, a rotating three-dimensional picture of a virus appeared. When he spoke again, his voice had softened. "This is the nasty little creature the Gau created. It is very unique. Remember the Lego set? You see many viruses are difficult to detect because once they enter a cell, they discard the bits and pieces of themselves that they used to gain entry through the cell wall. So composition of the virus before and after entry to the cell is quite different.

The virus Kleis created is in some ways much more sophisticated. Once it enters the cell, it is able to break apart once again into several sections, and attach itself to specific genetic components of the cell, causing the systemic inflammatory reaction I described before— almost like being incinerated in a microwave oven. Horrific."

The ghastly imagery made her lean against the computer table. Hans put his hands on her waist pushing her hips against the table to steady her. She thought it was strange, but his voice brought her back to reality.

"My dear, you have to be strong to fight against evil when it exists. Evil depends on shock, fear and helplessness. No, no. You have to be strong." Hans let go of her and poured a capful of brandy from a half-empty bottle beside his keyboard. "Open your mouth, I'll pour it in. You could use it, I think."

She swallowed and coughed as the harsh, alcoholic taste burned her tongue. "It is hard to believe this is really happening," she sputtered.

"You must believe it. As I said, the Gau had planned to start the first wave in Montreal. The next move was into the United States sequentially as soon as they had a fix on how rapidly the virus could spread. After that was Israel then Europe and so on."

"Can they be stopped?"

Hans looked at her. "That is beyond my predictive capacity. I have done all I can. It is up to Karl to destroy the Gau."

She pushed for more. "I still don't understand why he didn't do it long ago."

Hans replied, "As I said before, he couldn't trace Kleis's centre of production, plus he had satellite laboratories diffused through the Brazilian Rain forest. Karl had to be sure all the virus was accounted for and where to find it. When enough of the virus was developed, those labs were shut down and all of it was sent to the central lab. Karl knew he would only have one opportunity to obliterate the operation. He hoped any serum I developed would never be necessary."

Before Hans could continue, the door burst open. A man barged in holding a long-barrelled gun in his hand. A blood soaked rag covered one eye, but she could tell it was Agent Wirt. His injury looked hideous, but didn't seem to slow him down. Concern and relief flooded her in a split second. Now she could help them all understand. Everyone would be safe. The room was filled with the energy of Wirt's entry. She smiled hesitantly at the Interpol agent.

The air seemed to still for a split second as she looked back to Hans. He seemed genuinely startled, his eyes wide, his grey hair still in a mess like a mad scientist. He even seemed afraid. She would speak. Reassure him. Only a few words just to say— 'It's all right. I know this man from Interpol. He will help us.'

Hans raised his arm, palm forward as if he imagined he could stop Wirt from advancing towards them. She saw Hans attempt to speak, his voice squeaking, "Sto..."

He didn't finish the word. Megan heard a kind of spat as his head whiplashed back, forcing his body to ram the computer table against the glass behind it. She stood in amazement as Hans slumped to the floor. Blood started to trickle through a single bullet hole in the middle of his forehead.

Megan was stunned. In disbelief she stared down at his inert body. She didn't even hear the scream that came from her own lungs. Tears started to fall from her eyes.

She looked at Wirt and crying, "My God! You've made a dreadful mistake. He could have helped us."

Megan then noticed how ugly he looked with the blood-drenched rag. She felt compelled to remain very still when he turned his remaining eye on her.

Chapter 23

Ménard guided his car onto Roxton Crescent, acutely aware that Wirt was sitting easily in the passenger seat as if he was being chauffeured. Embers of fading sunlight created angled shadows across the pavement as if pointing accusing fingers at the Treiger mansion's unorthodox murder with its obscure mismatched evidence. He glanced at Wirt who was scrutinizing the place as if he had X-ray vision. Ménard turned off the ignition in front of the Ogilvy residence. He couldn't help, but be irked by the ease with which Wirt swayed Megan, convincing her of his Interpol expertise. But, like Bullard had unceremoniously reminded him, emotional distractions could destroy a professional investigation. Still, in that few minutes, she had warmed up to this athletic agent. He didn't relish Wirt meeting up with Megan again, but business was business. He got out of the car and made sure he climbed up the thick stone steps ahead of the well-muscled Wirt. Ménard extracted his ID from the left inside pocket, briefly showing a gun and holster strapped to the side of his chest. As he raised his hand to use the massive brass knocker, the door swung open.

Deirdre Ogilvy stood before, him looking dressed for a party in a floor length black taffeta dress. The shining fabric pulled over her abdomen as if the size was too small at the waist and the bust strained with silvery safety pins holding several different straps of black lingerie. A lengthy bohemian silk scarf of mottled lavender swirls was draped across one shoulder. The filmy tissue extended around her back and ended up hooked over her arm on the other side like a narrow shawl. Her soft white hair was pinned in an elegant swirl of curls and bright red lipstick had run up along the creases of her upper lip, but her smile was radiant and welcoming. Her small poodle, half hidden by the hem of her dress, was growling lowly beside her. Ménard noticed that the dog seemed to focus on Wirt who was behind him, leaning on the stone-sided steps still watching the Treiger mansion. The little dog stood up and shoved his snout forward almost between his legs to get a better view of Wirt and gave a short, threatening yap. Ménard couldn't help feeling a little smug. Dogs either like you, or they don't.

Deirdre had a somewhat questioning expression until her eyes fell on the badge in Ménard's hand. "Oh my! You must be Detective Ménard. Megan isn't here, but I expect her soon. We usually have tea together. How thrilling! Did Megan tell you I saw the whole thing? I can't wait to tell you the story. We shall have a very interesting time." Her voice petered out in a distracted way as her head sort of bobbed up, straining over his shoulder to peer at Wirt.

Ménard moved aside because Wirt had remained innocuously silent in the background, however his striking blue eyes were now narrowed onto Deirdre Ogilvy. Oddly, his body seemed poised with tension, like a tiger ready to pounce. The posture seemed out of place, but reminded him of Bullard's lack of decorum, which never engendered co-operation. Ménard said quickly, "*Pardonnez-moi, Madame Ogilvy.* Let me introduce Agent Wirt who is helping us with this particularly difficult case." He stopped speaking momentarily then, more words following before he could stop them. "I expected Mademoiselle Brodie to be here."

"Well, that's a lot to expect from Megan," Deirdre tittered lightly and turned to lead them inside, "but she'll be home soon especially if she knows two handsome gentlemen are expected."

Deirdre grandly ushered them through the spacious foyer. Her taffeta swished in unison with her step as she led the two of them along the hallway into the drawing room. She stretched her arm out beckoning them to enter and said, "Relax in here while I arrange the tea. It's almost ready. Its good for me to do a few things for myself, don't you think?" Deirdre stopped speaking as if expecting an appropriate response.

Ménard stared blankly. These elderly English people swimming in old money always made him feel awkward. He grasped around for the proper etiquette, but twinges of worry over Megan still percolated in his mind. Finally, he just smiled because Deirdre had already continued her flight of conversation. "It's so EX-citing to have DE-tectives in the house. I don't believe that has ever happened before." As if the audience had ended, she swept her black taffeta out of the room, lavender scarf and all.

The little poodle pranced up beside Ménard and pressed his warm body against his pant leg. He put his front paws on the toe of Ménard's left shoe and turned his head back to snarl at Wirt. Having made his preferences clear, the white bundle of tiny curls turned tail and raced after Deirdre. Ménard turned around to look at Wirt. As soon as they entered the house, the Interpol agent's wary demeanour toned down to a quiet respect and he was certainly keeping a low profile. Perhaps he had been far too judgmental about the Interpol agent. But something about the expression on the man's face still left him cold.

"I do not think we will get very far on this lead. She seems to be demented." After offering this non-committal view, Wirt looked bored.

Ménard's defences reared up. He didn't want to be manipulated by Wirt's opinions especially when they were delivered with such subtle arrogance, but he knew there was value in co-operative work with another agency. Reacting from a polarized emotional basis could be dangerous. Ménard had to entertain the thought that, perhaps Bullard's terse criticism was right and his feelings were overriding his professional acumen. Ménard induced some emotional self-discipline and responded evenly, "It's difficult to say. There are many elderly eccentrics living in Westmount. That doesn't mean they're inept." The comment was tinged with an understated, but notable reprimand. Wirt's eyes almost burned into his head, but the agent said nothing. Ménard added with professional directness, "I'll just check in with Bullard. I saw a phone in the hallway." He could have used his cell phone, but he preferred not to in front of Wirt.

Ménard retraced his route to the foyer to where a red touch-tone stood on a carved stand, accompanied by a small satin-covered French Renaissance chair, looking far too fragile for him to sit in. Ménard was dialling as Deirdre came down the hall, rolling a shiny wooden tea trolley laden with china and silver. Her little poodle trailed behind. Holding the receiver to his ear, Ménard nodded a pleasant acknowledgement in her direction. She returned a generous smile before pushing the trolley through the drawing room doorway. He heard her lilting voice swing into social action. "Tea, Mr...? Oh my, I seem to have forgotten your name, but somehow you do look familiar." Ménard's mind turned to the phone as Bullard answered.

Suddenly, he heard a crash and Deirdre Ogilvy's voice was replaced with the spiking yowl of the little dog. The phone dropped to the floor as he bound down the few yards of hallway and through the entry. Blood was spurting from around Wirt's eye, but his arm was raised, ready for a powerful thrust. The dog's back was upside down with Wirt's fingers encircling his ribcage. All four legs were scrambling madly through the air writhing to get out of Wirt's grasp. The feisty mongrel snarled angrily with his head twisted back, snapping his jaws to bite Wirt again. The Interpol agent turned to Ménard, but that did not stop him from flinging the little form towards the wall. The helpless creature gave a pitiable yelp before thumping into silence near the doorframe. Deirdre Ogilvy lay in a black motionless heap beside Wirt's feet.

Wirt ignored her and without a word of explanation slipped his hand into his inside jacket pocket. Reactively Ménard did the same, grabbing for his own weapon.

Unexpectedly, instead of a gun, Wirt whipped out what looked like a set of fine wires. He snapped the bundle between his fingers. The wire mesh extended, exposing several steel ball bearings on the ends. Wirt flicked his wrist with well-practised expertise. The device launched in a fluid spin with the low frequency hum of a hornet, but electrically fast. The wires flew like a bullet.

Ménard had wrapped his fingers around his gun, but there was no time to withdraw the barrel. Instinctively, his other arm swung up. He wanted his hand in a protective position near his face, but he was too late. His palm had only reached the level of his neck before the spinning mass made contact. The thin filaments encircled his neck consecutively making a rapid whooshing sound. In less than a second the ball bearings came to an abrupt halt, melding his hand against his vocal cords. The wire edges cut through the flesh at the back of his neck. The squeezing pressure of the wire grip gagged his windpipe. The compression was so fierce that he knew he was being choked to death with the bones of his own hand. His gun slipped from his other hand and fell to the floor. He dropped to his knees and tried desperately to unlash the criss-crossed wires. Panic overcame any sense of reality. He couldn't think of how many seconds he had left as he writhed on the floor helplessly. His body screamed for air.

Stoltz had remained slightly behind Ménard when he first encountered Deirdre Ogilvy. He wanted to observe yet be slightly obscure. He was prepared to react the second the old lady showed any sign of recognition, but she hadn't in the initial few moments, so he figured he was safe. When she rolled that ridiculous tea table across the room and started to speak, he knew she had forfeited her life. His lethal blow targeted her neck. She had bent over the table, innocently presenting the most vulnerable area. Unfortunately, she was shakily lifting the hot teapot when he charged. Unpredictably she jerked at his sudden lunge and the fucking silver had seared his arm. He ended up only striking her head. Still, she toppled like a dead tree. He would have given her a second blow, but that feral mutt of hers nearly ripped his right eyelid off. He was glad that speck of vermin was now out of the way, but the blood running into his eye would slow him down considerably and speed was essential

Stoltz looked at Deirdre Ogilvy, his nearest source for a possible bandage. He grabbed the lavender scarf that lay across the black mass of fabric and deftly wrapped it around his head, putting pressure on the wound. He wiped away the worst of the sticky blood on his face, then twisted the rest of the material around his head, tucking the remaining edge at the back. Ménard was on the floor halfway across the room struggling ineffectively, blue in the face, and dying slowly in agony, which is just what the conceited French bastard deserved. He hated dealing with competitive morons.

He walked over briskly and grabbed Ménard's gun; and was just about to give his quarry a bullet through the head when a female voice calling from another part of the house stopped him. *She's back.*

Firing would make too much noise, so he left his victims to their fate and darted out of the drawing room. The detective and the old lady were tangents to his cause, but his own strength and perfection were paramount. He moved as fast as he could with the impaired vision, thirsting over the fact that he would now get his hands on Megan Brodie. She would be the prize that would make this Treiger foul-up worthwhile. He moved up the hallway in the direction of the voice, which came from the kitchen. The bandage would startle her, but that would confuse her into letting him get close. Uncertainty led to indecision, which made people more vulnerable. He strode through the doorway. Across the room, on the threshold of a sliding door, stood another woman.

For one second they both stared at each other until the woman, supporting herself on the doorframe, said, "Shello, yi-am Fiona. Whash'appened tu yu?"

Stoltz shifted his head to one side, focusing his aim with one eye. Simultaneously he raised Ménard's gun and fired. His aim was off target. The glass door beside her shattered and she jerked into an intoxicated frenzy of action. Stoltz ran across the kitchen in time to see the woman half run, half slide down the steps of the deck and slip through a gate. Stoltz sprinted after her, his feet landing on the lower deck in one leap. As he lunged to follow the drunken woman, he heard the sound of distant sirens. She was just another tangent. He had his priorities. He changed direction and ran down the side of the house. The sun had now fully set and there were enough shadows to give him cover. Within seconds, he was across the street and up the front steps of Treiger's home. He quickly jimmied the lock to the front door and slipped inside. The flashing lights of police cars strobed through the door-side windows into the dark foyer.

In his haste, Stoltz failed to notice a figure crouched in the dark. As police cars screeched onto the street, the secretive shape cautiously pulled further back into the shadows, then again settled into a completely motionless state, watching Treiger's house.

Stoltz stumbled. He would have to let his one eye adjust to the dusky visibility. Unilateral vision was a bastard to get used to, especially in the dark. The intensity of the throbbing was deep enough to make him wonder if the little bugger punctured his eyeball. He ignored the spasms from the raw nerve endings, and focused on his goal.

The pain would give him more energy; make his mind sharper. He shoved Ménard's gun in his pocket and walked down the hall. Where is the entry to your precious hiding place? He let his mind swirl in thought about what type of devious pattern Treiger's cunning and betrayal would take. Just like the specially designed fortress in Rio, Treiger would have ensured that any devices or secret exits were accessible, perhaps obvious if you knew about them, but completely concealed if you didn't know about them. He thought back to his visit here a few months before. Treiger had told him to search the house. The circumstances were different. He didn't know about the tunnels then. But given that he was looking for some sort of underground passage, the upper part of the house was not a priority. Overall, there looked to be no renovations to the inside. The house seemed to be essentially original except for the garage. He walked slowly towards the elevator. The solution seemed to slide into his mind. How obvious.

The compartment stopped smoothly at the garage level. As there were no windows in the garage, he switched on the overhead lights. Looking around he found some tools in a small storage room not far from the elevator. Sorting through them, he grabbed a crowbar and a flashlight. These two items would do the job. He headed back to the elevator, got on, and pressed the first floor button. The heavy door slid closed and the elevator proceeded to glide upwards. After a few seconds, Stoltz pressed the emergency stop and jolted to a halt. He wedged the crowbar at the opening edge of the door. The thick metal slabs resisted at first, but then unwillingly gave way. The compartment was suspended between the two floors. He jammed the crowbar across the opening and crouched out into the garage. He squatted to look at the space underneath the elevator. There was room enough for the cabin to descend another level. Treiger would have some way of bringing the elevator down there, but he didn't have time to figure out how. Using the garage floor edge to hold himself, he dropped down into the dark and switched on the flashlight. There it was, a simple wooden door, which he only needed to push open. And Treiger thought he was so ingenious.

The ceiling was fairly low and had an air vent. He was at the beginning of a granite walled tunnel that was old, but definitely man-made. The width was about four feet. The cold grey rock was dry. A thick wire was strung along the roof and a light bulb. There were probably going to be others along the path. He'd not switch that on. No need to notify Treiger ahead of time. On the floor in some fine dust were small prints, probably from a woman, probably the dead sister-in-law. There were other larger tracks in both directions. He moved on. Treiger would soon be in his grasp.

Soon the tunnel blended into a more open channel with a shallow stream. This space was higher and wider. Stoltz figured he was now under Mount Royal because the walls were natural formed with what looked to be a mixture of crystallized and igneous rock, probably volcanic. Almost immediately, the shallow tributary joined a deeper, more rugged passageway and a river. He continued following the wire. He passed an opening to another passageway, which was smaller and looked to be partially man-made with some of the same granite slabs that formed the tunnel from Treiger's place. This second passage was most likely another route leading into this labyrinth of caves. He let the beam of his flashlight play along the floor. The damp sand had been disturbed very recently. He crouched down to examine the details. Along with the other tracks, he found another set of small footprints in the same direction he was going. A small soft-soled shoe made the light indentations, again, probably female. He hoped they belonged to the luscious half-breed. He liked mixed-culture females for his kind of entertainment. Somehow they had more ingenuity and fight. His mind flitted over the ways he could toy with her body before getting rid of her. As his imagination played, he felt power and strength rise in his loins. The surge of energy spurred him to move faster. His most expedient option to finding Treiger would be following this more frequented route rather than sidetracking.

Water spray filled the air. The thick humidity made his injured eye throb. Further along there was a side gorge where a raging torrent entered in a foaming fury. The walls of the joining branch were sheer. There was a rock ledge alongside of the raging tributary with enough room for a person to walk. The ledge disappeared into darkness. More interestingly, there was a rope-sided bridge with a wooden slat base, like ones he had seen in South America for crossing chasms. The primitive crossing spanned the main river to meet up with the path he was following. His eyes surveyed the layout. The wall on the other side of the water was vertical except for the short ledge. Obviously that forceful tributary led to another exit from the tunnels. That's why the bridge was there. A very useful maze of underground rivers for Treiger to use, Stoltz mused.

A stretch later his light beam fell upon another similar bridge, and further on the river went underground. There was a door, slightly ajar with light around it. This was what he'd been looking for. He took hold of the rope rail. Just as he put his foot on the first wooden slat, some water splashed up onto his bandages. The cold spray stabbed his eye. His arm jerked up, catching the flashlight on the rope. The lightweight metal flipped out of his hand and the front glass shattered on the rocks at his feet. Worried that someone would have heard the noise above the sound of water, he charged across the bridge, concealing himself against the dark wall on the other side. Ménard's gun was now securely in his hand. He waited for a moment. There was no sign of activity, so he slowly crept near until he heard the voices from inside. He listened carefully. Two people were talking. He was certain he couldn't hear Treiger, so that meant the deep voice was his feeble-minded brother. Disappointing but, at least, he would be able to set off more destruction on Treiger's treachery. His nostrils flared as adrenaline surged through his body in anticipation of a kill. Stoltz inhaled, then lunged forward shoving the door wide open. He saw Hans Treiger across the room standing with the half-breed.

In startled recognition, the old man started to call out his name. Stoltz fired. He did not want to be identified to the Brodie woman just yet. Sinking the bullet into Hans Treiger's brain was such a little thing, but unsatisfying because the death was instantaneous. Afterwards, Stoltz wasn't surprised at Megan's reaction. He wanted to laugh when she declared he had made a mistake. For him the game had just begun. He twisted the meaning of her words around. "On the contrary, it seems to me I am in the process of rescuing you." Stoltz let the tension out of his trigger finger. Killing her would be necessary, but he wanted more and there was just enough time to play.

The coldness in his voice caught Megan off guard. Shivers crawled across her neck and shuddered down her spine. She noticed Wirt made no move to rush over and untie her hands. She looked down at Hans. Tears stung her eyes. She attempted to explain. "You don't understand. They are innocent. Karl Treiger is not a war criminal. He is trying to stop a terrible disaster from happening. There is a conspiracy concocted by post-war Nazis to destroy Semitic peoples. They're demented fanatics. Hans Treiger was just explaining to me how they were going to stop them."

"This man was obviously colluding with his brother. It amazes me that you can have such sympathy for him especially since you have been held prisoner."

His sharp expression made her stop. Something deep inside felt wrong.

"Go on." Wirt prompted.

But she'd made up her mind. If Wirt was here, Ménard must be on his way. She would wait for Ménard. She tried to delay his insistence by saying, "There's nothing more, really. He didn't have a chance to say a lot before you mur...I mean, shot him."

His smile became tight. "You are so transparent. It is obvious that you are lying. For what reason I cannot fathom because, from my perspective, I just saved your life."

"It's just that I get the feeling you are not who you say you are." Her discomfort increased as she decided he was smirking in response to what she said.

He answered obscurely, "Nobody really is, if you think about it. Now, tell me what Hans said."

"Don't you think you could untie me first?"

He started speaking slowly. "Freeing you would be imprudent of me. Detective Bullard told me how you were let off for manslaughter on a technicality, and now I find you in a cave scheming with the Nazi criminals. Such details make it difficult for me to trust you. Thus I would be unwise in setting you loose prematurely. First, to gain my confidence, you must tell me what was said."

He took a few steps towards her, but with the table to her back she had nowhere to go. Megan's intuition made her stubborn. "Well, if that's the way you feel then, take me to Detective Ménard and we can get this straightened out."

He looked like he was ready to use the gun on her just like he had on Hans Treiger. His reaction was so swift that she could almost feel his red-hot anger as he strode forward, grabbing the front of her T-shirt and slamming her back down on the table. Wrenching down, the T-shirt stripped open like tissue paper. His hand was around her throat, pinning her down. Only a small amount of pressure would crush her trachea. In disbelief, she glared at his harsh, wild features. Another nightmare had become reality. She gasped in some air to force herself to react and then tried to fight with her legs. Bending her knees towards her chest, she tried to kick out at his waist. He twisted sideways forcing himself to wedge between her feet. With some struggle he thrust himself between her legs. Her arms were pinioned underneath, crushed against the table.

"You are such a pretty little animal. Half-breeds like you really know how to fight. I've been looking forward to this." He didn't even look at her face as he spoke. His one eye lingered on her breasts and he leaned down covering his mouth over one of her nipples and sucked hard using his teeth to graze back and forth against the tender protrusion. She tried to shift her chest away and bit her tongue at the pain. Tears sprang to her eyes. His torso moved up so he could enclose his free hand over her left breast "You taste so succulent I don't know where to start." His fingers closed in a brutal crushing fist compressing the single bare bosom he had ensnared. She had to whimper, "I beg you...st...stop."

Her back-muscles released in relief as the oppressive squeeze stopped. But his fingers remained hatefully on her skin. His hand moved down across the flat of her stomach to her jeans. Tears ran down the side of her face into her hair. She gritted her teeth. Frantic thoughts shot through her mind like lightening bolts, but her body lay imprisoned by his hold. She strained her neck forwards and moved her head back and forth. He gripped her throat harder until she choked. There seemed no way to fight back. The horrific violation was repeating itself. She prayed silently to Dekanewidah, hoping for courage, then lay completely still.

"Ah. You know how to take the fun out of it. We'll see about that." He pulled away from her and stepped back. He did a short little strut as if showing himself off and said, "Soon I will explode in you with sublime satisfaction." He rubbed his hand over the bulging length of his hard groin watching her face. She could tell he loved the anticipation. The main thing was he had released his hold on her. Now she could think. When she continued to lie unmoving, he snarled, "Get up."

She pulled herself up off the table, watching him warily. The bloody covering over his eye made him look grotesque. His one-eyed focus was intent on her body, yet the eye returned momentarily to her face as if he was making a critical judgement. Somehow she knew he was looking for a flicker of fear. Her mind raced for options, a route for survival. One thing was certain. The bastard thrived on victimisation. If submission was what he wanted, then that was what he would get. She let her shoulders shrug back helplessly, leaving her breasts exposed. "Please don't hurt me any more," her voice quivered.

He laughed as if well entertained. "You don't know the meaning of the word hurt. My only problem is I won't have the time to make it last as long as I had hoped. " His arm lashed out to swat her across the face.

She had been expecting some sort of move to inflict pain. Giving wrong cues worked the last time. In her position, faking the role of victim wasn't difficult. When his hand whipped out at her, she ducked. He missed. She forcefully rammed her crown into his solar plexus. A zap of momentary success suffused her as Wirt bent over with the air knocked out of him.

The door to the cave was still open. That was her escape route. Handicapped with her hands bound behind her, she dashed for the exit and leapt through the doorway just as a splinter of wood from a ricochet bullet struck the side of her face. She lost her balance and fell heavily to the ground. He was on her in a flash. His vice-like hand wrenched her shoulder forcing her on her back. Her hands crushed against something. Her knife. She wrapped her fingers around it, but that was all she could do.

He slapped hard across her face. His distorted features glared down at her. "Scream as much as you want, bitch. Hopefully your cries will bring Treiger to us." He laughed, " I'm really going to enjoy splitting your tail, and then I'm going to kill you." He laid his gun beside her head. There was nothing she could do. She was frantic. Then she thought if Treiger was still in the caves somewhere, noise was her only hope. She started to scream.

He slapped her so hard that warm blood seeped into her mouth. "I could easily strangle you. On the other hand, I like a moving target. Death would make you far too co-operative." His voice was calm.

Megan spat in his distorted face and resumed screaming as shrilly as she could. He struck her chest with one fist. She thought another blow would crack her sternum. She let out a moan and then became silent.

"That's better. I may only have one eye at the moment, but you make it difficult to have ears." He grabbed the end of her belt and tore the leather band back mercilessly, making her feel like she was being sliced in two. The constriction forced the air out of her. "You sick bastard," she gasped.

"Save your breath, you delicious little squaw. Today you're on the menu and I deserve this reward." He busied himself pulling her pants down to her hips.

She looked around frantically for something. She felt panic rise and knew her only hope was self-control. As her head turned, a dark movement caught her eye. She wasn't sure what it was, but instinct told her someone was there. Perhaps it was Treiger. She didn't care. She only hoped it was some sort of help. To buy time she would have to distract him.

"I don't think you are an Interpol agent at all. I think you are a man Treiger called Stoltz."

He didn't even look at her. "It took you long enough to figure that out."

She engaged his single eyed vision. Making an additional effort to sound in control, she said, "Well, I like to know who's raping me. You know I could make this more interesting for you if my hands were untied. You said you wanted a moving target."

"Don't worry, I've planned the way to make you move."

"What an ingenious plan you have, handsome."

Stoltz sneered down at her, "I'm going to strangle you at the same time." He reached up and encircled her throat with his right hand. A surreal kind of numbness invaded her leaving no room for fear. Her mind clung to the wisp of movement she had just seen. If what she saw was only an illusion, then there was no hope.

Chapter 24

Treiger finished slapping his clay sealant over the hole Megan had made in the old stone wall. The patching looked solid, but the repair wasn't adequate and he knew it. However, the sun had set and that would likely mask his work on the outside. Some sweat dripped along his cheek as he shoved a final stone in place. The repair had taken more time than he had anticipated, even though the actual exterior opening had been quite narrow. Using the light of propped up Maglite, he washed his hands with bottled water from his knapsack and wondered how the Brodie woman managed to squeeze through.

As a monthly routine, Treiger checked the tunnels, but he had always judged this area beneath the coach house to be the most vulnerable. Days ago, Kendall unwittingly broke through the floor, exposing the irregular cavern. As far as Treiger knew, Kendall had not climbed down, probably fearing that the floor would collapse. Upon discovering Kendall's chance infiltration, the thought of blasting this tunnel closed crossed his mind, but he decided to use scaffolding to stop Kendall from going further. An explosion might bring attention to the area or, worse, expose the monks' tunnel to the river. He'd only needed a few more days before the Gau's objectives would be in ruins and the caves wouldn't matter. At the start, Treiger considered Kendall's interference an unimportant fly in the ointment. He had obviously underestimated the trouble, because the meddling dermatologist had begun searching for the old plans. Then unforeseen problems had started falling over like dominoes.

At this point, his decision against an explosion still held, even though the knapsack contained hi-tech explosives with timed detonators. He would have to gamble that no one would find this way to the lab. Just to be certain his job would hold, Treiger took a few extra boards from the scaffolding and wedged them behind his makeshift patching then stood up to leave. He had just set his knapsack by the crawlspace exit when some thuds rumbled from the other side of his repair. The movement sounded human. He shut off his flashlight and shoved it into his pocket. Crouching to the wall, Treiger laid his ear close to the replaced stones and heard a distinctly stiff German accent. It was unmistakable. Higler was on the other side of the wall. Treiger listened intently.

"Well, I see someone has recently preceded you. By the looks of the soil, this hole has been freshly dug." The paced words were modulated with an occasional hi-pitched ring conveying a distinctly dangerous condescension towards his companion.

"The husband must have done this. He's the only other one trying to find the tunnels." It was Durn, the lackey with Stoltz at the hospital. He sounded unsettled.

"Or could our elusive Herr Treiger have been repairing the mess you made?" There was a slight pause after the curt observation. As if in answer to his own question, Higler continued, "I doubt it. He would never have left evidence like this around. That is not his style, unlike you. Nevertheless, it is time for you to get to work."

"And just what the fuck are you going to do while I hammer through this shit?"

Durn sounded resentful, but his voice lacked the necessary defiance to keep Higler in control. Durn would have to watch his step if he wanted to stay alive. Treiger distastefully remembered Higler growing up. A brilliant mind, fastidious worker and irritatingly precise. He also loved to torture. He had started with insects and small animals until he worked his way up to humans. He was well known in Sao Paulo for disfiguring male and female prostitutes and had murdered countless of the poor wretches living in favelas. There was no body count amongst the destitute in Brazil. Higler made the right connections and covered his tracks scrupulously. He was never caught. Treiger listened to Higler's sarcastic snort followed by a dry announcement. "I am going to hold the flashlight, Durn. I might also have a drink of water. You're making me thirsty."

Treiger could almost picture the conceited bastard toying with his temporary vassal like a malicious cat. Higler was now noisily glugging some water. When Durn asked for a drink, Higler snappily told him to keep working, then laughed. It sounded like Higler threw a bottle over the wall out of his pawn's reach. A token torment. More scraping sounds ensued. Higler's voice gloated in enjoyment at Durn's slavish submission. Treiger knew that Higler's ruthless requirement for control was his most significant weakness. He intended to use that flaw against Higler when the time came.

Some of the newly packed soil fell on Treiger's feet. The cold stone wall now seemed very thin. Treiger's mind raced over his options. Return to the crypt and clear Hans and the Brodie woman out or find some way of getting rid of these two. Higler would be pushing Durn to hack through the wall in the shortest time possible. The muffled conversation on the other side of the wall continued. Durn's voice filtered into Treiger's thoughts. With a defensive thrust, he ventured an ineffectual taunt. "You act pretty tough. I'll bet you never killed nobody."

"Anybody." Sarcasm laced Higler's hissed correction. "I suppose you are too thick to believe that my last victim was a Brazilian Indian in the Amazon. I disembowelled him just before I travelled to your fair city." Higler's shrill laugh seemed to cut right through the stone.

Treiger was momentarily stunned. Joao? Dead!

Rage ignited like a gas-drenched inferno. His hands formed granite fists as he hardened himself from the ravaging emotion. He knew what to decide. Treiger quickly swung himself up onto the scaffolding. The top level was layered like a sub-floor with rocks supporting the floor above. The sound of Durn's digging and clanking against stone would have to be enough to occlude any sound he made. He began shoving the stones off in rhythm with Durn's digging. Soon, enough floorboards were exposed to get him inside the coach house. With little effort, Treiger punched out several wooden slats. A dusty tarpaulin happened to dampen the sound.

He hoisted his body through with the precision of an acrobat and turned on his flashlight to get his bearings. A large toolbox, which looked more like a metal bureau on wheels, took up the space beside him. Surprisingly he found the door latch open. A padlock was hanging on the outside and there was a sliding bolt fixed to the inside. He let the door swing out an inch or two to give himself a view. The cool air contrasted with the heat radiating off his skin. The noise from Durn's shovel continued. The effort would wear him down. Treiger wished he had brought his Rugar with him to simplify matters. Instead, some tools from Kendall's utility box would do. The explosives in the cave he would use after dealing with Higler. This entrance needed to be completely destroyed.

He laid a plan in his mind, gauging the height of the stone wall behind the coach house and estimating the position of the two figures on the other side. The German was lethal. Durn was secondary. The situation and the physical layout required that Higler be caught off guard. Higler's best weapons were his gun and his wits. Treiger recalled how Higler, when twelve years old, had spun around and in a split second shot a large Brazilian beetle off the bark of a tree at two hundred feet. Hopefully tonight Higler wouldn't have his gun drawn and his attention would be focused on Durn's labour. Treiger pushed the door open further. The shrill screech of a woman cut through the air.

The clanking stopped immediately. Treiger leaned back into the coach house and stayed close to the door, waiting for the two on the other side of the wall to react. Keeping the door open a crack, he watched and listened. He heard scraping over stone, as if someone were trying to mount the wall. Higler or Durn would be trying to figure out what was happening just like he was. As the cries came closer, he saw Fiona Kendall, white faced and panicked, racing to the back of the garden, screeching, "…KILL ME! HE'S…GOING TO KILL ME!"

Treiger looked back to the wall. The dark shape of Higler's hooded head came over the top edge, along with his gun. The darkness made him almost imperceptible. Sensor lights flashed on as the Kendall woman dashed passed in a frenzied sprint. Treiger looked beyond to see who was chasing her. There was no one. Was the woman mad? Running desperately from a ghost into the arms of a killer. He didn't need to be faced with such a precarious dilemma. Treiger crouched down and stuck his hand through the slit in the doorway. He flung a small stone with enough force to hit the wall. Higler's silenced gun spit a shot at the sound. The screaming woman had almost reached the coach house door. Treiger could see by the wild expression on her face she didn't know where to go next and was about to run right past heading straight for Higler.

Treiger used his shoulder to widen the opening. He grabbed her arm. Her feet almost flew out from under her at the jolting hold. His move caught her in mid-screech, silencing her. He whisked her into the coach house with such force that she flew through the air. Her collision with the floor seemed to knock the wind out of her. Treiger slammed the door shut. Bullets smashed into the wood on the other side. He rammed the bolt into place. Such a simple contraption wouldn't hold Higler for long. He rolled the tool-chest against the door, crashing the oversized metal hulk onto its side. Perhaps the weight against the door would stall them. He then bent towards Fiona and said, "Can you follow me?" She reeked of alcohol.

Brutal pounding on the door made the hinges strain. His mind functioned on two levels simultaneously; rational logic, where his thoughts judged the significance of every action; the other level was raw primal instinct. He brought his fist up and gave her a tough clip on the chin. Her eyes rolled back and she collapsed into unconsciousness. Treiger threw the old tarpaulin over top of her as the small window beside the door shattered and bullets hit the floor. He disappeared through the floorboards.

They would follow and he would trap them in his territory. Higler probably felt empowered now that he was engaging in a hunt, but he wouldn't be one hundred percent certain who had saved the girl, until he discovered the hole in the floor. If they didn't look under the tarp then Higler might assume she was with him, hampering his speed. That would be a useful deception.

At the crawl hole, Treiger grabbed his knapsack and slid through, but not before hearing the scraping of the metal cabinet grate on the floor as his two pursuers forced their way in. Treiger selected a timed explosive from the back of his pack. He set the mechanism and placed the plastic mine beside the hole then stooped in a run, using the flashlight to guide his way. With any luck, both Higler and his buddy would be crawling through the access hole at the time of the explosion. Treiger tried never to depend on luck, but he hoped for some now. However, Higler was smart enough to anticipate the unexpected. Nonetheless, Treiger was determined to destroy every one of the maniacal conspirators along with their virus. At least if he failed, Hans would be left to help find the antidote.

Treiger continued to scramble along the tunnel as the explosion powerfully shook the ground under his feet. His hand hit flat on the side of the wall, stabilizing his footing. A whoosh of dust funnelled like a whirlwind. He choked briefly in the thick air. When the rumbling of falling rock subsided in the background, almost as an echo, he heard retching coughs. Then Higler's accent filtered through the tunnel. He was demanding in half German, half English for Durn to hurry, but the reply was weak. By the sound of the muffled speech, only Durn had been injured by the blast.

Once the ear became accustomed to the rolling sound of water, movement through the caves could be heard echoing off the walls. This was now an advantage for Treiger. He made enough noise for them to follow, again hoping Higler thought he was following two people. Sweat rippled along his forehead as he turned a sharp corner of the cave joining the main river. Treiger intended to lead them away from the central cavern where Hans and Megan were. As he hurried alongside the rushing water, Treiger recognised that the pieces of the puzzle weren't fitting together. If Higler was following him, then where was Stoltz? Stoltz would want to spearhead the total destruction of a traitor to their cause. The irritating thought simmered on the back burner of his mind.

He ran through the fine mist until he came to the first suspension bridge and crossed over the furious current. This tributary was not overly deep at this time of year, but treacherous because of the sharp rocks spiking up through the overpowering current. On the wall was a torch. He ignited the oil-soaked head then switched off his Maglite. He slipped his Bowker hand-knife from his belt and began hacking at the rope ties holding the bridge. He wanted to give Higler a clear message that this was the route to follow. He worked at the hemp fibres until he heard the sound of thudding feet. Higler and Durn had no light so they were like moles searching for a route to follow, slowing them down.

Treiger called out as if he had the woman with him and said, "Move faster." He heard the dull sound of quickening footsteps just above the din of the river. He waited until he thought Higler could see his torch. A bullet ricocheted off the rock wall near him. He disappeared out of the main cave, following the ledge along the tributary. Where the shelf came to a narrow end he saw his pulley. Treiger doused his torch in the river and threw the smoking baton on the ledge. Such evidence could lead Higler to think he had made a mistake. Still if Higler chose to use the torch, then Treiger's job might be easier. Treiger hoisted himself up to the rope pulley slung near the wet, dripping roof, and gave a forceful shove so that he sailed obliquely across the tributary, over the spiked rocks and foaming turbulence below. Once he had safely traversed the treacherous water, he disconnected himself and sent the harness back to the other side. The exit tunnel was only a short distance away.

Treiger again used his knife, slicing into the pulley rope. The fibre frayed badly, exactly as he had wanted. He took some binder twine from his pack and wrapped the fibre around the weakened section. This time he didn't want Higler to see the damage. He barely managed to finish the faux repair when muted sounds bounced down from the ceiling. Higler would appear shortly. He had to keep the smart Aryan away from Hans. Treiger slid into the shadows a split second before hearing the echo of someone stumbling onto the ledge across the river, followed by Durn's barely audible voice. "I think I've found some sort of light. This club is still smouldering."

After a moment or two, the torch was re-lit. An uneven flame from the sodden rags cast uneasy shadows along the wet walls, as if the river disliked being revealed. Treiger couldn't see Higler, but Durn came stumbling forward. He looked like he had been shoved out into the open. Obviously Higler was using him for bait. In the shadowy torchlight, Durn's left arm hung limp at his side. His face was dark as if blood was smeared along the side. He stood for a moment, looking unsteady on his feet and glancing back fearfully at the hidden form of Higler. His decoy was still alive. Treiger let out a long, silent exhale. The German would not expose himself easily. Treiger eyed Durn again. If the man had been in top shape he would have risked thrusting his knife. The three-metre stretch to the tottering Durn would have made him a fairly easy target, but the knife was most effective at close quarters, even though he probably could inflict a nasty wound from where he stood. Keeping the blade near was the wiser decision. Treiger continued to watch the unsteady form. In his injured state, the thin lackey probably hadn't the strength to cross the gorge. Durn was more of a danger to himself. In these situations, anything could happen.

Higler suddenly appeared in a brisk move out of the shadows. The torch was burning more brightly. The hood from his jacket still covered his head, casting a sinister outline in the erratic yellow firelight. The Aryan had presumed, and rightly, that there was no gun, as Durn was not attacked. Cautious as usual, Higler was keeping his body behind that of Durn. There was no clear aim for a decently incapacitating knife throw. Treiger watched Higler manoeuvre Durn to the rim of the gorge, all the time keeping his sharp eyes scanning for Treiger across the gap.

"Come out, Treiger. I know you are there. Or are you under the impression you have to protect the woman. Such chivalry is out of character." He spoke with sawdust-like humour.

Treiger knew to stay put. The taunt and bait approach was a favourite technique of Higler's. The comment was a test to discern if the woman was still present. If Higler wasn't certain if there were two, then that was an advantage. He would keep up the deception as long as he could. Treiger waited. A moment or two ticked by. When it seemed like Higler was questioning whether to head back into the tunnels, Treiger threw a small stone up to the ceiling. The sound was slightly above the thrashing of water, but loud enough for Higler to make his decision. Higler set the torch onto the ledge. The end continued to burn. With totalitarian authority, Higler grasped the back of Durn's neck and reached up for the pulley. Checking that the roller was secured to the cable, he hooked it onto Durn's belt while Durn protested nervously.

"Hold tight," Higler said, giving Durn a hard push across the gap.

The frayed rope gave way. Durn flailed for a second before his body fell directly on an outcrop of rock. The crack of bone was followed by a harrowing cry. Durn's scream ended abruptly. His dark form smashed against more rocks then snagged as if he was caught like a carp on a trawler's line. The rope around his body pulled taut. Higler's eyes were not on Durn's downfall. He had a hold on the cable at the top of the line. He used the force of Durn's fall like another pulley, enabling him to swing across the river over the mangled body. Lithely his feet caught the far edge of the gap and he lurched forward to escape a fall back onto the jagged rocks and Durn.

Treiger wasted no time when he saw Higler's plan, and began to act out his decoy sequence. By the time Higler landed Treiger had already footed down the tunnel. He hoped he hadn't left himself too short of time. However, manoeuvring through the tunnels was difficult if you weren't used to them, and that would hold Higler up. The tunnel ended at the narrow stone stairs. He climbed the steps two at a time until he reached the door at the top. He waited to listen for Higler. Once they were on the mountain he would end the life of that mutant snake. Then, for everyone's sake including Luisa, he would go after Stoltz.

A boot hitting stone notified him that Higler was at the base of the steps. He knew Higler would waste no time. Treiger vaulted through the door. The thicket was pitch black. Treiger started to belly crawl in order to keep himself hidden. All of a sudden the echo of a woman screaming came from the tunnel exit. Trouble! Hans and the girl. Sweat poured off Treiger's forehead. Something had gone wrong. If Stoltz got to Hans first then all this life's work would be destroyed. And people would die... he knew he had to get back to the lab. Making his way over to the exit Luisa had used would take too much time. That would also leave Higler as a wild card on the mountain. The most effective alternative was to backtrack. Treiger stood to face Higler.

The hooded German was not there. Treiger's mind raced over the possibilities. Had Higler turned back or was he lying in wait for him in the tunnel, hoping to lure him to return? Treiger felt the full impact of being a loner. There was no one to back him up. No saviour. No friend. He was on his own. That was the way his life was. The way life would always be. He palmed his blade and quickly retraced his path to the entrance.

Hearing nothing, Treiger hurriedly uncovered a can of kerosene hidden near the entry. He poured the contents down the stairs, reached for the torch matches, lit one, and flung it onto the slick. He had to dodge away as a rage of red-hot flames gushed out in a flash explosion. No human sound was heard— just the rush of mass oxidation. The flames quickly subsided, leaving an acrid smell of burnt oil. Treiger rushed down the stairs, knife in hand. Again there was no sign of Higler. Warily, but swiftly, he made his way back to the rushing tributary.

Reaching the end, Treiger quickly looked to the river edge. The torch on the far ledge had continued to burn. The black, dripping wetness of the gorge was covered with an eerie pallid film. In the dim light, Higler was in motion at the side of the water. He had already retrieved the rope, still attached to Durn's body. Torchlight reflected on the blue corpse; even though his form was firmly wedged amidst the rushing torrents, sharp stalagmite-like rocks and the cold pummelling water continued to maul movable parts horribly. His head rammed continuously against a limestone outcrop.

Treiger raced forward, ready to slam his knife into a vital artery, but Higler's moves were fast and calculated. The devious mind knows no boundaries. *Higler* leapt towards Durn's carcass, planting his boot on the flaccid torso. Durn's extremities bounced in a life-like dance from the weight of Higler's pounce. Blood shot up. One of the sharp-rising projections ripped through Durn's abdomen, splaying him wide open. His corpse fell back like a gutted fish in the rushing current.

The tip of another stalagmite helped Higler to project himself to the other side. He barely made the whole distance, but managed to scramble a hold onto the ledge. With a great hoist, one of Higler's legs hooked over the shelf, enabling him to crawl out of the water. Higler swung around in a small stagger. His gun barrel pointed over in Treiger's direction. The crossing couldn't have been easy as he was panting noticeably. He stooped to pick up the torch keeping his eyes, livid with anger, on Treiger's side of the water. He held the flame high and tried to fire his gun. The mechanism failed, but his shrill scream cut through the air. "Are you there, old man? Soon you will be dead just like your Yano punk. He was no match for me!" Higler let an ugly cackle resonate through the caves, as he extracted Joao's bowie knife from inside his sodden jacket.

Treiger's Bowker soared like an arrow across the river. The short blade sunk into Higler's forearm. Higler didn't flinch, but the torch dropped into the river. There was no more light. There was no more laughter. Treiger heard the German's retreating footsteps. Only then did he notice that Megan Brodie's screams had stopped.

Chapter 25

Police cars squealed onto Roxton. An ambulance swerved behind. Windows in the Treiger mansion caught flashes of blue and red lightening as vehicles screeched to a halt in disconnected confusion, scattering on the street and lawn in front of the Ogilvy manor. Officers exited their cars, crouching behind their doors with their guns out. One man in a plaid jacket, both hands holding a gun in a straight-armed aim, ran up the steps and kicked in the door.

The dark figure continued to sit absolutely still in the shadows. He watched the activity only to make certain that no one targeted the Treiger property. A light switching on in the window across from the Ogilvy manor caught his eye, but he ignored it. He would wait just long enough to ensure he would not be caught. Finally he rose up from his crouch. A sharp pain reminded him that he was human. Long ago he had learned that pain could be an inhibitor or a motivator and always chose the latter. In his uncomplicated philosophy, enduring pain was a choice for life.

He entered the house by the same route as his predecessor and immediately smelled old blood. The stink hung in the air, but did not bother him; he had an objective and would function only to achieve that end. He walked through the foyer hoping to encounter the man called Stoltz, but the house was silent and, he was fairly certain, completely empty of life. Although he'd never been in the house before, he'd seen a fairly precise, hand-drawn map of the tunnels below. He pushed for the elevator, but there was no movement. Unable to open the metal door with his bare hands, he went to the kitchen and found a large screwdriver amidst a mess of utensils on the counter. Using the tool skilfully he was able to slide the door wide enough to squeeze through. He jumped onto the top of the elevator and kicked open the small door on the ceiling leading into the compartment. All the time there was a discernible sense of urgency in his movement. As quickly as he slid into the compartment, he slid out the propped open door and underneath the base, as if following a route that was laid out for him. He pushed open the door to the tunnel cautiously.

In the dark, the wall was his guide along the stone tunnel, until he reached a shallow tributary. When it joined a river, he checked the water to feel how fast the current was moving. He was about to continue on when the muted sound of one gunshot sounded above the rush of water. He started to jog. After a short interval a woman started screaming. The noise bounced off the ceiling and hung in the thick vapour rising from the river. Further on, he came upon a rope bridge and then saw a light ahead where the screams started again. He slipped quietly into the icy water to avoid meeting anyone from either direction. The current was strong, but he could manage because the water was only up to his hips. He bent forward until his chin nearly touched the surface. His powerful legs propelled him forward. He had advanced to within several metres of two figures struggling on the ground. One of them was Stoltz. A rag tied about his head made him look like a wounded animal in a frenzy and ready to kill. He was straddled on top of a woman, viciously striking her even though it was obvious she could not fight back. Her clothes were torn and her arms were pinned under her. She was no longer screaming.

The woman turned her head and looked right at him. He sank down to neck level and pressed his back against the river wall to stop the current from dragging him back. The whole time he kept his focus on the woman, hoping she wouldn't give any indication of his existence. She lay just before a rope bridge. Stoltz was facing away and seemed completely absorbed with his victim. Like a hyena eating his prey, if disturbed, he could be doubly vicious. He couldn't afford that.

Keeping to the river wall, the forceful current glided past his body as he moved under the bridge. The cold water had numbed his pain so he stretched up, grasping hold of the wet ropes at the base. His biceps bulged as he swung his legs up. As soon as his feet touched the edge of the stone bank, he used the hard surface to drive his body forward, leaping high into the air.

The German seemed to know he was besieged without looking and twisted in defence, releasing his hold on the woman's throat. Moving in unison with his body, Stoltz grabbed the gun lying on the ground.

Knowing a simple shot would kill him in mid-leap, Joao torqued, using the momentum to flick out his leg. His great toe hit Stoltz's head close to the patched eye. Stoltz grunted in pain, but kept hold of his weapon and rolled off the woman, swinging up to shoot.

As soon as the weight of Stoltz's body lifted, Megan rotated to the side, her mind bursting with release from the powerlessness. She knew Treiger would come back, but gasped in dismay. Stoltz was facing a dark figure much shorter than Treiger. Megan realised that if her rescuer had a gun he would have fired because that's just what Stoltz was doing. His arm was rising in aim, targeting point-blank at the chest of his opponent. His body moved with almost robotic precision. She could almost see the muscles of his hand contracting to pull the trigger. She listened for the shot.

The shadowed figure's legs flicked out in rapid motion. A kick deflected the gun, followed by precise kicks to Stoltz's body. One kick hit the chest, another the head, then back to body and arm. After the flurry of powerful foot jabs, the last kick sent the gun clattering across the stone near Megan's feet. Stoltz backed away. He was surrendering. The fight was over. Megan inhaled, realising that she had been holding her breath. But something was wrong. Stoltz had crammed his hand into the inside of his jacket. In the dim light she saw him pull out a bunch of thin wires weighted with tiny ball bearings.

Without thinking she loosened the moccasin on her foot and flung the sole directly at Stoltz. He was neatly releasing the wires with a professional toss from his wrist just as the leather heel struck his arm. Instead of whirling evenly, the projectile twisted through the air in a disorganised swarm. The wires hit the rescuer's forearm encircling the muscles so rapidly that the force spun the man sideways. Stoltz didn't even turn to her; he lunged for his gun.

The barrel lay inches from Megan. She kicked wildly aiming at Stoltz's head, whacking him near the eye. With her bare foot she lashed out at the gun trying to kick the pistol into the water. Her toe hooked the trigger. The butt arced through the air sailing the revolver into the darkness. Some distance away metal hit stone and slid noisily to a stop.

Enraged, Stoltz swatted violently at her. She wrenched away and expected another try, but instead of continuing his attack, he dodged into the shadows.

From behind, one arm of her rescuer powerfully lifted her body and, without a word, tipped both he and Megan into the icy water. She heard two shots fire before her body hit the water. She barely had time to gasp in air before being completely submerged.

The swirling cold engulfed her body and constricted her lungs. In desperate need of air she panicked. The instinct to survive drove her to struggle against the man, but he wrapped his body around hers, holding them both under the water. She lightly scraped the bottom as the current swept them along. With her arms still restrained there was little she could do, but writhe in his arms. They seemed to rotate over and over as the twisting current carried them downstream. Pain built up in her chest to the point of bursting. Her mind was frantic with the absurdity of being saved only to drown. To cry out would only allow water to suck in and she wanted to live as many more seconds as possible. She felt herself going numb and knew then that she would soon give in to the water. Survival didn't seem possible any longer. She felt a huge pressure on her abdomen, trying to force out the last of her air.

Suddenly her head came out of the water. Her whole body reacted explosively. Humid air sucked into her lungs. She coughed violently and weakly flailed at her captor, trying to struggle away from him. The river was now much shallower and he dragged her to shore with a vice-like hold. The bank was a huge rock slab lying flat like a beach.

"You nearly killed me, you bastard!" she said in a gasping sputter.

"No," was all he replied.

She wasn't certain how to respond. He had, after all, saved her life. She couldn't really see him and wondered what he was doing. There were too many questions in her mind, but she was still out of breath, but managed to gasp, "I wish there was more light."

"Torch on wall." He said. The words were spoken in perfect English, but the phrasing sounded like some sort of pidgin dialect.

She gritted her teeth at his clipped words, not knowing if she was angry, scared or just cold. Silently, he reached behind her and loosened her bonds. It was then she realized her knife was still in her hand, but her arms ached in spite of the freedom, and the darkness made the wet cold bitter. It didn't seem very clever to sit there freezing to death. He certainly wasn't making any move to look for the light. She got up and did her best to tuck her torn T-shirt around herself. Feeling her way over to the dripping wall, her hands ranged over the surface until one struck a club smelling of kerosene. On a stone jutting out beside the torch was a lighter. The torch ignited immediately, creating a flash of warmth against the freezing wet of her skin.

She looked at the man who was still crouched on the ground. He was dressed in a black turtleneck, black jeans and some soft cloth shoes, also black. He was preoccupied with his arm. She noticed how quiet he was, intently struggling to unwrap the wires strangling his forearm. She realised that he had dragged her away without thinking of himself. Biting her tongue, she thrust the torch towards him saying, "Hold this." He stopped his work and took hold of the end.

She sat down beside him and hunched over his disabled arm. She was startled that his sleeve was sodden, not with water, but with blood. Nimbly she started to untangle the wires. The filaments had sharply severed his sleeve, slicing severely into his arm. There was as yet little swelling. She figured that was because of the damn cold water. The dark cloth made the injury difficult to evaluate, but her fingers were soon wet with the warm ooze as if the fluid was being siphoned out of his arm. She flicked her knife open and cut the wires, trying not to injure him further. When she was done, she picked up the torch to have a better look. Not only were there seeping gashes on his arm, but also the front of his shirt seemed to be sticking to his abdomen. She pointed at his stomach, "What happened there? You're bleeding."

He shrugged his shoulders and remained silent.

Taking a better look at his face, Megan thought he looked like some sort of Indian, but not from any tribe she knew. "Are you Inuit?"

He looked blankly at her.

"You know. From Northern Canada?"

"Yanomamö."

Feeling frustrated at his monosyllabic responses, she said, "From Brazil? Oh, well that explains it then." Megan cut herself off, realising that he must be in considerable pain. "You'd better let me have a look at that," she said, pointing again to his midsection. When he made no move to stop her, she gently eased up his shirt.

"My God!" She saw the length of an awkwardly placed long slash from one side of his abdomen to the other. "This wound is huge. I think the cold water has stopped you from losing much blood. Well, whatever it's tied with is holding, but what's this green stuff? I hope its not infected. I can't believe you rescued me in this condition." She felt that he would feel uncomfortable if she thanked him more obviously. Besides, the usual social necessities didn't seem necessary with him. She then realised in an odd way that she felt comfortable with him. "My name's Megan Brodie. What's yours?"

"Joao."

"Jowh?" she copied his sound.

He nodded.

"Well, Joao. I'd say we've got ourselves in a bit of a mess. I don't know how you got in here, but you must know Karl Treiger."

His expression showed acute interest. She wasn't certain then if he was on Treiger's side or not. Tentatively she said, "I wish I knew what to do next."

"Go home."

"You mean me? I can't do that. Luisa Treiger died because she wanted to save me. Somehow she thought I was worthwhile enough. If that isn't enough, this situation is much more important than I am. A lethal virus has been created as some sort of biological atom bomb. Many millions would die horribly if this thing got out." She hesitated then asked, "Do you know where Karl Treiger is?"

Joao shrugged, but looked straight at her. There was a level of intelligence that he seemed to disguise with his bushman-like mannerisms. He obviously understood English perfectly and, for some reason, she thought that she wouldn't be surprised if he spoke the words with better diction than her slight Scottish lilt. Still nothing in this seemed clear-cut so she probed. "That man— the one you attacked— says he's from Interpol."

"Ernst Stoltz. No."

"What do you know of him?"

Joao looked at her as if evaluating what to say, but then answered, "Terrorist, killer, well-trained."

"He is a killer. He murdered Hans Treiger and his wife...Luisa." She said the words as if to herself. Death seemed to follow her like a spectre.

Joao shrugged his shoulders as if there was no more to say.

Megan bit her lower lip. The focus had to stay on stopping a disaster. "Hans told me Karl Treiger is fighting against this guy Stoltz. If Treiger dies then this bastard is home free with the virus. The police are after the wrong person." She paused then decided to be direct. "Now you. Where do you fit in this puzzle?"

"Friend."

"Well, I guess you must figure that says everything, but for me the relationship means absolutely nothing. Do you think you could try giving me a few details?" He looked at her again and she wondered if there was a hint of amusement in his eyes. He took a breath to continue. She was prepared to interpret another staccato of sparse syllables, but he replied speaking well-bred English.

"Ernst Stoltz is not the only fanatic. There are others here and elsewhere. But if the main operating body, called the Gau, is destroyed, then the whole organisation will fall apart. Treiger has almost accomplished that except for two, Stoltz and Higler."

Well, what do you know. At least she was getting somewhere. "How do you think the Gau kept all this secret?"

After a short pause he answered thoughtfully. "They operate that way. Secrecy and subversion are the moral principles they incorporated from the original Nazi regime. Treiger knows that is the primary vulnerability in their structure. He also knows the organisation well enough to use that weakness against them. He will die stopping them if he has to. I will try to help."

Megan looked him over, knowing that both this succinct edition and Hans's version were congruent. She now asked, "Where did you learn English?"

"Long story."

"Don't tell me you're switching back into that pidgin-lingo."

He looked at her in a way she couldn't figure out, then put his hand up to her mouth as if to say 'be quiet'. The flame from the torch flickered. Joao cocked his head and listened then said resolutely, "I will find Treiger."

Megan knew she would go with him, but couldn't help looking back at the cold water. Joao moved towards the wall, using the torch to light the way. At the far end of the clearing along the water's edge he disappeared into the wall. This startled her, until she saw it was an optical illusion. The jutting of the rocks obscured another tunnel cut through the underground terrain. This tunnel was much lower and she had to hunch over, almost crouch, in order to fit. The narrow passage seemed to run parallel to the main river. She figured the monks had constructed this one as a safety net. The cramped route was difficult to navigate. She thought she was in a pretty fit state, but found she was out of breath keeping up with Joao. The struggle helped her to regain some warmth even with her damp clothes. She remained silent, intent on following him. She observed the power of his body as he forged ahead, thinking of what pain he must be in with his injuries. Some people knew how to use their strength to survive. His stoic endurance appealed to her. She kept her eyes on Joao's form and contemplated for a moment. He's extremely powerful, quite capable of speaking English fluently when he chooses, and apparently, limitlessly loyal to Karl Treiger. Yet he bothers on his crusade to stop and help me, or was he just focused on killing his enemy Stoltz? When she thought over the events, Treiger had done similarly. One thing was certain, they both valued life. Megan took a deep breath. Intriguing. Her blood tingled.

The tunnel ended at a cross section. Joao had just crossed over and started to enter a continuation of the low passageway. Megan was now close behind. She took the opportunity to ask how much further, but Joao turned slightly, signalling for silence. Of course! Stoltz or whoever he was might be near. Megan clamped her mouth shut and followed him. She let her body accommodate to Joao's pace and steadied her breathing.

Suddenly he stopped and again motioned for silence. As she crept up to him, he signalled for her to remain where she was, pointing to a faint light coming from the end of the tunnel. He rolled the torch on the ground snuffing out the flame, and crawled out the opening. Megan shivered in the dark, feeling like a mouse about to be trapped. She edged forward. Her adrenaline began to race. She swallowed then sneaked her head around the end of the tunnel.

She was near the bridge to the lab, and light still shone out of the doorway. The place where she had nearly been raped was vacant. Her eyes fell on Joao's darkly-reflecting body. He seemed to be intently stalking his way to the bridge along the uneven wall. She desperately wanted to follow him. Shivers went down her spine, giving a cold chill to her bones. Uneasiness hit her in the form of a premonition that if she stayed put she would die. With only one moccasin on, pain started to throb in her bare foot. Gathering her courage, she set her aim to the wall just to the side of Joao. She knew she could move silently. When she neared the wall, a pointed shard dug into the skin under her foot. Sharp pain made her inhale. Only then did Joao turn his head. She thought he seemed to look surprised that she moved so close without him noticing.

Suddenly, a hand clamped over her mouth and the force behind the grip pulled her down. Fear forcefully injected itself almost paralysing her, but she knew she would rather die than let Stoltz molest her again. In no time at all she had been snatched behind some rock, out of Joao's sight. Twisting with all her might, she tried to strike out at his groin with her knee. She realised only too late that such a move was a mistake. He used her rotation to spin her onto her stomach. He stretched himself along the back of her body, pinning her down. Her head was turned to the side held down by his head. His hand was still over her mouth. She felt hot breath against her ear before he uttered a gruff, barely audible warning. "Lie still."

A second later Joao's legs passed rapidly through her line of vision. She felt him press against their feet in the close space. She wanted to shake the hand off her face, but realised that she must indicate that she would be silent. She let her body relax and nodded her head hoping the signal would be understood. The hand dropped. She turned her head to make sure. Karl Treiger shifted away and pulled her to a standing position between himself and Joao. They all squeezed closely back in the shadows of the rock niche.

A German voice became audible. Megan felt Joao's body tense. Someone came out from the lab and crossed the rope bridge. Boots stamped on the rock base. A light beam appeared in their line of vision, roaming the area. They waited. The boots made an arrogantly loud echo on the stone floor near to their recessed alcove. Suddenly the shadow of his gun materialised on the floor in front of her. He took another step. She kept her eyes open even though she wanted to squeeze them shut. Her breathing seemed screamingly loud. Blood pounded in her ears.

His boots scraped closer. The light swivelled away, but the back of his shoulder came into view. One half turn more and he'll surely see us. Her mouth was open. Air panted shallowly from her lungs. Her throat became so dry that one sharp breath refused to grate through her trachea. The trapped tickle created an irresistible impulse to cough. Tears ran from her eyes and she held her hand over her mouth, concentrating every ounce of her being to withhold the demanding urge. Higler stood only a foot away while she continued to stifle her breath.

"Egon! Kommen-sie." Stoltz called. He sounded like he had already crossed the bridge. That meant they were both close. The man obeyed. His noisy echo faded into the distance. Joao relaxed beside her. Megan gathered saliva in her mouth and swallowed.

Treiger hissed, "Do we have a chance?"

"Guns," Joao whispered.

"We'll wait then."

Megan stood silently between them, wondering if she should tell Treiger that his brother was dead, but the two Germans had begun talking and Treiger was listening intently. They spoke so fast that Megan didn't have a clue what was being said. Normally she would have been able to decipher at least one or two words. Stoltz sounded excited yet in control. A few seconds later, the sound of boots stomping through shallow puddles told them the Germans were hurrying down the river, probably back to Treiger's place.

Megan found herself shuffled rapidly from their refuge. Treiger pushed past her and raced across the flat plain of rock plain towards the bridge. Joao followed closely behind. By the time she reached the river's edge, Treiger had already crossed the expanse. Joao was halfway over. She stood at the end of the roped suspension. She didn't want to see Hans again. Treiger was about to enter the lab. She became frantic knowing she had to tell him. More loudly than she wanted, her voice echoed across the river, "He's dead."

Her voice only made Treiger hesitate as if he already knew. His hand moved to shove open the door, but as he did so, his expression changed. His other arm went up to pushing Joao aside. Treiger dived in the opposite direction. Megan found herself flung off her feet by the force of an explosion. In the midst of her fall, she saw the crypt door blast across the spot where both men had been standing. A huge block of the wood hit one of the rope stays to the bridge before spinning into the water.

Megan put her feet on the slippery slats and steadied herself across the wobbly contraption. She almost leapt to the other side and ran to Treiger. He was dazed and shaking his head while Joao was already on his feet. Somehow she had known he would be all right. She looked down and saw her moccasin. With relief she shoved the damp leather on her aching foot. Treiger had moved inside the cavern, but came out looking seriously grim. All he said was, "They must have it, Joao."

Joao nodded.

Looking back and forth at them, Megan uttered, "Have what?" Treiger's stare penetrated her as if he was trying to dissect her mind. A shiver went through her.

He responded, "A disc of the viral antidote Hans is...was working on." He didn't say anything more and the rushing sound of river current filled the space between them.

She spoke up hesitantly. "He was showing me how he succeeded. The treatment was nearly ready to try on Semitic people. Stoltz interrupted us before he could explain everything." She thought Treiger's look had turned cold, as if considering why she was alive and his brother was not. He said nothing. Guilt made an excuse stumble out of her mouth. "Stoltz tried to rape me." The simple statement sounded like such a weak explanation for her continuing existence.

Treiger turned and looked into the darkened crypt. Joao had retrieved a torch and started to enter. "Be careful Joao. Looks like Stoltz used the explosives in my other knapsack. That also means the two of them are armed."

Light flickered over the area where the lab had been. That section of the vault had completely caved in. Megan looked for any sign of Hans's body. The enclosed section that had contained the primitive lab was a pile of rubble. Hans must have been buried in the explosion.

Treiger sounded worried. "They probably attached the bomb to the incubator. This whole place must be contaminated with the virus. We could be carriers."

Some of her discussion with Hans came back to her. "Hans told me he had changed the virus somehow. It won't kill people."

Treiger put his hands up to his forehead in a brief display of relief. "That is only a small mercy because Stoltz took some of Kleis's virus for his own purposes. Stoltz is the one that matters. He has to be stopped and we have to get that disc."

A rumbling overhead interrupted him. All three of them dashed out of the decimated cave. Bits of shattered stone started to pelt them as they ran through the door. A second later, rocks collapsed the remaining space with thundering force. They barely crossed the bridge before the stays in the wall released. It plunged into the river.

Treiger shouted. "That blast...these caves are unstable. Run." Even as he spoke more stone from the cave roof started to fall. Megan found herself wrenched forward by Joao as more thundering began. The whole area began to crumble. They fled down the river. After several hundred yards the cave-in subsided, leaving the air thick with dust. Coughing, they stumbled forward with the foggy light of the torch, until they reached the tunnel leading to Treiger's garage.

When they neared the elevator shaft, Treiger extinguished the flame. Joao moved ahead, but returned a moment later, speaking fluently, "They are in the garage trying to get your car to start. It won't be long before they're out of there."

"The car is specially rigged against theft, but no doubt Higler will bypass the mechanism in no time. We must hurry. To go up through the elevator shaft would be foolish. Both of us are not in great shape." Treiger looked at Joao. "That reminds me.

You're supposed to be dead. Don't tell me you're one of those Yano ghosts."

Joao looked a bit sheepish, but managed a glimmer of a smile for Treiger. "Higler slit me open...shaman did a patch up."

Megan listened quietly while she busied herself tying small knots up the front of her T-shirt. Astonished by what she heard, Megan interrupted, asking, "When did this happen?"

Joao showed two fingers in response, but watched Treiger who was already removing a grate near the ceiling. Treiger explained. "Even though I showed you a map of the caves, Joao, I didn't tell you about this air shaft. I made it big enough for a backup route. It pays to be cautious." He looked sternly at Megan. "You stay here for now."

Her insides rebelled. "No way. If you don't take me with you, I'll start screaming."

Joao tilted his head and nodded shortly. "Screams good."

Treiger looked at Joao then at Megan and without another word crawled into the air duct. The metal canal was fairly easy to scale with iron-rungs welded up one side. Joao was the last to exit into the foyer. Treiger moved immediately into the first room just off the hallway. He strode to a wall covered with shelves of books. Quickly removing a select book, he stuck his hand inside the empty spot and pressed a lever inside. The bookshelf swung away from the wall revealing another room. Megan's jaw dropped when she saw the arsenal of weaponry hanging from the walls.

Treiger entered purposefully. First he switched on his computer. Several screens lit up. He then turned to the weapons and pulled one for himself. Megan noticed how comfortable he looked in handling the pistol. He checked with Joao saying, "Higler's got your Bowie. Want anything else?"

Joao grasped hold of a streamlined crossbow with steel-tipped arrows. The hilt fit like a glove. Some how the Brazilian aboriginal was a mystery of contrasts. He looked like he belonged in the jungle, but was obviously adept with modern technology. She knew well how to use a bow and arrow. Treiger blocked the entry, stopping her from examining the array of weapons at the back of the compartment, and had a strange searching expression on his face as he looked towards her. Megan realised he was measuring her up, probably wondering how she could defend herself.

"Have you any knives?" she asked figuring she would handle that the easiest. He stepped to the side revealing a large selection of long and short blades hung on the wall. She chose a slender sheathed stiletto, which she was able to snap onto her belt. Dekanewidah had taught her about bows and arrows, but old Brodie had taught her about knives, the only useful thing he taught her besides distrust and deceit. Treiger watched her and said, "I hope you won't be put in a position to use that."

She looked up at him and said seriously, "I know how to if necessary."

Treiger nodded once and turned his attention to Joao. "Our best advantage will be to divide and conquer."

"Higler." Joao replied with an intensity that gave Megan shivers.

Treiger nodded then turned to Megan, "Come here. Do you know how to use a computer?"

She moved beside him confidently, a signal for him to go ahead and explain. There was a red flashing icon on one of the screens along with a map of what looked to be the local area. Treiger said simply, "That spot represents my body. The homing beacon was for Hans to keep track of my whereabouts."

Treiger clicked the mouse to change the program. A display of eight videos flashed onto the grid of screens. Treiger explained. "This whole house is surveyed by hidden infrared micro-cameras. We couldn't afford to take chances." Clicking again, four scenes divided one screen. She immediately saw movement in one, displaying the eerie forms of Stoltz and Higler working on the Mercedes in the garage. The other focus was the inside of the garage door. The next was a stairwell and the last, a widescreen view of the front yard including the garage door. The infrared made the views look surreal. Treiger instructed her, "I need you to open the garage door to let Joao in. When you get my signal from the stairway screen here, just click on this icon. Can you manage that? Otherwise I'll be a sitting duck for those two."

Megan nodded seriously, feeling strangely rewarded that he trusted her. She listened to his other directions. Treiger finished abruptly and left with Joao, not even looking back. She turned her attention to the screen, observing the two Germans. They both looked quite sinister with their red skin and clothes. Stoltz had been so convincing and charming when he was with Danny. Danny? She'd completely forgotten about him, and suddenly felt shaken and distracted. Surely he wouldn't have left Stoltz on his own. She wished she had time to call him and kept her eyes focused on the screen. The one named Higler was again fiddling under the hood of the Mercedes. Stoltz took a knapsack lying on the floor and tossed the pack into the car. That bag probably contained the weapons and the explosives Treiger had mentioned in the lab. All of a sudden, Stoltz looked right up, directly into the camera. Megan jerked back. A clean, narrow black band was tied over his injury, making his one-eyed look more fanatical. He was carrying what looked like a semi-automatic machine gun. They were heavily armed. Her eyes briefly scanned the other screens. She couldn't see either Joao or Treiger yet.

There was an icon that looked like a volume control. She clicked on it. Stoltz's voice became audible. He was hissing commands impatiently at Higler. While Stoltz continued with his German tirade, Higler managed to start the engine running. He lifted his head out from under the hood and slammed the latch shut. Megan was startled at how similar Higler and Stoltz looked once she had a good look at them together. A flicker of movement flashed in the corner of her visual field. Only then did she see Treiger madly signalling her on the screen. She raced the mouse onto the icon and clicked. The door started to open. Stoltz was already in the driver's seat when Treiger started to fire. The car gunned forward. Treiger dived out of the way. She couldn't see Higler. Her eyes scanned frantically as the garage door finished opening. He had ducked out the opening door. She looked for Joao in the bottom frame. He was moving towards the garage door, right in the line of fire. She had to warn him.

Megan ran to the front door and onto the steps. The property out from the house was too dark. She couldn't see Joao. Almost too late, she saw Higler cast in the light from the garage, standing at the corner of the house. Suddenly bullets struck the doorframe beside her. She collapsed against the stone siding, realising the blonde-haired Nazi was shooting at her. Cornered and alone, her heart pumped at a blasting pace. At least the bullets would have warned Joao. But there were no more shots. She crouched behind the stone, waiting. She wanted to see what was going on, but didn't want to risk getting her head blown off and shuddered at the thought of Higler sneaking towards her.

Suddenly tires squealed. Treiger's Mercedes burst past the steps. Stoltz was at the wheel and Treiger was holding desperately to the sides of the roof. His gun was missing. The car swerved furiously, but Treiger managed to stay on. His legs swung precariously from one side to the other. The car was out of sight in a second.

Megan took a chance. She lifted her head over the edge of the stone railing. Higler was aiming his semi-automatic rifle at the car. One short blast and Treiger would be dead. She dropped her head down and extracted her knife. Higler's gun never fired. She took another chance and quickly peeked over the stone balustrade. Higler's gun lay on the ground, with a metal arrow piercing the shaft. Neither Joao nor Higler were in sight. The racing car and Treiger had disappeared down the street.

But she was safe. Perhaps it was time to walk away.

In the moments that follow, Megan Brodie has no choice but to go on with the chase. The story continues in the sequel:

RUNNING THE RACE

Check out N.A.T. Grant's webpage at www.llumina.com.

About the Author

N.A.T. Grant has a Masters of Science (Nursing), which led her into a variety of health care positions, including clinical practice, teaching and management. She lives in Pointe-Claire, a suburb of Montreal, Québec, with her husband, a professor at McGill University.

Printed in the United States
22588LVS00004B/150